The Settler

Brian Duncan

THE SETTLER

A historical novel set in
Southern Africa in
1890-1902

by
Brian Duncan

Author's Note

In 1890-1902 the region of Africa south of the Zambezi River went through a period of extraordinary turmoil. In 1890 the Pioneer Column, consisting of volunteer troopers and settlers financed by Rhodes' Chartered Company, entered and occupied Mashonaland (in what is now north-eastern Zimbabwe). Friction with the tribe to the west led to the Matabele War (1893). Then followed the Jameson Raid (1895/6), and the Matabele and Mashona Rebellions (1896). The culmination of this period of history was the protracted Boer War (1899-1902). These twelve years of sporadic warfare between white settlers and black tribesmen, and between British soldiers and Boer commandos, is the background to my story.

I have tried to make the background historically accurate. When I lived in Rhodesia/Zimbabwe I was steeped in the country's history and was fortunate to meet the descendants of early settlers. Some anecdotes have been gleaned from the publications of the Rhodesiana Society, but mostly I've been inspired by great books, notably Thomas Pakenham's *The Boer War*, Deneys Reitz's *Commando*, and John O'Reilly's *Pursuit of the King*. If I have erred in historical facts it is my own fault!

The main protagonists are fictional. However, several historical figures appear in the story, albeit often briefly, including Cecil Rhodes, Leander Starr Jameson, Winston Churchill, David Lloyd George, and Generals Botha, Smuts, Roberts, and Kitchener. I have drawn from the writings of a number of them, notably Frank Russell Burnham, the American scout (*Scouting on Two Continents*), and Christiaan de Wet (*Three Years War*). Short biographical notes on some historical persons are given at the end of this book.

I am deeply grateful to Tess, to my daughter Caroline, and to my late mother, Elizabeth (Betty), for their constant encouragement.

The map entitled 'Political map of South Africa' was first published in the late 1890s, i.e. during the period in which 'The Settler' is set. The railway from Mafeking (through Palapye) reached Bulawayo in October 1897. The eastern railway from Beira on the coast reached Umtali in February 1898, and Salisbury in May 1899. The railway between Bulawayo and Salisbury (not shown on the map) was completed in October 1902.

The map can be studied on the Internet at: http://commons/wikimedia.org/wiki/File:Southern Africa 1890s Political.jpg

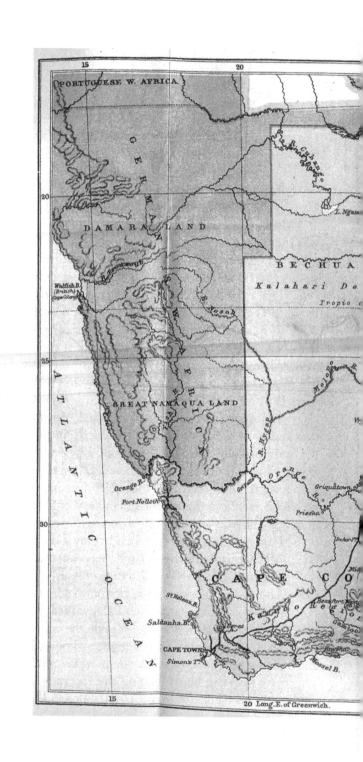

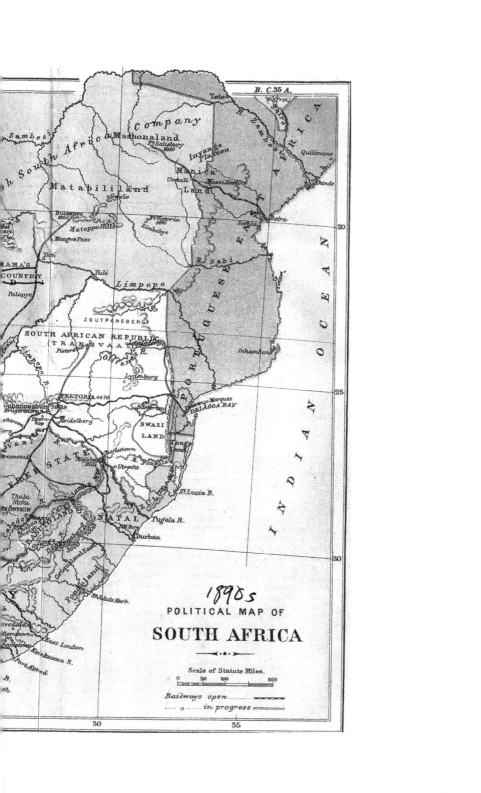

B. C.35 A.

1890s

POLITICAL MAP OF

SOUTH AFRICA

⟶ ‹ ● › ⟶

Scale of Statute Miles.

0   50   100   200

Railways open _____

_____ ,, ____ *in progress* ═══

CHAPTER 1
England — May 1890

Late on a May evening a tall young man with upright bearing arrived by train at Tackley station in the Cherwell Valley of Oxfordshire. He was greeted by an elderly groom, short, stocky, gnarled and solid as a tree stump. They shook hands and walked out together. The groom carried the young man's worn leather suitcase and heaved it onto the back of a pony trap that creaked in protest. He then climbed onto the high seat and watched as the young man moved to the pony's head and fondled its ears, conversing with it in a low voice.

Fred Cowley the groom had seen this young man grow from a child of three when the Russell family bought Middleton Hall. That was twenty years ago, when Fred was forty and already held the position of head groom. The Russells gave him the task of teaching their children to ride and he soon discovered in this boy a more natural talent than any he had known. The horses seemed to detect an innate liking for them. Many were the times Fred had watched these little ritual conversations. When others would merely climb into the pony trap or carriage Martin Russell would want to know which animals were in harness, and would discuss their disposition and exchange little pleasantries with them.

"Hello there, old Wally," he was saying. "Bored with waiting, are you? Want to get home for your gruel I'm sure. Well it's a heavier load than you came with, but it won't take long." He patted the pony's neck and climbed up beside Fred.

When they drove off along the country lanes the still dank air dulled the ring of the pony's hoof beats. Fred noticed the young man was unusually quiet, as if something weighed heavily in his thoughts, so he kept silent. Though he despised servant's gossip he'd heard that visitors were invited to the Hall that evening to help the young man decide his future.

Martin Russell's face was strong, the symmetry of his features marred only by a slightly crooked nose, broken in a childhood riding accident. He looked out over the hedgerows at the fields of young wheat and barley, breathing the cool scents of the spring flowers. How can I leave? he thought. Should I not live the rest of my life here, and die here, an Englishman? Then he remembered the stooped figure and rasping voice of Cecil Rhodes speaking to the Oxford students. 'There is a land of unimaginable space, of unfound riches, unexplored, waiting for men like you. Go there. See for yourselves.'

He dragged himself back to reality. "How are your family, Fred?" he asked the groom.

"Fair, Mr Martin. Young Fred be made a cowman." The Oxfordshire accent was strong and slow.

"That's good. Does he like the work?"

"Oh aye. Always liked the milkin', an' all the business of the dairy—and the maids." He laughed shortly and glanced at the young man beside him. Martin was his favourite of the Russell family, and as close to him as the son of a master could be with a servant. Never did the young man give the impression that he had been born to higher status. The groom had watched Martin teach Young Fred to ride, while he had lost patience with his own offspring. Now, whenever Martin visited the Hall he would seek out the groom's family to enquire after their welfare.

"You'll be riding tomorrow?" asked Fred.

"I may not have time, Fred." Martin answered ruefully. "My final exams are going on. I shouldn't really be here at all. It's only because of the visitors..."

"Well, it's a pity, Mr Martin. The 'orses need more exercise. Your brother don't ride enough."

"I know, Fred, I know. I'll hate staying indoors." He added more cheerfully, "It's only a few more days—then I'll be free again—to do whatever I wish. I'll exercise the horses then, you can be sure. Perhaps play polo again..."

"Ah, but for 'ow long?" The old man turned to Martin with a gloomy expression. "There's talk about you goin' away—to Africa, is it?"

Martin laughed. "So there's talk, is there? Well, Fred, I may go to Africa. Perhaps the visitors this evening will help me to make my decision."

"If you ask me, I don't think you should leave 'ere," Fred grumbled. He resumed his contemplation, gazing ahead over the sleek back of the pony. He wished that Martin were the son to inherit the estate instead of the elder brother, who seemed to have little interest in the farm, who rode to hounds but cared little for the horses, who invited his friends from London to shoot, but scarcely spoke to the farm workers when they were asked to beat. How different were the two brothers; one could scarcely believe they were from the same parents.

Fred turned the trap off the road and down a long avenue of lime trees. The pony's ears pricked up in anticipation of his evening feed. Martin lifted his eyes to admire the avenue. They had a timeless quality, and he liked to remember that they had been there since before his birth, and would be there when he died, and for long after. At the far end of the avenue was a Georgian country house, large but not grand, built with mellow honey-coloured stone from a quarry on the estate. The same stratum in nearby quarries supplied the stone used to build much of the city of Oxford. It had a strange capacity to reflect the soft English light, to magnify the slightest warmth to a glow. The surrounding park, scattered with mature oaks, complemented the simplicity of Middleton Hall's design.

The trap turned into the yard, wheels crunching on gravel, and drew up at the entrance to the house. The pony stamped impatiently, lowering his head as he settled. The groom hitched the reins and climbed down to unload Martin's bag, while the young man went to the pony's head, murmuring his thanks. Fred noticed this and smiled to himself.

A dog barked inside the house, followed by a woman's soothing voice. The front door opened, and a young girl emerged, bending to restrain the dog for a moment before letting it go. The yellow labrador rushed forward to greet Martin, weaving round his legs ecstatically while he fondled its head and urged it to calm down. The dog soon left him to survey the pony and then the trap, his moist glistening nose drawing in a heady bouquet of scents brought from the sortie into the countryside.

Martin strode up to his sister Beth and kissed her cheek. She was a tall girl of eighteen, with long dark brown hair in a thick plait brought forward over her shoulder. She was radiant in greeting her brother, with whom she had a great rapport. He was her best friend, and her mentor. They entered the house together arm in arm, following the groom. In the tall central hall of the house, Donkin the housekeeper greeted Martin, and received his suitcase from the groom, with a nod that sealed the handing over of responsibilities between the two servants. She passed the case to a maid to carry up to Martin's room, but he remonstrated, saying it was too heavy because it contained his books. The maid relinquished the case with a curtsy and went back to the kitchen.

Beth drew her brother aside, saying in a quiet warning voice, "The guests are here, Martin. They've already started to argue. Father said he's invited them to help you decide. But I suspect one of them, at least, is supposed to make you change your mind. There's an..."

"I think he knows I've already made up my mind." Martin felt a tingle of irritation as he was reminded of his father's attempts to manipulate him.

"Have you?" She understood something of the pressures that her brother had been subjected to. "There's an American mining magnate who's full of gas. And another man, a banker, I think, who doesn't say much." She squeezed his arm fondly. "Father's still trying to prevent you going, isn't he?"

Martin sighed. "Yes, but at least I can take comfort from knowing that they're not indifferent. Though if they didn't care, it would be easier for me to go."

She smiled up at him. Like her parents, she wished he would not go to Africa, but had given up trying to dissuade him. He would not interpret her silence as indifference, but it was difficult to keep her counsel when her whole being yearned for him to stay, to shield her from the dominance of her father and to plead her cause about the young man she wished to marry. She pushed Martin gently in the direction of the stairs. "You have to wash and change for supper. They're waiting for you. I can tell it's going to be men's talk." She made a moué.

Martin patted her on the shoulder. "I'm sorry Beth. It must be a bore for you. The only reason I left Oxford was because they invited these visitors to meet me."

He ran up the stairs, with Ranter the labrador bounding after him. On the landing a marmalade cat advanced to meet him, mouthing a silent greeting but keeping a respectful distance from the boisterous dog. Martin set his bag down to tickle the cat behind the ears, then went into his room.

The young upstairs maid was lighting the fire. She stood up hurriedly and bobbed a curtsy, smiling shyly, her cheeks flushed from her exertions. Her hand moved instinctively to check the opening of her blouse as she bent to push away the dog. She looked at Martin apprehensively. She was new to the house and had not seen him before, but the other two maids had told her about him. He was the second son, and would inherit nothing. He would soon graduate from Oxford University and go out to Africa to seek his fortune. When Edna asked the other girls if he was married, they giggled, and said that he was still available if she wanted him.

The tall young man was smiling at her, trying to put her at ease. "You're new aren't you? What's your name?"

She bobbed again. "Edna, sir."

"Well thank you, Edna, for starting the fire. Now let me take over." He took the poker from her and she retreated, dipping another curtsy.

He bent to tend the fire, remembering another maid. He was sixteen then and he found her in similar circumstances. As she had passed him to leave the room, something made him put out his arm to stop her. She moved towards him and he kissed her. She was a year younger, but knew far more about kissing. When his hands touched her breasts she made no resistance, allowing him to unfasten her blouse and stroke the hidden warm skin. He wanted to do more, but she stopped him, saying that there would be another time. That time never came—with that girl.

Now, he walked to the window and gazed out in fading evening light at a familiar scene. Mature oaks standing statuesque on a long gentle slope, and beyond them a field of young wheat, burnished by the setting sun. Farther still, dark yews surrounded the church that stood beside a cluster of thatched cottages. Smoke from freshly lit fires hung over the village, layered in still evening air. He wondered again how he could even contemplate leaving this lovely place, this house where he'd grown to adulthood. How he had yearned for it when he was away at boarding school, and when serving in the Army in India, summoning up this very scene.

Turning away from the window he surveyed the room that had been his since early childhood. So often he remembered the contents— the heavy oak furniture, the bookshelves above the wainscot that he had built himself, the dense hang of the heavy velvet damson curtains. He sighed as he washed quickly before changing into evening clothes.

The Russell family moved to Middleton Hall when he was three years old, and he had no earlier memories. The furniture had scarcely moved in all that time. He touched the heavy four-poster bed with affection, as he had when a child. At its foot was a long chest, a blanket box, whose surface was worn to the colour of caramel. Against the wall opposite the window was a gun cabinet, a present from his grandfather. It held his two shotguns, left to him when the old man died six years ago. A matched set of Purdeys, a twelve bore and a sixteen bore. Next to them was the Lee-Metford rifle that he had bought against his father's wishes.

He bent to stroke Ranter, who lay patiently at the hearth, and the dog looked up with limpid hazel eyes. This would be another parting difficult to bear. He had trained the labrador to behave well enough to be allowed in the house. He gave Ranter to his sister when he went up to Oxford, but the dog stayed close to him whenever he visited the Hall, and when he lived there during the university vacations.

"We must go down now," he murmured, and the dog went ahead down the stairs, pausing to look back every few steps. Martin waited at the door to the drawing room, feeling for the first time a sense of foreboding. Soon he would have to confirm his decision. Would this evening's discussions help him, or would they lead to more recriminations?

There were four men and three women in the room. Their conversation died as he entered. They looked at him expectantly, as if he were an actor emerging onto a stage. He glanced around, making a short bow. Beth was seated at the grand piano; she was nodding to him in encouragement.

He greeted his father first. A solid portly man, Bentham Russell smiled with confidence. His sandy hair had receded from most of his head to leave a semi-circle of locks hanging over his collar. Solicitor, farmer, and Liberal Member of Parliament, he had risen from middle-class origins. A London firm of solicitors recognised his worth, made him a partner, and sent him to Oxford, to start a branch of the firm. Two years later, on the death of the owner of Middleton Hall, a widow without family heirs, he borrowed from the firm and bought the property. Five years later he was elected to Parliament.

As he shook his son's hand he felt mixed emotions. Admiration for the young man's ability was mitigated by disappointment that he would soon be leaving. The long-standing fantasy was now becoming a finite plan and Bentham admitted to himself that he had little hope of changing his son's mind, but wished something might happen to dissolve the dream before he left. If only the boy could get the idea out of his system and take up a decent profession. Of course, he couldn't have the farm; it would go Arthur. But another farm could be bought. He sighed; it would have been much better if Martin had kept his commission in the Army.

Next, Martin bent to kiss his mother Isabel, who sat on the sofa facing the fireplace. Matronly and rosy-faced she raised a cheek and murmured his name. She knew her son better than his father and had almost resigned herself to his going. She was already turning her attentions to her daughter-in-law and the prospect of grandchildren.

Martin kissed the cheek of his brother's wife Sylvia, who sat, thin, pallid, and awkwardly straight-backed, beside her mother-in-law. She smiled wanly in greeting. He nodded to his brother Arthur who stood behind the sofa, his hands touching his wife's shoulders. He was four years older than Martin, shorter and already growing rather stout. He smiled, but Martin knew that he was put out because the evening had been set up for his younger brother. He had let it be known from the beginning that Martin's idea of going to Africa was crazy enough to have him certified.

Bentham Russell took his son to meet the two visitors: first, a very tall stooped man, standing with his back to the fire. His eyes were hooded under thick brows, giving the appearance of a huge raptor surveying potential prey. He was there because he knew the MP slightly, through a mutual friend. It was suggested that he might draw Martin's attention to the hazards of Southern Africa.

"George, this is my younger son," said Bentham Russell. "Martin, meet Mr Davenport. He's the President of Consolidated American Mining. They have big investments in the Transvaal."

Though tall, Martin had to look up to Davenport's sharp eyes as they shook hands. The older man offered a smile and keenly appraised the young man. "Pleased to meet you," he said, with a New England accent.

Martin then followed his father to the other guest who sat deep in an armchair near the fire. He had a broad, rather solemn face, and his expression scarcely altered when he held out his hand to Martin. Bentham Russell was less enthusiastic than in the previous introduction. "Mr Grainger, my son Martin." He turned to Martin. "Mr Grainger is a banker. He has spent some years in South Africa. He's a friend of your mother's cousin Charles."

There followed awkward silence. Martin felt an ominous tension, as if he were in some grand inquisition led by his parents, though for different reasons, using the two guests as their inquisitors. Arthur and Sylvia would probably not need to participate, but they would not help him. Only Beth was on his side.

"So, young man, you soon complete your studies at Oxford?" asked Davenport. "Studying agriculture? Your father says you plan to farm in South Africa."

The interrogation had already started. Martin replied, "Yes, sir, I have plans—to go out to Africa." He took a glass of sherry from his father and caught his eye. There was no hint of sympathy there.

Davenport laughed gruffly, aware of the tensions. He spoke in short clipped sentences. "Want to go up north of the Limpopo, eh? Wild country. Very little known about it. Grainger and I have both lived in

South Africa. I still visit every year. Perhaps you should consider the Cape instead. Good land to be bought there. Quite civilised."

Grainger joined in, his tone priestly pompous. "I certainly have no desire to return to the other parts of South Africa, like the Transvaal. Greed and corruption have overcome the decencies that one expects from one's fellow men..."

Davenport's deep laughter rumbled. "Come, come, Grainger; you paint too depressing a picture. Rough, tough place, I grant you. But that's true of all frontiers. I've prospected in California and Australia, and the Transvaal's not much different. You cannot deny the great opportunities for young men..." He stopped suddenly, remembering his brief; he should not appear so optimistic.

Beth spoke from the distant piano. "And are there no opportunities for young women, Mr Davenport?"

Her parents both frowned at her, discomforted by her interjection. Arthur's throat rumbled at his sister's impertinence. But George Davenport smiled; he liked women with spirit.

"Not an easy place for young women, Miss Russell. Dutch Boer women at the frontiers, of course, but most British and American girls prefer the civilisation of Cape Town. Well-established society there; fine old family houses, gracious hospitality."

"With good reason do they stay in Cape Town", added Grainger. "I would not like my daughter to live in Johannesburg—nor my son for that matter."

Davenport turned to Martin, deliberately ignoring Grainger. He sensed that the young man was beleaguered and sympathised with him. After all, in his own youth he had been drunk with the spirit of adventure. "This new territory north of the Limpopo. Went on a short prospecting trip there five years ago." He noticed the young man's eyes brighten and this disconcerted him. He mustn't be accused of being enthusiastic. He added, "May be wiser to stay south of the river."

"What is to be done there besides prospect for gold and hunt wild animals, Mr Davenport?" asked Isabel Russell. She seemed distracted and her tone was mild, but Davenport suspected she was more keenly interested than her demeanour suggested.

"Good potential for farming, ma'am, so I'm told. Not a farmer myself, but I know the Boers have been trying to get up there. Good cattle country, they say. Gold's there too, but so far we've found only small deposits. By some accounts it was the biblical 'Land of Sheba'".

Grainger snorted and passed a conspiratorial glance to Isabel. He turned to Martin. "Why on earth do you want to leave England, young man?"

Martin had been asked this question many times, and knowing his reply seemed rehearsed, he said, "I served two years in the Army, mostly in India. It gave me a taste for a different life. I decided to go to University. Then I heard Mr Cecil Rhodes speak about the new territory of Mashonaland. He said they may give farms to settlers—or at least he indicated that land might be bought cheaply..."

"No certainty about that. Why not farm here?"

Before Martin could answer, his father spoke. "You see, Grainger, this farm's too small for two families. Isabel and I will move into Oxford next year. I'm getting older and it'll make it easier for me to travel up to Parliament. Then this house and the farm will belong to Arthur."

Grainger nodded. "I see." He looked at Martin, and his expression hardened. "Africa's not as easy as you may imagine, young man. Rhodes wants to settle very remote land, which is scarcely known at all—except by missionaries and hunters—and a few prospectors like Davenport's men. There are no roads, there are wild animals, and plenty of diseases we don't know how to cure. Besides, the natives are fierce fighters—they won't take kindly to white men taking their land."

Isabel Russell stood up, a slow process because she was heavy and arthritic. She looked up at Davenport, who still stood at the fireplace. "A situation not dissimilar to your occupation of the Indian territories, Mr Davenport?" Before he could reply, she added, "Shall we go in to supper?" She offered Grainger her arm.

☙❧

The family and guests were seated in the dining room. A dense quiet magnified the occasional small sounds that seemed to echo round the dark walls. The trickle of the wine poured by Donkin, the scrape of cutlery on plates, and the hiss of flickering candle flames, created an almost sinister atmosphere in the room. The walls, wainscoted in oak, seemed to crowd in, forcing the diners into an intimacy they did not want.

Martin looked up and found a sympathetic glance from his sister, but it was Arthur Russell who broke the silence. "What about this man Rhodes? We often hear his name now. How can he offer to give out tracts of land in an unexplored country?"

"How indeed," mumbled Davenport, finishing his mouthful. "Strange man. Brooding, powerful. Not easy to talk to. Made a fortune in diamonds, y'know. Now meddling in high politics..." He turned to Bentham Russell. "No offence, Bentham." He went on, now to the table at large, in the manner of addressing a board meeting. "Won't be satisfied with the Cape. Wants to spread the Empire up the continent of Africa. Heard him say he wants to build a road from the Cape all the way to Cairo. Anyone else said it you'd think him a madman, but Rhodes makes things happen."

Grainger's deep ironic laughter interrupted. "But the Transvaal Boers stand in his way, don't they? They're an intransigent lot. What will he do about them, Davenport?"

"'Go round them', he says. Through the northern Cape Colony and Bechuanaland..."

Isabel Russell's voice was hard edged. "And will the people who live there accept British rule?"

Davenport peered down his long nose at her, realisation growing that she was a formidable woman. "Surely your British rule will be good for them, Mrs Russell? Only savages, after all. No long centuries of civilisation like your East Indians. Nor even the culture of our Indians. The Africans have no writing. Not yet invented the wheel—can you imagine that? They fight all the time against each other—in primitive fashion, you understand—spears, and shields made of ox hides..."

Mrs Russell persisted. "But will they resist the expedition that Rhodes is sending north of the Limpopo?"

Davenport paused to consider his answer, sipping more wine. He had reservations about the Column, thinking that greater numbers were needed to prevent a disaster. He was also concerned about the inexperience of the commanding officer. "The Matabele may put up a fight. The Column will avoid their territory—passing to the south-east, on the way to Mashona country. Suspect the Matabele will be aggravated—incursion of white men. Might be intimidated—by greater numbers than they've seen so far."

"And the Mashona people? Will they stand back and allow white settlers to occupy their land? Or will they fight?"

Davenport shook his head emphatically. "Too weak to resist, ma'am. Seen the poor devils—small and scrawny—not like the strongly built Matabele, who raid them—steal their cattle and women. They scatter like rabbits into the rocky hills."

Martin joined the conversation with some diffidence. "Surely the Matabele won't allow their vassal state to be settled by our people? It would put an end to their raiding. Could they field large fighting impis like Cetewayo did in Zululand?"

"You're right, young man." He looked keenly at Martin. "They won't take it lightly. You British have a concession from the Matabele king, Lobengula. It'll mean little to them when they see the settlers. Not familiar with written treaties—as we are. Could they come out in force?" He paused to consider. "Yes. They say he has thirty thousand warriors— perhaps more. Fearsome prospect. Don't forget Isandhlwana. The Zulus wiped out one of your regiments. 'Course, if the Matabele give trouble, you have the Maxim gun. And the machine-gun is mightier than the spear, to coin a maxim!" His deep laugh reverberated in the room.

Isabel Russell did not join in the laughter and chose this moment to change the direction of the conversation. She sensed that enough had been said. This man that her husband had invited did nothing but whet Martin's appetite. He'd dominated the conversation, leaving her own man with little to say. With a sinking heart she realised the evening was a failure. Her son would leave England; if only she could be confident he would return. All she'd heard had closed a cold hand round her heart. So many perils.

The meal continued with no further discussion about Africa and Martin's plans to leave England. When the Russells and their two guests returned to the drawing room, Donkin brought a tray with coffee and set it in front of Mrs Russell, who poured, and the maid carried the cups to the guests.

As Davenport took his cup he looked at his pocket watch and said. "Mrs Russell, would you excuse us?" He turned to Martin. "I would like to talk to you alone for a while, young man."

"You two can talk in my study," said Bentham Russell. "I'll tell the coachman to be ready to take you to Oxford in half and hour."

Martin showed Davenport to his father's study, a spacious room dominated by a large desk on which lay some of Bentham Russell's legal papers. The walls were lined with bookshelves filled with bound volumes. Davenport seated himself in a leather-upholstered armchair, lit a cigar, and squinted through the thin blue smoke at the tall young man who stood near the desk. There was something most likeable about him. He had not argued with the older men, but the set of his jaw suggested that he was more determined than ever to try his luck in Africa. To stand up to a father like Bentham Russell would need plenty of character. And that was what he could see in Martin's face.

"Look, I'll get straight to the point," said Davenport. "Wanted to talk to you about my nephew, my brother's son. Want him to go out to South Africa." He gave a short hollow laugh. "Need to get him out of the Boston salons." He paused to examine his cigar. "What I propose is this. You're determined to go out there. Can tell you are. I want my nephew to go with you. Would you let him join you?"

Martin was taken by surprise. He had planned to travel alone to the Cape, and imagined long hours on the boat for reading. He did not relish the prospect of travelling with a stranger, yet he felt it would be ungracious to refuse. "I had expected to travel alone, Mr Davenport, but..." He sat down on the movable library steps, as if it would help him to think.

Davenport held up his hand to interrupt. "Course, I don't want you to commit yourself without meeting Perry—his name's Peregrine Davenport, but we call him Perry." He stood up and walked round to the front of the desk where he towered over the seated Martin. "He's in London at the moment. I can arrange for you to meet."

"How old is he? Has he travelled abroad before?" Martin was trying to think quickly.

"Twenty-two—so a bit younger than you—but...I'll be frank with you, Russell..." He paused and re-lit the cigar. "My brother died when Perry was a baby. Lad was brought up by his mother's family in Boston. I funded him through Harvard—he studied geology—but the boy seems to prefer dances and the company of women. Should be going out into the world to earn his living. Want him to experience the rigours and manly life in Africa..."

Martin wondered how the nephew felt about this formidable uncle. "How have you persuaded him to go?"

Davenport smiled wolfishly. "He has no money—and I made a good enough fortune with my mining investments. But I've no children. Never married, you see. Never had the time. Perry knows he must respect my wishes—if he wants to benefit from my estate."

"So he'll be going against his will?"

The older man cleared his throat. "In a manner of speaking." Then his voice became quieter and conspiratorial. "He may be a trifle reluctant, but he's not without spirit. Some sense of humour too. Could make an agreeable companion, eh? Now you're a man who's attracted to adventure—away from the comforts of your family." He bent forward towards Martin, almost defying him to refuse. "So, Russell; agree to meet him, eh?"

Despite his doubts Martin couldn't help muttering, "Yes, of course."

"Good man! As a quid pro quo, I can promise you a position in my mining company. Has good prospects in Africa—probably better than farming! Think it over, my boy."

Martin found it difficult not to like this keen old fellow. He thanked Davenport and showed him out to the hall where Bentham Russell was waiting for his guest, then moved back to the drawing room, where he found Beth alone. She sat at the piano playing snatches of Schumann's Sonata in G Minor, and he paused at the doorway to listen. His sister was making a name for herself in Oxford as a recital pianist. He thought she looked disconsolate, and remembered tensions because the young man who was courting her did not meet her father's exacting standards. He moved forward to sit down in the armchair near the dying fire. She noticed him and stopped playing.

He asked, "What's happening about Peter? Is Father any better disposed to him?"

Beth's expression was defiant. "He still thinks Peter's not good enough for me." She left the piano and came forward to stand next to her brother's chair. "Teaching's an honourable profession, isn't it? His father's a don at Oxford. Sometimes I think Father won't be satisfied unless I marry into a title."

Martin laughed. "Our brother started the rot by marrying a baronet's only daughter." He saw the distress shadow Beth's face and started to speak soothingly. "I like Peter. I think you'd suit each other well. If you love him that's all that matters. I'll see what I can find out from Father when we talk tomorrow morning."

She grasped his arm and looked down at him pleadingly. "I wish you would. He won't even talk to me about it any longer. He just dismisses the subject—as if he's made his judgement, and that's that. Mother frowns and tells me not to bother him." She paced back towards the piano then turned to face him. "I have to pursue my life, Martin. I'm eighteen now; an adult. But to them I'm only a daughter. I find it so galling that because you're a son you can oppose their wishes, while I have to obey them."

He thought for a moment of some of the emancipated young women he'd met at the University. They had told him about their frustrations with the unequal treatment of women. They were not entitled to vote, nor to be awarded a university degree. They felt discrimination in many other ways, and parental dominance was often mentioned.

"You'll be able to leave home when you're a bit older, Beth. Be patient."

                                         ઢ઼ઢ

Next morning Martin rode round the farm at dawn. He knew the four hundred acres so well that he could appreciate the little changes since his last ride here two months ago. The lambs had grown and would soon be sold. An old elm had fallen in a storm, and was being sawn for timber; they would bring some of the smaller branches to the Hall for firewood. After his ride he visited the byre and talked for a few minutes to Young Fred. He walked the lines of warm cow bodies as they contentedly ate and waited their turn to be milked. He stopped now and then to appraise the condition of his favourites; some he had milked himself.

He was in the dairy when his father came in and they walked together round the farm buildings. Martin relished the familiar sounds: horses stamping in their stables, milk buckets clanking, cows complaining about their full udders. Ranter the labrador, and old Sheba, a cocker spaniel, gambolled beside the two men.

Martin sensed that the impending conversation would be seminal. He had tried to analyse whether he was being selfish in leaving England to seek his fortune in Africa. He'd been to India for two years in the Army and his father raised no objections to that, even encouraged it, regarding it as a start to a career. There had been much anguish when he abandoned his commission and entered the University, though his parents were mollified when they anticipated him renting a farm for a settled life in England. Then his increasing desire to go to Africa led to many arguments and accusations that he regretted.

Bentham Russell wore his weekend clothes, breeches and a tweed jacket. He carried a thornwood walking stick, and Martin noticed that he seemed to walk rather stiffly, though it was a mild morning. "Well, Martin? Have you made up your mind? Did the conversations last night help you?"

Martin smiled; his father always went straight to the point. "They only confirmed my decision to go."

"I was afraid so."

"Mr Davenport was fair, I thought. Mr Grainger was too...well, perhaps a bit one-sided in his arguments."

Bentham Russell grunted and nodded, frowning. "You must understand that I respect your desire to go abroad, son, but why not try business somewhere in the Cape? Davenport will give you a good job in his company. Or if you don't like that, I'm sure he'd give you introductions."

"I haven't the slightest interest in mining...or business." Martin tried to conceal his exasperation.

"Well, I believe you're making the wrong decision. And you know your mother can't come to terms with you going. What we don't like about you going to Africa is that you will be facing all sorts of dangers alone..."

"Father! I'm twenty-five years old. Surely that's old enough to make my own decisions and fend for myself?"

Bentham whistled impatiently to the dogs, who were chasing the scent of a rabbit. "It's not a question of age. You heard last night how primitive and dangerous the place is. Your mother was most upset last night."

"I'm sorry, truly I am. But I want to see for myself..."

"I don't mean the Cape, or Johannesburg—if you were going to stay there I, at least, would not have such rooted objections."

"Objections, Father? I was expecting you to lend me some support."

"You have enough money of your own—if that's what you mean."

"Scarcely. Most of Aunt Clare's legacy went towards my fees at Oxford. I have enough for my passage to the Cape, but I was hoping you'd stake me for the journey north? I'll pay you back, of course."

Bentham shook his head angrily. "No, Martin. You cannot expect me to finance you doing something in direct contradiction of my express wishes."

"As you wish." He was saddened rather than angry. "I plan to return soon, you know."

"I wonder if you will. Isn't it more likely you'll settle out there?"

"Not if it's as bad as you think." Martin tried to raise a smile from his father, but failed. "I don't know. I want to come back regularly to see you all. England will always be my home."

They walked on for a while in uncomfortable silence, and on reaching the far side of the farm turned to walk back to the house.

Martin broached a new subject. "Father, why are you so averse to Peter Jacobs? Beth is quite stuck on him, and he seems a decent enough young man..."

"I'm not really 'averse'—as you put it. You probably don't understand, son, that a girl's station in life depends very much on the man she marries. I know times are changing fast, and it may not be long before women are making their own careers." He paused. "Peter's a decent lad, I'll concede, but he has no money at all—except for his teacher's salary..."

"But you had only your solicitor's salary when you married."

Bentham smiled wryly. "True, but I had old family money behind me—an inheritance to expect."

Martin decided to grasp the issue. He felt honour bound to make his sister's case, but he feared his father's reaction, knowing that this was stepping beyond his right as Beth's brother to question a parent. "She won't be happy if she can't marry the man she loves."

"Love?" His father puffed out air, his face darkening. "Love? She's hardly in love! Let her wait a couple of years." He struck the ground irritably with his stick and the dogs turned to look at him, startled by his change of mood. "She should spend a few months in London."

Another exile, thought Martin, deciding to drop the subject.

∻

Four weeks later came one of those baking June days that herald high summer. The sky was cloudless, the air still and thick with the scent from wild flowers in the hedgerows. Martin paced the platform at Oxford station, waiting for the train to take him to London to meet Perry Davenport. He wore a suit, but has taken off the jacket, which he slung over his shoulder, and had loosened his tie. His mind, as often in these days, was consumed with thoughts about going to Africa, and the adventures that might lie ahead.

He noticed, further down the platform, Mrs Jacobs, the mother of Beth's beau Peter. Standing beside her was her daughter Amanda. Mrs Jacobs was tall, with a pouter-pigeon bosom and an imperious demeanour. Amanda was almost as tall, but slim and seeming fragile as she stood next to her mother. She wore a light cotton dress to suit the hot day and carried a linen jacket over her arm. Her straw boater had long ribbons that trailed down her back.

Martin walked down the platform to greet them. He knew both only slightly, having met them a couple of times at dinner parties given by mutual friends. Amanda had completed her first year at the London School of Medicine for Women. A sharp sensation that he recognised as physical attraction ran through him. Something about her bearing that reflected her reputation as one of those girls who was breaking out of the mould of Victorian strictures. He'd met a few of them at the University, and enjoyed their company. They were so independent compared with the officers' daughters he'd met in India, who seemed bent on marriage despite having barely left school.

Mrs Jacobs spotted his approach and said something to her daughter with an arch smile. Amanda turned to watch the young man as he approached. He noticed that she touched the loose hairs that had escaped from her plait at the nape of her neck; they were pale blonde and had a fine almost infantile texture. Her eyes were lively in their movement and attention.

"Martin, dear boy," gushed Mrs Jacobs, proffering her cheek to be kissed. "Congratulations! I hear you have a good degree." Then she said commandingly, "Would you escort us for the journey to London?"

Martin smiled and bowed in acknowledgement. He looked at Amanda and stepped forward to shake her hand. She blushed slightly then turned to point to the train, which approached from the West, all steam and hissing brakes. When Martin helped the two women into a compartment Mrs Jacobs settled in the centre, while he and Amanda sat opposite each other next to windows.

The girl was pleased at this opportunity to get to know Martin Russell; she had heard his praises sung by Beth. At a couple of parties when they had both been present, he had been inaccessible, usually talking to young men of his age. The snatches of conversation she'd heard were about hunting and polo, or the merits of alternative careers. Now he was sitting in front of her, a captive for her to interrogate, but her accustomed confidence evaporated as she sought an opening gambit.

She was an unusual girl for her generation, involved in the periphery of the suffrage movement at her College in London. Her feisty interjections at student meetings had already given her a reputation as an exemplary modern woman. To some of the male students she was intimidating, because she had a sharp tongue. But her beauty overcame their misgivings, so that she had many suitors, none of whom had succeeded with so much as an invitation accepted.

Mrs Jacobs fanned herself vigorously. "It's going to be terribly hot in town. What takes you there, Martin?"

He glanced at Amanda before replying; although she was gazing out of the window she was evidently listening. "I'm meeting someone who's going out to the Cape," he said. "We may travel together. We're going to discuss it...and we'll visit a man who knows the situation out there."

"Oh Martin!" Mrs Jacobs' tone was both disparaging and patronising. "I don't know why you young men are always tearing away to foreign places. Why ever do you want to go there? How long will it take?"

He stifled a smile, not wanting Amanda to suspect that he thought her mother was living up to her reputation as a busybody. "It takes about two weeks, Mrs Jacobs. And the reason I'm going is that there's so much opportunity out there—and adventure..."

Mrs Jacobs shook her head doubtfully. "It may be very exciting for you, but I expect there are a lot of difficulties. And what do your mother and father think of the idea?"

Amanda stirred and looked away from the window, embarrassed that her mother should question at this level. "Mama! Martin probably doesn't want to discuss..."

He laughed to reassure the girl. "I'm afraid they don't really approve. They prefer that I settle down in England, but I won't be away for long. A two-week journey is not too far away, is it?"

"It is for a mother, " said Mrs Jacobs relentlessly. "I can understand how Isabel feels. I would hate it if my son decided to work abroad."

"Mama!" Amanda remonstrated. "If Martin wants to go, it's not for us to dissuade him."

He laughed again and said to her, "Nothing will dissuade me, Amanda."

For a short while the two young people looked out of their respective windows at the summer fields. Amanda was smiling to herself, thinking that here was a young man who was willing to do what he wanted in opposition to his parents' wishes, just as she had when she decided to study medicine. Martin had both determination and a sense of humour that made him very attractive. She recognised feelings that had been discussed with her closest friends. A woman's desire for a man was beyond contemplation in her mother's generation. But she saw no reason why desire should be an exclusively male preserve. Her friends acknowledged that to want a man was one thing, but to indulge one's needs was really not practical. The best that a girl could do was to present herself as desirable and hope for the consequences.

She leaned forward to catch Martin's attention. "You are coming to my party on Saturday, aren't you?" she asked.

He stumbled in his reply. "Oh, yes—of course. And your father said I could bring Perry Davenport. That's if he can come. He's the man I'm meeting in London."

Amanda said, "There will be people you know at the party, and perhaps some that you don't. You must come."

He laughed. "I will, Amanda. I'm free from my studies now."

They talked easily for the remainder of the journey, mostly about mutual acquaintances and about life and work at university. At Paddington Martin helped the mother and daughter into a hansom cab before taking one himself to the Farmers' Club in Whitehall Court.

A few elderly men hidden behind newspapers occupied the oak-panelled rooms; the air was redolent of cigar smoke. Martin chose the main lounge, seated himself in a large leather armchair and started to read The Times. A short while later, a well-dressed, rather foppish young man entered. He looked around with an amused expression, and walked up to Martin. He was quite tall, but of slender build, with long dark hair and a nervous ironic smile. He moved with a swagger, seeming over-conscious of his appearance.

"Are you Martin Russell? I'm Perry Davenport. Sorry if I've kept you waiting." He had a slight American accent.

Martin stood up, folding his newspaper, and shook Perry's hand. So this was the companion, the reluctant traveller, looking like a caricature of the salon habitué that his uncle described. He offered coffee or tea.

Perry grinned. "What about a whisky? Is the bar open?"

Martin summoned a steward and ordered a whisky for his guest and coffee for himself. He waved Perry to an adjacent armchair, already filled with apprehension about this prospective companion.

"I hear you graduated from Oxford—congratulations." Perry spoke in a slightly affected manner, tending to over-emphasise some words. "I made it through Harvard by the skin of my teeth. My own fault of course—as I was told by my tutor—'Not enough dedication to work'." He sighed. "I'm afraid I wasn't cut out for academe. What about you? A natural student?"

Martin laughed "Not at all. Besides I had two years in the Army after I left school, and that was long enough to forget my books."

"Ah yes, my uncle told me. You served in India. But now you want to get back to adventure again." There was a hint of mocking as he spoke. "For my part, I really want to stay in England—or in Boston. But I had to make a deal with my uncle—the truth is, the old chap's bribing me—to do the manly thing, you know. To do what he and my father did. They used to prospect for gold and shoot lions—heroic stuff like that. He has this idea that I should go to Africa."

Martin was dismayed at the apparent lack of enthusiasm, even ridicule. "What has he told you about it?"

"The life out there? He tried to make it sound interesting, poor old buffer." Perry laughed with some bitterness. "But I haven't been very good at listening. I try to steer clear of him." He paused and looked carefully at Martin. "One of the reasons I'm here is to find out more—without his bias. What do you know about it?"

Martin suspected that whatever he said would not convince this fellow. Yet he felt an obligation, having given an undertaking to the elder Davenport. "I heard from Rhodes himself, when he visited Oxford. He's given a contract to a young man called Frank Johnson to recruit and train men, and then lead them into Mashonaland. You know where that is?" Perry shook his head so Martin explained with a map, roughly drawn on a piece of Club notepaper. "Here's the Cape, at the southernmost tip of the African continent—and here's the Vaal River, with the Transvaal above it—'trans', across the Vaal. It's a Boer Republic. The gold mines and Johannesburg are in the Transvaal—about here. Now here's the Limpopo River, flowing east into the Indian Ocean—it's the northern boundary of the Boer republic. It's almost *terra incognita* north of the Limpopo River. A few prospectors and hunters have been there—and missionaries, of course..."

"Of course; Livingstone and his fellow bible thumpers."

Martin ignored this interjection and continued. "Johnson's only twenty-three—that's younger than me—but he's been up there before. He must know a lot to get the contract from Rhodes. They're called the Pioneer Column, men with special skills. They've chosen only about two hundred out of two thousand applicants. They have over a hundred wagons, and plenty of labourers to cut through the bushveld—oh, and they have machine guns, and an electric searchlight to frighten off the Matabele."

"And we're too late to join them for their epic journey?" Perry affected to be slightly bored. "I wonder if they would have selected us—if we'd applied."

Martin smiled uneasily. "We're certainly too late; they started this week. And no, we'd have been too young and inexperienced to be selected. But I plan to follow them. Your uncle said he wants you to go with me."

"Yeah. He told me." Perry was grinning wryly. "I follow his scheme—that was the deal I made. If not, he cuts me out of his will—simple as that. And you're to be my chaperon." He laughed. "Could you bear that? When do we leave?"

"We have to leave soon. The wet season there starts in November. If we reach the Cape by the end of July we can be in Palapye by August, and then have ten weeks or so to make the trek." Martin looked at his pocket watch. "It's time we went to see Lord Eyre."

"Oh yeah." Perry heaved a sigh of resignation. "Uncle George's old pal."

The two young men left the Farmers' Club and took a hansom cab to Lombard Street. Martin's sober suit and solid conservative appearance contrasted with Perry's swagger and foppish clothes. When they entered the offices of the Chartered Company they were shown into the office of Lord Eyre, a tall supercilious man known for his impeccable connections in the city. He invited them to be seated, noted Perry's attire and lifted an eyebrow in disapproval. He pulled out a large gold fob watch, as if to indicate that his time was limited, then started talking in patrician tones.

"Let me tell you about this company first. The Chartered Company—of which I'm a director—has absolute rights in the territories of North and South Zambesia—you know where they are?" Not waiting for their reply he waved expansively at the large map of Africa on the wall. The colour pink covered much of the fringes of the continent, but there were large blank areas in the centre. "We are authorised by our Charter to develop mines, to farm, and to allocate land. In fact, we are the governing authority." He paused to allow these portentous words to sink with gravity into the minds of the two young men.

"Is it an indefinite charter, sir?" asked Martin. "Or will the British Government eventually take over?"

Lord Eyre cleared his throat noisily. "The Charter runs for twenty-five years, and it can be renewed. A great deal could happen in that time. It is possible that the territories will ultimately become dominions of Britain."

Perry leaned forward and spoke eagerly, though Martin knew he was playing a part. "And will men like us be welcomed in the new territory?"

Lord Eyre looked piercingly at Perry. George Davenport had warned him that his nephew needed to adjust his attitudes. "The administrators will be looking for talented men, preferably those with some experience in the services, or with skills—doctors, miners, and so on. They certainly don't want adventurers."

"And will it be possible to buy land?" asked Martin.

"As I said, er...Russell, the Charter gives the Company the authority to do anything it pleases, including the allocation of land. I can say no more now. All will depend on circumstances as they arise, which will determine the decisions of the administrators out there. But you can be sure that we will expect the settlers to buy land and start farming."

After a few more minutes, Lord Eyre stood up to indicate that the discussion was closed. He shook hands with his visitors, wished them well, and they left his room.

Out on Lombard Street, they started to walk towards Piccadilly. Martin decided that he could not refuse to take Perry with him to South Africa. At least he was cheerful, and amusing in a rather mocking way, and perhaps he could be resourceful. He had ample funds from his uncle and that would be valuable when they gathered equipment in South Africa. There was so much to buy, and without his father's financial support Martin had only a few pounds left after paying for his passage.

Perry started declaiming as he sauntered down the pavement, in flippant imitation of Lord Eyre. "Well, what do you say, old chap? Will you take me on? Allow me to go with you to the depths of Africa? Or will I be too much of a burden to you?"

"If you become one, I'll dump you." Martin laughed as he shook Perry's hand. "We must go to the steamship office and confirm the booking of your berth—I made it provisionally, because they're so difficult to get. And then you must come to visit my family in Middleton."

For the first time Perry shed his casual attitude and mocking smile. "I would like that very much."

Martin thus glimpsed a different personality lurking behind the glib façade. He suspected that Perry was lonely, because he agreed with such alacrity to visit the Russells over the coming weekend. In reality, Perry was making a supreme effort to accept the inevitability of going to Africa with this earnest fellow. Perhaps kind fate would appear to rescue him, some lost Aunt with thousands to squander on him, some wealthy heiress to buy his favours. Yet he was reduced to the company of a man consumed with thoughts about the best cattle to rear in sub-tropical countries, and the likely dates for the onset of the monsoon. How droll it would be to make this adventure. He would dine out on the story, summon flutters in the hearts of the salon girls, and arouse the envy of his friends, who had little to offer besides the latest antics of the Quorn or the Beaufort.

CHAPTER 2
Amanda—June 1890

On the following Saturday morning Martin met Perry at Tackley station, and drove his visitor in the pony trap to Middleton Hall, where he introduced him to the other members of the Russell family. Perry became the epitome of charm, making a particular effort to capture the attention of Beth. His politeness was exemplary with Bentham and Isabel Russell, who were soon won over. Only occasionally could Martin detect the mocking irony that Perry had displayed when they met in London. His misgivings about taking Perry to Africa began to dissolve.

That evening, Martin, Perry and Beth drove to Oxford in an open landau drawn by two bay horses. The weather was fine and mild as they spanked down the Banbury Road into north Oxford in high spirits. Martin drew the landau up at the Jacobs' house in Norham Gardens. A couple of grooms, hired by the hosts for the occasion, took care of the horses. It was a large house, built in the middle of the century, and brightly lit for the party. Before they entered, Beth smoothed her skirt and checked that the men's bow ties were straight.

In the hall, Amanda Jacobs advanced to greet them, wearing a blue taffeta ball gown. Martin again felt a strong attraction, admiring the sheen of her hair, and the smooth swell of her breasts under her low-cut bodice. He thought she glanced at him for longer than the occasion demanded, before introducing her brother to Perry. Peter Jacobs, slender and studious, with horn-rimmed spectacles perched on his long nose, took Beth away, to Perry's evident chagrin. Amanda led Martin and Perry to a table in the large parlour where a group of men helped themselves to drinks, then left them to greet another group of guests.

"Your girl, Martin?" asked Perry.

"Who? Amanda? No."

Perry laughed nervously. His eyes were darting round the room. "I don't want to be accused of poaching."

Martin greeted Amanda's father, who was helping a maid to ladle punch, and introduced Perry. Mr Jacobs, a don at St. John's College, amiably welcomed the young men as he handed them glasses.

"So, when are you going out to South Africa, Martin?" he asked. "Is it true that you're to settle there? Or are you just going for a holiday?"

Martin laughed. "It won't be a holiday, Mr Jacobs—that's certain."

"We have a guest who's been out to that part of the world, a geologist—Dr Ramsey. Come, you should meet him. You come too, Mr Davenport."

Jacobs led them into the drawing room, which was filled with guests standing in small groups. On his own, near the piano, stood a short, thickset man, with a heavy black beard, holding a glass of whisky and watching the other guests with an air of disdain. Jacobs made brief introductions and left them, when there followed an awkward moment of silence that Martin felt obliged to break.

He said, "Mr Jacobs told us you'd been out in South Africa, sir."

Dr Ramsey regarded the two young men with suspicion, his dark eyes glittering. His voice was deep and rasped like a rough file. "I've worked there for several years. Why do you ask?"

"Perry and I leave for the Cape in a fortnight. Our aim is to follow the Pioneer Column to Mashonaland."

The older man smiled condescendingly. "Has anyone told you about the trouble that's brewing in South Africa? You fellows may think it's some sort of playground for adventurers, but I assure you it isn't." He eyed them over his glass as he sipped his whisky. "There are thousands of foreigners flocking into the Transvaal. Some of them are professional people, but many of them are fortune seekers—traders, gamblers, prostitutes. Soon they'll outnumber the Boers, but they're regarded as outsiders—'uitlanders' the Boers call them. They're complaining because they have no vote, and no say in the taxes they have to pay." He paused to glower round the room. "Greed reigns supreme. The Boers are greedy for the mineral wealth. The fortune-seekers are greedy for money. The imperialists are greedy for territory. Mark my words, gentlemen, there's going to be an explosion before long."

Perry spoke with mock ingenuousness, broadening his American accent. "What, another war? After you chaps were defeated at Majuba Hill?"

Dr Ramsey seemed not to react to the implied slight. He nodded slowly. "Yes, we were soundly defeated then. Gladstone was right to settle with the Boers. We should have learned something, but the defeat rankles with the army and the government. They want to teach the Boers a lesson they won't forget, and put them back on their farms where they belong. Chamberlain is too belligerent by half. Wait until you meet the Boers. They're a rum bunch. I rather like them—for their fundamental religious beliefs. And I admire their pride and their hospitality. But they're out of their depth trying to run a country, dealing with the likes of Rhodes and Chamberlain."

"And their fighting ability?" asked Martin. "I hear they're first class shots."

"True; they've had plenty of experience of fighting the natives— been doing it off and on for two hundred years. But when it comes to fighting us?" He shrugged. "If we had better generals the Boers would be no match for us."

"Have our generals really been at fault?" Martin remonstrated.

Ramsey sneered. "Most of our generals are incompetent aristocrats—amateurs. The rest are aggressive professionals. None of them has experienced fighting well-armed and well-mounted men. Our army hasn't fought on level terms since the Crimea. Just chasing a few Afridis on the North-West frontier, or fuzzy-wuzzies in the desert, or Zulu warriors armed with spears. It's no preparation for the likes of the Boers, I assure you—as we found to our cost at Majuba."

Beth came up to invite them to help themselves to food from the buffet. She gave Perry an empty plate and directed him to the table, then drew her brother aside, holding his arm so that she could speak quietly to him. She had a ploy that might make her brother change his mind about leaving England.

"You know Amanda likes you, Martin?"

He laughed. "What do you mean? Is this some sort of intrigue? I thought you modern girls were too proud for that sort of thing."

"Don't be obtuse," she retorted, fond but irritated. "She's told me she admires you, and a moment ago she said she's sorry you're leaving. Don't you like her? Don't you find her attractive?"

He looked across the room to where Amanda was talking to Perry in the line at the buffet table. Her face was animated, her eyes sparkling, and he felt a sharp pang of jealously. "Of course she's attractive, but I hardly know her. When we were on the train to London the other day she told me she's studying medicine there."

"Yes, and when she finishes they can't award her a degree. It's so unfair! She and I agree that women are treated wretchedly." She noticed that her brother was smiling. "It's not a matter for amusement, Martin!

We feel very strongly about it. You should talk to her about it. You might find it rewarding."

She left him and he joined the line for food. After helping himself he walked alone onto the stone-flagged terrace overlooking the garden. A brick wall lined with shrubs surrounded the long narrow lawn. Sitting on a low bench at the edge of the terrace he sniffed the mild damp air and thought he'd caught the scent of an urban fox. For a moment familiar doubts assailed him. It would be so easy to rent a farm in Oxfordshire, stay close to the family, and enjoy the company of friends at evenings like this. Then he looked up at the star filled sky and imagined what it might be like in Africa.

Amanda had watched Martin go out to the terrace and followed him, her long taffeta dress rustling. She wondered if she should interrupt his thoughts. He must have come to contemplate; it was the only justification for his coming out here. But this was an opportunity to talk to him alone, the first young man to stir feelings in her that she knew were natural. He had a maturity that her fellow students lacked, and she knew that he was older than most of them. He also had a calm assurance in the way he spoke to people, leavened by a ready smile. There was a strength to him, reflected in his determination. Thinking this, she was saddened that he would soon leave England.

"Are you being unsociable?" she asked. "Dreaming of Africa?"

He stood up. "As a matter of fact, I was." He pointed to the sky. "Those stars—there are more of them in the African sky."

"Will you have girls to entertain you there?"

He laughed. "I doubt it. When you're a doctor you must come out to Africa."

Her expression turned serious and she spoke vehemently. "Martin, you don't know how difficult it is for a woman to do something like that, do you? I envy your freedom to decide that you want to go to university, or travel to Africa. Such freedom is unimaginable for a woman."

"I'm sorry. Should I feel guilty? My father's quite sympathetic to giving women the right to vote. But unless the Government decides to legislate, there's little he can do."

She shrugged impatiently then took his hand and led him out onto the lawn. It was darker here, away from the pool of light flooding out from the house. "When do you leave?" She asked. "You're very determined to go, aren't you?"

"It's all planned now."

She wondered if she could undo his plans and stopped at the far end of the lawn facing the house. Someone had started playing the piano, and the strains of a song from 'Pirates of Penzance' drifted out into the night. She saw Martin was looking towards the house with its brightly lit windows and she moved to stand in front of him, forcing him to look at her instead.

He caught the scent she was wearing and wondered where the moment would lead, remembering a time when he was led out into semi-darkness by a girl in Simla. He had been to Delhi on Army business and having a fortnight of leave went up to the hill station. Young officers were welcomed to parties that were usually sprinkled with girls seeking husbands. On that occasion the girl left him in no doubt that he could have her, married or not. They fumbled in the dark with growing urgency, and opened some of their clothing, but it was too cold and close to the party. They met next day and rode up into the mountains, finding a secluded spot in the pine forest where they made love. It was his first experience, but he knew it was not hers. In the ensuing days he found her demands for attention intrusive, and return to his regiment brought an end to the affair.

Now, Amanda's face was in shadow but her long curling lashes, like those on a doll, glinted. "What will you do in your last week?" she asked.

"Well...I have to pack." He was cautious, wondering where her questions were leading. "Say my goodbyes to friends—that sort of thing."

"So you're not terribly busy?" She was trying to sound scarcely interested but he detected her nervousness.

"No. We'd have left earlier but the liners were all fully booked. Why do you ask?"

She swallowed, and he realised that despite her apparent confidence she was having difficulty asking him these questions. "Martin, would you take me punting? Beth says you're an expert. And I'd like you to tell me more about your experiences at the University."

He was taken aback at this sudden request. "Yes...of course I'll take you." Then he laughed. "But I must warn you that Beth's opinion of my punting skill is exaggerated. When would you like to go?"

"Tomorrow."

"I'm sorry—I can't take you tomorrow. I promised to take Perry riding. How about Monday? He leaves on the morning train, so I'll be free for the rest of the day."

"Monday would be lovely." She glanced over her shoulder. "I'd better get back to the party now, to do my duties as hostess."

They strolled back to the house together and parted without another word. As he entered the drawing room Martin noticed his sister sitting with her beau Peter Jacobs, listening to a young man playing songs from the Savoy operas on the piano. Some of the guests were singing.

Beth was sitting on a cushion on the floor, with Peter behind her, tall, thin and awkward. Martin saw him lean forward to whisper in her ear, his expression anxious. He had a habit of glancing round while he talked, as if he expected an acquaintance to enter the room.

⑽❧

"What did Martin find out?" Peter was asking.

"Not a great deal," Beth replied. "Father wants me to wait for a year or two—I suppose he hopes I'll meet someone else. He wants me to live in London for a while."

Peter sucked in his breath at this unwelcome news. "And will you?"

"Change my mind?" She turned round to reassure him and realised for the first time that she could not be sure. "I don't think so."

Peter noticed the doubt in her voice. "He knows you could make a better match." He paused while a guest moved past them. "If you went to the University we could see each other..."

"Oh, Peter. You know I'm not at all academic. I'm not like Amanda. It would be a hopeless waste of my time and my parents' money. I think Father will give me permission to study piano at the Royal Academy." She sighed heavily, then caught Martin's eye across the room and smiled to him. She said to Peter. "He's so obstinate. There's your sister—a lovely girl who thinks the world of him—and all he can do is rush off to Africa."

"I gather your mother hasn't prevailed on him."

"No. She hates the whole idea. Father wouldn't mind—if only Martin went into business there instead of farming."

"How I envy him," said Peter wistfully.

Beth turned to him in surprise. "Why should you envy him?"

"He has money and position. He can go where his spirit takes him..."

"Peter! You're so wrong." She was vehement in her impatience. "Martin has no money...at least barely enough to pay his passage to Cape Town. And he has no more position than you do. He's only the younger son of a solicitor. He has no income, nor a legacy to expect." She sighed. "But he does have spirit." And she realised that Peter lacked spirit—which was perhaps an unfair judgement. She ought not compare him with her brother and Perry Davenport.

み〜ふ

Returning to Middleton Hall in the landau Martin looked back over the Cherwell Valley. It was flooded with moonlight, with its scattering of hamlets—Kidlington, Hampton Poyle, and Hampton Gay. The horses trotted smartly, their hoof beats echoing through the hedges. Startled rabbits scattered down the road ahead. The night air was mild and heavily scented. He held the reins loosely, allowing the horses to make their own pace. This was the sort of evening he would remember when he was homesick for England. He recalled his conversation with Amanda. She was a lovely girl and so full of life, but it was madness to think of romancing her when he was on the eve of departure. He was enticed by her, but his better nature made him regret accepting her request. What did she mean about finding out more about his life at the University?

Perry was in high spirits, buoyed by plenty of good wine. "Why, Martin!" he shouted, as if he wanted the whole countryside to hear him. "Why are you so set on leaving this wonderful country—and all these beautiful girls?"

"Yes!" added Beth. "We think you're mad!" She turned to Perry, increasingly conscious of his attraction. "And so are you, Perry, for going with him."

Perry threw back his head and laughed. "Do you really want us to stay? Say something and I'll cancel my passage."

"Of course I want you to stay! Martin's my best friend."

"And what about me?" he shouted in protest. "Do you want me to stay too?"

She hesitated, and in a quiet voice answered. "You don't seem the type to go to the wilds of Africa."

Perry was serious for a moment. "I guess you're right."

"Then why go?"

"Hasn't Martin told you? I'll be cut out of the family fortune if I don't go."

"You could make your own fortune...here, or in America."

He laughed. "Not me, Beth. I'm too fond of the good life. Besides, I have no talent. Come on, now. No more of this serious talk. What shall we sing?" He did not wait for an answer, but started warbling.

∂∞⊲

Back at Middleton Hall, Perry went to his room, weary but cheerful, Beth and Martin met in the study by unspoken agreement. Martin glanced idly along the bookshelves recognising old friends from his childhood. Doubts about leaving England kept ringing in his mind and he tried to counter them with fantasies of rolling sub-tropical farmland stocked with glossy steers and fields of tall maize.

His sister moved restlessly, tidying some of the papers lying on a table. She felt that dull ache of sadness, almost physical in its unrelenting presence. It came from the knowledge that her love for Peter Jacobs had ended. Her analysis concluded that it had to do with both Martin and Perry. Martin was so much more active than the schoolteacher. He had served two years in India, studied for three years at Oxford, and was now on the brink of a journey to Africa. He played polo, tennis, and other sports. Peter seemed to have accepted a career in education because his parents wanted it, with scarcely a thought for any alternative. And Perry? There was an undeniable attraction about him. She knew he was irresponsible, but he was so busy enjoying his life.

She said to her brother, "Did Amanda try to persuade you not to go to Africa?"

"No—but she persuaded me to take her punting!" He laughed. "What did you tell her about my skill on the river?"

She raised her eyebrows in disguised surprise. "I told her you're an expert, which you are. And it shouldn't be any hardship to take a lovely girl punting." She suddenly lowered her voice. "Be careful though..."

He looked up from a book. "What do you mean?"

"She can be rather scheming—when she wants her way. I don't mean deceitful...It's rather hard to describe. It's as if...she's not innocent."

"Do you mean she's not a virgin? I don't know what you mean." He put the book back on its shelf and walked up to her. "Isn't she your friend?"

"She is, but..." She realised that she had gone too far. "Oh, I don't know, Martin. I suppose it's something a woman can sense, without recognising exactly what it is." She dropped into one of the leather armchairs. "Tell me about Perry. Will he be a good companion for you?"

"Not ideal. I even doubt he'll stay the course. He's treating our journey like a joy ride. I won't be surprised if he drops out at Cape Town. But it wouldn't matter to me if he did. I have no obligations..."

"What is he like as a man?"

Martin looked sharply as his sister. He'd already observed that she found Perry attractive, but this was becoming a serious interrogation. "I hardly know him," he answered evasively.

She would not let it go. "Come, Martin. You can do better than that...for your sister."

He moved to sit on the edge of the heavy table, on which were piled some of his father's legal papers, and looked indulgently at her. "He's a type that seldom entered the army. Those that did never prospered." He stood up and started pacing the room. "I might be wrong. I haven't seen him in a situation that would show his character. He strikes me as wanting to spend too much time with women—almost like a gigolo."

Beth smiled. "Perhaps he finds them better company than men."

"Perhaps. But I suspect they're gratifying something that he badly needs. Approbation?"

"We all need that." She moved to get up.

"Some more than others. For some it's a kind of narcotic." He held out his hand to lift her from her chair. "There's something strange about him. I gather his parents died when he was quite young, so he may have had an unhappy childhood." He paused to remember his impressions. "You know, it's difficult to have a sensible conversation with him. He's generally flippant." He smiled. "Better not take to him too much, Beth. Stick to that steady fellow Peter."

She sighed, knowing that he was wrong. The brief acquaintance had shown her that she no longer wished to marry Peter Jacobs.

સ્જ્જ

The following Monday, at Oxford station, Martin saw Perry off to London, then cycled up to Norham Gardens. The sky was clear, and he had taken off his blazer and rolled up his sleeves. A bottle of champagne in an ice-filled canvas bag was strapped to the carrier. As he passed his old college in St Giles he felt a lightness of spirit, knowing that three long years of study were ended. Arriving at the Jacobs' house he wheeled his cycle across the gravelled drive and rang the doorbell.

Amanda opened the door wearing a cool blue cotton dress, cut low enough to reveal a glimpse of the cleft between her breasts. She guided him inside, where he was greeted by her parents, who were about to set off for Newbury to visit friends for the day. He chatted to them in the parlour for a few minutes before they left, then followed Amanda to the kitchen, where she completed packing a hamper on the kitchen table. They left on foot, Martin carrying the hamper on his shoulder and collecting the champagne as he passed his bicycle. Taking a book out of the other pannier, he handed it to Amanda.

"'The Story of an African Farm'; Beth told me you wanted to borrow it." He laughed. "You know, when I bought it I thought it had something to do with farming and might be useful."

"Did you know she used a man's name to have it published? The things women have to do! Did you read it?"

"Yes, I did. Very intense, and strong. Amazing that it was written by a...such a young woman. You'll see Beth has marked some passages."

They strolled along quiet tree-lined streets to the Cherwell boathouse. Martin chose a punt from a serried collection on the bank, and the rotund proprietor assured them they would have the river to themselves. Martin expertly poled out the punt, while Amanda settled herself on the cushions, leaned back and opened the book.

"What did you think of my travelling companion?" asked Martin. "I noticed you had a conversation with him."

She looked up from the book distractedly. "Perry? Oh, a charmer, like many Americans I've met. But he's not very sure of himself, is he? I wonder how useful he'll be in Africa."

"It's not so important." He steered the punt smoothly along the narrow river between banks of drooping willows. "We agreed that we might decide to go our separate ways when we reach the Cape. He doesn't want to settle out there, you know."

She seemed not to be listening to him. "Here! It's the first passage Beth marked. 'I once heard an old man say that he never saw intellect help a woman so much as a pretty ankle'. Isn't that the root of our problem?"

He frowned, wondering if the morning would be spent in debate about the role of women in society. "There are deeper sentiments later in the book...Do you feel you have that power over men?"

She looked up at him. "Yes...but not all men are susceptible." She put down the book and watched the effortless ease with which he lifted the pole and leaned his weight to drive the punt along. It was as if he had been doing it for his livelihood.

"Most are..." said Martin, grinning at her.

"Your friend Perry is. Are you?"

He smiled, but did not reply. She pretended to read the book, with occasional glances at the passing bank. Later she suggested that he remove his blazer and he took it off, draping it over the central thwart. She lifted it up, folded it, and placed it in the space beside her as if it were a companion.

Amanda had experienced her first affair during the recent summer term. Cathy Evans was a junior lecturer, a Rubenesque dark-maned woman of thirty, full of the fire of enthusiasm for the causes of women. She took her time seducing Amanda, first with words and ideas and then with her fingers and tongue. Only months from school and the close protection of her home, Amanda drank deeply of the freedom in Cathy's rooms, shedding her clothes and luxuriating in the orgasms the older woman summoned.

Cathy had talked to her about experiences with men, warning her that they were often brutal and single-minded in their desire to penetrate. She herself had found it painful and messy, and besides there was the risk of pregnancy. Yet even as she warned Amanda she sensed that the feisty young girl would need to find out for herself. 'If you do,' she had said, 'try to find a man who is kind—and laughs.' Then she told the girl at length how she could avoid having his child.

Now, Amanda watched Martin and wondered if he was a man who was kind enough to show her what it was like. As a student of medicine, she knew enough about the theory of the sexual act, and as she thought about it a shudder went through her, and she blushed.

"Where would you like to go?" he asked.

"Let's find somewhere quiet where we can talk and have our lunch..."

"It's quiet everywhere here, Amanda."

"I mean somewhere the other boats won't come."

He feigned misunderstanding. "What other boats?"

"You know what I mean," she retorted impatiently.

In fact, he knew a suitable place. Within minutes he manoeuvred the punt expertly under a canopy of a weeping willow into a little creek. The light softened to a pale lambent green. Cows and sheep grazed in the meadow behind the tree. It was so quiet that one could hear them cropping the grass.

Martin tied the punt to a convenient root. "Well, here you are, Mademoiselle. Does this meet your requirements?"

She resisted a smile and answered briskly. "For the time being. Come and help me unpack the hamper."

She had brought bread rolls, pâté, smoked salmon, and salad, to be followed by raspberries and cream. Martin opened the champagne. They spoke little while they ate, but watched each other occasionally. When they finished they packed up the hamper and Martin took out his pipe. Before he could light it Amanda patted the cushion beside her. He put the pipe down and moved up the punt to sit beside her. He lay back, looking up at the dome of greenery above. Then he turned to find that Amanda was watching him. He put an arm round her and cautiously drew her down to kiss.

Feeling her respond, he became excited and started to touch her body. She made no protest at first and he began to unfasten the buttons on the front of her dress. Her position was awkward and cramped, and he remembered friends telling him of hilarious antics in punts that tipped over. He was surprised at the passion of this girl's reaction, having expected that she would be shy and reticent. Her hands were on his neck and made no interference as he opened her shirt, but her bodice obstructed his exploration. He tried pulling it up but it was caught at her waist and she helped him loosen it, until he was finally able to free her breasts and kiss them. She became intensely active, stretching and twisting her body, but when adjusting his position he rocked the punt too much. Its wavelets startled a moorhen, which clattered away with raucous cries. They both laughed and disengaged.

"Let's go back to the house," said Amanda. Her cheeks were flushed as she re-fastened the buttons on her dress. "You might have tipped us into the water."

On the way back to the boathouse she trailed a hand in the water, then used her wet fingertips to cool her cheeks. She watched Martin thrusting the pole with leisurely movements, whistling, and now and then glancing down at her with a smile. She knew it would happen at the house and she was prepared for it. It would be a difficult step for her because she recognised that her emotions were wrought by his impending departure.

On reaching the boathouse Martin paid for the punt and they ran all the way back to the house, arriving laughing and panting. Amanda unlocked the front door and they tumbled in.

"My parents won't be home until late tonight."

"And the servants?"

She shot the bolts on the back door into the kitchen. "They're away for the day," she led the way up the stairs. In her own room, surrounded by childhood keepsakes, she seemed younger and vulnerable. She stood looking out of the window, the light shining through her fine blonde hair. She had the sensation of being intoxicated, as she had been one evening when Cathy plied her with wine. She turned to see Martin watching her, then started to unbutton her dress, and wondered how long it would be before he came to her. His eyes showed puzzlement and it occurred to her that he might have no experience of women.

He waited while she removed her dress and dropped it on a chair. She looked at him steadily, standing in a short white petticoat—her last garment. Still he had not moved and she bent to take the hem of the petticoat with both hands. With a long-used movement she peeled it off her body and stood naked, her cheeks burning. He walked up to her, lifted her off her feet and carried her to the bed.

෴

He saw her once more after that first summer day. His round of farewells and her social engagements kept them apart. They had to meet in the park to speak in private, knowing it was the last time they would see each other for a year at least, perhaps longer. In an area of tall shrubs Martin took her in his arms, and they held each other for a long time before she pulled away, sobbing. He walked with her back to the Jacobs house. Finding his bicycle near the tool shed, he stood with it, reluctant to leave her.

She said, "I know I can't stop you from doing what you've always wanted to do."

"Any more than I could ask you to stop studying medicine." He paused. "Amanda, until now I haven't had any strong reason compelling me not to go…"

"And now?"

He took her hand firmly. "You must understand. I have to go."

"Oh, I understand. It isn't 'a love that blots out all wisdom…', is it?"

He frowned. "What do you mean?"

"Something Olive Schreiner wrote. "Its '…bitter with the bitterness of death, lasting for an hour…', but is it worth having lived a whole life for that hour?" Her eyes filled with tears.

"Do you regret it? Are you bitter?"

"No, I shan't regret it. And I'll try not to be bitter."

As he cycled away down the darkening streets, Amanda watched him, deeply grieving. She did not know whether she would see him again, nor indeed whether he really wanted to come back to her.

∂∾⊸

CHAPTER 3
Cape Town—July 1890

Martin Russell stood on the deck of the liner *Dunottar Castle* gazing up at Table Mountain. He had heard and read many times about this great seaport, and now he was in awe, facing the huge flat-topped mountain, its famous cloud 'tablecloth' draped over it, the margins dissolving like ancient ragged damask. The gigantic amphitheatre was in early dawn shadow, some lights still twinkling in the city at its base. To his right, the Lion's Head was amber in sunlight, and he could see tiny figures moving near the lookout point. He imagined that among them were relatives of passengers on this liner come to greet its arrival.

It was mid-winter at the Cape and he pulled his scarf tighter. He had not expected it to be as cold as this. No wonder they could produce fine wines here, with cold wet winters and hot dry summers to ripen the grapes. He saw Perry swaggering along the deck to join him; a young woman wearing a fur coat clutched his arm. He nodded a greeting and the three of them stood together in silence, drawing in deep draughts of sea air. A pilot tug approached with regular hoots to guide them to the dock. This signalled the liner to increase the pace of its engines, and their throb made the deck stir as if a giant creature was coming out of hibernation.

"I must go and get ready," said the young woman. She offered her cheek for Perry to kiss and touched Martin's arm as she left them.

Perry watched her go. "I did my best, but she remained faithful to her husband."

"It must have been difficult for her," said Martin with a wry smile. He felt no envy for the other man's relentless pursuit of women, suspecting that it was a ceaseless quest for approbation. His thoughts led him back to Amanda, and the memory of his flippant suggestion that she might like to come out to Africa when she graduated. How vehemently she'd answered, with the impulsive spirit that he wished was with him now. Throughout the voyage he'd thought of her, regretting the separation. Only his excitement at the prospect of arriving in Cape Town prevented him from descending into melancholy. How strange, he thought, that that the act of sexual intercourse, so physical in essence, could strike an emotional bond; and it must be a stronger sensation for a woman, because she sacrificed more. The invasion of her body must be like the storming of her soul.

Lieutenant Carter, one of the ship's officers, a short, burly young man, came to stand beside them. "Soon to be ashore, eh, lads? How long will you spend in Cape Town?"

Martin answered guardedly. He'd heard that the liner's crew spread gossip about the passengers that was around Cape Town within a day of arrival. "A couple of days perhaps. We want to go north as soon as we can."

Carter smiled indulgently, his tone patronising. "It'll be tough, you know, especially for you fellows who haven't been in Africa before. I suggest you take the advice of the old hands."

"That means we can ignore you, Carter," said Perry, and laughed as the officer turned on his heel and walked away. He said to Martin, "Are we always to be plagued with a surfeit of advice from people like him?"

"We should at least listen—discard what we judge is useless."

Perry shrugged. "That fellow isn't worth my ear." He laughed. "I think he's been used to playing the field of young women without competition." He nudged Martin. "Are you serious about spending only two days here?"

"We've been through this so many times." Martin sighed in mild exasperation. "If we don't move quickly we won't get to Mashonaland before the rains start in November and the rivers become impassable. That means we have barely three months, and we must make every day count..."

"You use 'we' rather freely, my friend." Perry regarded Martin with amusement. "I've come as far as this; I may go no further."

Martin looked at him carefully. Although they had shared a cabin he had seen little of his companion during the voyage. Martin spent most of his time talking to passengers who knew the Transvaal, gleaning as much as he could about conditions in that territory. He read copiously from the ship's library about the history of Southern Africa and about its farming and mining. He tried to learn the Shona language from a missionary publication. The other passengers of his generation regarded him as rather dull, though good at deck games when he could be persuaded to join in. At least one girl watched him wistfully after a brief conversation but was too shy to make an approach.

Meanwhile, Perry participated in every social activity that brought him into company with the score or so of young women passengers. There was a dance almost every night, as well as whist drives and charades. Martin was a light sleeper and would be woken by the American returning to the cabin in the early hours of the morning, wafting cigar smoke and perfume.

"You bargained with your uncle to go to Mashonaland."

Perry turned to lean on the rail. "Don't remind me. You behave like my keeper; as if I'm tied to you by a leash..." There was an edge of irritation in the way he spoke.

"You don't have to stay with me," replied Martin calmly. "That wasn't part of the bargain. I'm just a convenient companion for you, but you could go with someone else—or even on your own."

Perry faced him, his smile now uneasy. "Is that a hint that you want to be rid of me?"

Shaking his head, he took Perry's elbow to steer him along the deck. Sometimes he found the American exasperating. After all, a deal had been made with the uncle. Perry had to keep his side of the bargain and he might as well do it with good grace and efficiency.

&∞§

On the quayside, while the two companions assembled their cases, a man of about forty came up to them, wearing the uniform of a major in the 16ᵗʰ Lancers. He introduced himself as Major Farrington, a friend of George Davenport, who had written to say that his nephew was arriving on the *Dunottar Castle*. He had a friendly demeanour as he appraised the two young men.

"Well, on African soil at last!" he announced, and noticing Martin sniffing the air keenly, he added, "All the smells are different here, aren't they? You know where to go? Up to the top of Adderley Street and turn left. You'll find the Chartered Company offices near the corner. There's a Captain Rogers there, who's expecting you. I asked him to find you some accommodation." Then he handed each of them an envelope. "These are invitations to Government House this evening—a reception—seven sharp—and black tie." Seeing their concern about this, he added, "Dress as best you can."

They thanked him, then hailed a spring wagon and helped the porters to load their belongings. They each had a tin trunk, a large leather case, and two capacious saddlebags. The wagon was driven by a small Cape man with wrinkled yellow skin, short grizzled hair, and a snaggle-toothed grin. He took them up the city's main street towards the Botanical Gardens, turned left, and stopped at an office bearing the brass plate of the Chartered Company. A Cape Coloured guard wearing a starched khaki uniform showed them into a large, sparsely furnished office with a scrubbed wooden floor.

"Russell? Davenport?" barked a stocky man in a blue serge uniform who came forward to greet them. "I'm Captain Rogers, the Chartered Company's representative in Cape Town. I've been expecting you. Lord Eyre wrote about you—and Major Farrington came here—asked me to brief you." He waved them to chairs and studied some papers from his desk. "Now, first things first," he said fussily. "I've arranged for you to stay with Mrs Phipps in Van Riebeeck Street. She has a boarding house where our younger men stay when they pass through Cape Town. And I've booked you on the train to Kimberley the day after tomorrow. I suggest you take the coach from there. At Palapye you can buy horses and a trek wagon, and of course oxen. I warn you, horses may be hard to come by. The men in the Pioneer Column have cleaned up most of what was in the area."

Rogers puffed out his chest and looked keenly at the two young men. The English lad was serious, and looked quite tough, as if he'd be able to cope with the rough conditions of Africa. In contrast, the American seemed rather soft and languid. "You haven't been in Africa before, have you?" He grinned as they shook their heads, and went on. "Let me give you some advice. Don't trust anyone. There are plenty of crooks up there—here too—waiting to part you from your money. Get advice from local British people when you buy your outfit. And be careful, only buy horses that are salted—that means they've had fly sickness and can't get it again—like being inoculated."

"When is the latest we can leave Palapye to head north?" asked Martin eagerly.

Rogers nodded to acknowledge the merit in the question. Beckoning them to look at the map on the wall, he pointed out the route of the journey. Martin was struck by the large blank areas on the map. He had been used to the survey maps used on the North-West Frontier in India, where every village was named and every prominence and river had a title. On this map there were only a few rivers marked, arising on the fringe of a blank area, and with courses known only in the vaguest terms. There were no mountains marked, and no towns or villages. The most important feature on the map was a thin red line that indicated the route of the Pioneer Column. Rogers was pointing a stubby finger at it.

"It'll take at least two months. You'll travel by coach from Kimberley north to Palapye, where the Column set up their base camp. Then you'll trek to their destination. You'll have to get there before the main rains start in November. So you should leave Palapye by the beginning of September at the latest. You don't have time to waste."

"Where is the Column now?"

Rogers pointed. "About here. They started last month, so they're roughly half way. It's slow work for them, cutting new tracks through the forest, and getting their wagons over the rivers. We reckon they should reach their goal by mid-September. It'll be easier for you, because you can follow their track." He looked up at them sharply. "I suppose you lads can shoot?"

The two young men nodded, glancing at each other. Perry said, "Why do you ask?"

"Well, you see, the Matabele may cut up rough." Rogers stroked his moustache and grinned, relishing his role as mentor. "You know they're an offshoot of the Zulu tribe, don't you? They speak the same language. You'll be passing through the southern part of their territory. They haven't given the Column any trouble yet—so we hear—but our chaps are a hundred and eighty civilians and two hundred troopers, with two Gatling guns." He grinned. "A couple of lightly-armed young men may be more inviting. I suggest you team up with some others—strength in numbers, eh?"

After giving them more detailed advice, Rogers showed them out, pointing them in the direction of Van Riebeeck Street. The spring wagon, which waited outside, took them past the Botanical Gardens, where the white colonial bulk of Government House could be seen through bare-branched trees. A few people strolled in the gardens, the women wearing bonnets and shawls in a chill morning breeze.

"What do you think about Rogers' warning?" Perry tapped his boot nervously on the rim of the floor.

"I think he's right about joining up with some others. We know that we're not the only ones going after the Column. Let's see who we can find in Palapye."

The house in Van Riebeeck Street was small and white, built in Cape Dutch style. Mrs Phipps came to the door, plump, cheerful, and rosy-cheeked. With peals of laughter she supervised the men as they unloaded their luggage, and counselled them on paying the driver. She showed them to a room on the upper floor at the front of the house, with two beds and a window with a view down to Table Bay. After stowing their belongings they joined their landlady in the neat little drawing room, facing a crackling fire. Mrs Phipps served tea and digestive biscuits and told them that her husband was a trawler skipper, now at sea. The room contained many nautical objects, the most prominent being a model schooner in a glass case, and a large brass telescope pointed towards the bay.

"You must be very careful," said Mrs Phipps kindly, looking from one to the other. "I've seen several young men return sick from up north. Sufferin' from the fever they were. One 'ad terrible sores on 'is arms and face. Another one was a sorry sight; 'e could scarcely walk, poor man."

Perry grimaced. "Your tea is so good, Mrs Phipps, I believe I'll stay here. I'll leave the adventuring to young Martin."

The kindly landlady noticed that behind his cheerful demeanour this young man was rather afraid. She had known enough men in her life to recognise it in his eyes. By contrast, his quieter companion seemed eager to experience the rigours of the journey north.

∾⇛

That evening they set off on foot to attend the reception at Government House. They wore dinner jackets and black bow ties under raincoats—they had not been able to bring overcoats. Their evening suits had been aired and carefully ironed by the kindly Mrs Phipps. It had been old George Davenport who had insisted they bring these clothes. "Standards are high in the Cape," he had said, "and in Jo'burg too. I doubt you'll need them when you go further north, but you never know. I've been to mines in remote areas where the manager dressed for dinner."

Following the gas-lit path through the Botanical Gardens they approached the imposing gates of Government House, where a military guard in a pillbox indicated they should sign the visitors' book. A young subaltern showed them up to the entrance hall, where a servant took their coats. Standing in uncertainty for a moment, they could hear dance music played by a military band inside. Then Major Farrington came striding up to greet them and led them into the huge banqueting hall, where about a hundred guests were gathered. Many of the men were officers in dress uniform, while the women wore long evening dresses and shawls. Servants in starched white uniforms moved among them carrying trays of drinks. The major ushered Martin and Perry up to the High Commissioner, Sir Henry Loch; two men who had been talking with him moved away.

"Excuse me, Sir Henry," said Farrington. "These young men are going north to follow the Pioneer Column into Mashonaland." He introduced them. "Mr Martin Russell—his father is the Member of Parliament for North Oxfordshire. And Mr Perry Davenport—the nephew of George Davenport, who you'll remember, sir—the President of Consolidated American Mining."

The High Commissioner was a portly man in his fifties, with a pallid complexion. "Indeed I do remember Mr Davenport. I met him here last year." Addressing Perry, he said, "I hope your uncle is in good health." His voice wheezed, suggesting that he suffered poor health himself.

"He is, sir," answered Perry, reluctantly impressed at the extent of his uncle's acquaintances. "He hopes to come out to the Cape later in the year."

"Ah. Well, please advise him that we hope to meet him then. And what brings you from America?"

Perry managed to contain his ironic laughter. "Duty, sir. I have to report to my uncle about the potential for mining in the territory north of the Limpopo."

The High Commissioner nodded sagely. He was accustomed to listening attentively and storing large amounts of information in his head. "Indeed—and Mr Russell, what is the political leaning of your father?"

"He's a Liberal, sir—on the back benches."

"Russell has just graduated from Oxford—in natural sciences," interjected Major Farrington.

"Then I expect your training will serve you in good stead when you go north, young man. I wish you both good fortune. Now please help us to entertain the young ladies." He indicated the direction they should take.

They left the High Commissioner and accepted drinks from a waiter carrying a tray, before surveying the room as they walked round its perimeter. In the centre swirled dancers, wheeling to a polka, their faces reflecting contrasts between exhilaration and apprehension.

As the dance ended Perry stopped suddenly. "Well I'm dashed, Martin. There's Helen Bateson. Come along, I'll introduce you. I met her in London. She's engaged to Lord Robert Onslow, whose father's the Earl of Bury. Remember, I told you they were coming out to South Africa?"

He led Martin to a group of young women, one of whom turned towards them as they approached, recognising Perry. She left her companions and advanced to greet him. Taller than average, she held herself very straight. The curve of her bosom was accentuated by a strip of frilly lace on her dress that ran from neckline to hem. Her large brown eyes regarded them rather haughtily.

She held out her hand. "Perry, we heard from your uncle that you were coming to Cape Town with a friend." Regarding Martin enquiringly, she tilted her head slightly.

Perry introduced his companion and looked over the girl's shoulder. "Is Robert with you?"

She looked steadily at Martin as he took her hand, then turned to the American. "He went north to Palapye, to find out more about journeying to the Mashona country. He knows that you two gentlemen are coming. He hopes to meet you there. When will you leave Cape Town?"

They explained that they were booked on the train to Kimberly the day after tomorrow. She smiled graciously. "Then we shall be fellow-passengers. My father and I plan to go straight on to Palapye, where we will meet my fiancé and find out whether he has decided to go across the Limpopo. He had originally intended to buy a farm here in the Cape, you know. But he heard so many stories about the land that will be sold to settlers in Mashonaland..."

At that moment the band started to play a waltz, and Helen glanced at the young women to whom she had been talking earlier. She said, "You must come and meet these ladies." Leading them to the group she made introductions, and as she did so male partners came to claim some of the women, including finally Helen herself.

Perry found a plump freckled girl who did not have a name on her programme. He whisked her away, leaving Martin on his own. He noticed Major Farrington beckoning and circled round to him, avoiding the dancers. Farrington introduced him to a tall gaunt officer in the uniform of a Colonel of the 7th Lancers, with beetling eyebrows and a kindly smile. Standing next to him was a portly clergyman with ruddy cheeks and snow-white hair.

"This is the Mr Russell you were asking about, Colonel. Martin, this is Colonel Bateson, and Doctor Portman." Farrington then took his leave.

"I've just been talking to a Miss Helen Bateson, sir. Is she your daughter?" He shook the colonel's hand. "She tells me that we'll be travelling on the same train to Kimberley."

"Excellent!" Colonel Bateson laughed heartily. "We'll be able to talk more easily on the journey than we can here." He evidently found the noise from the band intrusive. "We heard that you plan to follow the Pioneer Column to Mashonaland. Dr Portman here"—he nodded to the clergyman beside him—"has just been telling me that Matabele warriors have been raiding the Mashona in recent months."

Dr Portman nodded his round head and spoke wheezily. "So I've been told—by missionary friends. And the Matabele will not take kindly to the occupation of the Mashona territory by Rhodes' Column. We must be very wary of the Matabele; these warlike tribes are not to be underestimated." His protruding eyes stared at the Colonel as if challenging him to deny this judgment.

"Indeed," responded Bateson. "Our military learned some salutary lessons in the Zulu Wars. But we now have the Maxim gun, you know. Its firepower is overwhelming—perhaps 500 rounds per minute—that's equivalent to about a hundred rifles. We've already shown it to the Matabele; I'm sure they know it would be futile for their *impis* to march against us."

"But what if they use stealth, sir," demanded Portman, "as the Zulus did at Isandhlwana?"

"A fair question, Doctor. But, even that was a daylight attack, and our weaponry is much more advanced now. Besides, everyone tells me the natives do not like to venture out in the dark. They have no means of lighting their way, other than embers, or a torch of burning twigs. Their night is full of hazards—wild animals, snakes, scorpions, thorns. Their culture keeps them in the security of the hut at night."

Dr Portman looked unconvinced. "We may have the Maxim gun, but I wonder about the wisdom of relying on a single weapon. What if its mechanisms failed? Surely these new weapons are not infallible?"

Colonel Bateson laughed gently and shared his amusement with Martin. He patted the clergyman on his broad back. "Each regiment normally has three guns; and I'm told they are extremely reliable. The mechanism is designed to function even when dirty—or wet."

Portman turned to Martin. "You must learn the language, Russell, if you plan to settle there. Bantu languages are quite easy to learn; they have the most basic grammar. Find a native tutor. We British are deuced lazy. We lose much local knowledge through our failure to converse with native people."

The dance music stopped and Helen Bateson came up to join them. Martin was struck again by her graceful, almost stately, manner, and her cool beauty. She seemed much more mature than the rather frivolous young women he'd met at social occasions in India and on the recent voyage.

She introduced her dancing partner as Arthur Forrest, a stout, balding man of about forty, and informed them that he was a banker from Johannesburg.

Dr Portman had evidently heard of Forrest and said in a provocative tone, "We hear you are an advocate of votes for the immigrants to the Transvaal."

The banker was still out of breath from his exertions on the dance floor. "I am, sir," he panted, "After all—we pay enough to—the Boers in taxes. They shouldn't tax people—without giving them the right—to say how the proceeds should be spent."

"But surely one can—and does," retorted the clergyman. "In most of our colonies we tax the natives, without giving them votes, or seats in the legislature."

Forrest frowned, and when he spoke his tone was defensive and rather pompous. "A simple modest poll tax—levied on uneducated natives—hardly the same thing as the exorbitant income taxes we pay in the Transvaal. Besides, it would be pointless to allow—such native people to vote..."

"But we do in England!" Dr Portman was enjoying the argument. "We permit uneducated farm labourers to vote."

"But not educated women," interjected Helen quietly.

The four men turned to look at her, and Martin admired her for having the nerve to speak up like that. She caught his eye but did not smile, and he wished he could tell her that he sympathised with her point of view. Wondering if she was as vehement as Amanda, he started to compare her. Helen was slightly taller, and her features more defined. Though not conventionally pretty like Amanda, her skin was soft and clear, and her large brown eyes seemed to bore deep into him.

Forrest ignored the girl's remark and continued. "In the Transvaal the Boers have all the votes; yet they are uneducated people with no experience in governing..."

"That may be, sir," said Colonel Bateson, "but they believe the Republic is theirs—by right of conquest. They will not surrender a controlling majority of votes to those they see as a rabble of gold-diggers and shop-keepers...most of whom arrived in the last three years."

Forrest's face reddened. "So you support the Boers, do you, Colonel?"

"I didn't say that," replied the colonel calmly. "I was merely describing their stance for Mr Russell's benefit. They're stubborn and determined people. That's how they've been able to survive on this continent, despite the deprivations of a harsh environment. They have fought off the Xhosa, the Zulu, and the Matabele. I'm willing to concede that they've conquered their territory."

Martin was somewhat relieved when the band started to play. He caught Helen's eye again and asked her for the dance. She took her card from her purse and studied it carefully. He realised that a girl as attractive as her would have her programme fully booked, especially at a ball where the women were so heavily outnumbered, so he was surprised when she looked up with a smile.

"I must make an excuse. Come." She led him across the crowded ballroom towards a group of young officers, one of whom came forward to greet her and claim his dance.

"William," she said, "please forgive me if I have this dance with Mr Russell. I have a really important matter to discuss with him, and I may not have another opportunity."

The young lieutenant regarded Martin with a disdain that men in uniform sometimes display towards civilians. He bowed ironically and nodded to Helen. She and Martin moved together into the slow waltz. She relaxed a little when she realised that he was a capable dancer.

"I feel very privileged," he said with a laugh.

She smiled, but not warmly. "Truly, I have something important to discuss with you. Perry has told me about you—that you are level-headed and a good shot." She took a deep breath, then said in a rush of words. "If my fiancé decides to go to Mashonaland, would you allow him to travel with you?"

Martin looked at her carefully. It was almost as if she was pleading, and he realised she found it difficult to ask for help from a virtual stranger. He presumed she was deeply concerned about her fiancé's safety.

"I see no reason why not, Miss Bateson..."

"Please call me Helen. You see Robert has had no experience of trekking..."

Martin laughed. "Neither have I!"

She smiled more easily now, and he could feel the stiffness leaving her. "Yes, but you could help each other. I would deem it a great favour. Robert has ample funds, and that might be helpful."

He was amused that she thought they needed money; then remembered that Perry might have revealed the facts about his straightened circumstances. He looked into her eyes and saw that she had read his thoughts.

She said, "Perry told me that your father has not given you any financial support."

"That's true," he replied. "But I did not expect him to. I'm a second son, and have to make my own way now—especially if I decide to follow my own pursuits."

"Is that how your father sees it?"

He changed the subject without answering her question. "What will you do while your fiancé's in Mashonaland?"

She looked over her shoulder, almost as if afraid someone might be overhearing. "My father and I will wait in Johannesburg...that is, until we hear whether Robert intends to buy a farm. If he does, I will go to join him."

Martin was astonished. "Surely it's no place for a woman to live?"

"Sooner or later women will go there—to follow the men." She regarded him steadily. "Some wives of missionaries have already been in the Matabele country—have lived and died there." Watching her partner nod in acknowledgement she was disturbed at the sensations invading her body. This tall young man was guiding her firmly round the floor without a hint of impropriety, yet she felt her cheeks burning and found it difficult to concentrate. She had danced with dozens of young men, mostly young officers in India, but could not recall one for several years who had stirred her like this. She thought the sensations were certainly inappropriate in an engaged woman.

Trying to find a new topic, she asked, "Don't you find Perry rather—frivolous?"

"Frivolous? Perhaps. I think he's making light of a journey he regards as some sort of penance. I expect he would rather stay in Cape Town attending functions like this. How well do you know him?"

"Not well." She looked up at his face, thinking that in contrast she already seemed to know this man quite well. There was something about him that was like her father. Perhaps it was his calmness and the rather slow and deliberate way of speaking. She also sensed his integrity, and then chided herself because she'd known him only a few minutes, and could not reasonably make such an assumption. "What do you hope to find across the Limpopo?"

He replied with a certainty that surprised her. "A farm, where I can settle and be my own master..."

"Do you have a girl who will come to join you?" There was hint of playful teasing in her question, and Martin realised that she might not be as haughty as she had appeared at first.

"As Robert has? No."

He could tell from the music that the waltz was drawing to an end, and whirled Helen round at a faster pace, expecting her to resist, but to his surprise she seemed to relax in his arms and float on lighter feet. When the music stopped he saw she was smiling, her cheeks reddened.

"Why did you do that?" she asked quietly.

"I suppose to find out whether..." He had meant to say, 'To find out whether you're really a young madam', but the term was inappropriate. He escorted her to her group of women friends, bowed to her, and took his leave.

✿

The two young men spent the next day combing the city for items that Captain Rogers had advised them to buy. Their weapons were brought from England, though with limited ammunition, so they purchased several hundred cartridges for each gun, wondering how they would carry the extra weight. Spare bridles and two saddles were essential, since they'd heard that these things were virtually unobtainable on the frontier. Mosquito nets, insect repellent oil, quinine, and other medicines, were only a few items on a long list Martin compiled on the voyage, and were quite easily obtained in the city.

Next morning they said farewell to Mrs Phipps and took a hired Cape cart to the station. Arriving early they found their compartment on the train and stowed their luggage. While Perry dozed off, Martin stood on the platform and lit his pipe, watching the other passengers arrive. There were smartly dressed businessmen destined for Kimberley, their wives in fashionable woollen dresses and large bonnets. Some Boer families stood in groups, wearing coarse loose clothing, men in broad-brimmed felt hats, and women in white bonnet-like *kappies*. Coloured servants carried their luggage and ran errands.

Martin noticed the Batesons arrive and went forward to greet them. They did not need help with their luggage because the colonel had a batman in attendance, loaned by Major Farrington. They found their compartment was in the same carriage as Martin and Perry, but at the further end. After exchanging pleasantries, they climbed on, the guard blew his whistle, and the train coughed steam as it wound out of the Cape peninsula, through spectacular mountain scenery. An hour later, it emerged into the Karoo a plain of stunted grass and low scrub stretching to shimmering distant ochre hills. Scrawny sheep and wild ostriches browsed on the harsh vegetation.

On reaching the dusty little town of Laingsburg the locomotive took on water and coal, while the passengers left the train to lunch at the hotel. The Batesons, with Martin and Perry, settled on the broad verandah, where they were served bread, cheese and wine. They had scarcely started to eat when the portly Afrikaner station-master appeared, wiping his face with a dusty handkerchief. Approaching them diffidently he spoke in broken, halting English. "I'm afraid your journey will be delayed about four hours, people. We have a fault on the line ahead. You may remain here—it will be more comfortable than on the train." He stumped off hurriedly back to the station, wishing to avoid their questions.

Colonel Bateson waited until the station-master was out of earshot, before saying in his usual calm manner. "I could think of worse places to spend four hours. We must do something to amuse ourselves."

They discussed possibilities with little enthusiasm. Martin watched Helen surreptitiously and thought she seemed preoccupied with her own thoughts. She answered questions, but volunteered nothing. On a couple of occasions she caught his eye, but her expression revealed nothing.

When they finished their meal the colonel walked over to talk to the landlord of the hotel. Perry stood up, stretched, and looked out at the dusty street. "What a bore. I was told about these dusty Boer *dorps*, but this is worse than I imagined. Time and life suspended."

Helen smiled slightly. "I expect they become even more primitive near the frontier..."

"...until they cease to exist," added Martin, "and then we have to put up with the bushveld."

Perry grimaced peevishly. "I know all that. You don't have to remind me." He scuffed his foot on the ground in a childish gesture. "I feel sure I'm in the wrong place. I don't understand you Martin—nor Robert..."

He was interrupted when Colonel Bateson returned from his talk with the landlord, wearing a triumphant smile. "Mr de Bruyn says there are partridges—francolins, to be precise—on the plain. What say we take a walk with our guns, lads? You come too, my dear?"

Martin saw an opportunity to talk to Helen again. He said, "I'll walk with you, sir, but I won't shoot this time. Perry, why don't you use my shotgun?"

"Martin doesn't shoot for sport," said Perry to the Batesons, with a trace of scorn in his voice.

The colonel looked at Martin in surprise. "But you will shoot for the pot, I presume?"

"If I have to," Martin nodded.

"He's too fond of animals to kill them," persisted Perry in a tone that was almost deriding. "Isn't that right?"

Martin refused to rise to the bait. "Just that I prefer to leave them as they are?"

The colonel was mildly interested. "And people, Martin? Have you had any compunction about killing them?"

Looking at him steadily, Martin replied, "Not if it's in the cause of duty, sir…in war. I've shot at, and killed men—on the North-West Frontier."

"I know what you mean," said the colonel. "I've been in some nasty incidents, and I'm sad to say I've had no choice about taking a man's life."

They waited on the hotel verandah for an hour in desultory conversation until the sun dipped lower towards the dusty brown hills. Then they walked north away from the station, where their train still waited patiently. The colonel and Perry walked ahead, their shotguns at the ready. Helen and Martin followed. Further behind was an African servant, provided as a guide by the landlord; he carried a canvas bag containing a flask of cold water.

The first pair of partridges took both armed men by surprise. The birds had crouched in the scrub until the men were a few yards away and flight became imperative. They rose with clattering wings and skimmed low and away from danger.

Colonel Bateson grumbled at his slow reaction. "At least we know what to expect now," he muttered.

"They were far too quick for me," Perry laughed.

Further on they put up another pair, this time on Perry's side. He fired both barrels but was too late. He looked at the Colonel ruefully, knowing that he should give up; the francolins were safe while he held a gun. He turned to Martin, who was walking with Helen, and held up the shotgun, indicating that he wanted to hand it over. But Martin shook his head and waved him on; he was enjoying his conversation with this enigmatic girl.

"Your views about shooting animals won't find any sympathy in this country," said Helen.

"I know. But I won't join in the popular slaughter. Oh, I don't mean this," he added hastily. "This sort of shooting is harmless enough. But I've been told these Karoo plains once teemed with antelope until they were all shot by the Boers. They say immense herds of springbok and oryx used to graze here...as far as the eye could see."

A couple of shots echoed over the flat ground. Colonel Bateson at last made a hit, and the party changed direction to find the fallen bird. The servant discovered it lying on a saltbush. They moved on, next putting up a covey of five birds. The Colonel shot another, but their search failed to recover it.

Bateson came back to where Helen and Martin were standing. "Fine sport, these little blighters," he said enthusiastically. "Eh, Helen? But we need a retriever like my old labrador. I wonder if they have these partridges in Palapye."

"Shouldn't we be going back, Father?" Helen looked anxiously in the direction of the station, now in the distance, a mile behind them.

"One more put-up," said her father, as he set off again eagerly, shotgun poised.

The next time, three birds rose on Perry's side and he fired both barrels, but missed. He said to the Colonel, "I'm no good at this. The irony is that Martin's supposed to be one of the best shots in Oxfordshire—at clay pigeons."

The older man turned to Martin. "Perry says you're a good shot. One bird won't give us supper. Won't you change your mind?"

When Martin smiled and shook his head, Bateson shrugged and started to walk back, holding his empty gun on his shoulder. It was getting dark quickly, and was suddenly much colder. He felt uneasy that his daughter was so keen to talk to this young man, Martin Russell. Her engagement to the titled and quite wealthy Robert Onslow was not to be jeopardised. He quickened his pace and engaged Perry in conversation, looking back now and then at the other couple, who followed about twenty yards behind.

Martin was saying, "You seem to be taking this journey—and its interruption—in your stride, Helen."

"I've lived virtually all my life abroad. My mother died when I was very young, and my brother and I went with my father to his army postings—mostly in India." Sighing deeply, she added. "Sometimes I thought we'd drift for ever—through the backwaters of the Empire."

"Your father could have sent you to live with family in England?"

"Oh, I'm glad he didn't. But sometimes it's been lonely, especially after my brother died." Seeing Martin's questioning expression, she explained, "He caught fever in Burma, eight years ago. At least I'm capable of looking after myself. But I often envy you men. You're so free to follow your dreams. Look at you two, setting off on your adventure. A woman could never do that..."

"But you are going north—if Robert finds a farm."

"I mean, I could never go on my own—only as an appendage." She sounded philosophical about it rather than bitter.

Watching her stride lightly through the scrub, he thought she was would be an asset for any man venturing into the wild interior. She knew plenty about wild animals, insects and tropical diseases. She seemed hale and self-assured, and she would probably want children.

"And Robert? Why is he going so far? If he has 'ample funds', as you said, he could farm in the Cape."

She shrugged with a trace of impatience. "He has his reasons—perhaps rather like you. He's a younger son too, you know. Perhaps he's trying to prove something. Are you?"

"That I can make my own way in life?" He laughed shortly. "I don't have Robert's resources, so I need low cost land. That's what makes this new territory so attractive. There may even be free grants of farms to those who are willing to settle there."

When they reached the station they found the train was ready to leave. The servant was dispatched with a note to thank the landlord for his suggestion about the game birds. They agreed to meet in the dining car for supper and climbed aboard to their separate compartments.

☙◦❧

Colonel Bateson sat on his bunk cleaning his gun with practised and meticulous attention. Helen looked out of the window watching the sun set over the Karoo Mountains. She was thinking about Martin and her conversation with him. He had been so easy to talk to, with none of the stilted shyness of some young men, nor any hint of flirtatiousness. His slow relaxed way of speaking appealed to her, and encouraged her to say things that she would not normally have discussed with a virtual stranger.

Her father coughed and said. "You seem to like Russell, my dear. Much the steadier of those two young men. What d'you think?"

She pushed her thoughts away to give attention to her father. "I agree. Perry doesn't seem to belong here. He's what you've sometimes called a 'drawing room type'. I really wonder why he came—and how long he'll stay the course. I hope he doesn't become a burden to Martin—and Robert—if they go north together."

The Colonel put his gun away, carefully setting the burnished pieces into their compartments lined with green baize, where they nestled into the shapes. "He'll find out soon enough that there are no drawing rooms where he's going. And Russell? What do you make of him? Odd that he doesn't like to shoot..."

"I rather agree with him about that. But he *does* seem to fit in here, Father. Don't you agree? He seems the type to persevere. There's a sort of quiet determination about him. I just hope Robert can go with him..."

Bateson smiled fondly, but with a trace of apprehension. "I see that you do like Russell. If Robert were here, I think he might be a bit jealous."

She turned away to hide her embarrassment, and said, "I'm not sure that he would, or that he would even notice."

"You know, my dear, you're going to meet other men like Martin Russell, who may test your affection for Robert...No, Helen," he held up his hand when she made an expression of remonstration, "you must make your decision very carefully. I can advise you, but ultimately the decision is yours alone." He sighed, and added quietly, "I only wish your mother were here to help you."

"Oh Father," she put her hand on his shoulder. "I've already decided to marry Robert..."

"But it's not too late to change your mind."

"I know, but I'm not going to."

ॐॐ

The clear night brought even sharper cold, that surprised the passengers and forced them to dress informally to keep warm for dinner.

Martin and Perry wore khaki bush jackets over thick jerseys; their dinner jackets were packed in trunks. They met the Bateson's in the dining car, the Colonel in a thick serge uniform, Helen wearing a heavy shawl over her long woollen dress. Over the meal, and for an hour afterwards, they talked about the countries where the Batesons had travelled. They had stayed in many parts of India, Ceylon and Burma. They urged Perry to tell them about America, and he complied with his accustomed flippancy. When the Colonel excused himself to go to bed, Perry went too, complaining that he felt 'whacked' after his late night at the High Commissioner's reception and all the shopping on the following day.

Seeing they were the last guests in the dining compartment, and that the waiters wanted to clear the tables, Martin and Helen moved forward towards their carriage but lingered talking in the corridor. The regular chuffing sound of the labouring steam locomotive carried back to them, while sparks from its furnace flew past the window like shooting stars. Helen talked with more ease now that she was alone with Martin, and he thought her unusually animated.

She was emboldened by the intimacy of the dark passageway, and intoxicated by the cold air roaring past the half-open window. To hear her better, he moved closer, bending his head to hers. There was a question that she needed to ask, although her upbringing warned her it was unwise. "Who did you leave behind, Martin?"

"Do you mean family? My father..."

She saw that he was smiling, and said, in exasperation, "No. I meant a girl—a steady?"

Pondering for a moment, and knowing she was engaged to another man, he decided he could tell her. "There was a girl, in Oxford, but we have no attachment any longer. It would have been a great complication if there had been..."

"So those years in India and at Oxford failed to produce someone that you wanted to marry?"

He laughed in reply. "Not many years, Helen. There was..." He hesitated.

"Yes?" she prompted.

"No one serious."

"Are your standards too high?" She tried to sound light and cheerful, but was perturbed at her almost querulous tone.

"Perhaps I was hoping to meet someone interesting, like you."

She smiled to herself, thinking it was the answer she deserved. "You don't know me, Martin."

"Enough to admire you."

She felt him move closer and said to herself, 'I shouldn't be here. This could get out of hand, and it would be my fault.' To Martin, she said, "What do you admire?"

"You have strength and character...and you're lovely."

She savoured his words. Then she told him, "I must go." But she made no move.

At that moment her father approached down the corridor wearing a paisley patterned dressing gown, with an old khaki bush jacket over his shoulders. When he spoke, his voice was crusty, but indulgent. "You two going to stay here talking all night? Better get some sleep—both of you."

"Sorry, sir. We were about to go." Martin gave him a little courteous bow.

The Colonel nodded in acknowledgement and turned back down the corridor.

Helen touched Martin's arm. "We'd better go. Good night." She reached up quickly to kiss his cheek, then turned away. He pulled her back, and for a moment felt her yield against him, her breasts pressed against his chest. He bent to kiss her mouth, but she turned her face away and tried to disengage. Slowly, he let her go, and watched her walk unsteadily up the corridor. He hoped there was a hesitation in her step, a reluctance to leave him. When she reached the door of her compartment she looked back at him, lifting her hand in a brief salutation.

In his own compartment he found Perry already asleep. He undressed and lay awake on his bunk for a long time, images of Helen and Amanda revolving in his mind. It was only a few days ago that his thoughts turned constantly to the girl in England, and now they were overcome with Helen. Was he so fickle, so capricious? Was it the dominance of the present over the past? Helen was here—he could still smell her light scent, and remembered the warmth of her body.

But it was futile. She was engaged to an aristocrat, a titled, moneyed man. She probably had little income, and Lord Onslow would ensure her future. In contrast, what could he offer? He had blown his savings on the liner ticket, and his only wealth was in a few paltry possessions. Yet, she was not married, and in his slight social experience he had encountered several girls who broke their engagements. Furthermore, she was willing to brave the unknown in Mashonaland. They could scrape by. Perhaps she was not a forlorn hope.

CHAPTER 4
Palapye — August 1890

The train from the Cape took two days to reach Kimberley. After a brief visit to the great cavity of the diamond diggings, they took the horse-drawn coach for the five day journey to Palapye. Martin and Perry hired horses when they reached Mafeking; they rode in front of the coach to avoid its dust. The party spent nights at Gabarone and Mahalapye, staying in ramshackle inns. The lurching dusty coach travel was not conducive to conversations. Helen was so tired at each destination that she went straight to bed.

Many residents of the small frontier town Palapye were at the hotel to meet the coach, shouting greetings to their friends. The men wore khaki cotton clothing and broad-brimmed felt hats. There were a few women too, in long skirts, carrying parasols to protect their faces from the harsh sun and drying breeze. Martin and Perry helped the drivers to hoist out their baggage, while Colonel Bateson and Helen disembarked, stretching stiff limbs.

Martin felt weary and dirty. It seemed that dust and grit had permeated his clothes and become ingrained in his hair and skin. The close company of Perry had been irksome, and he believed they might have quarrelled seriously if Colonel Bateson and Helen had not provided relief. Every mile away from Cape Town made Perry more anxious about the perils ahead, and the American's reaction was to alternate between high spirits and depression.

Their worst quarrel had been about Helen. Perry could see that his companion admired the girl, and he started hinting that she might ditch her fiancé if given encouragement, or that she might indulge in a temporary liaison—a 'fling' as Perry described it. Martin was riled by the implication that Helen might be 'loose', even though he could see that she might be interested in his suit if he was prepared to offer it.

Lord Robert Onslow came hurrying through the throng to greet them. A man of average height, in his late twenties, he was decidedly overweight, an almost comical figure. Even though the season was early spring, the morning was hot, and he dabbed at his forehead with a large handkerchief. His skin was peeling from sunburn, and his long pale hair was plastered to his head with sweat. His loud braying speech had an aristocratic accent, and was at a higher pitch than one would expect from a man of his size, affected by exaggeration of certain words.

"Colonel, sir! Helen, my dear, how delighted I am to see you again." He kissed his fiancée decorously on the cheek she proffered, then shook the Colonel's hand. Finally he grinned at the two young men, who waited a few steps behind.

"And you must be Russell and Davenport?" He shook their hands vigorously. "I'm Robert Onslow."

"You make us sound like a music hall turn", said Perry. "And I met you in London." He ignored Robert's embarrassment at his forgetfulness, feeling tired and a trifle sour. How could the cool elegant Helen engage herself to this bumbling caricature of an English gentleman?

"Of course—foolish of me—I remember." Onslow gave a high-pitched whinnying laugh. "I say, I've kept a room for you chaps. I'm afraid you'll have to share—sorry about that. Deuced difficult—this tiny hotel is the only one in the town—always crammed full. Come on! Cold beers are in order, what?"

In the afternoon Robert took the men on a short tour of Palapye in a pony trap that he rented for the duration of their stay. It took them through the dusty frontier town on broad roads, lined with tin-roofed shops and stores. Some were substantial, made of brick, while others were mere shacks. From here on there was a dirt road to Francistown, but to the north-east, their intended direction, there were no real roads, only cart tracks through the bushveld as far as the Limpopo, then nothing. Furthermore, there were only crude maps, because the land to the north had never been surveyed.

æ∞

That evening Colonel Bateson was the first to join Robert Onslow sitting on the hotel verandah. They had bathed and changed into dinner jackets, and settled deep into canvas chairs. After ordering iced gins the Colonel told Robert about their journey from the Cape, before the conversation turned to future plans. He sensed that his prospective son-in-law was deeply apprehensive about the journey ahead. The perspective was now very different when viewed from this frontier location, where news of problems and potential danger seemed more urgent and real. They had heard all manner of alarming stories about malaria, wild animals, and not least the threat from Matabele warriors. Robert confided that, though he was still enthusiastic, he could not contemplate the trek to Mashonaland on his own. He had ridden to hounds, but knew too little about the care of horses and oxen. When he lived in England the horses were always looked after by servants. Furthermore, he could not speak the local languages.

Martin and Perry came out to join them soon after, looking spruce but arguing about who was the wearier. They greeted the other two men and ordered beers from a servant waiting nearby. It was dusk and growing quite cold when Helen joined them, wearing her heavy cashmere shawl from India.

As Robert talked to Martin and Perry, his enthusiasm was rekindled by their supporting presence. He said to Helen, "I've been telling them that I'll definitely go north to Mashonaland if the three of us can travel together. I've taken lots of advice—it sounds like a fabulous place. They say land will be sold for a shilling an acre! Imagine that! I've been told it's swarming with antelope and game birds. Rich fertile soil, reliable rains, and a cool climate. Not much risk of fever, they tell me. What do you say, chaps?"

Martin watched Helen's expression, and thought she seemed rather disconcerted that Robert was so eager to go north without consulting her. He smiled politely in response to Robert's enthusiasm. "I've already decided to go, Robert. But the most important question is—can we get there before the rains break?"

"Yes, old man, I think we can. I've bought a wagon..." He sighed ruefully. "It was deuced expensive. It's a light wagon, for eight oxen..."

The Colonel cut in. "And have you found the beasts to pull it?"

Onslow beamed. "Yes, sir, I have – twenty-four oxen – sixteen to haul and eight to spare. They're not in good condition, but I had little choice. I'm doing my best to feed them up for the journey—some of them look as if they've never had a proper meal. And I've also bought a little donkey cart. It needs two beasts to pull it, but I've bought four..."

"And horses?" asked Martin.

"Well, that's been more of a problem." Robert was instantly deflated, slumping forward, his plump hands wringing each other. "Actually, I'm afraid there's none to be had. Even people who know I'll pay well haven't been able to find me anything."

"Do we have to have horses?" Perry affected boredom. "We can ride on the wagon, can't we? Much more comfortable."

Martin replied thoughtfully. "We could travel without them, but the problem will be at the other end—when we want to search for farming land, or go shooting for the pot. We can't trundle around in an ox-wagon. It would be far too unwieldy, and remember there are no tracks there, so a wagon will easily get stuck in the rainy season."

"Quite right," agreed the Colonel. "You'd be unwise to leave without at least one horse each."

They continued their discussion, sipping their drinks as the night darkened. Helen caught Martin's eye and she smiled slightly, though her expression reflected her concern for the impending departure of the men. She was dismayed to find that her thoughts were concentrated more on Martin's safety, and she blushed in guilt.

"I can't help feeling worried about your trek," she said to the three young men. "You have no experience of this country. Sometimes you make it sound as if you're planning a trip from London to Brighton. What about the risks—the wild animals, the Matabele...?"

Seeing that the others were waiting for him to reply, Robert started. "You mustn't worry, dear. I've been talking to some men who might join us. We'll light big fires at night to keep the lions away. The Matabele won't bother us—they know if they give trouble it would mean war. The men around here say the beggars won't step out of line."

"And what about fever?" she added. "I've heard stories about black-water fever..."

"We'll be careful," he reassured. "And we have quinine—ghastly stuff."

In the days that followed, these discussions became features of their sojourn in Palapye. Assembling on the verandah for drinks before lunch and before supper, they recounted their attempts to buy provisions and particularly to find horses. Helen reminded them of the food and clothing they needed, and her father added his advice about equipment, based on his long campaign experiences.

Like Perry, Martin wondered what Helen saw in her fiancé. It was easy to imagine Robert as a schoolboy, large and timid, the type who usually became a target for bullies. He was good-natured, but he veered alarmingly between a cheerful demeanour and melancholy. His confidence was ephemeral, and pessimism erupted each time their plans met an obstacle.

⁂

One morning, soon after their breakfast, they met an Afrikaner on the verandah of the hotel who had been given their names by a horse trader. He was a burly man in his late thirties, with a thick rufous beard, and deeply tanned skin, like well-cured leather. They sat down to coffee and in broken English he told them about a Boer family who were leaving the district to return to the Transvaal.

"They lost too many cattle to lions, man. I know they have some salted horses. Why don't you go and see if they'll sell you some. They need money."

"How much does he want for them?" asked Perry. His smile was patronising, as if amused by this specimen of primitive pioneering stock.

"*Gott*, I don't know", answered the Afrikaner, blowing out his cheeks. "There's not many horses for sale up here, as you know."

"Don't you have any idea?" persisted Perry.

"Ten pounds?"

Perry whistled. "That would be daylight robbery. You can get a good horse for half that in the Cape."

"Yah, man, but this isn't the Cape," replied the Afrikaner.

Martin knew they had no alternative. He could ill afford to pay such a high price, and would have to ask Robert Onslow for a loan. Robert had already guessed that he was short of capital and had offered help. So Martin asked for directions to the farm and wrote them down carefully.

"Ask for Kokkie de Wet—the *kaffirs* all know him."

Early next morning, the three men set out for the de Wet farm, Robert and Perry in the donkey cart, and Martin riding a borrowed horse. They followed a rudimentary track through thorn scrub, consisting only of two deep, dusty ruts; sometimes they forked, which led to arguments about the correct route. There had been no rain for five months and little grass was to be seen. Martin wondered how cattle could survive, let alone thrive, in these conditions. Then he remembered that sheep prospered in even more hostile environment of the Karoo. Occasionally they saw small buck scamper away through the dusty bushes. Twice the horse was startled by flocks of guinea fowl that flew off with loud cackles and clattering wings. They encountered few natives, but all seemed to know the de Wets, and pointed the direction for them.

By early afternoon they came upon a group of pole and *dagga* shacks that comprised the Afrikaner homestead. It was surrounded by a rough fence—a *kraal* or zariba—made of interlocked thorn branches, designed to prevent wild animals from getting in. A lanky middle-aged Boer, emerged, wearing tattered khaki shorts and a dirty white singlet. Behind him was his thin wife, a small naked child on her hip. Three tawny hunting dogs bounded forward to greet the visitors. The men shook hands before de Wet led them to another *kraal* where seven scrawny horses stood in the shade of a thorn tree, their tails swishing away the flies.

The Boer leaned on the fence; he knew only a few words of English, and spoke in guttural Afrikaans, a problem that the three young men had not anticipated. When he saw they could not understand him, he gestured with his fingers—two horses for him, five for the visitors. He pointed to the best two animals, indicating that he would keep these for himself.

Martin said to de Wet, "How much do you want for them?"

De Wet held up both hands to show ten digits, then one hand.

"Fifteen pounds—each." Robert whistled, and looked anxiously at his two companions. "That's a hell of a price. I suppose we have no choice."

Perry held up both hands, and said loudly, "Ten pounds each."

De Wet laughed and shook his head; he knew it was a seller's market. Finally, Robert nodded his acceptance of the price and pulled the notes from his pocket.

It was too late for them to return to Palapye before dark. De Wet offered them a room in his homestead, a pole and *dagga* rondavel that the Boer couple normally used to store their maize. It was nearly empty, and there was enough space for the three men to spread their groundsheets on the beaten earth floor. Later, they joined the de Wet's for roan antelope steak and *boerwors* sausages grilled over an open fire. Conversation was virtually impossible, since neither of the de Wets could speak English, and the three young men knew only a few words of Afrikaans.

Robert and Perry were so tired that they went away to sleep soon after the meal. Perry complained volubly about the sleeping conditions and would not accept Robert's attempts to make him more comfortable. Martin stayed out a while longer to smoke a pipe, enjoying the night sky full of stars, and the sparks rising from the fire. Now and then the dogs lying outside at the door of the de Wet hut would prick their ears at the sounds of wild animals in the surrounding bushveld.

He could hear the Boer couple murmuring to each other occasionally. It was a perilous life, he thought. Even if they and their cattle survived the tropical diseases, there was the risk of marauding lions, the reason they were going south again. Their meagre herd, like the horses, were in *kraals* ringed by high fences of thorn branches, that needed constant maintenance to keep them high enough and wide enough to prevent lions from breaking in.

ঌৎৡ

Next morning, the Boer helped the three visitors to catch their five horses and put on bridles; the horses were docile and seemed to lack energy. They had brought three saddles with them, and purchased another two from de Wet, as well as a set of leading reins. Robert groaned as he dug into his wallet again. On the way back to Palapye, Robert drove the cart, while Martin and Perry rode horses. The other three horses and the one borrowed in the town were on lead reins, two tied to the cart, and one led by each rider. It was an exhausting business leading the horses through the bushveld. They were hungry enough to want to graze any tuft of palatable grass, and were easily spooked by guinea fowl. Loss of a horse would have been a calamity, but luckily the bridles and reins held.

By late afternoon they at last reached Palapye, weary and coated in dust. Martin led the horses to the water trough near the hotel, where they drank heavily. Colonel Bateson and Helen were on the verandah having afternoon tea, and came to the railing to greet them. A dozen other people gathered round to assess their purchases.

"They're awfully thin," said Helen doubtfully. "Have you made your personal choices?"

"We gave Robert first choice," replied Martin, "because he put up the cash—though we'll pay him back our share, of course."

Robert giggled. "I chose the biggest chap—for my weight." He indicated a black gelding, half a hand larger than the other horses, but with all his ribs showing. "Martin had second choice, because he'll probably ride more than any of us."

Martin dismounted; the chestnut gelding had a strong frame, and seemed of a calmer disposition than the others. "I've called him Chandra. It's a Hindi word for 'moon' – see he has this crescent on his forehead. He's quite a gentleman. You might like to take him out some time, Helen."

Helen looked from Martin to his horse, appraising and wondering if there was a hidden meaning in his words. She felt a real ache of apprehension about the impending departure of this young man, who had suddenly invaded her life, casting all manner of doubts about her future.

"And this one's mine," announced Perry. "I've called her Scheherazade, because she has lots of Arab blood—so Martin says. See her ears." He pointed to the inward curving tips of the little mare's ears, which were twitching away the flies.

"The two others are spares, I suppose," said the Colonel. "What have you named your horse, Robert?"

"I haven't, yet, sir." He looked up at Helen. "I thought you might help me, dear."

☙❧

On the eve of their journey north the group had supper together at the hotel. Excitement was tinged with sadness at the prospect of parting. Perry's flamboyance seemed shallow; Martin dwelled only on the practical; Robert was almost silent, gazing mournfully at Helen; he felt she was ignoring him.

The Colonel toasted the three young men and wished them good fortune. "I wish I was going with you," he said, lifting his glass of wine. "Robert, be careful. I hope you find farming land soon, and that I'll be able to see my daughter settled on it. Perry, I hope you find gold, so you can make the report to your uncle that he's hoping for..."

"...that will allow me to return to America?" interrupted Perry with an ironic laugh.

Bateson next lifted his glass to Martin. "And Martin, I hope you too find a farm. And I thank you for taking my future son-in-law with you..."

"Here, here!" added Robert.

A while later Martin got up and made to leave, saying that he wanted to check the horses. As he left he saw that Helen was watching him guardedly. He walked out of the hotel into the cool night air, paused to light his pipe, and then walked slowly down the main street towards the livery stables where the horses were kept. A bright half moon lit his way. He had almost reached the stables when he heard his name called, and turning he saw Helen running after him, holding up her skirt.

"Can I come with you?" She was out of breath.

"Of course." He looked back towards the hotel. "What did you say to the others?"

"That I was going to my room." She did not smile and looked over her shoulder nervously. He knew that she was risking social censure by going out alone to meet him.

They walked on in silence and on reaching the entrance of the stables he greeted the African night guard, took his lantern, and entered the long shed, where about thirty horses were tethered along the walls. He found their five, and they stirred and stamped as he checked their water buckets. The confined air was filled with their cidery scent. He stroked them, and whispered a few words, while Helen followed him, watching him carefully, sensing that he was preoccupied and chagrined that he seemed hardly to notice her presence.

After several hesitations she spoke to him, almost inaudibly. "When am I going to see you again, Martin?"

He stopped and looked at her, and when he spoke, his tone held a hard edge she'd never heard before. "I suppose when you come up to Mashonaland to marry Robert. And when will that be?"

She looked down shyly. "Next year, after the rains." Drawing in a deep breath, she summoned her courage. "I'll miss you."

He took a step towards her. "Will you? Is that what you came here to tell me?"

She touched his arm lightly. "Yes. I'll miss you more than I should admit." Detecting no response in his expression, she added, "You will look after Robert, won't you?"

He turned away and said with a bitter laugh. "I've already promised, haven't I?"

"You must be careful yourself. Those two will be depending on you—I can see it. They seem so naïve."

An awkward pause followed as the lantern guttered, sending shaky shadows over the stable walls. She still had her hand on his arm, and Martin looked down at the diamond engagement ring. It had been the symbol of her exclusion since he met her in Cape Town, reinforced by Robert's presence here in Palapye.

"Are you in really in love with Robert?" he blurted.

She regarded him carefully. "I felt quite confident about marrying him—until I met you. Now I'm not certain..."

"Are you under some obligation to marry him? Is it for your father's sake? For the security of his money?"

She shook her head in despair, knowing she could not offer a truthful denial.

He did not wait for her reply. "I've tried to contain my feelings about you—because you're engaged to Robert. But...Helen, I have to tell you. I'm in love with you."

Now she was frustrated, almost angry. "Why are you telling me now? You're leaving in a few hours. Isn't it too late now? We don't know when we'll see each other again..."

"Damn it! I haven't said anything because you're engaged to another man. I thought I was behaving honourably." He turned away, touching Chandra on the flank, feeling the depth of the horse's chest. "Would it have made any difference if I'd told you before? You know I started to feel it when we talked on the train that first night. It's grown stronger in the last two weeks—even though I told myself you're committed to another man."

They heard footsteps and a cough. Helen's father entered the stables and approached them slowly, leaning heavily on his stick. Martin could tell that he was reluctant to interrupt them.

Bateson coughed again. "Hello. Oh, you're here, Helen. I thought there might be something wrong."

Martin answered before she could speak. "No, sir. Everything's fine."

"Is it?" The Colonel had a shrewd idea of what had been going on. "Better get some shut-eye, Martin. You have an early start." He turned abruptly, and started walking slowly out of the stables.

Martin watched the Colonel until he was out of sight, before turning to Helen. She was watching him with reproach, but he pulled her into his arms and held her, then kissed her hard, almost violently. She pressed herself against him, shaking with sobs and he finally released her, seeing an expression of anguish that would haunt him in the months to come. Turning, she hurried after her father, while Martin stayed to hand the lantern back to the watchman. Then he walked slowly back to the hotel.

☙❧

CHAPTER 5
Into Mashonaland — 1890

The trekking party left Palapye on a bright September morning. There was a chill in the air and Martin noticed a few wispy clouds, the first he had seen since they came here. He wondered if they were omens, heralds of the rains. The local people had assured him that the main rains usually started in mid-November or even December, although scattered heavy downpours might occur in October. He feared that the rivers would come down in spate and bring their journey to an abrupt halt. Meanwhile, several horsemen had returned from Mashonaland with news of the Pioneer Column. They had reached the high plateau, at an altitude of over four thousand feet, and were only days from reaching their objective.

Colonel Bateson and Helen bade their farewells to the three men. Martin watched Helen kiss Robert decorously on the cheek, and he was reminded of one of Perry's comments, that there was no hint of passion between the couple. She shook Perry and Martin by the hand. Martin looked for something in her expression, and thought he saw wistfulness in her eyes. If it was there, it lasted only a second before she turned to join her father.

The wagon rolled forward, pulled by eight pairs of oxen. It was followed by the donkey cart, and the spare animals on lead reins tied to the wagon. A young Shona, Enoch, walked alongside the lead oxen, while a Tswana lad drove the team from a seat on the wagon, wielding a long whip. A third African, their Tswana cook, drove the donkey cart, and his son, a boy of twelve, rode in the cart with the chickens. The three white men rode their horses, turning to wave their hats as they left the end of the long main street. At the outskirts of the town they made a planned rendezvous with two other trek parties having similar complements of men and animals.

So began their long journey to Mashonaland. Ahead was the route taken by the Pioneer Column, deeply rutted tracks, the desiccated droppings of oxen and horses still visible in the dust. The route passed through thornveld scattered with great bronze-trunked baobab trees. In the heat

of the days they outspanned to rest the animals. Martin usually took
the opportunity to shoot guinea fowl for the pot. There was no sport to
it because their cackles could be heard easily, and they were heavy and
slow in their flight. He never went far, and was careful not to get lost;
it would be easy enough in the featureless bushveld, where there were
no hills from which one could take bearings. They had an arrangement
that a shot would be fired from the camp every fifteen minutes after the
arranged time of the hunter's return.

At night they built fires to keep lions away from the animals, and
the white men took it in turns to stand watch. There was always some
light from the cloudless sky, from the moon, and even from the stars.
They could hear the yaps and howls of jackals and hyenas, and sometimes
grunts of hunting lions.

After a week they had to cross their first large river. The oxen
waded it through belly deep pools. Perry shot at a crocodile on the river
bank, but missed. That night a thunderstorm broke over them with tor-
rents of rain that lasted only a few minutes. The tarpaulins kept the wagons dry, but it was difficult to light the night fires, and the rain seemed
to bring out clouds of buzzing biting insects.

Martin had employed Enoch partly because he wanted to learn
Chishona, the language of the Shona people, as soon as possible. When
he wanted a lesson, he would hitch Chandra's reins to the wagon, and
make the herd boy lead the oxen so that Enoch could drive the team. The
young Shona man had been captured by Matabele at the age of eleven.
He had lived with a Matabele clan near the Tswana border, and had been
brought to the Transvaal by prospectors. There he received some education at a Christian mission, and had revived his native tongue.

Sadly, Enoch had now forgotten much of his English. Nevertheless, Martin was able to have simple conversations with him in Chishona,
based on a grammar and dictionary written by a Portuguese missionary
who had penetrated the Eastern districts of Mashonaland. The slim volume, purchased in London, had been translated from Portuguese to English. The Chishona words were written phonetically, and Martin added
his own versions when listening to Enoch.

A few days later they came to the left bank of the Limpopo River.
At that time of year it was not Kipling's 'great, grey-green, greasy' river,
Most of the bed was sand and too soft for the wagons; they did not have
the resources to lay branches to make a road over the sand. When they
reached the Mzingwane River the only rocky ford was through a pool

that held water. The oxen struggled to cross, and Martin had to swim with them, nervous about crocodiles. Near the far bank they used a rope and winch to drag the wagons out. It was desperately hard work in blazing sun, and by the end of the day, the men and draught animals were exhausted.

A couple of weeks later Robert showed symptoms of malaria. Their fellow trekkers, who had been brought up in the Transvaal, agreed that the pattern of fever was consistent with the disease. The patient lay in the wagon, his shirt soaked with perspiration, while Martin tried to spoon quinine into his mouth. He retched at the horrible taste but Martin persevered, then sat beside his shivering companion.

Perry peered into the wagon. "How is he?"

Martin moved to the sill of the wagon and spoke quietly. "Near the peak of the fever, I would guess. We can't trek until he's better. It's going to delay us at least another couple of days."

"Will the others wait here that long?"

"It's in their interests to stay with us. They know we have better equipment. Also, our extra rifles will be useful if there's any trouble. We're in Matabele country now, so there's sense in staying together." He climbed out of the wagon. "Your turn. Try to keep him cool. I'll stand guard for a while."

As they passed, Perry grinned conspiratorially, "It would be in your interests if he snuffed it."

Martin reacted angrily. "What do you mean?"

Perry laughed. "It was obvious the fair Helen would prefer you—instead of fat bumbling Robert. She's only marrying him for his money..."

"Shut up!" Martin hissed. "He might hear you..." He went to throw more brushwood onto the fires that surrounded the camp. They had placed the three wagons in a triangle with just enough space to climb between them, over the *disselbooms*. The animals were in a nearby *kraal* made from thorn brush, a laborious undertaking that seldom took less than two hours. On the perimeter of the camp were three fires, kept burning through the night.

Martin sat for a while at the fire nearest his wagon. He could hear the deep coughing call of lions hunting, and checked the bolt action of his rifle. Suddenly, he saw two tall black figures standing at the edge of the circle of firelight. They carried spears and shields, and wore the plumes of Matabele warriors. Without turning his head he called softly, "We have company."

Perry poked his head out of the wagon. "Oh God!" His voice quavered. "Are we surrounded by them?"

"I don't know. They seem to be looking behind them, so perhaps there are others. I want to talk to them. Call the others—and get Enoch here. He can speak to them in Sindebele."

"But Enoch can't speak English? How will we know what he's saying?"

Martin growled at him impatiently. "Please get on, Perry."

The American hurried away while Martin stood watching the motionless figures, his rifle at the ready, heart thumping. After a few minutes Enoch come up beside him. At that moment, the little Shona drover saw the Matabele men and his eyes widened, gleaming white in the firelight.

Martin spoke to Enoch in halting Chishona. "Speak—ask...What they want?"

Enoch nodded. He called out in Sindebele, "What do you want?"

The two Matabele warriors looked at each other, then one of them moved forward a pace. Martin could see them better now. They were tall young men, well-built, and wearing warrior trappings. Their eyes gleamed in the lambent firelight.

The one who came forward answered Enoch who translated for Martin. "There are lions. They wish to sit by your fire."

"Say slowly," said Martin, not fully understanding. "Fire? Lions?"

Enoch pointed to the fire and spoke more deliberately, with actions. "They—want—sit—here—because lions."

"Tell—them—yes."

Enoch called to the Matabele men and they moved cautiously forward. When they reached the far side of the fire they squatted down to warm themselves, their spears within easy reach. They held their palms towards the flames in the atavistic gesture that is common to all men, then looked around. Martin watched them carefully, wondering how they felt about these foreigners encroaching on their tribal territory.

Martin's fellow trekkers came up to the fire, with Perry close behind. They all carried rifles and peered apprehensively at the two warriors.

"It may be a trick," hissed one of them, "to assess our strength before the others attack."

Martin shook his head, but kept his eye on the visitors. "I don't think so. But just in case, you'd better keep an eye open in the other directions." He held out a water bottle towards the Matabele, who at first looked suspicious. Then he walked round the fire and squatted down near them. He had some biltong in a pouch tied to his belt, and took some sticks out, offering them. The two Matabele sniffed the biltong, then grinned and started chewing. They eyed Martin warily as he beckoned to Enoch, who crept up, stopping a safe distance from these much feared men.

Martin then started a slow mono-syllabic translated conversation with the Matabele men that lasted through the night. Enoch grew tired, and there were as many gestures as words, but by dawn Martin had established the names of the two men, that they had been sent by their *induna,* their commander, to observe the people trekking up after the Pioneer Column. No, they were not really concerned, because the numbers were so few, but they had noticed no one moving in the opposite direction.

It was growing light when Martin heard a shout from one of the drovers. One of the trekkers ran up, gesticulating wildly. "One of my donkeys has gone!" he shouted. "Must have been pinched by these bloody Matabele, or their mates.." He pointed angrily at the two men, who were still squatting at the embers of the fire.

"Wait a minute," said Martin, trying to calm him. "There are only two of them and I've been watching them all the time."

They found the neat hoof prints of the missing donkey clearly visible on the dusty ground. It had somehow found a gap in the thorn branches and made its escape. Martin pointed in the direction of its spoor, as Perry stumbled up sleepily to join them and asked what was going on.

"One of the donkey's missing," answered Martin. "How's Robert?"

"Seems a bit cooler." Perry seemed uninterested. "What can we do about the donkey? It's probably run off into the bush."

"Come with me," said Martin. "I'm going to ask the Matabele to help us search for it. They'll be experts at tracking."

He went back to the fire, where Enoch was still sleepily talking and gesturing to the two warriors. Martin explained to Enoch that a donkey had run away, and instructed him to ask whether the Matabele would help to track it down. The two men nodded, grinning with flashing teeth. They all moved off together, the Matabele in front, and were soon following the donkey's spoor.

A short while later, about a mile from the camp, they found the carcass of the donkey, partly eaten. The huge pug marks around the body showed that it was the victim of lions. The Matabele men were phleg-matic, shrugging and telling Enoch that there were many lions in this area and a donkey was good meat for them. They pointed north to indi-cate they were leaving. Then they raised their spears to Martin in fare-well; he waved back, smiling.

Perry asked, "What were they doing here?"

"I can't be certain," Martin replied. "It's difficult having to talk through Enoch. They seem to be keeping watch on the people coming up this route."

"Spies for Lobengula?"

"Something like that."

Martin went back to the ox wagon where he found Robert sitting up in his litter. The crisis of his fever had passed, but he was exhausted, his skin pale and wet with sweat.

"I'm sorry I've held you chaps up," he said in a weak voice.

"It wasn't your fault," Martin reassured him. "It could have been any one of us."

"Perry said you were my nurse..."

Martin laughed. "A poor substitute for Helen."

☙❧

The trekkers moved on, following the broad track cut by the Pio-neer Column. They seemed to cross an interminable succession of rivers and streams—some of them with large sand beds, such as the Tshabezi, Shashi, Bubye, Mtchwani, and Nuanetsi. These larger rivers still flowed a little and enabled the men to collect enough water to last at least a week. Eventually they reached a rocky defile, named Providential Pass by the Pioneer Column, and the track started to rise to higher country. It still continued diagonally across the slope that drained the plateau into the Limpopo River. There were many more rivers and streams to cross, but now they flowed more strongly, with clearer water.

Occasionally they encountered small groups of native people—known as the Banyai tribe. They seemed to live in miserable conditions, fleeing to hide in the rocky hillsides and *kopjes*, and emerging only when encouraged by gifts of venison.

The rolling country was covered with an open forest of *Julberna-dia*, *Brachystegia* and *Acacia* species. Martin had learnt that the density of the tree cover, and the height and straightness of the trees, indicated the fertility of the underlying soils. He was impressed by his first sight of the highveld; it seemed to have great potential for farming. The grassland supported plenty of antelope, mainly bushbuck, sable and roan antelope, besides occasional small groups of eland. Because the countryside had seen little or no rain for several months, these wild animals congregated at pools in late afternoon and early morning. Martin was able to provide a plentiful supply of fresh meat, which the white men and the Africans cooked over open fires.

About a week later they reached the tiny settlement of Fort Victoria, staffed ten weeks before by a small group from the Pioneer Column. They were greeted enthusiastically, and treated to their first civilised meal for two months. They were told that the column had taken a month to travel from this point to Fort Salisbury, but Martin's party should make the journey in three weeks because the route had been cleared.

It was early November when they emerged onto the Mashonaland highveld, with its rolling grassland and patches of open savannah woodland. Almost every day they came across herds of sable and roan antelope grazing; ostriches and giraffe were common. The streams were crystal clear. Every day the sky was a great blue vault with gatherings of massive thunder clouds that heralded the main rains. From this place the Pioneer Column had cleared a double track so that the length of the line of their many wagons was reduced by half.

One day they came across a group of Shona people, the first they encountered. They were collecting firewood and ran off to a rocky hillock about a hundred yards away. It was only when Enoch called to them that they ventured back. After a short conversation these people confirmed that they knew about the settlement made by the white men. They pointed up the rutted track, and estimated that it would take another week to walk there.

The following day they met a prospector on horseback, a tall gaunt Australian named Tom Ellsworth. After they invited him to join their evening meal he told them he had been present when the Pioneer Column established their camp near Mount Hampden. He had been in Mashonaland since the previous dry season—a so-called 'pre-Pioneer'—and was searching for gold. Though too laconic to sound enthusiastic, Martin thought he detected a guarded optimism in Ellsworth's answers to Perry's questions about the potential for ore bearing strata.

Ellsworth was astonished at the naivety of this little group of trekkers, and considered them extremely lucky to have come so far unscathed.

It struck him that the portly aristocrat was a misfit in this wild territory, and the American appeared to want to return to South Africa as soon as possible.

When Ellsworth left them next morning, Perry said, "I only need to meet a few more men like him and I can write my report and get out of here. It's not my idea of a place to live, I'm afraid. I'll leave it to you." He had long ago decided that he was unsuited for this way of life. The discomfort was constant, the food utterly basic, and not a woman in sight— if you discounted the occasional glimpses of scrawny Shona females. The risks were considerable—not from wild animals as he had earlier feared, but from diseases, especially malaria. He was determined to extract himself at the earliest possible moment.

The trekking party arrived at Fort Salisbury in the middle of November. It was two months since the Column had planted the Union flag on the grassy plain and declared their occupation of Mashonaland. Martin and his companions were not the first of the so-called 'followers', but the Pioneers greeted them warmly, and helped them to find a place to set up their camp. They were shown where they could draw water from a well that had just been dug to provide clean drinking water.

A week later the Town Clerk leased them a plot of land in the embryonic township, on which they built a pole and mud shack with the help of hired Africans. By this time the rains had started in earnest. The thatched roof of their shack leaked during each heavy downpour. Their clothes become damp and mouldy. Food was difficult to obtain. Within a couple of weeks the dirt roads in Fort Salisbury were deep in mud, and the livery stables where their horses were kept had to be moved to higher ground. The proprietor used the opportunity to raise his charges, and also cited his difficulties finding food.

∂∽∾

Now it was Perry's turn to contract fever. It took him two tedious weeks to recover, leaving him pale and drained but thankful to be alive. When he eventually stumbled out onto the little verandah of their house he found Martin smoking his pipe as he wrote a letter home. The American slumped into a canvas chair and watched his companion listlessly.

Martin wrote: *'Living here is proving harder than we expected. The route from the south is still blocked because the rivers are flooded after very heavy rain. We have had no supplies or mail for six weeks. Of course we will not starve—venison is plentiful and guinea fowl are easy to find—but the maize from local Africans has all been bought and eaten. Bread is just a dream...'*

He looked up to see Robert hurrying along the dirt road that led past their pole and *dagga* shack. He was out of breath, his forehead beaded with sweat; he flapped a letter held in his hand.

"A couple of mail riders just got through," he panted. "Helen's father—he's been ill. Helen's gone back to England with him. It means she won't—she won't be able to come—here after all." He slumped into a chair, his face a picture of gloom.

Perry suddenly perked up. "You didn't really think you could bring her here, man! You must have been mad. Now what will you do?" In his opinion, quite often expressed before he was stricken with fever, Robert ought to return to a life to which he was better suited.

"I suppose...I'll go back to England. There's a trek setting off south next week. We can always come back when we're married."

Perry shook his head, sighing as he slowly stood up, easing his aching joints. "Listen," he announced. "I was going to tell you this evening, but you might as well know now. I've already decided to go back. This isn't the place for me. Call me a hedonist if you like, but you know I'd rather be in Cape Town, or enjoying the company of my friends in Boston." He turned to Robert. "Do you think I can join your trek?"

Robert nodded. "As long as you're fit enough."

Martin started to re-light his pipe. "And the deal with your uncle, Perry?"

"I've made quite a lot of enquiries about the mining potential. I have enough to make a report. Besides, I can tell him truthfully that I've had fever and need to recuperate. So I'm going to Johannesburg—that's it. What about you, Martin?"

"I'm staying. I'm determined to find a job on a farm. This heavy rain won't last forever. I'm sorry you're going, both of you."

A week later Perry and Robert left on the journey south. They joined forces with a dozen other men in a small trek that would bring the safety of extra numbers. They took the donkey cart to carry their belongings, leaving the ox wagon with Martin, who bought out their share, using a loan from Robert. Mounted on Chandra he waved farewell to them they rode off towards South Africa.

A feeling of loneliness and isolation descended on him, and intensified that night as he sat reading by the light of his hurricane lamp. He was thousands of miles from his home country and his family. In India he had the camaraderie and protection of his regiment. Here he was largely on his own, one of only a hundred and fifty men of his own race, in a vast country, largely unexplored. Doubts began to invade his thoughts. He could have rented a farm in England, married a girl like Amanda, and raised a family. It would have been a comfortable life in the countryside he loved. It would not have taken much to persuade him to quit.

CHAPTER 6
Mashonaland - 1891

In early September 1891, Martin offered to break in a recalcitrant horse for Henry Borrow, known to his friends as 'Harry', one of the men who came to Mashonaland with the Pioneer Column. Since his arrival a year earlier Martin had worked as an assistant manager—a sort of apprentice farmer—with a Pioneer settler who had previously farmed in South Africa.

He set off early in the morning riding Chandra. The *Hyperrhenia* grass alongside the path was tall enough to brush its dew-laden leaves against his legs, wetting his khaki trousers. The sun had just risen and the dew droplets sparkled with jewel-like brilliance. Chandra was full of energy, shying playfully as birds flew across the path.

Harry Borrow owned a farm north-east of Fort Salisbury, having acquired the land free of any charges as his reward for participating in the Column. His house stood on a broad ridge overlooking a long valley running in an easterly direction. He had thinned out the trees to create a park effect, and to enhance the view. He and his African workers were re-thatching the roof. He greeted Martin, pointing to the bundles of grass on the roof. "Roof leaked like a sieve last rains. I don't want it to happen again." Laughing, he added. "What I wouldn't do for some good Norfolk reed and a professional thatcher."

Borrow was tall and rugged, one of the most popular men in the Column. He had formed a syndicate with friends to help each other in finding land and the basic requisites for living and farming. Martin met him within a few weeks of arriving in Fort Salisbury, and they gradually forged a friendship through their interest in polo. During the dry season, when the ground was hard and the grass sparse, they organized regular weekly games on the outskirts of the town.

Martin dismounted and handed his horse to one of the Africans, while his friend clambered down off the roof. They walked together to some log seats in the shade of a *msasa* tree.

"Malaria's started again," said Borrow. "You've escaped so far?"

"Touch wood. One of the police chaps died last night, I heard—blackwater fever..."

A servant brought mugs of coffee for the two men, and they lit pipes, watching the blue smoke curl up into the branches of the *msasa*.

"Last of the coffee," muttered Borrow gloomily. "Hope a supply wagon comes soon. I say, have you heard that Philips is leaving? He offered his farm to me. It's over there." He pointed to the east, where the sun was already over the tops of the trees.

"Will you buy it?"

Borrow shook his head. "Our syndicate has enough land already. But what about you? I told him I have a friend who might like to buy it."

Martin felt his spirits soar. "What's it like, Harry? Do you know it?"

"Not very well. He wants three hundred pounds, which sounds a lot to me. It's about three thousand acres, so that works out at two shillings an acre. But he's done hardly any development—just a few patches cleared for cropping near the stream—and his house is a tumbledown shack." He looked keenly at his friend. "If you're interested, we could ride over now."

Martin's thoughts were racing. "I'd like to see it. I have less than a hundred pounds here. It's all I've been able to save, so far. I could ask my father for the rest. When I left, he didn't want to stake me, but a couple of months ago he wrote and said he would let me have up to five hundred..."

"I expect it would suit Philips to be paid in England. He wouldn't want the cash here—unless he has some debts. He knows virtually nothing about farming and horses. At least he has the sense to know he wouldn't make a go of it here."

Borrow called to his African groom who brought their horses onto the grass clearing in front of the house. They rode together through the savannah woodland along the broad crest of the ridge. As they rode eastwards the ridge started to dip slowly and widen, and beyond Martin could see in the far distance the grey granite dome called Domboshawa.

Borrow pointed to a slash cut in the bark of a tree. "Here's the boundary. Ah, and there's the beacon." It was a rough pile of dull red stones.

The broad valley stretched in front of them, its sides heavily wooded, the floor scattered with flat-topped acacias. The great height and girth of the trees showed that the red soil was deep and fertile. There was no sign of any African settlement. They reached a group of ramshackle huts that was Philips' homestead. The stocky ex-sailor sat outside smoking a pipe. He stood up to greet them as they dismounted, and Borrow explained that his friend was interested in buying the farm.

"Three hundred is the price," said Philips bluntly.

"I need to know how much arable..." said Martin.

Philips eyed him shrewdly. "Take a ride over the place. See for yourself. Borrow can show you the way."

The two friends remounted to ride down a well-used path to the valley floor. Here the grass was tall and lush, and Martin was surprised that it was still green, even though there had been no rain in the winter months. At the stream, where a little clear water flowed slowly, thick reeds lined the banks. They rode their horses through, letting them drink at the far side.

"Water," enthused Borrow, "that's the key. You can do nothing without water; that's why I'm going to build an earth dam. But you'll have running water all through the year, and it will be stronger when I've made my dam. You could grow vegetables to sell in town. We could market together. So do you want the place? Philips got the farm for nothing, like me—because he was a Pioneer—so offer him two-fifty. He's being a bit greedy. On the way home we'll ask him to give you an option for a week."

"Do you think he'll accept two-fifty?"

"I don't know. Try him. But if you're in any doubt, ride around the farm tomorrow. I'll lend you a couple of boys to dig some pits. Look at the ant bear holes. Watch out for laterite, or anything that gives a hint of shallow soil. The trees will always give you a clue."

In his mind Martin could see broad fields of maize such as those he had seen on the train journey up to Kimberley. His teams of patient oxen would ply the rows, turning the rich red-brown soil, burying the few weeds. He looked up to the ridge ahead, where Harry had suggested building the homestead. He would build it up there, among that clump of *msasas* that spread serenely like great cedars on the ridge top.

Borrow seemed to sense where Martin's thoughts were. "I'm convinced it's healthier living away from the streams. All this fever comes from people hanging around near marshes and the mosquitoes...."

"Have you ever had fever?"

"Oh, I have—in Bechuanaland. And I don't ever want it again. The cure is almost as bad as the sickness. I gather Doc still has some quinine left."

Martin grimaced. "I had a temperature last week, and he gave me some. I vomited most of it up, so it must have been something else."

"You were lucky. I would get out of that place if I were you. Buy a tent and pitch it here until you can get a thatched house put up. If you like, you can stay with me while you build."

They turned back, and Martin asked for an option for a week while he inspected the farm carefully. Philips agreed, realising that he had a serious buyer who was backed by Borrow.

❧

Next day Martin watched Borrow's two men dig deep into the rich red earth. His intention was to examine a dozen pits like this, at different locations on the farm, to sample the soil types and their depth. He took a handful of the earth from the top of the pile and poured a trickle of water from his bottle. He kneaded it between his fingers, recognising it as sandy clay. The Pioneers had already established that this red doleritic soil was very fertile, but it was sticky and difficult to work when wet. The local Shona tribesmen preferred the lighter sandy soils derived from granite, which were easier to cultivate.

They dug quickly to a depth of three feet, as Borrow had advised. Before moving on, Martin scanned the trees for signs of stunting, or twisted trunks, but found nothing to cause suspicion. He left the two labourers and set off on foot. About ten minutes later he put up a flock of cackling guinea fowl. Three of them flew up into the branches of a *msasa* tree, where they peered down at him, warbling in alarm. He shot one of the birds with his twelve-bore shotgun. It tumbled out of the tree, a bundle of feathers. When he brought it back to where the two men were digging, they greeted him with broad smiles and quickly lit a fire, plucked and gutted the guinea fowl in seconds, and drove a spit through it.

Martin spoke to them in his slow careful Chishona. He had been learning for over a year, and had made good progress. "Where are your homes?" he asked.

"Domboshawa—over there." The taller of the men pointed to the north.

"Why are there no Shona people living here? Have they never lived here?"

"The clay soil is too sticky when it rains and too hard when it is dry," the shorter African said. "As well, the trees are too big to dig out.

Sandy soil is easier for us to cultivate. Besides, it is better to live near the river, where we have water throughout the year. We only come to these places for hunting."

"What do you hunt?"

"Reedbuck, duiker, sometimes roan antelope come here—and we trap guinea fowl, like this one." He pointed to the remains of the bird.

Martin was struck by the simple good humour of these African labourers, as with their compatriots on the farm where he worked. They had had no formal education, like most farm labourers in Britain, and an idea was germinating in his mind, to provide basic schooling for his workers and their families.

ᘒ◦ᕲ

By the end of the week Martin finished traversing Philips' farm, and he discussed his findings with Borrow. At least half the farm was first class arable, while another five hundred acres might be affected by rocks or laterite. The remainder was *vlei*—poorly drained land at the bottom of the valley. He rode up to Philips and made him an offer of two hundred and fifty pounds. They settled for two hundred and seventy-five, subject to payment in London by the end of the month, confirmed by the bank. Martin would have clear title through the Administrator's office in Fort Salisbury.

The Administrator confirmed the Deed of Sale early in the following week, and Martin deposited with him an undertaking to pay Philips. He moved onto the farm and hired two young Shona men to help him make a more detailed survey of the soils. Their names were Mpanda and Ngwiri, his first permanent employees. Together they built grass huts to live in. For himself, Martin chose a spot under the *msasas* with a commanding view of the valley. Mpanda and Ngwiri preferred to live nearer the stream, knowing that proximity to water would save them much energy fetching water.

Borrow's headman recruited a dozen other Shona men to work for Martin as daily paid labour. He came out of his hut one morning to find them squatting around a makeshift fire, waiting for him. They wore ragged cotton shorts, and cloaks made of animal skins to ward off the early morning chill. He marked out the foundations of the homestead and started the labourers clearing grass and cutting poles. The house was made from pole and *dagga*—the African equivalent of wattle and daub. He took two of the men down to the stream, where they located an anthill and started to make the sticky mud paste that would be plastered onto the framework of rough poles and laths. This paste was carried up to the ridge in baskets. His house consisted of two round huts joined by a rectangular room, which was his dining room cum drawing room. One of the round huts was a bedroom, the other a storeroom, which could be used as a makeshift bedroom if he had visitors. Having seen the trouble caused by Borrow's leaking roofs, he ensured that the grass thatch was doubly thick. Down the slope and well away from the house they excavated a deep pit to serve as his latrine. It was roughly walled and roofed with grass; the seat was made of *msasa* branches.

There was no shortage of meat. Martin shot enough guinea fowl and duiker to give them an unlimited supply, to the delight of Mpanda, Ngwiri, and the other labourers. The men also gleaned green herbs from the forest, but to Martin their diet seemed the rather unappetising fare of hunter gatherers.

While building his house Martin stayed with his friend Borrow. He wrote to his parents:

'I'm so grateful to you both for lending me the money to buy this farm. I have a marvelous feeling of possession—knowing that this land belongs to me— the earth, the stream, the beautiful big trees, even the rocks. I've calculated that I can make a profit of about fifty pounds in the coming summer rainy season. I'll grow maize and vegetables, but I have many development expenses. I'm paying a dozen Shona men to clear the fields for planting maize; and I have to feed them—food is scarce, but they'll work better if they have their favourite maize meal.'

'It takes two hours to ride—at hacking pace—from Salisbury to my farm, so you can tell it is a journey of about eight miles. My friend, Henry Borrow, has invited me to stay with him, and my daily journey from his place to mine is a mere fifteen minutes! I've changed the name of the farm to Long Valley, which is a rough translation of the Chishona name.'

'I'm building a wattle and daub house on the ridge. The settlers say the risk of malaria is less if you live on a ridge, though it means carrying up water. My latrine is a small hut, built over a deep pit. It has no door, so I can sit and admire the view! The settlers call this sort of convenience a 'long drop".

❧

One day, when the house was nearing completion, Martin went on Chandra to look for guinea fowl. Riding slowly through the trees, his shotgun lying across his lap, he suddenly noticed a movement in the shadows near a strange heap of granite boulders. He put his thumb on the safety catch of his shotgun, then realised that he was looking at the figure of an African man. He held his gun tightly.

"Hello, how are you?" he called, in Chishona.

A small man emerged cautiously from the shadows. He wore only a kilt of skins and a ragged brown cloth jerkin. His frame was thin and wiry, and Martin guessed his age at about forty. In one hand he carried a short spear, in the other a calabash and a small bark parcel that gave out a wisp of smoke. He watched Martin warily like an animal tensed for flight.

"My name is Martin." He pointed at his chest, then pointed to the man inquiringly.

For a moment there was no response, only the flickering of wary eyes. Then the African slowly pointed the spear at his chest, his face impassive. "Nyendi." He said.

"What are you doing?" Martin tried to sound friendly, rather than interrogatory.

After a short pause, "Collecting honey."

"Is there much honey here?"

The man nodded and made a sweeping gesture with his spear. Martin unfastened the water bottle from his saddle and took a drink, then held it down for him to take. The little man advanced cautiously; he had a pronounced limp.

Martin pointed at the bottle. "Water."

Nyendi took the water bottle, sniffed at the opening, and then sipped warily, keeping his eyes on the white man. He turned and called softly, and a young boy of about seventeen emerged from the long grass. Taller than Nyendi, his face was broad and open, with wide eyes looking fearfully at the man on the horse. He turned towards Nyendi, clapped his hands softly, dipping at the knees in the Shona gesture of deference to an elder, then squatted on the ground.

Martin indicated that Nyendi should pass the water to the boy. "Your son?" he asked.

The little man nodded. "His name is Mpata." He held out the water bottle to the boy, who drank from it without hesitation.

"Will you sell me honey?" asked Martin.

Nyendi said something to his son, who returned to where he had hidden, then emerged with a large tube made of tree bark. Nyendi laid the tube on the ground and opened it to reveal several combs of honey. He lifted one of them and offered it to Martin, who made a cutting gesture to show that a small piece would suffice. The African produced a short knife and cut off a piece of comb the size of a slice of bread, and handed it to Martin. As he ate the piece of honey comb, Martin noticed a smile on Nyendi's face. He was evidently amused that the white man found it so appetising. He started to eat too, but his son stood waiting respectfully behind him.

Saliva spurted in Martin's mouth as he ate the honey comb. It had a strong smell and taste of wood smoke. Looking up he saw the honey gatherer watching him, his face relaxed for the first time. Then Nyendi started to eat a piece of comb filled with white grubs. The boy remained standing aside; Martin knew that in Shona custom the children will not eat with the father.

"Where is your home?" he asked.

Nyendi pointed with his spear, high, and to the north. "Over there, but I sleep here sometimes." Now he pointed to the granite boulders.

Martin turned in the saddle and nodded in the direction behind him. "I live up there. I have bought this land." He felt a sense of the ridiculous as he said it. This man had probably walked this valley all his life, and here was this foreigner claiming to have bought it. The whole idea seemed preposterous.

"The other white man has gone?"

"Yes. You can live here. I will buy honey from you. How much can I pay you?"

Nyendi smiled slowly with a hint of cunning. "You give me meat, I give you honey."

"You show me how you find honey." He laughed. "I show you how I find meat."

He waved to them and rode back towards his homestead. The honey gatherer and his son watched his departure impassively. They had heard that these white men would prevent the Matabele from raiding, and that was good.

⌒∾⌒

Every week Martin rode into town and collected his mail from the post office—a thatched hut with a rack to hold the letters for settlers; mail was carried, for a fee, by travellers who came up occasionally from the Cape Colony. He sat on a canvas chair on the crude wooden verandah of Salisbury's only hotel, a ramshackle single story building. About a dozen other settlers were gathered there, drinking beer as they read their letters. They sat around trestle tables exchanging tidbits of news from South Africa and England. Martin looked at his only piece of mail, a gold embossed wedding invitation. There was a short letter enclosed with it, which he read first.

'Dear Martin',

'Robert has asked me to write to you. He says he is no good at writing letters, and I have to agree with him! We would have been so pleased if you could have come to the wedding. We both regard you as a close friend, even though our time together, especially mine, was brief. Sadly, all we can do is send the invitation and I fear that it will reach you long after the event. My father is not at all well, but his spirits have risen with the assurance that I'm marrying Robert, and will become Lady Onslow. As you know, the title means nothing to me!'

'As long as my father is unwell, Robert and I will remain in England. So, dear friend, we cannot tell when we may see you again. Perhaps you will return to England before we see Africa again?'

'Yours affectionately, Helen.'

Martin looked up to see Henry Borrow and Captain Forbes approaching and invited them to sit down at his table, a crude but serviceable affair of rough planking. He beckoned a waiter and ordered drinks. Forbes was the senior military officer in the country, a dark brooding man who took his duties seriously. He was not popular with the settlers because of his abrupt manner.

Borrow nodded towards the letter in Martin's hand. "Good news?"

"Robert Onslow's married—you remember him? He came up from Palapye with me a year ago. The wedding was a week ago, but I've only just received the invitation." He handed Borrow the card.

"A society wedding, eh? You know the bride don't you?"

"I met her in the Cape—on my way up here."

Borrow returned the card, and looked shrewdly at his friend. "I was telling Forbes about your honey man. You're certainly different, Martin.

Most settlers would have sent those two Shona hunters packing...trespassing and all that. Be careful, Martin. We know very little about the Shona—except that they're fed up with being preyed on by the Matabele for the last fifty years."

Forbes entered the conversation for the first time. "They're quite capable of sticking a spear in your back, Russell. Be wary."

∾∾

One morning, while out shooting, Martin encountered Nyendi again. The little man limped warily out from behind a tree, and, after exchanging pleasantries Martin asked him to demonstrate how he found honey.

Nyendi nodded. "Tomorrow. Here." He pointed to the sun, then indicated the low angle of early morning.

When Martin returned next morning to the same place the honey gatherer and his son came cautiously out of the thick grass. Suspecting that they had waited to see that he was alone, Martin dismounted and followed them, leading his horse. They walked quite quickly, picking their way through the trees, brushing aside the long grass. Occasionally they stopped and seemed to be listening. Nyendi said something to his son, who smiled, then they started forward again, faster now. Despite his lame leg the little man moved at a steady lope that Martin could scarcely keep pace with. In a short while he stopped and pointed into a tree ahead. Martin could now see a small light brown bird, about the size of a thrush, chattering excitedly. So this was the honey guide he had heard about. This bird would lead you to a hive on the understanding that it would be left one of the combs as a reward.

The honey guide moved on, leading them from tree to tree, until they came to a tall *mpondo* with a stain half way up the trunk where honey leaked from a hole. The little bird was moving around the branches, chattering and fluttering its wings as if urging them to do something. The two Africans gathered a few twigs and arranged them in a pile at the base of the tree. They added kindling in the form of dry moss from a pouch and then lit the fire with a piece of charcoal carried in the green bark parcel. A thin column of smoke rose up the trunk and Martin could hear an angry hum as the bees registered their dismay.

Nyendi then started to cut down the tree with his little axe. The trunk had a diameter of about a foot, but the little man made the task look easy. Buzzing from the hive grew louder and some bees emerged, dropping down to circle around the father and son. Martin stayed with his horse at a safe distance, but Nyendi and Mpata showed no concern for the bees. They were slightly protected by the smoke from the fire, but received several stings. Each time they would stop and pull away the bee, then pinch out the sting that had been left behind.

Within a few minutes the tree fell with a crash that echoed through the open forest. Nyendi quickly scooped up the fire on a strip of bark and carried it along to the entrance of the hive. Striking a few well-placed blows to open up the hollow place in the trunk, he exposed a cluster of five fat honeycombs and one breeding comb. This latter he broke in two, throwing half away from the tree for the honey guide to feast on. The remaining combs were quickly bundled into a bark cylinder. The Africans left the area to the angry bees, walking up to Martin with the pride of men who had completed a skilled task.

࿐࿐

In the weeks that followed Martin met Nyendi and his son several times. They became accustomed to chatting for a while, and Martin would sometimes give them a guinea fowl. Once, Nyendi pointed out where he had seen a reedbuck, and when Martin shot it, he presented the haunch to the little man. Their conversation became easier, as the little man lost his suspicious reserve. Martin discovered that he had formerly lived further to the west, beyond the Hunyani Range, but the Matabele had raided his village. The refugees from the raid moved to land north of Domboshawa, on the upper slopes of the Mazoe valley. Now, the honey gatherer explored widely, but he kept clear of the white men who were opening farms and starting to mine for gold. He found the valley of Martin's farm to be rich in honey, made from the flowers of the *msasa* trees, and came there regularly in the dry season, sleeping in the open and living on maize meal brought from his village, supplemented by the many wild plants that he knew so well.

Martin realised that Nyendi was more at home in this savannah country than any man he had met. He knew the trees and plants that gave sustenance, or spiced his rather bland maize meal, and he knew all the animals and their habits. He could move silently through the open woodland, and with his sharp eyes and keen ears knew all that was happening in the valley. Mpata was being taught by his father, and was already an expert woodsman. He would sit quietly, behind and some distance away from his father, listening intently to their conversation, but saying nothing. When Martin asked him a question, he would smile but not reply.

Nyendi and his son were intrigued by Martin's horse and his gun. They had never seen a horse, nor any man ride an animal, until the year before, when they caught glimpses of the white men foraging out of Fort Salisbury. Now they were having their first close encounters with the strange creature, and would glance apprehensively at Chandra as he cropped the grass, swishing his tail at the flies. They had seen guns before, but only old muzzle-loaders that were effective up to barely fifty paces. Martin's rifle and his double-barreled shotgun were the first they had seen, and they were fascinated with the accuracy and consistency with which the white man used his weapons. He used them sparingly because ammunition was scarce and expensive. He would put guinea fowl up into the trees, then line up a couple and drop them with a single cartridge. *'Not very sporting,'* he had written home, *'but economical.'*

It became their custom on meeting to cook a meal of guinea fowl followed by honey. They would sit on the dry ground tearing off the delicious grilled white meat, talking about many things as the mood took them. As Martin's Chishona vocabulary improved he learned more about Shona customs, and their names for trees and animals. Later he went with Nyendi on foot, sometimes tracking game, but always within the boundaries of the farm.

One day when they were talking about Nyendi's upbringing, Martin asked, "When the Matabele fought your people, did they use guns?"

Nyendi sighed. "When I was younger, when Mpata was a baby, they attacked our village. They did not have guns, only spears, but we know they have guns now—given to them by the white men. When they raided I fled with my wife and child. I knew places in the hills where we could hide—where I had stored water in pots. The Matabele killed all the men of the village, and the old women and young children. They took only the young women and the children who were old enough to walk."

"Took them as slaves?"

"The women were made to be wives, I have been told. They and the children became members of the Matabele tribe."

"And have you seen the Matabele since then?"

"Yes, many times. We moved further east to escape their raids. Even here, many days walk from their country, we were not safe from them. Now the white men are here, we think the Matabele will not raid again."

"Are you glad that the white men have come?"

"If they keep the Matabele away I am glad. If they make slaves of us I will be afraid."

ॐॐ

One morning, as Martin sat drinking coffee on the verandah of his half-constructed house, he saw a horseman approach, a tall lean man with a straggling beard. When he dismounted Martin recognised him as the Australian miner they met on their journey to Fort Salisbury in 1890. He greeted Martin, reminding him that his name was Tom Ellsworth.

"And you're going to tell me you've got a prospector's licence?" Martin knew that prospectors had the right to peg claims on farms, and this was a serious problem on the mineral-rich ridges east of Fort Salisbury.

Ellsworth looked down, embarrassed. "Yes, and I'd like your permission to look round the farm."

"I'm afraid I've already pegged most of it myself," said Martin. He liked the Australian when they first met, and now something about the man's demeanour made him relent. "I may have missed something, and there's a formation you could advise me about."

He offered the prospector breakfast and he watched Ellsworth eat the maize porridge and cream with a gusto that suggested he had been a long time without decent food. Later, he took the Australian to a place where granite intruded into the dolerite ridge near the eastern edge of the farm. He had already pegged the area and registered a claim, though he knew this would arouse the interest of prospectors. Sure enough, six or seven had come onto the farm that week to ask his permission, as they were required to do, which he could not refuse. However, they found that the promising area of the intrusion had been amply covered by his claims.

He asked Ellsworth to appraise the claim, and the Australian walked it thoroughly before announcing that he would need to excavate adits before he could assess its worth. "You see, the gold was melted out of the rocks by the great heat of the molten granite intrusion," he explained. "When the rocks cooled, the gold solidified in veins and pockets. See this rusty colour? It's a good sign."

Martin offered ten pounds and food if Ellsworth would supervise the digging of the adits. He hired extra labourers to supplement men he could spare from his own gang, and for three weeks they dug trenches, taking samples of ore, which Ellsworth took to Fort Salisbury for assay. When he had the results he advised Martin that it would be worth opening a small mine and gave him a rough estimate of the cost. Martin discussed Ellsworth's report with Henry Borrow, who in turn sought advice from a miner friend. He came back to Martin later to say that the estimate seemed reasonable, and as long as he was aware that mining was a risky business he should go ahead. Martin and Tom Ellsworth then decided to form a partnership, completely separate from the farm business. The Australian set off for Johannesburg to have the sample assays checked and to get quotes on mining equipment.

CHAPTER 7
The Matabele War — 1893

By August 1893 Martin had been in Mashonaland for almost three years and had owned his farm for nearly two years. His second crop of maize had been successful, and he now sold modest amounts of fresh vegetables in Salisbury. Meanwhile, Tom Ellsworth had finished exploring the gold-bearing reef and was busy installing a small stamp mill to process the ore.

Martin wrote a letter to his parents:

'They say the younger Matabele warriors are becoming restless, and have made several sorties into Mashonaland. They seem to have been up to their old habits of preying on the Makalaka and Banyai tribes in the areas near Fort Victoria. Dr Jameson went there for an indaba (that's a discussion) with the Matabele leaders. He told them to go back to their tribal area; otherwise they would be driven back. It was a bold statement, because there were only a few police there. I gather there was an exchange of shots between the police and some warriors. We've heard that there was criticism in the press in England as 'firing at defenceless natives'.'

'There's a general sentiment among the settlers here that the Company should take punitive action against the Matabele, otherwise they'll continue to cause trouble in Mashonaland. I think it would be better to negotiate with Lobengula, the Matabele king, before taking military action. Besides, we have only about six hundred white men in Mashonaland—and not all of them potential combatants!—whereas the Matabele have perhaps thirty thousand warriors! Of course we have better weapons, but it could lead to disaster.'

'As you know, I used to be an active member of the Mashonaland Horse— sounds like an act in a pantomime!—an efficient little outfit, well trained, and keen to practise riding and shooting skills. Our CO was Major Patrick Forbes, and we got a good deal of help from the Company, but they disbanded the police force and some of the fellows thought our voluntary force gave the Company an excuse to save money! We disbanded a few weeks ago, but most of us meet for informal practices.' 'I've bought a Ridgeback dog – Lolloper – to keep me company.'

He rode on Chandra from his farm into the dusty little town of Salisbury, making his weekly visit to buy provisions and to post and collect mail. Finding the town buzzing with news that Jameson was calling for volunteers to invade Matabele territory, he went straight to the Administrator's office, where Jameson was standing on the verandah of the office building talking to Major Forbes. Dr Leander Starr Jameson was a small, dapper man, with a neat beard, and a way of pacing around that suggested pent up energy. Beside him, Forbes looked laconic and lethargic. Both men looked up as Martin arrived.

"We were talking about you a moment ago." Jameson was in jocular mood, his eyes twinkling. "Coming with us?"

"To invade Matabeleland? I hoped it was only a rumour."

"We're reviving the Mashonaland Horse, and it's going to be an essential part of our force," announced Forbes. "I want you to come as section leader in Borrow's troop. We need men like you with military experience. Come to my office about an hour from now and I'll give you a letter of appointment." He went on to explain that he would lead the force from the Salisbury area. The job had been requested by Frank Johnson, but Forbes was chosen because it was thought that he had more experience in military activities.

"Wait a minute..." Martin held up his hand.

"You know Forbes well. You can trust his leadership." Jameson was trying to forestall Martin's objections. "We leave on Thursday..."

"May I ask, sir, what is the real reason for the invasion? Have the Matabele broken the treaty?"

Jameson's smile started to fade, and his voice grew colder. "In my view they have. I'll give you men all my detailed reasons when we assemble on Thursday." He turned to walk into his office.

"Have you any idea how long this will take, sir?" Martin called after him.

The Administrator turned. "Why? Are you worried about your farm?"

"Of course I am. My livelihood depends on planting a maize crop in November. As you know, the last couple of years have not been easy. I can't afford to plant late."

"I'm aware of that, Russell. But if we don't sort out the Matabele now you may never be able to plant any maize again. All I can say is that I hope we'll all be back in good time. Remember, our aim is to preserve the integrity of this country—including your farm."

Martin observed Jameson's obdurate face for a moment, then nodded to Forbes and turned to ride away.

Jameson said to Forbes "I suspect young Russell has the liberal sentiments of his father the MP. Are you wise to make him a troop leader?"

"I know him well enough. He's well respected by people like Borrow."

"Very well. I leave it to you."

⤟⤞

When Martin entered Forbes' sparse office on the edge of the parade ground the major was standing at his desk poring over a large map. He waved Martin to a chair and continued studying the map for a while, then folded it up and picked up a sheet of paper from the desk, handing it to Martin.

"That's a list of the men in your section. You have the rank of lieutenant. Your troop commander is Henry Borrow—he's a captain and he probably knows most of your men. Your job now is to find them and give them my instructions, which are simple—parade at 0900 on Thursday morning to hear the Doctor and final briefing. We leave at dawn on Friday. Every man must bring a spare horse—if he has one—and a spare rifle. He must also bring as much provisions as he can manage—biltong and mealie meal are essential—the usual gear for a long trek."

"How many of us going?"

Forbes took a pipe and tobacco out of his bush jacket pocket. He offered the tobacco pouch to Martin and they both prepared for a smoke. "We'll have an officers' meeting tomorrow but I can tell you now it'll be about four hundred. I know it's not enough but don't dwell on that." He watched Martin's expression carefully, then laughed. "Well...you'll be in uniform again! Have you anyone to look after your farm?"

"Tom Ellsworth will keep an eye on it. He's too old to come with us, surely?"

"I did think about him. Yes, he is too old. But he'll have to move into town. He can go out to visit your farm, but his first priority must be to help look after the town, and at night to guard the women left behind."

⤟⤞

That evening Martin and Tom sat on the verandah of Borrow's house, drinking mugs of beer with their host. The beer had been brewed by Borrow using hops sent up from South Africa. Moths flitted round a paraffin lamp in a thin cloud of pipe smoke that helped to drive away mosquitoes.

"I think Jameson's using a flimsy excuse to invade Matabele country," said Martin. "Those incidents at Fort Victoria don't justify a war—a few noisy, drunken warriors. No one was killed..."

Borrow drew on his pipe. "What excuse would justify war? One death? Two? There've been a rash of incidents, Martin. The African takes advantage of weakness—and he respects strength. You call it war, but it's really just a show of strength."

"But I know the Matabele," said Ellsworth, ".... better than you two, and better than the Doctor. "They'll never allow you fellows to march up to Bulawayo without testing you with a fight."

Martin leant forward urgently. "But if they do that—if they 'test' us—attack us—it will give Jameson just the excuse he needs to take over their territory." He turned to Borrow. "Don't you see, Harry, it's *us* who will be provoking them. I'm convinced that Jameson and Rhodes have cooked up this expedition to occupy Matabeleland..."

Ellsworth added, "What Rhodes doesn't realise is that you'll never be able to settle in Matabele country as you did here. The white men here simply don't understand that the Matabele are completely different to the Shona."

☙ ❧

The officers' meeting was an occasion for Major Forbes to explain, in confidence, the broad strategy for the invasion of Matabeleland. There would be three columns, each consisting of about two hundred and fifty men. The 'Salisbury Column' would consist of the voluntary Mashonaland Horse under Forbes. The 'Victoria Column', under Major Allan Wilson, would meet them at the Iron Mine Hill, on the frontier with Matabeleland. Meanwhile, a third column was being formed in Johannesburg, under Captain Raaff, and would join forces with a body of Bechuanaland Police under Colonel Goold-Adams to march north to Bulawayo.

Forbes explained that the Salisbury Column would be armed with Martini-Henry rifles, and each man would have a hundred rounds of ammunition. "If you want to take your favourite hunting rifle it has to be unofficial, and not to be used in engagements with the enemy. We have to standardise for reasons of ammunition—imagine picking up a rifle from a comrade and finding it uses different cartridges. Also, and vital, we'll have two Maxim guns, a Gardner, and a Nordenfeldt. We spend most of September training at Fort Charter."

Early on the Thursday morning Martin was ready to leave the farm. Chandra was saddled, and he took Robert Onslow's former horse as his reserve; Beauty carried large saddlebags, and a roll strapped over the saddle. Martin's two servants waited for him as he finished writing a letter home.

'This may be my last chance to post a letter for some weeks. By the time you receive it, I expect you will have heard about our expedition. Harry Borrow says the Little Doctor has the bit between his teeth. We will hear his reasons this morning—or at least those reasons that he's willing to divulge.'

'I question the wisdom of advancing into the Matabele territory. As it is, there are not enough of us to occupy Mashonaland! And as far as I know there's no longer any other foreign power lurking beyond the borders.'

'Tom will watch over the farm while I'm away. However, he can't plant the maize crop—he's a miner, not a farmer—and if we're not back by early December I'll miss a year's income. Perhaps the gold mine will keep me going.'

He mounted Chandra and set off with a wave to the servants, leading Beauty on a long rein.

෧∘ঙ

The Salisbury Column assembled at the parade ground in front of Forbes' office. There was an air of excitement as they waited to hear the address by the Administrator. Martin stood at ease beside Chandra, the ten men of his troop in a loose group behind him. They had no uniforms, but they all wore khaki bush jackets and felt hats. Some had khaki breeches and boots, others wore trousers and *veldskoene*, shoes made of soft leather.

The subdued murmur of conversation stopped when Jameson walked briskly out of Forbes' office to stand on the verandah. He almost strutted, and Martin surmised that the little man was being carried away by his position of power. By all accounts the Matabele had become belligerent, but there was a common view that Chief Lobengula could be reasoned with. In any case, he had about thirty thousand warriors at his command. Yet here there were only a few hundred mounted men, a similar number of Mashona servants and grooms, three machine guns, and a small cannon.

When Jameson spoke, his voice was high-pitched, full of the excitement of the occasion. "Good morning, men. I want to tell you where we are going, and why." He paused to ensure full attention. "We're going to Bulawayo to demand the obedience of Lobengula, King of the Amandabele. No doubt you've heard how some of his *indunas* have caused trouble at Fort Victoria? Well, I've decided that they need to be taught a lesson..."

A muffled cheer rose from a few troopers, followed by a murmur from other men as their tension overflowed. Jameson waved his hand for quiet, then raised his voice.

"You may think we are too few in number, but we will be joined by a column from Fort Victoria. That will double our numbers. Together, we will have five Maxims, and our cannon—which most of you know we captured at Macequece. Forbes is our commander. Colenbrander is our scout—he'll talk to you when I have finished. I will go with you—to represent the Queen. And now, men, three cheers for our Queen."

The men gave three cheers and waved their hats. Chandra snorted and pulled at his reins. Discussions broke out among the men as they walked over to the shade of some big trees where Johann Colenbrander, tall and dark-bearded, waited to address them. He signaled them to sit on the ground around him. The men tied their horses to a nearby fence or handed them to Shona grooms.

Colenbrander spoke slowly and with deliberation. His English was fluent but with a strong Afrikaner accent. "The Doctor has asked me to tell you men something about the Matabele—the tribe we may have to fight. First, I'll give you a little of their history. They were originally a clan of the Zulu nation. They broke away when Chaka was King of the Zulus—that was sixty years ago. They moved into the Transvaal under their leader, Mzilikazi. There they clashed many times with the *Voortrekkers*—the Boer settlers—and finally they were defeated at the Battle of Vegkop. Then they moved north of the Limpopo, into the territory they occupy today. Mzilikazi died twenty-five years ago and their present Chief—some call him King—is one of his sons, Lobengula."

Colenbrander paused to drink from his canvas water bottle. He looked around his audience, the men lounging, relaxed, lighting pipes, wondering what he could tell them that was new. He wanted to shake them out of their complacency, to make them understand that this was not just a trek through the bush.

"Now, I want to tell you how they fight. I don't suppose they'll allow us to reach Bulawayo without a scrap! Think of them as Zulus—they speak the same language, and their customs, including the way they fight, are the same. They always fight on foot, in regiments, called *'impis'*. Each *impi* is led by an *induna*—a senior warrior. They are armed with assegais—stabbing spears—but remember that they also use throwing spears, and carry *knobkerries*, which they can throw, or use as clubs. We know that they have several thousand old Martini-Henry rifles, and older guns—muzzle-loaders. Although they are poor shots they can point a rifle in the right direction."

There followed a ripple of laughter, but Colenbrander's expression turned serious. "Don't underestimate them. The main risk when fighting the Zulus, or the Matabele, is to be overwhelmed by their numbers. That's what happened at Isandhlwana in '79, when one of Britain's finest regiments was wiped out almost to a man—I believe three men escaped from a whole regiment! There have been other instances of well-armed groups of white men being defeated by sheer numbers. Any one of you alone will be extremely vulnerable—for instance, if your horse is killed and you're on foot and surrounded. On your horse you have a chance. On foot, you're dead!"

Colenbrander noted with satisfaction that he had succeeded in sobering the men's expressions. He continued, "We know that the Matabele have about thirty-thousand warriors, but they've had a small-pox epidemic, and we don't know how that might have affected their numbers." Some low whistles and exclamations broke out to interrupt the scout, and he waited until the disturbance subsided. "I know that sounds a lot compared with our few hundred, but Lobengula won't commit them all at once. The key to our fighting supremacy is firepower, and the most important element in our firepower will be the Maxim guns; each is equivalent to about a hundred Martini-Henry rifles—let's hope they don't let us down. The classic defence against these tribes is to form a *laager*. There have been many battles when the *laager* enabled my people—the Boers—to fight off much greater numbers of Zulus and Matabele—battles such as Blood River and Vegkop. Remember, too, that a handful of British soldiers in a *laager* held off great numbers of Zulus at Rorke's Drift."

Colenbrander noticed that Forbes wanted to speak so he stepped aside in deference to the young commander. Forbes took over the address, looking fiercely at the men. He had become increasingly concerned that Colenbrander was being too negative and he saw no point in frightening the troopers. They had plenty of spirit, and now was not the time to break it.

"So, men, if we're threatened by Matabele we'll immediately form a *laager*. We'll practice every day on our march so that we know exactly what to do, and how to do it quickly—in a few minutes. Our lives will depend on it."

One of the men wanted to ask a question and Forbes invited him to speak. He had a Cockney accent. "Surely the *laager* is vulnerable if the Matabele have rifles?"

"Yes, that is true. But we think their firepower will be too weak—their rifles are old, and their aim too inaccurate—to do much damage."

Another man, with a broad Glaswegian accent, shouted. "The Boers us'ter to ride oot the *laager* in pursuit. Wull we do that, soor?"

Forbes nodded, pleased that they were thinking more positively now. "If an attack is defeated and the Matabele withdraw, we'll certainly leave the *laager* to chase them. However, we must be cautious because they were known to use ruses to lure Boers out."

Martin held up his hand, looking at Colenbrander rather than Forbes. The scout nodded to him, inviting the question. "Is it simple to recognise an *induna*? And if one can shoot him, will it reduce their morale?"

Colenbrander stroked his beard thoughtfully. "The *indunas* can be distinguished from mere warriors by their dress, but they usually stand well behind to direct the attack—being older men. Yes, I think it would reduce morale, but they would probably be out of range. But you must remember that the Matabele are very brave men. Their bravery comes partly from a common excitement. They work themselves into a fever pitch—stamping and beating their shields, and shouting. It can be very frightening for people like you who aren't used to it."

A voice from the back shouted, "Is it true that they cut their victims' balls off?" There followed a ripple of nervous laughter.

Forbes frowned and deferred to Colenbrander to answer. The older man continued in his serious vein. "Their custom is to cut out the heart and the liver—the Zulus did that at Isandhlwana. But if the enemy has fought well they leave the bodies unmutilated. It's a way of showing their respect." Then he smiled slowly. "Anyway, if you're dead, you won't know about it."

"Couldn't we make surprise attacks—instead of waiting for them?" shouted another trooper.

"No." Colenbrander shook his head. "They'll always know where we are before we find them. And they camp in small scattered groups, which makes it very difficult to attack them. You must accept that our tactics have been developed by generations of Boers fighting these tribes. Draw them into attacking the *laager*—that's the best way."

At this point Forbes decided it was enough. He was afraid that the men might be dismayed at the prospect of serious conflict, so he dismissed the men.

☜∾☞

The Salisbury Column reached Iron Hill Mine on 14 October 1893, where they met the forward scouts of the Victoria column, which reached the rendezvous two days later. Resounding cheers rang over the open grassland as comrades greeted each other and exchanged news. For about half an hour they manouvered their wagons into a joint *laager* for the night, and then groups of men from the two columns mingled as they sought friends.

Martin watered and fed his horses, encouraging the men of his troop to take care of their mounts before doing anything else. Then he walked slowly around the perimeter of the *laager*, checking the defences. After a few minutes he was astonished to see Perry Davenport. The American was instantly recognisable from his dandy clothes and long dark hair. He seemed taller, and Martin looked down at his boots, but though they seemed new there was no evidence of raised heels.

He shouted. "Perry! What on earth are you doing here?"

Perry feigned casual ease, but was actually pleased and excited to see Martin. "I couldn't let you go off to battle alone, could I, my limey friend?" They shook hands. "Actually, I'm working for Uncle George—or at least his company. He sent me up here to make another report on the gold prospects. Paid me a handsome sum—I couldn't refuse. Now I find myself at war! Just my luck."

"But surely you don't have to fight? Couldn't you come with the Column as a civilian?"

"It's the only way I could get into the Matabele country. I'll be out again in a flash!" His cocky demeanour seemed to evaporate. "There won't be any fighting, will there?"

Martin clapped him on the shoulder. "Perhaps not—you can always keep your head below the parapet."

The American invited him to a nearby fire, where he was cooking. "Hey, Martin, there's some countrymen of mine I want you to meet."

Martin said that he would return soon, wishing to make sure his troop had settled into defensive positions in the *laager*. He returned to his sector of the ring of wagons and spoke to each of his men in turn, arranging for two of them to be awake and on watch at all times. When he was satisfied he told the men where they could find him, and walked over to Perry's campfire.

It was now dark, and he could just make out five men, one of whom was Perry, sitting with a mug of tea; he stood up to welcome Martin. They talked for a moment, before Perry introduced the others. A short while later, two other men walked up to join the group.

Perry said, "Here's Burnham and Ingram—they're American scouts with the Victoria Column. Frank, this is my friend Martin Russell. He's a troop leader—a lieutenant—with the Salisbury Column."

Martin walked over to shake hands with the Americans. Burnham was short and slight, wearing khaki fatigues; a stiff-brimmed stetson hat hung on his back. He had long fair hair and a full moustache, and his blue eyes, set wide apart, deliberately appraised the Englishman. When he spoke, Martin recognised his accent as being from the American West.

"Say, my middle name is Russell—my mother's family name. Who knows, we might be related." His smile showed even white teeth.

"Are you also in the mining business?" asked Martin.

"Not now," Burnham laughed, "though I've done some silver mining in my time..."

"He was a scout in the Apache Wars," explained Perry.

Martin and Frank Burnham sat down next to each other, and one of the men handed them mugs of tea. Perry sat on the other side of Burnham, who glanced around at the faces lit by the firelight. He was gnawing a stick of biltong, and it occurred to Martin that he sought an audience, as he seemed to wait until the other men were listening.

"Yeah, I was a scout in the Indian Wars. I'm new to Africa, but I think the principles of scouting are the same anywhere—don't you?" It was a rhetorical question.

"He's a good shot too, Martin. Maybe better than you."

Burnham smiled slowly. "Perry has told me about your reputation. The British excel at target shooting but I wonder how well can they hit a moving object?"

"We use shotguns for sport—mainly for bird shooting—but we don't practise much with rifles at moving targets. In fact, in Britain, rifles are used only for stag hunting—other than target shooting, of course."

"That's what I thought." Burnham bent to sip his tea. "The Boers are marvellous shots over long distances—the best I've ever seen. We have some good shots with us now; I reckon we should use them as snipers."

Perry spoke to Martin anxiously, "Do you think there'll be a fight? What does Doctor Jameson think?"

"He doesn't know much about it, but Colenbrander and Forbes have no doubt that we'll fight. The only questions are when and where."

"Whenever—we'd better be ready for them," added Burnham. "Thank God for the Maxim—it's an American invention, y'know, so perhaps I should say 'Thanks to Hiram Maxim'." He was smiling, but seemed almost furtive in his awareness of the men sitting round the fire. Sometimes he seemed to cock his head, as if listening to sounds from the bush, and Martin imagined that this must be part of his scout's apparatus. Yet how could an American understand the sounds and smells of Africa?

The conversation changed to the topic of Captain Campbell, one of the scouts, who had been shot and killed the previous day. Burnham explained that his colleague had been checking some deserted Matabele huts, when a shot had been fired from one of them, mortally wounding Campbell. "Shows that we're not dealing with mere savages with spears", muttered Burnham.

❧

Next morning, at dawn, when the oxen had been outspanned and Martin was feeding his horses, Burnham appeared alongside him and held out his hand. "Frank Burnham. We spoke last night, at the fire."

His eyes are extraordinary, thought Martin. Pale blue-grey, set very wide apart, they made his head seem too large for his small body. The eyes flickered from appraisal of Martin to points behind him, then to his sides, then turned to glance into the misty trees behind, then back to Martin again. One might think he was nervous, Martin thought, but it's more likely that he's very cautious.

Burnham started to rub down his horse with a hard brush and curry-comb. "Furthering our conversation last night—the British seem to be restricted to stationary targets. Yet it seems to me that an ability to hit a running buck, or even a man, would be more valuable, especially from horseback."

"I agree," said Martin, "and it can be practised. I've tried—galloping past an antheap. And on my farm near Salisbury I arranged a running deer contraption. It was a buck hide stretched on a wooden frame, and ran down a slope on a wire hawser. We even had some competitions, but the scores were hopelessly bad."

"It doesn't surprise me. Our nationalities are all specialists in their way. In America many of our greatest exponents of shooting were proficient only at short distances. In competition with the Boers at more than two hundred yards they would have failed miserably." Burnham paused and regarded Martin with a penetrating gaze. "Your friend Perry does little credit to my country. He has no stomach for fighting. Men such as him, who are here by accident, could be a liability."

Martin felt uncomfortable hearing this blunt attack on Perry. He said nothing, and Burnham went on pedantically. "Young Perry may think he's God's gift to womankind, but what a woman really needs is a man who can defend her, and fight to protect her. Not necessarily a man with military experience, such as yourself, but a man who has courage and a cool head when the attack comes. What do you think?"

"You make it sound rather primitive. Perhaps in these modern times it's more important to be able to provide—in a material sense..."

Burnham shook his head vigorously. "These times? We're at war now, Russell. There will always be wars—even in Europe."

☙❧

The combined columns reached the Shangani River ten days later. There was scarcely any water, but a few pools allowed their thirsty horses and oxen to drink. The scouts, including Burnham, rode out every day, and found that the Matabele were gathered in some force about two miles away. Their numbers were estimated at about seven thousand, so out-numbering the white men by about ten to one. Yet this was not even their main army.

Forbes immediately ordered the usual *laager* formation for the night; it took about ten minutes to accomplish in daylight, and he wanted to take no risks. In this place, scrubby thorn trees were scattered wide apart for several hundred yards around the *laager*, so the Matabele would have to run across open ground if they attacked. The wagons were drawn into a circle, their lengths along the circumference, and the *disselbooms*—towing poles—and oxen turned inwards. The oxen were outspanned, and the wagons moved closer together by manpower, pulling the *disselbooms* into the circle. The canvas covers of the wagons were removed, so that they could not be set on fire. They were so close together that a man could not easily squeeze between them. Oxen and horses were loosely tethered within the *laager* so they could not stampede nor escape.

Before dawn, the favoured time for the Matabele to attack, a tremendous hubbub was heard from another camp containing four hundred Shona men, under Captain Quested. It soon became clear that this camp, within a thorn zariba, was being attacked by Matabele, and a detachment was sent to relieve them, firing concentrated volleys into them, which drove them off.

As soon as it grew light, the occupants of the *laager* could see about three hundred Matabele approaching. At first they were thought to be friendly, but they suddenly started firing their ancient weapons. When they were driven off, a group of mounted troopers was sent out after them, only to return when faced with a larger Matabele *impi*.

The commanders positioned the three Maxim guns at equal distances on the circumference of the *laager*, their barrels poking out from between wagons. They could be moved quite quickly to take up new positions, as could the single 'Macequece' cannon. All the troopers found places where they could get a clear sight, some lying on the ground under the wagons, some on top. Martin stood at the wagon of a farmer named Pete Brewster, one of the men in his troop. His other men were close by, their horses held by African grooms, ready for the troopers to ride out of the *laager* if the opportunity arose.

Brewster was a thin wiry Yorkshireman who chewed tobacco incessantly. He was lying on the ground, under his wagon. Despite having no military experience, like all the men in the column he was steeped in stories about the battles between white men and the African tribes. He spat a stream of brown liquid onto the ground, and swore.

"What d'you think, Russell—will they attack again?"

Martin was trying to distinguish signs of the Matabele among the trees, about six hundred yards away. "I expect they will. Remember, Colenbrander said they would test our strength."

Brewster grunted. He felt confident that he could scramble out backwards if he had to, and Russell, sitting above him, would warn him if the wagon was set alight.

About an hour later they caught sight of warriors emerging from the trees. More and more of them appeared, dark figures forming a long line about five men deep. They came to a halt, standing several hundred yards away, and a murmur of their voices drifted across the plain. Major Forbes ordered his men to hold their fire; the message was passed round to the troop leaders, who in turn informed their men. Martin went to each member of his troop making sure that they understood that they must wait until the cannon blasted, or if that failed, until a Maxim started firing.

He had just settled back into his position on Brewster's wagon when the Matabele warriors started their advance. They strode quickly forward to about two hundred yards away, a dense line of dusty figures, dressed in animal skin kilts, carrying shields and spears. Suddenly they started to chant in deep booming voices, beating their shields, and stamping their feet. The sound was ominous and made the hair on Martin's neck rise. He remembered Colenbrander telling them that the Matabele did this to work up their courage for the attack, and to terrify the enemy. Brewster and his other men were shouting curses as they tried to counter the chanting of the Matabele warriors, but after about ten minutes the troopers began to accept that this was just a show of bravado and they fell quiet.

Perry was behind a wagon next to Frank Burnham. He was very frightened, imagining in graphic detail a ferocious charge by the black warriors that would overwhelm them by sheer numbers. A spear in the chest might be his fate, or in his guts, to die in agony—and all because his uncle would not let him live in comfort in Johannesburg. He felt terribly out of place in this hot and sweaty clamour. The rifle in his hands stank of oil; his arms were sunburnt, and his eyes sore from the incessant dust. He could hear Burnham muttering and asked what he had been saying.

"Discipline," said Burnham. "Our firepower alone is not enough. We need the utmost discipline too. Volley firing is fearfully difficult for an enemy to overcome. That's what saved those Welshmen at Rorke's Drift—discipline."

"Don't the Matabele have discipline?" asked Perry, dismayed that his voice was querulous.

"I asked Colenbrander that question. He said they have, but their *indunas* give orders from the rear, and sometimes the warriors become confused. We'll soon find out."

After about half an hour of chanting and shield beating there was a sudden rush as about a thousand Matabele warriors ran forward. They were firing their old muzzle loading muskets and rifles as they ran, and bullets started to fizz into the *laager*. Martin shouted to his men to hold their fire, as did the other officers. The first shot from the *laager* came when the Matabele were less than a hundred yards away.

Later, Martin wrote in a letter to his sister:

'When we opened up firing, it must have been a terrible shock for them. Colenbrander says that these young warriors had never been exposed to rifle fire before. They fled, but shortly after, another regiment of older men attacked, but they never reached our laager. We saw them off with only one of our people killed. They lost about five hundred, killed and wounded, out of about five thousand. They had no chance against the Maxim. It's an amazing weapon, and must terrify them. I hate the killing. They are brave men, and we're invading their territory.'

As the second wave of attack turned back, Forbes called his company and troop commanders together. He ordered them to choose one or two of the best riders from each troop to break out of the *laager* and pursue those Matabele who lagged behind the retreat. "But be careful of ruses," he warned. "That's why you must use only the best-mounted men."

Martin picked Pilling, a man of similar age, who had served in the police force in the Cape, and was one of the best riders in his troop. He mounted and joined the others of the select pursuit group. One of the wagons was shifted aside and they galloped out to a chorus of encouraging shouts.

The main body of the Matabele force was almost at the tree line, but there were small groups left behind, either because they were wounded, or because they were helping comrades who had fallen. The troopers separated and galloped around, firing at these remnant warriors. Watching from the *laager* Martin found the proceedings increasingly distasteful, and made his own decision never to shoot at wounded men. After about twenty minutes, a bugle call from the *laager* sounded the retreat, and the men turned to ride back.

At that moment, there was a shout and they saw Pilling wheeling round a solitary Matabele, who had stuck an *assegai* into his horse's flank. An officer galloped towards him as Pilling jumped off his collapsing horse. The warrior had extracted his spear and turned to face the trooper, who had dropped his rifle, and was struggling to take his revolver out of its holster. Worse still, a group of four or five Matabele stragglers were running towards them, *assegais* raised. The situation was desperate for Pilling.

The officer was now a mere twenty paces away. Aiming his rifle carefully, he shot the warrior in the chest, then rode up to Pilling and shouted to him to get up. He held down his hand, grabbed his wrist, and swung him up. They galloped off, just in time to escape the threatening group of warriors.

Back in the *laager,* the men in Martin's troop gathered round to congratulate them on their escape. "I thought the bugger was dead," growled Pilling in Martin's ear. "Now I've lost my bloody horse." He was shaking uncontrollably in reaction to his narrow escape, and fell to his knees to vomit.

Major Forbes summoned his troop commanders and their deputies to a 'post-mortem' that evening. He sat outside Dr Jameson's tent, which was pitched near the centre of the *laager*; Jameson was beside him but said nothing. The men were in a semi-circle on the ground with mugs of tea laced with brandy. Forbes was tired but elated as he reviewed the orders for guards to be placed at intervals around the circumference of the *laager*.

"We did well today, men. We showed them that they attack us at their peril. We proved that we can handle their numbers..."

"It was not their full number," Borrow reminded him.

"True, Harry. They may bring their whole army against us next time. Can we hold off thirty thousand? What do you think Colenbrander?"

The Chief Scout stroked his beard. "My view is they'll test us again, before committing a larger force. We're so close to Bulawayo now. It could happen at any time."

"There you are, men. Be sure your troopers remain alert."

∽⁓

The Column continued its advance into Matabele territory with the opposing *impis* maintaining a respectful distance. At midday on October 29 1893, a *laager* was formed near the Bembesi River, about twenty miles from Bulawayo. The scouts reported that a large body of Matabele warriors had massed ahead, and it was presumed that they would make a concerted effort to prevent the capture of their capital.

When the attack came, although the *laager* had been completed, some horses escaped. Henry Borrow hurriedly asked Martin to help him gather them in, which proved extremely difficult, because the horses were frightened by the gunfire and the shouts of the warriors. Poorly aimed Matabele bullets whizzed among the small group trying to round up the horses, but none of them was hit, and they managed to get them all back.

When the Matabele *impis* attacked the *laager* a second time the fight lasted about three-quarters of an hour. It was estimated later that about four thousand warriors were involved, of whom about five hundred perished or were severely wounded. Only three men in the Column were killed, by stray bullets. As before, it was the relentless steady fire of the Maxim guns that carried the day, and Martin wondered what would have happened if they had fought without these amazing weapons.

Later, he rode out with others to see if there were wounded Matabele who might be interrogated. He was sickened by the sight of dozens of young men lying dead or mortally wounded on the dusty ground. They had died bravely in defence of their territory, facing a numerically small enemy force, yet mown down by vastly superior weapons. The sight of their stricken bodies was deeply poignant to him, and he muttered imprecations against Rhodes and Jameson, who had instigated the affair.

❧⸱❦

CHAPTER 8
In Pursuit Of Lobengula

When the Column reached Bulawayo, capital of the Matabele Kingdom, on 4 November 1893, they found it a smoking ruin. The great village was the size of a small town—Bulawayo means 'The Place of Killing' in the Sindebele language. The white men rode along the lines of charred grass huts, cautious of ambush, but there was not a single person left behind. It was concluded that Lobengula had fled, and that his tribe had dispersed into the surrounding countryside. The so-called 'Southern Column', under Commandant Pieter Raaff, was still ten days march from Bulawayo, and was being harried by an *impi* of at least four thousand Matabele. The invasion from the south was deemed to have divided the strength of Lobengula's army.

Martin left his men packing their saddlebags and rode up onto a small *kopje*, where he could look down on the smouldering ruins of Bulawayo. Henry Borrow, who had attended a meeting of troop commanders, rode up to join him and they watched the desolate scene for a while.

Martin spoke first. "What now, Harry? Can we go home now?"

Borrow shook his head. "No, I'm afraid not. Jameson has decided to capture Lobengula. There's a meeting of all the officers this afternoon, so you'll soon hear."

"But it could take weeks to find him! What purpose will it serve? We've shown our strength. They've been defeated in two battles. Their capital is in ruins." He pointed at the scene of blackened destruction before them. "When we were in Salisbury, Jameson told me he wanted to teach them a lesson. That's enough, surely."

"Obviously he and Rhodes don't think so. And there are others who support them. I want to get back to my farm too, but we'll have to finish it off."

Martin was exasperated. Just when his farm was beginning to prove viable, and when he had the resources to plant a decent area of maize, it now looked as if he would miss the ploughing and planting season. The red doleritic soils of his farm were fertile, but brick hard in the dry season. He had to wait for the first rains to soften the heavy soil so that he could plough. The maize seed had to be sown quickly, because early planting was known to give better yields.

On 12 November Martin wrote to his family in England:

'Jameson has decided to send a flying column of three hundred volunteers, myself included, under the command of Major Forbes, to capture King Lobengula. I'm one of the section leaders, and we're the best-mounted of all the men who came from Mashonaland.'

'We officers were told that Jameson wrote a letter to Lobengula offering him safe passage if he came back to Bulawayo. The messenger—a Cape native—found the King about thirty miles north of here, and brought back the answer that seemed to prevaricate and make no sense. I'm not surprised—the fellow probably does not trust us white men, and who can blame him.'

'So here we are, about to set off, and I must get this letter to you, as I don't know when I'll be able to send another one. We are ninety volunteers from the Salisbury Column, sixty from the Victoria Column, ninety enlisted men from the Bechuanaland Police, and sixty Rangers from the Transvaal under Commandant Raaff. We have four Maxim machine guns, and also there are a couple of hundred native carriers, mostly Shona—and a scared lot they are!'

'I felt I had to volunteer because Borrow and most of my men were keen to go. They feel we have to finish the job, but I'm uneasy about the justification for the war, and this mission seems foolhardy. I don't want to alarm you, but Father in particular should know the facts—there are upwards of twenty thousand warriors in the bushveld! Some say they are disorganised, but Colenbrander always tells us how disciplined they are.'

'Surprisingly, Perry Davenport volunteered. He says that his uncle insisted he go at least ten days walking north of Bulawayo, and he sees this as a way to do it—under the protection of an armed force! I fear he does not understand what he's letting himself in for.'

On 28 November Martin wrote another letter—it was never posted:

'We had a small skirmish last week at Inyati, the old mission station. It was sad to see the old stone buildings in ruins, and books and papers scattered around the place. The missionaries had done much good, and now their work has been spoiled. We left some of our chaps there—about eighty. Then some of the men decided they wanted to go no further, so Forbes asked us to declare whether we wanted to go back to Bulawayo or carry on the pursuit of the King. Borrow and I, and our troop all volunteered but a large number of the men decided they'd had enough—food is short, and the rains have set in with a vengeance. Luckily some reinforcements have been sent from Bulawayo.'

'So there we were at Shiloh—a tiny mission outpost; it means 'Place of Peace'. Do you remember, that's the Battle where Grant won a victory in the Civil War. We reorganised the force: Borrow and 22 men of the Mashonaland Horse, Major Allan Wilson and 170 men from the Victoria force (100 of them have no horses), 20 men with Raaff, and 80 Bechuanaland Police. This was our new Column, a total of about three hundred men. We were a motley crowd and moved far too slowly, because our wagons with the food and ammunition kept bogging down. Our scouts told us that Lobengula was keeping well ahead of us, and we wondered if we were being led into a trap. Today (28th) Forbes decided to send 130 men back to Inyati—now we have only 160, and two Maxims.'

'It's now 30th of November, and we've reached the Shangani River, several miles downstream from where the battle took place three weeks ago. The rainy season seems to be well under way. I wonder if the rains have come to Mashonaland too. How I wish I could be on my farm now.'

'We're really short of food for both men and horses. This so-called 'flying' column, is fairly well mounted, although our horses are not in the best of condition— we are certainly not flying!—just hard slog through the muddy bushveld.'

'3rd December: Several men have fever. We haven't seen much of the enemy, but there are scattered small groups of Matabele camped in the woodland around us. We captured a little Matabele herd boy who told us that the King's Regiment is close by. Forbes decided to send a small patrol, mounted on the best horses, to find the King. Twenty-one men, under Major Allan Wilson, set off at sundown. Perry's American friend Frank Burnham is their scout. I and my friend and neighbour, Henry Borrow, wanted to go with them. I wish I could have gone—at least it would have been more exciting than waiting here.'

❧

The officers gathered round Forbes; it was shortly before midnight. The commander stood under the fly of his tent, and had to shout above the sound of the rain drumming on the canvas.

"I have some good news! Napier has reported back. Major Wilson and his men have decided to stay out all night—they're on Lobengula's tracks. I've decided to send another twenty men." He picked out Borrow from the group in front of him. "Harry, you're to be in charge. I want you to pick your men—but not any of these officers. The men you take must have good mounts. You can take Trooper Robertson with you—he came back with Napier, so he can show you the way...and take Ingram as your scout. Leave as soon as you can."

An hour later, Borrow approached Martin, who was standing guard at the stockade. "Cheerio, Martin. I wish you could come with me."

"I wish I could. It concerns me that Forbes won't commit the whole Column, but he's willing to risk you fellows. Anyway, good luck, Harry."

Borrow turned away, then stopped and came back. Raindrops streamed from the brim of his hat. "If anything happens to me, write to my people, will you? I haven't had time."

Martin felt uneasy as he watched his friend walk off into the rain. Borrow had become a good friend. Both men shared misgivings about this expedition in pursuit of Lobengula, and they suspected Forbes was less than enthusiastic, though he would never admit it. They had been away from home for over two months and were weary of the grinding marches and short rations. Their horses had lost condition because food and fodder were always difficult to find. Now they were plunged into hazardous circumstances. The heavy rain had reduced visibility to a couple of hundred yards, and the going was heavy for the horses. They knew the Matabele were not far away, forcing them to stay alert in case of attacks. Forbes kept repeating the warning that several thousand warriors might descend on them within a few minutes. It was his way of ensuring that they did not become complacent, but the constant tension gnawed at their nerves.

❧❦

At first light Forbes moved his column towards the drift where they planned to cross the Shangani River, but they were soon attacked by Matabele warriors who fired at them from the nearby forest. Using the Maxim guns judiciously, after about an hour, the column retreated, with only five men wounded, but sixteen horses were killed. During this engagement they heard distant rifle fire from across the river, and rumours spread among the men that Wilson's party was involved in a fight.

At about 7 a.m. the Forbes Column set up a thorn zariba. Martin started cleaning his rifle in the shelter of a canvas groundsheet that he had rigged over a crude frame of branches. Rain dripped from his hair, and beads of water hung on several day's growth of beard. Perry was under a similar shelter near him, playing with his terrier Towzie, that he had bought in Fort Victoria. The white men huddled in small groups within the thorn bush stockade; a third of them were on guard at any time.

Martin heard sudden scattered rifle fire from outside the stockade. Jumping up he peered through the thorn bushes, but could see only the teeming rain and scattered trees. All the men in camp picked up their weapons and strained to see where the shots came from. Then followed a concentrated volley. He quickly inserted the bolt into his rifle and scrambled to look over the thorn fence, squinting to see through the rain. Moments later he saw three men galloping through the trees, urging their mounts with flailing heels, and hunching as they fled the shots of the Matabele. He ran to join other men in pulling away some thorn bushes to make an opening for the riders, who rushed past spattering mud.

He recognised one of them as Frank Burnham, haggard and dishevelled. In turn Burnham spotted Martin as he reined in his horse. He slid out of the saddle and staggered towards Martin before his knees gave way and he fell to the ground. The American's hair was matted with rain, sweat and mud, his clothes soaked and filthy. His pale eyes had sunk deep into their sockets, and his cheeks had hollowed, seeming to make his moustache more prominent. Martin ran forward and propped him up, while other men gathered round. Someone shouted for brandy, another suggested a mug of tea.

"Russell. Thank God!" Burnham croaked. "Where's Forbes?"

Perry had rushed up to join Martin and together they helped Burnham to his feet. They stumbled together, with the other two men who had ridden in with Burnham; they were Ingram, the other American scout, and an Australian trooper named Gooding. Their boots squelched in the mud as the rain beat down on them relentlessly.

Forbes emerged from his shelter to meet them with Commandant Raaff close behind. "Well, Burnham?" he asked brusquely. "What's happened? Did you find Lobengula?"

For a moment Burnham did not reply. His normally keen eyes were dulled by fatigue, and Martin felt he was estimating how much bad news the commanding officer could absorb. The American scout nodded slowly, and the men who gathered round to mutter their speculations quietened when Burnham started speaking.

His voice was slow and hoarse. "We found the King's wagons—but he'd gone. We had a skirmish and some casualties—men wounded—horses killed. Then we were surrounded by an *impi*—so Wilson sent me to tell you. He wants the Maxims. But I'm afraid it's all up with them..."

"What do you mean?" Forbes was angry and impatient.

Burnham let out a long exhausted sigh that brought a sense of dread to Martin. He had heard that sound from dying animals. "I mean—sir—that it's likely Wilson and all his men have been killed."

A collective gasp of dismay burst from the men around. Forbes looked away, then glanced round the anxious faces of his officers. Mugs of tea were thrust into the hands of the three survivors, and they drank greedily. Gooding started to sway, and one of the officers supported him.

"How can you be so sure, Burnham?" asked Raaff. "How far are they from here?"

"About three miles." He looked at his two companions for confirmation. "But the river's between us. We nearly drowned. The horses got us across."

"How many Matabele are there?" demanded Forbes. "Where are they?"

Again Burnham looked at Ingram for confirmation as he started to speak. Martin noticed the glance, thinking it uncharacteristic of the usually confident American, whose voice was very tired. "Five thousand, I guess. They were all around us. Many of them were between Wilson's group and the river. It's difficult to estimate—but I'd say several thousand." He looked at Ingram again, and the latter nodded his agreement.

Forbes and Raaff look at each other disconsolately. It was clear that they could not mount a rescue attempt. It would have meant crossing the flooded river with one *impi* at their backs only to face another. Besides, it would be impossible to get the Maxims over the surging water, and both men realised that the guns were their only salvation in the days ahead. Forbes turned back to Burnham, angry with the messenger who had brought him the problem.

"How many of them did you leave? Was Borrow with them."

"He was. He was still alive when we left. Two were killed, so there were about thirty—say a dozen of those were wounded before we left. Our ammunition was running low and we were under continuous fire..."

"How did you get away?" asked Raaff quietly, and Martin wondered for the first time whether he suspected the three men of having run away. It seemed unthinkable that Burnham could have bolted.

"I told you." The American was wearily defensive. "Wilson sent me to get word to you. He told me to take Gooding—I asked for Ingram as well. I told him I doubted we'd get through. But he insisted we try." He sipped from his mug, and, looking up, caught Martin's eye. "We galloped through what I think was the tip of the *impi*'s horn. But they trailed us. Our horses were dead beat. We back-tracked towards Wilson, then rested and came back towards the river. Then we could hear the chatter of your Maxims. When we reached the river we didn't know which side you were on. We decided to take the risk and swim across. Thank God we made the right choice."

For a while no one spoke, each imagining the ordeal. Martin thought about those thirty men—Wilson, Borrow, Judd, and others he knew less well. Was there nothing that could be done to save them? Was it already too late? Why did they not flee, as these three had done? Surely some would have come through. There were the wounded, but they could have been left with loaded revolvers. Perhaps Wilson decided he couldn't leave the wounded. How awful to die at the end of a Matabele spear, to have your body mutilated, your remains left for the jackals and hyenas to gnaw. He bowed his head, thinking of his friend Borrow, who might still be alive, hoping for rescue. There must be something they could do. They were only three miles away. They might even have heard the rifles if it were not for the deadening drumming of the rain.

With a sudden urge Martin said, "Forbes, I could cross the river and see if..."

"It's no good, damn it!" retorted Forbes dismissively. "We'll be lucky to get out of here ourselves."

Someone put a hand on Martin's shoulder. "I'd go with you. My mate's with Wilson."

At that moment they were interrupted by a new burst of gunfire from outside the stockade. The officers scattered to join their men at the thorn fence. Matabele warriors were dodging from tree to tree, firing ineffectually. The men in the zariba let off a few shots, trying to conserve their ammunition. Burnham and his two companions were led away and Martin heard the American scout asking about his horse.

Commandant Raaff, Forbes' second in command, came up to stand beside Martin. He was slightly built, older than the others, with a large moustache and straggling beard; his face was twisted with some internal pain. He put his hand on Martin's shoulder. "We need to get word back to Bulawayo—to ask for reinforcements. Will you go?"

"And have everyone think I fled?" Martin tried to conceal bitterness. "Could you see how they were looking at those three men."

Raaff nodded. "You know Burnham. Do you think he bolted?"

"No. He doesn't seem the type to run away from a scrap, but..."

"Did you notice, Burnham was the only one who spoke...as if they agreed he would give the story."

"Yes, but he was the one chosen by Wilson to take the message."

Raaff sighed. "Yes. It's unfair to suspect Burnham."

"Look, I'm sorry, sir. I'll go to Bulawayo—if you need me to."

Raaff patted him on the back. "Good fellow. It'll have to be tonight..."

They were interrupted by a chorus of shouts from the men in the zariba. "Here they come!" Raaff and Martin ran to join the men at the thorn stockade as about a hundred Matabele warriors emerged from behind trees and anthills and run full tilt at the thorn stockade, led by a tall *induna*. The troopers held their fire until the Matabele were fifty paces from the stockade. Then, as their first volley of rifle fire faded, the Maxim started its deadly rattle. The *induna* fell and the Matabele warriors, seeing their leader killed, lost their spirit and fled back through the trees.

Raaff found Martin again and led him back to the commissary tent, where Forbes stood under the shelter of the awning, lighting his pipe. The rain had eased to a drizzle, and the cooks were trying to reactivate a fire in the centre of the camp. One of the sergeants was shouting about the amount of tea that should be used, and ordering a ration of biscuits for the midday meal.

Raaff spoke to his commanding officer in a somewhat diffident tone, which made Martin suspect they were uneasy with each other. "We should send a message back to Bulawayo. Russell has agreed to go."

"Yes, Raaff, we should send a message," said Forbes, "but not with Russell. I've already decided to send Ingram and Lynch."

"But Ingram's done in," Raaff protested.

Martin could see that Forbes was finding it difficult to contain his irritation at his decisions being questioned. "Look, Raaff, I've worked this out. I want to send one of the men who was with Wilson's patrol—to report first hand to Jameson. Burnham is too valuable as a scout; I want to keep him with us. Gooding is an unknown quantity. Lynch is a good man to support Ingram. I'll give them two of our best horses".

Forbes turned to Martin. "Give the other officers my compliments, Russell, and tell them to meet me here at two o'clock—and tell Burnham to come too."

Martin plodded round the camp checking off the officers on a list as he gave them Forbes' message. They nodded acknowledgement to

Martin; all seemed to realise that this was to be a vital council. Finally, he searched for Burnham and found him in the horse lines rubbing liniment on his horse's legs.

"I thought I'd find you asleep," he said.

The American laughed wryly. "I am, to all intents. But this stout fellow saved my life. He nearly drowned crossing the river, when some grass got wrapped round his head. Guess he's strained some muscles, poor fellow."

"Burnham," Martin lowered his voice. "I could swim across the river and find Wilson. Lead them back here."

The scout looked at Martin, his eyes narrowed. "They're dead, Russell. You'd be wasting time—and your life. I'm real sorry about Borrow. I know he was your good friend—a fine man."

"How can you be so sure they're dead?"

"Because they had no hope of escape." Burnham resumed rubbing his horse.

"But you escaped."

"By a miracle. I wanted to stay with Wilson, you know."

"Why didn't they gallop out, like you? How did they allow themselves to be surrounded?"

Burnham stopped his work and leaned his head against the horse's flank. "We were always surrounded. We passed through several of their *impis* to find Lobengula's wagons. The warriors were everywhere. Wilson expected the rest of you to follow with the Maxims. He was very disappointed when it was only Borrow and his twenty men..." Then he turned away to resume his work with the liniment.

Martin looked at his fob-watch. "It's almost two o'clock. We should go to Forbes."

Burnham put the liniment and cloth into his saddle bag, which he kept wrapped in his groundsheet. They walked together to the meeting with Forbes, and found him standing in front of the group of officers. Commandant Raaff and the scout Colenbrander were beside him, waiting as he lit his pipe.

Forbes welcomed them and then announced, "Raaff and I have decided that our column must return to Bulawayo. We cannot advance because we would never be able to get the Maxims across the river. Nor can we cross without them—least of all while we have at least two *impis* of Matabele around us." He paused to judge the reaction of the men standing in front of him, then continued. "I've instructed Ingram and Lynch to ride back to Bulawayo, to inform Jameson. Before they leave we must decide our route. We could go back the way we came, but Raaff and I favour following the river. At least we would have protection on our left flank—and a sure supply of water."

There was a ripple of laughter at Forbes' comment about the water supply. Yet the men knew he was right; it would be easier to draw from the river that to dig holes in the ground.

"What's the difference in distance?" asked one of the officers.

Colenbrander answered. "We don't know, because we're not certain of the course of the river. It's probably the longer way, and it may be difficult country; but the direct route isn't easy either. There are three rivers between here and Shiloh."

Another officer asked, "Is it likely that the Matabele will follow us?"

"I think not," replied Colenbrander. "They may send one *impi* to harry us. But my guess is that the main force will continue north with Lobengula."

"So, gentlemen," said Forbes, obviously anxious to conclude the meeting, "as there are no objections, we'll follow the river. We leave at dawn. Keep your sentries alert. Burnham, for goodness sake get some sleep—I'm going to need you tomorrow."

Shortly after, Martin returned to his men. A majestic storm broke over the camp, forcing the exhausted and hungry men to huddle against the driving rain. Lightening bolts followed in quick succession, exposing for brief moments the dreary wet *mopane* trees around the stockade. The horses reared and whinnied in fear, while the men tried to calm them with soothing words. The dark river swept past in spate, its surface littered with floating debris.

Martin stood with Colenbrander watching the two messengers mounting their horses, their wet capes glistening in the flares of lightning. He imagined that Pete Ingram would be as tired as Burnham, yet he was now faced with a desperate ride for at least two days. The chosen horses, Brandy and Soda were from the Bechuanaland Police, emaciated shadows of their former selves, even though they were regarded by the men as the best mounts with the column. Martin was relieved that Chandra had not been selected for the messengers; he had rehearsed several excuses, including one that his horse was almost lame.

The two messengers now took advantage of the storm to make their escape, trotting through an opening made for them in the thorn stockade.

"What chance have they?" asked Martin.

"They're good men," replied Colenbrander. "Lynch is a fine scout. I give them fifty-fifty. They'll split up to increase the chance of getting the message through. Now get some sleep, Russell. We need you to be sharp tomorrow."

When Martin returned to his bivouac he noticed Perry was shivering. "Do you have fever?" he asked.

Perry laughed wryly. "No. But I'm shit scared."

"We all are."

"Not like me—oh no." He shook his head vehemently. "Besides you have some reason to be here. God knows why I ever left the comforts of Jo'burg. I must have been crazy."

"Come on Perry," said Martin, trying to encourage him. "We'll soon get back to the others."

"Oh yeah? Remember what Colenbrander's always warning us... about being overwhelmed by their numbers? That's what's happened to Wilson and his men—and we don't have wagons to make a proper *laager*."

"We'll make a square and fire volleys; and we have the Maxims."

Perry slapped his thigh in exasperation. "This isn't Waterloo, Martin. You bloody British are always so phlegmatic. Can't you see we're doomed?"

"Not if Colenbrander's right about the main army going north with Lobengula."

Perry seemed not to hear him. He started to play with his dog, his eyes downcast. Martin was disappointed in his friend. All his customary bravado had evaporated, leaving a cowering and rather useless young man. Perhaps Burnham was right to think he might be a liability. Yet he'd made his own decision to come with the Column—all for the right to say to his uncle that he'd ventured north of Bulawayo. It was almost as if he wanted to prove something, but lacked the necessary fortitude.

Martin went to the thorn fence and peered out. Flashes of lightening, now several miles away, outlined the trees, but the rest of the time the darkness had an ominous intensity. He stood on guard duty for three hours, until he was relieved at one o'clock, and fell into an exhausted sleep.

⧫⧫⧫

Next morning the bedraggled column set off along the Shangani River, constantly on the alert for a sudden attack. The Maxim gun teams were ready to turn their weapons at a moment's notice to face an onslaught. Martin rode ahead with Colenbrander and Burnham. His task was to guard the two scouts while they searched the ground; they had chosen him for his keen eye and quick shooting. After two miles they found the hoof prints of the two messengers' horses.

Burnham straightened and stretched his back. "I'll follow their spoor."

Colenbrander galloped back alone to the slow-moving column, while Burnham and Martin followed the spoor on horseback. Soon Burnham pointed to footprints overlying the hoof spoor.

"See, they've been followed—by at least two dozen Matabele, I'd say. I hope those two good horses can keep ahead. Pete will walk as much as possible to save his horse, in case he has to make a dash for it. I taught him to do that." He took off his bush hat and wiped his forehead. "They should be able to keep ahead. We can go back to the column." Then he added, "Lucky they're not being followed by Apache. Those devils can run for miles."

When they reached the column they conferred with Colenbrander and Raaff. "We mustn't tell the men that Ingram and Lynch have been followed," said Raaff. "They must be allowed to believe the messengers got through."

"I have good hopes for them," said Colenbrander. "The Matabele are barefoot and their feet will be softened by all this rain; they won't follow persistently."

æ∞ß

That evening Burnham flopped down beside Martin and Perry, who were lying on their capes, using saddlebags as pillows. The American scout said nothing for a while, staring up at the low rain clouds drifting above. When he spoke, his voice was uncharacteristically morose: "We're surrounded by an *impi*, you know. I think they'll attack at dawn. Forbes won't believe me. This is a bad location too. We really should move."

At that moment Raaff came up to them. "I'm sorry, Burnham. Forbes wants us to go over the ground again."

"At night?" Burnham was incredulous. "He doesn't trust me. Am I right?"

The Afrikaner laughed. "He wants a second opinion. Come on Russell, you come too."

Perry watched the three men leave the stockade on foot. He hated to admit to himself that he was a coward, but the suspicion had been growing since the campaign started. At least in the battles at Bembesi and Shangani he had been inside the *laager*, which gave him some feeling of security; he did not ride out after the stragglers because he was not judged a superior horseman. Yet in this pursuit of Lobengula he felt increasingly exposed—inside a flimsy thorn zariba. Why was he here at all? Now, the loss of Wilson's patrol, and the thought of literally thousands of vengeful Matabele warriors gathered round him, had gnawed away what little confidence remained. He started to shake uncontrollably and cuddled the terrier to conceal the tremors.

Martin again guarded Burnham and Raaff as they reconnoitered the terrain. They had to assume that the Matabele in the surrounding bush were all sitting or sleeping round their fires, which flickered among the trees. They might have sentries, but it had never been known for them to patrol at night. As the three men grew more accustomed to the darkness they moved to higher ground where they could see further. Burnham judged that despite the rain he could spot a small fire a mile off, and there were plenty of these fires further away, on both sides of the river. They spoke little, just a few muttered words between Burnham and Raaff, as they crept slowly from tree to tree, seeking higher ground. Martin twisted his head to and fro, peering into the gloom, fearful of wandering Matabele warriors who might leap onto them with their lethal stabbing assegais.

After an hour they returned to the stockade where they found Forbes drinking tea. He helped them to charge their own mugs, looking more tired and drawn than ever, responsibilities evidently weighing on him.

"Burnham's right," Raaff told him. "We are surrounded."

Forbes eyed the American sourly and sighed. "Very well. We'll move out. The Maxims must be unmounted. All metal-work to be wrapped with cloth to deaden the sounds. The dogs must be killed—a bark would give us away. We'll leave at two a.m. Pass the orders around."

"You don't have to kill the dogs," remonstrated Martin. "We can bind their muzzles with cloth..."

"And if one of the bindings comes undone? It's an order, Russell. Don't argue with me."

Martin turned away angrily. It was all very well for Forbes to make an order like that, but the dogs were helping to keep up morale. He was thankful he'd not brought one himself; but Perry had little Towzie. He found his friend looking out over the stockade. He had made a shooting stick out of a branch, and was sitting on it, his hat pulled down over his eyes; the terrier was curled up on his lap. Martin put his hand on Perry's shoulder and told him about Forbes' orders.

His friend was aghast. "No! Why, for God's sake?" He looked down in alarm at the sleeping dog.

"He's afraid that a bark will alert the Matabele. He's right, but I argued that we could bind their muzzles. He wouldn't have it..."

"I can do that!" Perry grasped at the idea, then spoke in sobbing bursts of words. "Help me, Martin. I'll stuff him into my saddlebag. Bind his mouth up—as you say. Perhaps we could stun him. He won't make a sound—I promise."

Unnoticed by the two men, Colenbrander appeared out of the gloom and was listening. He stood tall and commanding in front of Perry. "You can't jeopardise all your comrades for the sake of a dog." His deep calm voice, and clipped Afrikaans accent, gave his words an awful finality. He bent, and with a swoop of his long arms picked up the terrier; it wagged its tail sleepily and licked his captor's hand. Perry lunged to grab his dog but Colenbrander pushed him back and he crumpled to the ground sobbing. Martin went to him and tried to lift him so that he could regain his composure, but his friend was a dead weight. Colenbrander walked away a few paces, then pulled out his revolver and hit the little dog a sharp blow on the base of its skull. He checked on the pulse, then carried the limp form to the communal grave that had been dug for the bodies of the column's eight dogs.

After a while Perry got to his feet unaided, and Martin helped him to collect large stones to place on the dogs' grave, to prevent hyenas from digging up the bodies. Then they returned in silence and packed their saddlebags.

∂∽૭

At two o'clock in the morning the Column slipped quietly out of the thorn stockade. The night was now pitch black and it was almost impossible to see ahead, but darkness hid their escape. The horses stumbled, but their bits and stirrups were muffled with rags. The only sound was the occasional click of a stone or small rock dislodged. The men eyed the flickering Matabele fires with apprehension, trying to stay close together so they could form into a Waterloo square if they were attacked.

Eventually they emerged onto an open *vlei* and followed its edge as the morning dawned. It was almost six o'clock before they heard the first shouts from the Matabele behind them. The rearguard men could see a large party of warriors following. Colenbrander called Martin to join him, and they stayed behind to snipe at the followers from behind fallen trees and anthills. Their horses were among the best trained to stand on a long lead during gunfire. Whenever the rear of the column was about fifty yards away, they would cover each other as they rode to catch up.

By noon the men and horses were too exhausted to continue, and the column halted near a clump of trees where they cut branches to make a rough stockade. It would not stop a determined charge, but it gave the men gathered inside some sense of security. The two Maxims could not be mounted, because the carriages had been abandoned. They were placed on makeshift trestles and trained on the forest side, from whence, it was judged, the attack would come; the trees would offer attackers better cover than the open *vlei* behind them. Four of the fittest men dug furiously at the lowest point inside the stockade. Because of the heavy rain in the past week they found water at a depth of three feet. It was muddy and stained by the grey soil, but helped them to conserve their dwindling supplies.

The Matabele *impi* gathered among the trees, just out of range. Estimates started to flicker round the men; about a thousand warriors was the consensus. They could be seen squatting on the ground, shouting to each other. Colenbrander, and another man who understood Sindebele, said the warriors were afraid of the Maxim guns.

After about an hour, the volume of shouting gradually increased and suddenly the *impi* stood up and started beating their shields to a rhythmic crescendo. Although the men of the column had heard this sound at least twice before, at the battles of Bembesi and Shangani, it was terrifying now. There were no wagons to serve as a barrier against the hordes, and Martin's greatest fear was that one of the Maxims would jam. To bolster his confidence he insisted that his men clean their weapons, and practise disassembling them and putting them together again.

With a sudden concerted movement the warriors rushed forward through the trees. The Maxims fired 'sighters', and for a moment the Matabele checked their advance. Then they rushed forward again, bellowing to sustain their courage. In a few moments they were in range and the Maxims started to fire in earnest. "Don't stop", muttered Martin. "Don't fail us."

A strapping young Matabele warrior sprinted ahead of the others, ducking and weaving as if he could see the flying bullets, his stabbing spear held at the ready. He ran towards Martin, who stood at the stockade and sighted his rifle carefully, fired, and hit the warrior in the chest. But the young man kept coming, his assegai raised. Martin rapidly worked the bolt of his rifle to insert another round, and fired again. This time the young Matabele fell forward, a few feet from the flimsy barrier of thorn branches.

All at once the Matabele *impi* turned and retreated, firing occasional shots to deter pursuit. The white men of the column relaxed and counted their cost; none of the men was injured, but a horse was badly wounded and they slaughtered it for meat. Forbes then gave the order to move, explaining that they had to distance themselves from several score of Matabele who were dead or dying nearby. They saddled up and moved out slowly, keeping the Maxims assembled so that they could be brought into effect immediately.

This was a dangerous moment, since a return of the *impi* would find them exposed. After moving about a mile along the edge of the *vlei* they found a suitable place to stop and build another stockade, and dug another well. Later, at dusk, it started to rain again, and Martin and Perry huddled under a cape, brushing away the persistent mosquitoes, almost too weary to talk. The mournful whoops of a pack of hyenas could be heard in the distance, and Martin supposed they had caught the scent of the dead bodies.

"What would happen if we were killed?" asked Perry suddenly. "I mean, to our bodies?"

"Try to think of something else. Tell me about that girl..."

Perry continued as if in a trance. "It's been on my mind. Would our bodies lie here and be eaten by hyenas?"

"It doesn't matter, does it, Perry? When you're dead, your body is just an empty shell."

"Do you believe we have souls?"

This question was so uncharacteristic of his friend that Martin found himself smiling. "Yes."

"I wish I could believe that. If I could, perhaps I wouldn't fear death so much."

"I think it must be like sliding into sleep."

After a long pause, Perry said, "Martin, I've come to the conclusion that I'm a coward."

Martin glanced at him and saw only a pale serious face under the dripping felt brim of his hat. "You're just frightened—we all are."

"Yes, I'm afraid; but I know I'm a coward too, because my fear paralyses me."

"Perry, if you were truly a coward you'd run, or cower under your groundsheet. Look, anyone who isn't afraid either lacks imagination, or is stupid; it's a perfectly natural reaction to danger."

"With me, it's worse—believe me, Martin. Anyway, I suppose we should get some sleep."

ॐ~ॐ

Early next morning the column set out again. There were no signs of the Matabele warriors, but the white men were fearful of an ambush. By mid-morning they reached a tributary of the Shangani River, and Burnham, who had been scouting ahead, reported that several hundred Matabele were waiting in hiding near the obvious fording place. He led the column to an alternative crossing, where Forbes gathered the officers together.

"We're not certain where the Matabele are hiding," said Forbes. "I've decided that a decoy party will make a feint at the main ford, where they're expecting us to cross. The main column will cross here. When we reach the far side we'll fire a volley, and then the decoy detail can come over. Tancred, I want you to lead the decoy party, with Russell as your second-in-command. Take twenty men. Off you go, and good luck."

Martin rounded up his section of ten troopers and they rode over to join Captain Tancred's group. The twenty men trotted cautiously towards the main ford, knowing that at any moment they might be attacked. They were poised for flight; Martin kept Chandra on his toes, holding the reins tight and firmly gripped with his left hand. His rifle was in its holster, while in his right hand he held his Smith and Wesson .38 revolver. When the main ford came in sight, they advanced at a slower pace.

Suddenly a shot rang out from the other side of the tributary, about fifty yards away. Dismounting, they took shelter behind a rock outcrop, while heavier Matabele firing broke out. Martin suspected that the young warriors had been unable to contain themselves, and thus had given the white men enough warning. The decoy party fired sparingly; they were short of ammunition, but had to give the main column time to cross the tributary higher up. Colenbrander's warning of the dangers of being overwhelmed kept ringing in Martin's head as he imagined hundreds of warriors rushing across the ford.

The skirmish continued for thirty minutes. At the distance of less than a hundred yards the troopers were able to score heavily with their rifle fire. One of Martin's men received a flesh wound, and he was binding it to staunch the flow of blood, when they heard a concerted volley of rifle shots and knew that the main body of Forbes's column had crossed the tributary.

Tancred and Martin passed the word round that, on a bugle call, they were to mount and gallop back. They were all wary of being attacked from the surrounding bush, but eventually reached 'Burnham's' ford unscathed, and splashed across to the far bank, where their comrades lay resting.

↾❦

At noon next day the advance guard of the Forbes column saw a large party of uniformed men approaching. Cheers rang out as the men waved their hats, shouting hoarsely. It was the relief party from Bulawayo. They were soon greeting each other, and news circulated among the men that Ingram and Lynch had both reached Bulawayo. The relief party had set out within hours. Now, rations were broken out and eaten ravenously by the starving men of the column.

It took them another week to reach Bulawayo, where they camped at the outskirts of the charred remnants of Lobengula's grass hut capital. After Martin had looked after his troopers and their horses he fell into a long sleep of exhaustion. Later he continued the letter to his parents:

'We at least reached the safety of Bulawayo yesterday. We are all truly exhausted and emaciated—men and horses. But we are safe. I feel no elation, only sorrow for my good friend Borrow, left to die in the bush with his companions. Perry is not well, exhausted and feverish, so I will wait here with him for a couple

of weeks. We can feed up our horses too, before I set of on the long ride back to my farm.'

'Rhodes is here, inordinately pleased that we have driven out the Matabele. He chortles in that strange high-pitched voice. He told us that Lobengula breached the treaty, and now the Chartered Company will administer the Matabele country as well as Mashonaland. Land will be sold to anyone willing to take his chances in the conquered country. It's good ranching country, with sweet grazing. To be frank, I think the excuse for conquest was not sufficient. The Matabele are proud and brave. Some of us feel sure they will return and strive to drive the white men out.'

CHAPTER 9
The Venter Family— January 1894

It was January 1894 before Martin Russell was able to set off back to Mashonaland from Bulawayo; the Forbes Column had been disbanded, and its men were free to return home. He was anxious to return to his farm, even though he knew it was now too late to plant a maize crop. He simmered with resentment about the long absence.

He was accompanied by Perry Davenport, who had received a further sum of money from his uncle, and a commission to augment his earlier report on gold mining prospects in Mashonaland. Though reluctant to stay any longer in Rhodesia, he decided that he must consult with the Mines Department staff in Salisbury. He rode the horse he had bought in Johannesburg, and led the mare Scheherazade, that now belonged to Martin.

They had heard of an Afrikaner farmer named Gerrit Venter who lived not far from the route between Bulawayo and Salisbury. He was supposed to have brought good cattle from the Transvaal, and Martin hoped to buy a young bull from this man to improve his own small herd of native cattle.

So the two young men turned off the main watershed route at the small settlement named Que Que, and rode along a dusty track rutted by wagon wheels, that wound northwards alongside the Sebakwe River. They rode in silence, each absorbed in his own thoughts. By late afternoon they caught sight of the Venter farm and homestead. A beam of golden light from the low sun picked out a group of thatched buildings at the base of a large hill that had been their landmark. Below these buildings the trees had been thinned out to create open parkland stretching down to the river. A series of large pools glistened behind rock bars. A small village of round thatched huts huddled close to the river, and native women were carrying water in earthenware pots. The shrill voices and laughter of their children carried up to the two horsemen. A thunderstorm was brewing up in the north, and a gigantic cloud towered behind the hill, lightning flickering in its bowels. Thunder rumbled round the valley, and Martin's horse, Chandra, tired though he was, pricked his ears and shied at leaves skittering across the track.

As the two riders approached the farmhouse they could see that it was quite large by settler standards. The foundations were of rocks bonded with dried mud. A broad verandah ran across the full length of the front of the house, overhung by the eaves of a thick grass-thatched roof. Two large ridgeback dogs bounded down from the verandah and advanced, barking. They were not aggressive, and became calmer when they recognised that these were white men.

A tall, heavy, blond-bearded man loped down the steps from the verandah, calling off the dogs, but patting them as a reward for their vigilance. He shaded his eyes from the lowering sun to see the riders more clearly. Martin judged him to be in his mid-forties, noticing that he moved easily and confidently.

"Hello there!" the farmer called, with a heavy Afrikaner accent.

"Good afternoon. Are you Mr Venter?"

The Afrikaner smiled broadly, showing strong white teeth. "I am. My name is Gerrit Venter. And who may you be?"

The two riders introduced themselves, and the big man held their bridles as they dismounted. The two dogs circled round the visitors, taking in their scents, wary of the horses, who, in turn, eyed the dogs with deep suspicion. Martin explained that they were returning to Salisbury, and that he hoped to buy a young bull.

"You've come to the right place. This is my farm..." He swept his arm round the vista, then laughed as he turned to face the house, "...and this is my family."

Martin looked up to the verandah, where he saw a woman who he judged to be Venter's wife. A boy of about eighteen stood beside her. Two girls, a few years younger, one dark, the other blonde, were at either side. The family stood at the wooden rail of the verandah and looked down at the visitors with curiosity. Then the boy came down the steps. He was slight and dark, in marked contrast to his father, and had a cheerful smile and bright eyes.

"This is my son, Ben," said Venter. "Now come inside, *kerels*. We can talk over some coffee, eh?" He shouted in the Karanga dialect, and two young African men came from behind the house to take the horses. Martin had to soothe Chandra, who objected as the strangers tried to hold his bridle; he snorted and flared his nostrils. The two visitors then unsaddled their horses and carried their tackle and rifles up the steps.

Venter introduced his wife Jeanne, and daughters Louise and Pauline. Jeanne Venter was not the typical heavy-set blonde Afrikaner woman; she was the complete opposite, small and slight, with dark hair piled on her head in the French style. She wore a blue-checked dress with a clean white apron, and smiled gravely at the visitors. "You will stay with us tonight, won't you? There's a big storm coming."

Her English was clear, and Martin thought he detected a slight French accent. He was embarrassed about his dishevelled appearance and unwashed clothes, and replied, "We don't want to inconvenience you, Mrs Venter. We're used to sleeping in the open, so we could easily..."

Jeanne Venter laughed. "Sleep in the rain?"

"Yes, ma'am," Perry laughed, "we've slept many times in the rain."

"We wouldn't hear of it!" said Gerrit Venter firmly. He waved them to chairs on the verandah, while Jeanne sent her daughters to fetch the coffee.

She regarded Perry with concern. "You don't look well, young man. Have you men been in the fighting against the Matabele?"

Perry nodded, smiling weakly. The Afrikaners looked with keen interest at the threadbare clothing of the two young men, and at their worn rifles and bandoliers. Ben's eyes were wide he was itching to hear some stories about the fighting.

"Thank heaven's it's over," said Martin. "I need to get back to my farm—though I'm too late to plant a maize crop."

"Well, we must thank the Lord that you have come through the campaign safely." Gerrit shook his head. "We heard about the sad loss of your men at the Shangani."

"We still don't know much about it. It seems certain they were killed. I lost a good friend..." He was interrupted by a clap of thunder. "Mr Venter, I must go to see to my horse."

Gerrit held up his hand reassuringly. "You must call me Gerrit— and don't worry about the horses; they're in stables. We'll go out to see them after you've had your coffee. "

The two girls returned with a large pot. The elder daughter, Louise, had her mother's looks and colouring. She smiled shyly as she handed Martin his cup, then dropped her eyes as she blushed. She was very pretty, with a slim waist, dressed in a long pinafore dress. Martin judged her to be about sixteen. Her younger sister Pauline took after her father, with stronger build and short blonde hair. She had the youngest child's confidence and moved around restlessly, pausing frequently to examine the visitors.

Ben Venter could contain himself no longer. "Did you really fight the *kaffirs* in battles?"

"Yes, we did," replied Martin as he sipped his coffee. He looked at Perry to help him answer but his friend was absorbed in the young girl Louise, scarcely disguising his interest. He probably had not even heard the question, so Martin continued. "At the upper Shangani, then the Bembesi, we had pitched battles. Then some of us volunteered to follow them north from Bulawayo—trying to capture Lobengula—but we had to pull out—after Wilson and his men were killed..."

"We heard something about it," said Gerrit gravely. "Was there no chance of rescuing Wilson and his men?"

Martin explained what had happened, and how Forbes had judged it unwise to cross the flooded Shangani River without the Maxim guns.

"Do you think he was right?"

"I suppose so. It went against my instincts, but there were thousands of them—the Matabele. Our Chief Scout estimated about seven to ten thousand, and we were only a hundred and fifty. With the Maxims we could hold them off; without...well, we probably would have been overwhelmed."

Gerrit nodded. "Forbes was right, in my opinion. I have never fought the Matabele, but my father was in the battle at Vegkop..."

"Did you kill many *kaffirs*?" interrupted Ben eagerly.

Martin replied guardedly. "Many? We don't know how many were killed in the battles. Perhaps a hundred at each. Remember, we were in *laager*. They were no match for our machine guns."

"It was more than a hundred. More like two hundred, if you count the number who were wounded and died later—that's according to the commanders." Perry tore his eyes away from Louise and joined the conversation, regaining some of his former bravado.

"And do you think the Matabele will return to Bulawayo?" asked Gerrit.

"I feel certain they will," replied Martin. "After all, it's their country. They won't allow us to take away their grazing land."

"And your farm in Mashonaland? Did you buy it, or was it given to you?"

"I bought it. I wasn't a Pioneer, you see, so I wasn't entitled to a free land grant. Perry and I followed the Column by a couple of months. But my farm was virgin land, covered with trees, never used before. What about this farm, Gerrit, did you buy it?"

The Afrikaner nodded. "This land had never been used. It might have been grazed now and then by native cattle, but never cropped. I bought it from the local Chief—five thousand *morgen*—that's more than ten thousand acres."

A bright flash of lightning was followed almost immediately by the clap of thunder, and Martin insisted on going to check his horse. It was almost dark when he and Venter went out, carrying hurricane lamps. Behind the house stood a neat row of thatched stables for the family horses and draft donkeys, and a milch cow. Chandra and the other two horses were stabled together, and Martin checked that they had water and feed—some maize bran and hay. Chandra looked at him reproachfully, as if he resented having been stabled and fed by strangers, but was soon consoled. The first drops of heavy rain beat the dry ground as the men returned to the house. They ran in through the back door into a large kitchen, where Jeanne and her daughters were preparing the supper, the son waiting impatiently.

Jeanne wiped her hands on her apron. "Now, Ben. Take the guests to their room, and show them where they can wash." She said to Martin and Perry, "The servant has put some hot water there. Enough for a small bath—or at least enough for washing. I've had your saddlebags put in your room."

The two visitors followed the boy to a sparsely furnished bedroom with two low beds covered with duiker karrosses and a crude table standing between them. Ben watched the two visitors as they unpacked their saddlebags and took out clean shirts and wash bags. Jeanne had provided towels, which they took to the bathroom, a simple spacious room with a cool cement floor and a round tin bath. A table in the corner held an enamel basin and a large tin jug of water; a four-gallon can of hot water stood near the door that led to the outside. The two men stripped and washed, taking it in turns to stand in the bathtub. They had both lost weight and joked about their prominent ribs.

Ben joined in the laughter and told them, "Guests always have first use of the bathroom, but the women always have more water."

"Do you have many guests?" asked Perry.

"Not many. Some missionaries. One or two police troopers..." He laughed again. "I think they come to see Louise."

"I'm not surprised," muttered Perry.

Wearing clean clothes saved from the camp in Bulawayo, the two young men returned to the waiting family in the living room, lit by two large paraffin lamps. The chairs were of dark wood, with leather thongs overlain with soft karrosses made from antelope skins. There was a fireplace at one end of the room, but it was not being used, and at the other end was a large round table on which Louise was setting the table for supper, self-consciously glancing over her shoulder. The front door and windows of this large room opened onto the verandah.

"I'm sorry I cannot offer you beer or whisky." Gerrit stood at a cupboard. "We have a little brandy, but we'll save it for later this evening. We have some lime juice."

Martin laughed. "We've been drinking muddy water for six weeks. Lime juice will be a luxury."

Gerrit turned to his daughter, "Louise, please fetch us some. Now, sit down." He spoke to Martin. "Who is looking after your farm?"

"A friend—my partner in a small gold mining venture. He can't plant the crops, though he'll make sure my workers stay there."

The Afrikaner regarded him sympathetically. He had already taken a liking to this young British man. "So you've missed a whole season. That's a great sacrifice, man."

"Not compared to the one made by my friend Harry Borrow. He was killed at the Shangani—with Major Wilson."

"*Yah, yah.* That was a sad business."

"Will they go back to bury the men?" asked Ben.

"Yes, they were planning to send some men as soon as these heavy rains are over. They have to be sure the Matabele won't attack."

Venter sent his son to check the horses again, while Louise returned bearing a tray with balanced glasses of lemon squash. She placed the tray on the table, then took a glass to each of the men, starting with the two visitors. As she handed them to Martin and Perry she caught their eyes. Martin looked at her with guarded appraisal, but Perry gave her one of his captivating smiles, to which she replied with her own shy smile.

The younger girl came into the room and stood watching Martin drink. Then she asked boldly. "How old are you?"

Martin smiled. "I'm twenty-seven. How old are you?"

"Thirteen. Are you married?"

Martin spluttered as he laughed into his drink. "No, not yet, Pauline."

She frowned and said scornfully, "Nobody calls me Pauline. My name's Pookie."

"That's an unusual name."

Gerrit explained. "When she was little, she looked like one of those little creatures—We call them *nagapies*—night apes."

"A bush-baby?"

"*Yah*. The name stuck. Eh, Pookie?"

Gerrit gathered the young girl with his arm and hugged her. She squirmed loose and stood watching Perry, then asked him, "Are you married, Perry?"

Perry laughed. "No. But I'm looking for a wife."

Ben joined them, having returned from the stables, his hair wet and plastered to his head. Grinning cheerfully he took his glass of lemon squash and announced, "I think the storm is going."

Jeanne came in from the kitchen, and when the two visitors stood up she smiled and waved them to their seats. She took the remaining chair and Pookie handed her a glass of squash. Gerrit asked Perry about the prospects for gold in Mashonaland.

"It's all over the place," he replied. "But it seems to be in small pockets. The experts say there's nothing here like the Witwatersrand reef...where Jo'burg is."

"I thought *you* were an expert," said Gerrit, smiling.

"Not yet, but I'm learning fast. My uncle owns a mining company, and he's making sure I learn."

When Jeanne asked him about the company he told them, "It has a branch in Jo'burg which owns a big mine. But the main business is in the United States—gold and silver."

"Is America such a wonderful country?" asked Louise. It was the first time she'd spoken, and her voice was surprisingly clear and strong, with hardly any Afrikaner accent.

"I think it is," said Perry. "But I'm biased. Martin and I argue all the time about the merits of our countries."

Gerrit looked shrewdly at Perry. "Which country would America support if the British and the Transvaalers fight again?"

Perry turned uncharacteristically serious. It was a topic often debated in Johannesburg, and more recently he'd discussed the issue with his countryman Burnham. "I guess they would be neutral. Americans think the quarrel is too far away to get involved. Our concerns are mainly about Mexico—and Russia."

Jeanne asked, "Where does your uncle stand in the dispute?"

"Actually, he sympathises with the Boers—I mean the Transvaal-ers." He glanced at Martin with a sly smile. "He thinks the British are far too pushy."

Gerrit turned to Martin. "And what do you think about the dis-putes?"

Martin replied, trying to lighten the tone of the conversation. "Per-haps we are too pushy. But I think Mr Kruger ought to offer the *uitlanders* a vote when they've been in the country for some years—say ten years."

"Maybe he will," said Jeanne, in a tone that suggested this conver-sation should end. "Now, let us eat."

She led her daughters to the kitchen to fetch the meal, while the men took their places at the table. When the food came the visitors were delighted to see a roast guinea fowl, cooked vegetables—sweet potato and squashes flavoured with cinnamon, and fresh bread. Martin had not had such a meal for three months.

Gerrit said grace in Afrikaans, and they started eating. "Did you learn any Afrikaans when you were in the Transvaal?" he asked Perry.

"Only a few words. I took some lessons."

Pookie clapped her hands. "Tell us, please!"

"Well..." Perry glanced at Louise. "*Jou is'n pragtage meisie* (you are a pretty girl)...".

The Venters roared with laughter, and Louise blushed.

Heartened by their reaction, Perry went on. "*Ek het jou baie geliefde* (I love you very much)...".

Again the Venters laughed heartily, and Gerrit said, "We can tell you've been flirting with the local girls. But they may not understand, because of your American accent. Perhaps Louise should give you some lessons. Eh, Louise?"

Pookie bounced in her chair. "Yes, yes! Louise shall teach Perry." She turned to Martin. "Don't you want to learn too?"

He looked at Louise. "Yes, I would like to be taught too."

"Louise speaks French as well," announced Pookie.

Her sister glared at her. "That's enough, Pookie. You're getting over-excited."

Jeanne explained. "You see, my parents were both descended from French Huguenot settlers in the Cape. We continued to speak the lan-guage in the home; I think it has changed less than Afrikaans has from Dutch."

"And what about you, Gerrit," asked Martin. "When did your family come from Holland?"

He replied proudly. "Soon after Van Riebeeck—two hundred years ago. My father came up from the Cape with the Great Trek. He was just a lad at the time—a *voortrekker.*"

"*Oupa* was at the Battle of Vegkop," added Ben. "He was with President Kruger in the battle."

Gerrit sighed. "*Yah, yah. Oupa* and *Oom* Paul are still old friends. They've lived long lives. My father started farming in the Pietersburg area, in the Northern Transvaal. Now, my brother Jacobus looks after the farm. But, you see, I wanted my own place, so I came up here—first hunting—and I could see it was good cattle country. So I talked to the Chief. I gave him twenty head of good stock for the five thousand morgen. Your Doctor Jameson approved the deal. I think he liked the idea having farmers like me as a buffer between the Mashona and Matabele countries."

"And have the Matabele given you any trouble?" asked Martin.

Gerrit waited until the girls went into the kitchen with the plates. "I decided to keep well clear of their country. The people here are Karanga, more like the Shona. Oh, I've had some young Matabele warriors come here, but they've always gone away after a talk and some food." He went on to describe the problems of ranching in this area. "It's not easy here. There are plenty of lions and hyenas. We have to be very careful to bring the stock into *kraals* at night. The grazing is good, because we have large *vleis* that remain green in the dry season. The tsetse flies are well to the north. They tend to stay with the big game—buffalo and eland—and they're mostly confined to the Zambezi Valley."

Jeanne and her daughters returned from the kitchen bearing plates and a sweet *melktert*. Jeanne divided it among the seven people. "I wish Hendrik were here," she said. "He's our eldest son—he loves *melktert*. He's studying agriculture at the College in Pochefstroom."

"And is your family still in the Cape?" Martin asked her.

"Yes; my parents live in Hermanus now. My brother has the farm in Franschhoek. Louise will go to stay with them this winter, to finish her studies..."

"She should be at school, you see..." giggled Pookie.

"Hush!" Louise admonished. "And so should you be at school."

Jeanne said, "I can teach them myself, up to Louise's age. But a girl like her should have friends and go to parties—eh, darling?"

Louise pouted. "I wish we could all go..."

"Perhaps I'll save enough here to buy a farm in the Cape, who knows," said Gerrit. "I think farming there would seem rather tame compared to this. Or Perry might find gold for us?"

"Yes, yes!" shouted Pookie. "Will you look for gold for us?"

"I'd like to." Perry was delighted to be the centre of attention. "But I promised my uncle I'd visit the mines in the Mazoe Valley, near Salisbury. Perhaps I could come back here later."

"You would be very welcome," said Gerrit. "And you too, Martin. I have a young bull—you can see him tomorrow, but you'll have to wait a couple of months for him to be big enough to trek up to your farm." He took a bottle of brandy from a cupboard and poured tiny tots into liqueur glasses, then signalled for a toast. "To our visitors, with thanks for their successful campaign—and hoping to see them again."

They all sipped the fiery peach brandy, the visitors both catching glances from Louise's sparkling eyes. When the girls cleared the dining table Ben went to check on the horses and the cattle *kraal*. Jeanne brought coffee to the men, joining them to sit near her husband on the sofa. They talked about the war against the Matabele and the difficulties of farming in a country so remote from civilisation. Martin felt growing admiration for this couple; Gerrit was like a granite monument, strong and hard, a magnificent physical specimen, intelligent and well read. He seemed benevolent too, and it was easy to see how Jeanne would have been attracted to him. She was extraordinary—calm and gracious, and the sort of woman he liked, taking her place in men's company without reservation. To have a son of twenty she must be at least thirty-eight, yet she looked much younger.

Having cleared up in the kitchen the two girls came to sit in the living room, Pookie squeezing between her parents on the sofa. Although the two visitors stood up to offer her their chairs, Louise chose to sit on a cushion on the floor, curling her legs underneath her like a cat.

Later, Martin and Perry lay on their beds listening in silence to the Venters retiring for the night. The house had crude ceilings of jute sacking plastered with mud, which failed to exclude the sounds of the family washing, and the girls saying their prayers. The two young men knew they could not speak without being heard.

Perry's thoughts were dominated by images of the girl. He recalled that it was now four months since he left Johannesburg, where a young Afrikaner secretary had succumbed to his charm, and told him about her people and their language while lying in his arms. He saw Louise as another delicious prospect. She was at the age when she was just becoming aware of her sexual attraction, and he guessed that she would be willing to explore its opportunities. She would be limited by her strict upbringing, but it would make pursuit all the more exciting.

Martin, too, had been affected by the young Afrikaner girl, more as a reminder of Amanda and Helen; he constantly regretted lost opportunities with those two women. Although he wrote to Amanda every two or three months, and she replied, their letters now contained only words of friendship. She had graduated and was undergoing her practical training at a hospital in London.

ຂັ~ຈ

Next morning Martin woke early, dressed quickly, and slipped out of the house to see to the horses. Ben was already there, and they groomed the horses together, Martin answering the boy's insatiable questions about the recent war. When he returned to the house, he went out onto the verandah. He saw Louise at the far side of the garden and walked over to greet her. She was cutting roses, wearing a pinafore, with her sleeves rolled up. What a pretty sight, he thought. Like a flower bud herself, full of promise; but she was wasted here. No wonder the young policemen came to visit. They probably lusted after her, like Perry.

"Good morning, Martin," said the girl in her precise way. "Did you sleep well?"

"Like a log. I haven't slept on a proper bed for at least two months. I'm sorry that we put you and Pookie out of your room."

She smiled. "It's no matter. We have a guest room, but there was no time to prepare it. If you come again, we'll make it ready for you. Will you come back?"

"I will—to fetch the bull. And the route south through Que Que and Bulawayo is now much better than the Pioneer road. Because it's on the watershed it doesn't cross any big rivers. So, whenever I go south, I'll come this way, and I'll drop in."

"But I hope you will come before April? That's when I'll leave for the Cape."

"Then I'll make a point of coming before April." He laughed: "My bull should be ready by then."

She smiled mischievously. "If that's the only reason you're coming, I might not wait."

Her father came to join them. "Come and look at the young bull, Martin. Louise, you'd better tell your mother to wake that lazy American!" He led Martin to the *kraals* to the west of the homestead. In one of them was small bull, about six months old, a fine Afrikander, with rippling muscles under his loose tawny skin. "You're lucky; I had two born at the same time, so I can spare him. Would you like to buy him?"

"I certainly would." He thought this young fellow was just what he needed to put some weight and meat on the little Shona cattle that made up his herd. He could buy a bull calf like this in the Transvaal, but it would be a much greater undertaking to get him up to the farm.

At breakfast there was more discussion about the future of the territory, and the possibility that the Matabele might regroup and rise up against the white men. Martin could tell that Gerrit was concerned that there had been such a serious confrontation, followed by the Chartered Company's occupation of Matabeleland. The womenfolk would be going to the Cape for the express reason of putting Louise into final years at school, and Martin expected they might stay there if trouble brewed near the farm.

The young men left with full stomachs, rested horses, and entreaties that they should return. Martin handed over his last sovereign as a deposit for the bull calf. Perry had been given a last bewitching smile by Louise. He was determined to see her again.

శా❦

CHAPTER 10
Return To The Venters – April 1894

It was on a fine day that Martin rode up to the homestead of his farm. He had been away for five months, almost every day in the saddle, and almost every night sleeping in bivouac under the open sky. He had spent only one night under a roof—at the Venter's farm. He had lost over a stone in weight, but felt none the worse for it, though his skin was scarred from thorn scratches and bush sores. Chandra was thinner too, but stronger and calmer, his temperament seeming to have sobered with the responsibilities he had borne. He snorted at the dogs as they rushed out to greet their master, followed by the two servants, but he did not turn his rear to them and threaten kicks, as he would have done before.

Martin patted him on the neck. "Well, Chandra, we're fortunate to be back safely, aren't we? Now you can have a good rest and lots of good food to fatten you up—and two dogs to plague you—they would do well to stay away from your heels. Careful there!"

He greeted the servants and the dogs, then walked quickly through the house, relieved to find it as he left it. The roof had endured the rainy season without leaking, and though the garden was somewhat overgrown, he could soon put that right. A feeling of warm satisfaction came over him as he looked out over his valley, thankful he had been spared to return alive; but his thoughts turned immediately to Henry Borrow's affairs. What would happen to his farm? He had written to his friend's parents, but when he collected his mail on the way through Salisbury there was no reply—no doubt there had not been time for one to reach him.

Walking over to Tom Ellsworth's diggings he found his partner supervising the construction of a wooden framework, which Martin presumed had something to do with hauling earth to the surface. The Australian shook his hand heartily, and clapped him on the shoulder.

"I heard you were on your way back." He looked Martin over and said. "You've had a tough time, by all accounts." Pointing around with his pipe stem, he added. "I hope you find the farm in order. Sorry I couldn't plant your crop."

Martin thanked him for taking care of the farm, then peered down into the diggings. "How's it going?"

"Quite well. I'm getting the hang of the formations at last. There are little pockets of gold-bearing rock all over the place. The trick is to find a vein that's worth the effort of digging it out. As we don't have much equipment, I have to judge how much manpower is needed. These Shona boys are scrawny specimens, not like the big Zulus on the Reef. Seems they've never had a good feed."

Martin told him that Perry had gone to visit the mines in the Mazoe Valley, and Tom said, "Good idea. By the way, Martin, strictly between ourselves, I think the Mazoe River must have carried alluvial gold—washed down over the centuries from these hills. If we could think of a way to dredge it out..."

"Well, I'll be here to help for a while..."

"And then?"

As they walked back to the homestead together, Martin told him about the visit to the Venters, and the young bull he'd purchased. "I'll go back in a couple of month's time to bring him up here; he'll be old enough to walk the journey."

"I'm sorry about Harry."

"I'll miss him sorely." He told his partner about the tragic episode, then added, "When I wrote to his parents I offered to manage Harry's farm until they decide what to do with it. Of course, it might be entangled with his syndicate."

☙❧

In the weeks that followed Martin made preparations to plant vegetables in the dry winter season that started in May, having enough water on the farm to irrigate. This was the time when vegetables thrived; it was cool and dry, with fewer insect pests and less incidence of fungal diseases. The local Africans grew vegetables too, in tiny plots along the banks of the rivers, but they used traditional varieties, whereas he would sow the latest cultivars with seed imported from South Africa. To his great surprise Tom gave him twenty pounds from the first sales of gold, and he used the money to purchase more seed and fertilizer, and to pay his labourers.

The little school that he started before the war had been closed all the time he was away. He wanted to find a teacher, not having time himself, but he could find no Shona man who had even a basic education. There were a few white men and women in Salisbury who were willing to teach for one or two days a week, but their Chishona was too poor. Eventually he found a housewife named Emily Robertson, who had taught school in Scotland. She drove a dog-cart out to the farm, and taught with translation by a young Shona man who had worked for a missionary. The school building was rudimentary, consisting of a thatched roof over wooden benches. The blackboard was made of painted planks. The original pupils were children of his farm workers, but more soon came from neighbouring farms, and even from as far as Domboshawa.

One day, Perry rode out to visit, and told his friend that he'd finished his report on the gold prospects in the Mazoe Valley. Martin invited him to stay, but he was anxious to return to Johannesburg as soon as possible. After some discussion the two men agreed to travel together as far as Que Que and the Venter's farm, where Martin would fetch his young bull. Perry would then ride with the Venters via Bulawayo to Johannesburg.

Martin thought he detected changes in the American's demeanour. He seemed less confident and cocky. Whereas before he had been light-hearted and jocular, he now spent long periods in silence, his face clouded. He confided to Martin that the sights and sounds of violence during the war against the Matabele had affected him severely, and caused frequent nightmares. It was only when they visited Salisbury and had occasional social contact with the few women who lived there that his spirits seemed to revive. Otherwise, Martin saw few glimpses of the frivolous Perry that he remembered.

಄ఞ

The two men set off for the Venter farm in March 1894, a journey that would take them eight days. They stayed the nights at farms along the way, with settlers who were given land for serving with the Pioneer Column, or had purchased it from the Chartered Company. These farmhouses were miles apart, and sometimes required deviations of several miles from the main road, itself only a rutted track through the bush. There was camaraderie among the farmers that made it easy for the two men to ask if they could spend the night in a barn, although they were always invited into the house and treated as honoured guests.

It rained once, but only the sort of light shower that came at the end of the wet season. On the third day the weekly horse-drawn coach that plied between Salisbury, Bulawayo and Francistown passed them. Other travellers usually accompanied the coach on horseback, providing protection and support. There was still some concern that gangs of Matabele might take their revenge on isolated white people.

They arrived at the Venter farm in late afternoon, and found the family expecting them, having received a letter sent ahead. At supper the conversation was convivial, and only Gerrit was somewhat downcast, because Jeanne and the girls would soon be leaving for the Cape. Louise again captivated the visitors, laughing with them, and blushing when she caught their admiring glances. Soon after supper, a reluctant Pookie was sent to bed, and Jeanne served a last round of coffee before retiring herself. The others talked late into the night. While Martin sought advice from Gerrit about rearing cattle, Perry flirted with Louise.

This time the two visitors shared the guestroom, where a candle guttered on the small table between their beds. While they undressed they talked in muted tones, knowing that the pole and *dagga* walls were not soundproof.

"It's ironic, isn't it," whispered Perry. "Just as I'm leaving this god-forsaken country, I find this smashing girl."

"Don't be daft, Perry. She's too young for you."

"Sixteen? That's not too young. The Boers marry early."

"You're not thinking of marriage, are you?"

"Why not? A man could do worse. Imagine having a girl like that in your bed every night."

"Be careful." Martin was annoyed. "She's not one of your society flirts."

His friend laughed quietly, and whispered, "I think she's longing to be tickled by a moustache. And I know you fancy her yourself; I've noticed you watching her."

Martin pondered this last comment while his companion fell asleep. Louise seemed just a child compared with Amanda and Helen, but she had a vitality and sexual attraction that he could not ignore. Although Perry had tried to monopolise her attention, Martin noticed that she often turned to him, perhaps to ask his opinion on some topic, or to ask if he wished to have more coffee or cake. He in turn often found himself glancing at her, admiring her smooth skin and lithe body.

❧

Next morning Martin and Perry went out with the farmer and his son, to release the herd of cattle from their *kraals;* they milled and lowed in their anxiety to get out. Three African herdsmen would take them on foot to the grazing lands. They were local Karanga men who knew the land and were accustomed to herding, though not in such numbers. They wore ragged khaki shorts and a cloth over the shoulder, and each carried a long spear, generally used for poking recalcitrant cattle, and a *knobkerrie*—a stick with a round knob on the end, used as a club.

At the homestead for breakfast, Jeanne Venter and her daughters served them with maize porridge and cream, followed by fried eggs and salt bacon; the girls sat to eat only when the men had all they needed.

"You have a wonderful farm here," said Martin to the whole family, somewhat afraid of sounding portentous. "It shames my own modest efforts at Long Valley. You seem to have used an accumulated knowledge from generations of pioneering Boers. If more of your people come up here, this could become a great farming nation, like Canada or the United States. I just hope the Matabele don't make trouble for you."

"They might," said Gerrit. "Look what happened in the Transvaal. They gave us a bad time—for a while at least. It needed a fight such as at Vegkop to show them that they had to leave."

"Perhaps our battles last year taught them another lesson," said Perry.

Martin shook his head. They had argued this issue before. "What lesson? That they cannot live in their own country? They have nowhere else to go. To the west are deserts, to the east is Shona country, and the Chartered Company won't allow them there. To the north is the Zambezi Valley and the tsetse fly."

"I've heard they're drifting back to their former villages," added Gerrit. "They've even started re-building at Bulawayo. Perhaps they'll reorganise and become warlike again."

When the conversation lulled Louise said to the visitors, "Would you like to see the spring on the hill this afternoon? We could take a picnic."

"*Yah,*" said her father. "Good idea girl. Ben and I have to repair that fence, but we don't need any help for that."

Pookie started to dance around. "I want to go to the spring. Please, please!" But her mother, knowing that she would be an irritation to Louise, insisted that the younger girl had to do some schoolwork.

So it was that Louise led the two visitors from the house that afternoon. The sunshine had mellowed a little, and the harsh heat of the day was fading. Perry carried a picnic basket and a light blanket. Martin took his shotgun, because there were known to be leopards and baboons on the hill. The girl was conscious of being alone with the two young men for the first time; she skipped lightly along the path, humming occasionally like a child. The visitors followed just behind her, entranced by her slim figure, outlined under her light cotton pinafore dress.

A little stream trickled on their left and the vegetation here was greener than the surrounding bush. Louise moved quickly, knowing the path well, turning to urge the men on, and laughing as they clambered clumsily onto a boulder to turn and admire the view. She wore leather sandals on bare feet and hitched up her dress to her knees as she climbed the steeper sections of the path.

About half way up the hill, and several hundred feet above the homestead, they came to a place where the ground levelled into a shelf, and here the trees were somewhat taller. In a clearing lay a small pool about the size of a billiard table, surrounded by short grass and patches of moss. Walking over to it Martin thought there was something magical about the clear still water, so high on a hill. There was no sign that animals had drunk there; usually a pool such as this would have had broken banks, and the hoof marks of antelope muddying its edges.

"Pa won't allow the local people to come up here," announced the girl. "He wants to keep the water as clean as possible. He'll fence it one day."

She took the blanket from Perry and spread it on the ground, in the shade of an acacia tree. Then she sat on the rug and gestured for him to put the basket down and sit beside her. Small beads of perspiration had formed on her face from the exertions of the climb up the hillside. Watching her, Martin thought how childlike her gestures were, as if at any moment she might produce a doll and start to entertain it with a tea party. Yet the evidence of her physical maturity was plain to see; her breasts strained the material of her dress and her waist was tiny, accentuating the curve of her hips. Fearing she would notice and resent his frequent appraisals, he walked over to examine the pool. The water was about five feet deep and crystal clear, apparently seeping up from below and flowing imperceptibly out of the end, to feed the little stream.

While his friend was peering into the pool Perry sat down beside Louise, leant towards her, and whispered. "Louise, I would like to come here with you alone."

She smiled nervously but said nothing. Yet when she looked at Perry she shivered. Feeling her cheeks blushing she fanned herself with the handkerchief she had been using to mop her damp forehead. She had experienced nothing quite like the attention of these two handsome young men. At the few dances she had attended the young girls were always surrounded by older women, and the police troopers who visited occasionally were painfully shy, seldom staying for more than a few hours.

Martin returned to the others and looked carefully around, thinking it was surely quite safe here. He leaned his shotgun against a tree, after ensuring that the safety catch was on, and that no bark could fall into the barrels. Then he went over to the blanket and sat with the other two.

"What a beautiful place," he said to Louise. "Your father must have been tempted to build his house here."

"He considered it, but it would have been too much work to carry all the materials up here. He says he'll build a cottage here one day."

Perry moved his position restlessly, finding Martin's presence intrusive. After a while, he stood up and walked over to the pool. He knew the girl found him attractive, and suspected that she was excitable and might yield at least some way if he tried to seduce her. But it was impossible with Martin here. He dipped his hand in the water, then turned to the others.

"The water's so cool," he called. "We could swim."

"I'm a good swimmer," said Louise, as if it was a matter of fact. "I've been in the sea at the Cape. But Pa doesn't like us to swim here, because we use the water at the bottom of the hill for drinking."

In a challenging tone, Perry said, "Come on, show us how well you can swim."

She blushed. "But I don't have my costume."

"You can take your dress off," said Perry. "We won't look until you're in the water. Come on."

Her cheeks were burning but her brown eyes flashed. She wanted to rise to the challenge, but there was more. She sensed that both men desired her, and it gave her strength and purpose that she found unnerving. It was like the time a year ago, when she drank too much peach brandy at a party and danced in an abandoned way that surprised her, and caused her mother to make critical comments.

"Very well," she said suddenly. "But you must both turn round and promise not to look."

The American walked away from the pool to a large tree and Martin went over to join him; the two men stood facing away. When Perry looked at his friend with a sly smile, he said, "There are some girls who like a challenge, and this is one of them. The only question is how far she'll go."

"What do you mean?"

"Wait and see. Or you could go on back to the house. Yes, why don't you do that?"

Louise saw the two men facing away from her and she scrambled to her feet, unbuttoned her dress and slipped it off. She stood for a moment in her cotton petticoat, as she unfastened her hair, feeling suddenly cool and almost naked. She sensed her vulnerability, alone with the two young men, but she was certain that no one else would come to the place. Her father and Ben were fixing the fence; her mother was teaching Pookie; and besides, they would hear anyone who approached.

She skipped the few steps over the short grass and jumped with a splash into the pool, squealing at the shock of the cool water, then standing to test its depth. The water came to her chin, and she felt a sensuous soft sandy bottom on the soles of her feet. Her petticoat was floating up to her waist, and she could only move her legs slowly. She faced the direction of the men, her long dark hair drifting on the surface.

At the sound of the splash they turned round and walked unhurriedly to the edge of the pool; they looked down at the girl. She's like Ophelia, thought Martin, though she has no flowers. Her pretty face was shining up at them, triumphant that she was daring enough to defy her father by entering the pool, and to take off her dress in the presence of these two young men. Her olive brown cheeks were flushed.

Perry announced, "Well, I'm joining you."

He stripped off his shirt and sat down to pull off his boots and trousers. He did it very quickly, then stood up in his undershorts and jumped into the water, sending a shower of sparkling droplets into the air. Louise gasped as she backed away, watching him apprehensively as he slowly advanced towards her like a predator, his thin bare shoulders glistening above the surface. Martin watched from above, sensing that the usually light-hearted Perry was making a determined pursuit.

"Well this is very nice," said Louise nervously, "but I think I must be getting out to make the tea."

She backed away to the side of the pool away from Perry and started to clamber out, but it was difficult for her because the bank was too high. Perry waded over to her and stood behind her. He put both hands on her waist and tried to lift her out. Martin stepped forward to help, catching the girl's wrist and pulling her out of the pool in a single movement. For a moment she stood facing him, caught in sunlight, water streaming from her petticoat, which clung to her body, clearly showing its curves. Then she turned away from him and lifted the hem to wring it out. She pulled her hair into a thick tail and started to twist it. A sparkling trickle of water fell from it, as if from a faucet.

To Martin there was something primitive and beautiful about the young girl standing wet beside the pool. Her thin shift and her modesty made her even more enticing than if she were naked. He knew that he should give her the chance to dry herself in privacy, but could not take his eyes off her. She started to walk to the blanket, the wet petticoat clinging to her neat little buttocks. When she reached the blanket, she turned back.

"Please collect some wood so we can make a fire and boil water for the tea."

While his friend strolled to the trees to look for kindling wood, Perry heaved himself out of the water. He followed Louise to the picnic blanket. She had taken a small dishcloth from the basket, and was dabbing it against her petticoat in an ineffectual attempt to dry it. She moved into a patch of sunlight hoping it would assist the process, concerned to be in such dishabille in the presence of these men. She castigated herself; she was so stupid to have taken off her dress. There was only one thing to do; put it on over the wet petticoat.

At that moment, Perry came up to her, and without a word gathered her up and started to kiss her. She struggled soundlessly at first, then relaxed as Perry expertly fondled her. She felt her legs growing weak as he pulled down one of the shoulder straps of the petticoat and touched her breast. She spoke his name in protest, and made a half-hearted attempt to escape. But he held her strongly, his hand delving to find the other breast. He had pulled her petticoat down to her waist, and now ran his hand down her back to her buttocks, feeling them clench in response. The feel of her small lithe body and smooth skin had driven away all his caution.

When Martin turned to come back with an armful of small branches, he saw Perry embracing the young girl. Her petticoat was round her hips, leaving the top half of her body naked, and she seemed to have collapsed in his friend's arms. Dropping the kindling, he ran up to them and grabbed Perry by the shoulder, pulling him away. The American stumbled backwards, revealing for an instant Louise's bare torso, before she tried to hide her breasts with one hand, darting the other down in an attempt to pull up the wet petticoat that clung to her hips.

"Are you all right?" Martin asked her.

She said nothing. Her eyes were wide and slightly glazed, mesmerised like a hare facing a fox. Her head swam with the sensations of Perry's hands on her skin, and now this other man was watching her.

Martin turned to see Perry advancing on him, and he shouted, "What the hell do you think you were doing?"

"For God's sake! It was only in fun. I didn't hurt her." He grasped Martin's shoulder and pulled him round, then punched him.

Martin turned his head and the blow glanced off his cheekbone, but he was surprised at its force. He broke away and the two men faced off like prize fighters, glowering at each other. Martin had boxed at school and university, and felt capable of defending himself, especially with Perry so wildly angry. "You were a fool to start this," he growled. "She's the daughter of our hosts."

"Don't be stupid! Can't you see she wants it?"

"She doesn't know what she's doing."

The American turned away for a moment in disgust, and walked to where he'd discarded his shirt and trousers.

In that moment, Martin turned back to Louise and went up to her with the intention of helping. Standing in front of her he realised she was paralysed in her Botticelli's Venus pose, gazing at him intently. He reached out to lift the petticoat from her hips, expecting her to flinch in modesty, but she remained still. Impulsively, he reached his arms round her, and then kissed her. Her mouth opened and she was murmuring something; her body felt delicate and soft against him.

He expected that any moment Perry would interfere, but then he heard a shout; it was from a distance, from down the pathway. Louise's father was calling them from a long way away down the hill path.

He disengaged from Louise, but not before Perry saw. All three of them faced the path, trying to make out Gerrit's words. Louise, her cheeks crimson, pulled up her petticoat and struggled with her dress, which caught on the wet undergarments.

Martin's first thought was that Gerrit would discover what had happened. Would Louise tell him? Almost certainly not. He told Perry to put on his shirt and trousers, and would have set off down the path to stall Gerrit but was afraid to leave the girl alone.

Louise was terrified that her father would find her half-dressed with these men, imagining his wrath and the beating he would deliver. Her wet petticoat kept sticking, so she turned away and quickly pulled it up to twist out the water. She could feel that her thighs were slippery and was astonished to find herself in such a state, afraid that it would show and she would be disgraced.

Perry, too, was alarmed at the prospect of Gerrit bursting onto the scene. As he pulled on his clothes and boots, he looked anxiously towards the path and the direction of Gerrit's occasional shouts, coming closer. Thus he missed Martin's view of her naked back as she squeezed out her petticoat.

Having finished dressing they gathered up the blanket and basket and hurried along the path down the hill. Within a dozen yards they met Gerrit, red in the face and sweating from the exertion of climbing. For a moment he looked in suspicion at the rather dishevelled appearance of the trio.

"Lions—have got into the herd," he panted. "Come on—we must hurry." Turning, he led them down the path.

֍ ֍

CHAPTER 11
The Lions

Gerrit Venter hurried down the path; he carried a rifle in one hand. The two young men following a few paces behind. Louise stayed at the rear, fearful that her father would notice that her dress was wet; later she could explain it as perspiration. Now and then he turned his head to make sure they were keeping up with him. Though short of breath he blurted out information about the lions that had attacked his herd of cattle.

"About three of them—killed two steers—*kaffirs* ran off—I followed the spoor—round the other side of the hill—then we lost it. That's why I came for you—don't know where they are now—must wait up for them—tonight."

Running down the path behind Gerrit, Martin noticed his nimble movements. It surprised him that someone of his bulk could run like an agile young man. He set his feet almost daintily in the places least likely to be slippery, sometimes even straying into the vegetation beside the narrow path. When he grasped supple branches for support, he took care that when he released them they did not strike those behind.

When she could snatch a moment, Louise glanced anxiously into the forest; it had taken on a gloomy and menacing aspect. She reminded herself that it was not the normal habitat of lions—leopards perhaps, but they were shy nocturnal animals, and dangerous only when wounded. No, one would not normally expect to see a lion in thick forest like this. But one could never be certain, and she had been taught since childhood to stay alert. Those young men lumbering in front of her would see nothing.

Perry twisted his ankle, and yelped as he hopped on one foot. Louise passed him, and he followed her, hobbling. In the moments when he could look up his attention was riveted on her supple sinuous movements. She was tantalizing, and he wanted to reach forward to grasp the slim waist with both hands and twist her round, to bend her until she yielded. At the picnic she had been so close, and now the opportunity was lost. He supposed that she was now unattainable, as they would soon be off to Johannesburg. It might be better for him if she remained so, an image to conjure up in fantasies, unsullied by the inevitable flaws of reality and the banality of speech.

Gerrit stopped suddenly and turned to face them. "They'll be back—for their kills," he panted. "We must hurry to get into position before dark."

Louise nearly collided with Martin, and to stop herself put out her hand against his back, momentarily feeling his deep intake of breath; he felt thicker and stronger than Perry. Sensations of his embrace at the pool came back to her, and for a moment she wished there had been more time for him to caress her, as Perry had.

What a slut she was, to have allowed two men to touch her, and she half naked. God, if her mother knew, she would be in real trouble. It had been her first experience of a man's hands on her body. She had danced with boys and men, but only in folk dances. A couple of boys had kissed her, but she had fended off their fumbling attempts to touch her breasts. An older man, so drunk he could barely stand, had plunged his hands between her legs, but three layers of clothing protected her. If one of these young men had been alone with her, would she have allowed them to go further? She feared Perry; there was something relentless in the way he'd pulled down her petticoat. Martin seemed to be more in control of himself, and she felt that he would have allowed her to go as far as she wanted—and how far was that?

Gerrit had resumed running, steadying his heavy frame by catching hold of branches near the pathway, sometimes slipping, but never falling. As soon as they reached the edge of the woodland Louise ran ahead for the last hundred yards to the house, holding the hem of her skirt up, her slim legs flying. By the time the men reached the house she had gone to her room. They found Jeanne and Ben on the verandah packing saddlebags. Jeanne wore a worried frown, but the boy's eyes shone with excitement as he worked the bolt of his rifle.

Gerrit started barking orders. "Bring your rifles and bandoliers! Have we got water and biltong, Jeanne? We'd better take citronella—or the mosquitoes will bite us to pieces. And don't forget matches for the hurricane lamps." He rushed into the house.

The two visitors hurried off to the room they shared, occasionally glancing at each other angrily as they collected things for the night vigil. They said nothing, conscious of the flimsy partitions within the house. Martin took his Lee-Metford with considerable misgivings. The shotgun seemed to reproach him as he closed the latch on the gun case. After putting five cartridges in the rifle's magazine, and another half-dozen in a bandolier, he followed Perry back to the verandah.

Gerrit kissed his wife and Pookie. "Where's Louise?" he asked them.

Jeanne replied calmly. "In her room. She wishes you good luck."

Gerrit was suspicious and sensed that something had happened up on the hill. He looked quickly at the young men to read their expressions, noticing that Perry looked afraid; perhaps the lad was scared about the lions. Louise was not a 'fast' girl, but he wondered if she knew enough to control a situation with young men. He had been foolish to allow her to go to the pool with the visitors.

"From now on keep all the windows and doors locked," he instructed Jeanne. "On no account go outside the house. Even if you hear shots, or shouting, stay inside."

She nodded and took Pookie with her into the living room. It was now almost dark and the sudden silence menaced as the men hurried on foot to the cattle *kraal*. Two young African herders stood near the bodies of the steers, guarding them with ancient muskets. They were both shivering and wide-eyed, terrified that the lions would return. The steers lay on their sides, their necks twisted back at unnatural angles. The lions had been disturbed before they could eat much, and Martin expected they would be lurking not far away, waiting for cover of darkness before returning to devour their kills. He imagined their frustration and the saliva drooling from their lips.

A huge anthill, some fifteen feet tall, stood not far from the dead steers; it was thinly covered with thorn bushes. Gerrit pointed. "We'll sit at the foot of the anthill, with our backs protected." He instructed the young herders in the Karanga dialect, "Now go back to your homes. Tell everyone not to make any noise after dark." The two frightened youths hurried off, talking at the tops of their voices to keep up their spirits.

"There'll be a half moon—we should see the shape of the lions when they come to the kills. Ben and I will sit between you two. Sit close enough to touch each other. Keep your rifles ready. Don't talk. Let me fire the first shot. Are you clear about that?" His eyes gleamed in the dying light of the hurricane light as he blew it out.

They settled down on the base of the anthill, water bottles handy, and rifles across their laps. Martin put his back against an eroded buttress of compacted clay, fashioned by generations of ants. He checked for the third time that his rifle was loaded, and felt the safety catch. Ben's hunched figure was only a yard to his left, but almost unrecognisable in the last light. Beyond sat Gerrit, still as a stone statue, then Perry.

Half an hour passed. The half moon rose, bathing the scene with cold colourless light. Faint sounds from the labourers' village faded to silence. An owl hooted. In the far distance a jackal howled. After about half an hour, Martin gradually became aware of a shuffling noise, like the sound of an old woman's dress as she walked. He thought he could smell the sour scent of lions. The moonlight was casting ghostly shadows over the scene. His shoulders were stiff. Mosquitoes whined in his ears, frustrated by the strong scent of citronella. More minutes passed, perhaps twenty or thirty.

Suddenly, dark shapes appeared over the carcasses of the two dead oxen. One moment there was nothing, the next moment they were there, ghostly, looming in the moonlight. As he raised his rifle, from the corner of his eye, Martin saw Gerrit aim and fire. Then he fired himself, worked the bolt and fired again. The shape that he'd aimed at fell. With a muffled grunt another lion, on the side of Gerrit and Perry, bounded away.

"*Gott verdomme!*" shouted Gerrit, rushing down to the level ground. "Come on—stay together. Watch out—I think one of them's wounded."

They advanced, cautiously circling the dead steers and the fallen lion. Gerrit picked up some clods and threw them at its prone body. There was no movement, and he advanced further to prod it with the end of his rifle barrel. Still no reaction, and he felt confident enough to check whether it was breathing. Feeling its chest he could detect no heartbeat. Now satisfied, he announced that it was a large male lion. He lit the hurricane lamp, then started searching the ground on the other side, bending down to touch the ground gently with the tips of his fingers. "I can't see any blood from the other one," he announced gruffly. "I hope it wasn't wounded. We'll get some men to carry this one in."

The four men strode down to the labourer's huts, Ben chattering to his father in Afrikaans, his voice high-pitched in high excitement. Martin felt a sense of foreboding and held his rifle so that he could react immediately. The grunt from the second lion might be a sign that it was wounded, or it might have been frightened. After discussion they agreed that Gerrit and Martin had each fired two shots, and Ben and Perry one. That meant six in all, and surely one or two must have struck the other beast.

Gerrit called for the headman, who replied from inside his hut in a loud nervous voice. Gerrit shouted, "Mapini! We have shot one lion. The other one ran away. I want four men to carry the dead lion to the house."

The rough wooden door of the headman's hut opened with a creak, and then he peered out, his eyes wide, reflecting the moonlight. Acrid wood smoke flooded out of the doorway as the grizzled old African stepped out to stand in front of them, hitching a blanket over his thin shoulders as he listened to Gerrit giving instructions. Turning, he shouted to the other huts, calling for men to help move the lion. Gradually, dark figures emerged cautiously, gathering to listen to Mapini's instructions.

As he led the group to the cattle *kraal*, Gerrit impressed on them the potential danger if the second lion was wounded. He supervised them as they bound the paws of the dead lion over a pole, and four of the Karanga men carried it to the house, its body swaying heavily under the pole. How undignified, thought Martin; one moment to be king of the bushveld, now dangling lifeless, deserted by his pride. The dark mane that would have inspired terror in his competitors hung like a shaggy bearskin, the long tail trailed to the ground, its brush dragging in the dust.

They laid the lion's body near the foot of the steps leading up to the verandah. Gerrit sent the Africans back to their huts, then shouted, "Jeanne! You can come out."

The front door opened and she emerged, with Louise and Pookie huddled close behind her. They peered down at the group of men standing round the fallen lion.

"Was there only one?" Jeanne asked doubtfully.

"*Nie*," muttered her husband. "Another one ran away. We must go out at dawn—in case it was wounded."

The men trooped into the living room, narrowing their eyes against the sudden brightness of the paraffin lamps. Louise gave bashful glances to Martin and Perry, while Gerrit took out the brandy bottle and poured tots for the four men.

"I fired at the lion that ran away," said Gerrit, handing out the glass tumblers. "I must have missed. Martin, you fired two shots at the one that fell. Perry, you fired only once—why?"

"Because it all happened so quickly" Perry muttered reproachfully.

"You should still have fired again."

The American looked at him defiantly, then glanced at Louise. "I guess I was too slow. Anyway, it was your shot that frightened it."

Gerrit shrugged. "There's no sense in crying over spilt cream. Tomorrow at first light we must find out if the other lion was wounded. If it was, we must follow its spoor. That may be dangerous, *kerrels*." He pondered for a moment looking at Martin and Perry, then added, "You two don't have to go with us. This is our problem—our cattle, our lions."

"Of course I'll go," said Martin, "but I'll take my shotgun this time."

Gerrit nodded in acknowledgement, his respect for this young man growing. He turned to Perry. "What about you, lad?"

"I'll go too." Perry swallowed nervously. What else could he say in front of Louise? He had heard plenty of yarns about wounded lions, and he knew that they could be extremely dangerous. He hoped they would find that the second lion had merely fled the scene, or had died of its wounds.

"Very well. The four of us men will go. Now go and get some sleep. I'll wake you at first light." Gerrit signalled to Jeanne to come with him to the kitchen. He shut the door and turned to her with a sigh. "I'm sorry, my dear. I made a mess of the shooting…"

She went up to him and reached up to put her arms round his neck. "Never mind. You'll find the other lion tomorrow. And you have those two men to help you."

He sighed again. "That fellow Martin can handle himself. By the way, something was going on—up on the hill—with Louise. I noticed when I went to find them."

"At their picnic?"

"I think those two young men were fighting. Martin's cheek was red—as if he had been hit."

"Fighting over Louise?" she laughed. "She really should be going to the Cape, darling."

৯০৯

The air was cool and still next morning, and at first light the men assembled on the verandah, dressed for riding. Jeanne had mugs of coffee for them. The horses chewed their bits and snorted at the strong smell from the lion, which was being skinned under the headman's supervision. It looks even more undignified now, thought Martin. As a domestic cat becomes scrawny when wet, so this great lion's body shrank as it lost its tawny pelt. One of Mapini's men was probing its shoulder with the point of his skinning knife and dug out a bullet, which he gave to Jeanne. She handed it to her husband, who had just mounted his horse.

"I think it's your Metford," he called to Martin, grinning. "You should have the skin. Your first? I doubt it will be your last."

Martin mounted Chandra, and now carried his twelve bore shotgun on his lap, with two cartridges of heavy gauge shot in the breeches, and another eight cartridges in the large side pockets of his jacket. In the holster that hung from his belt, he had his .38 revolver, loaded with six rounds, and a further ten rounds in his leather belt.

In Afrikaans, Gerrit called to Jeanne, "You must stay inside again! I don't know when we'll return."

She reached up with prescient concern to touch his hand. "Be careful, won't you." To the other men, she called, "Be alert! Do exactly what Gerrit tells you!"

Just as they were leaving, Louise came out onto the verandah rubbing her eyes. As Martin and Perry watched her she smiled slightly, as if confused, then waved hesitantly, not sure whether she should.

῾῿

The early morning light was already harshly bright when the four men reached the cattle *kraal*. Gerrit dismounted and started searching the ground methodically. "*Agh!*" he shouted in disgust, "I feared as much. It's wounded. There's blood here—and here. It should be easy to follow, but we must be very careful. The spoor is quite small, so it's probably a lioness—she will be vicious because we've killed her mate."

Ben dismounted to join his father, and they followed the spoor on foot, leading their horses, while Martin and Perry rode on either side of them, their height giving them a better view into the grassland and among the thorn trees. After about a mile, that took them nearly an hour, they came to the wide *vlei* that was one of the farm's main grazing areas; it was a couple of miles long and about four hundred yards across, devoid of trees. A small stream meandered down the centre of the *vlei* where dense reeds and tall elephant grass grew in a strip about twenty yards wide. Most of the grass in the *vlei* had been burnt, and green grass shoots sprouted through the ashes. The pug marks of three lions, an adult and two three-quarter grown cubs, were clearly visible in the ashes, and led to the strip of elephant grass.

Gerrit stopped and pointed. "They may be laid up in the *spruit*. The wounded one wants to stay near water. We'll walk along the edge of the vlei. Keep at least fifty yards away from the reeds and long grass. Stay well apart. I'll lead."

He and Ben started to mount their horses. At that instant a deep angry 'oomph' came from the long grass to their right, startling the horses and making them wheel, with eyes wide and nostrils flared. All their atavistic fear surged in them, urging them to flee. Ben was left holding his struggling horse by the reins, while his father, caught with one foot in a stirrup, hopped around shouting angrily.

Suddenly two lions broke cover and headed straight for the group of men, their tails erect. They covered the short distance in long bounds, throwing up plumes of ash dust from the burnt ground. What happened next became a vivid memory for Martin, a sequence of images enameled in his mind for ever.

He brought his shotgun to his shoulder and was about to squeeze the trigger when Chandra leaped sideways in fright. Grasping the pommel with one hand he strained to keep his eyes on the lions. As Chandra pranced he had to raise his shotgun with one arm. The two lions were only ten paces away when he fired his right barrel. The leading lion tumbled forward; it was one of the three-quarter grown cubs.

During the same few seconds, Gerrit managed to extract his foot from the stirrup. Letting his horse go, he raised his rifle when the second beast, the lioness, hit him. He was bowled over, his rifle flying out of reach. The lioness's momentum carried her past him, giving him just time to stand up, and he swung round looking for his weapon. In that instant the lioness turned with incredible speed and reared up at him. He fell backwards, with the beast on top of him, trying to get its back feet onto his stomach, like a cat playing with a cushion.

Martin could not fire his second barrel, because Chandra was snorting and lurching in fear, desperate to flee, but trained to stay. He flung himself off the horse and ran towards Gerrit, glancing quickly to the long reeds to see whether another lion was following. The lioness did not see him approach, as she struggled on top of Gerrit's heaving body, her muffled growls mixed with his gasps. Martin walked quickly up, placed the muzzle of his shotgun against the lioness's shoulder, and pulled the trigger for the left barrel. The force of the heavy pellets knocked the beast off Gerrit. She lay on her side, struggling to get to her feet, but both her shoulders were shattered. He quickly reloaded both barrels and fired another shot that killed her.

Hastily glancing round he saw Ben still struggling with his horse, hands entangled with the reins. Perry had let his horse go, and stood about twenty few paces away, holding his rifle tightly and staring at Gerrit's body on the ground.

Martin took out his revolver and walked to the bodies of the two lions, shooting them, in turn, in the head; he wanted to be sure that they were not merely stunned. Then he turned and shouted to Perry: "Watch out for other lions!"

He started to examine Gerrit. The Afrikaner's big body was coated with ash, his face filthy, eyes shut; his clothes had been ripped from his chest and midriff, and an alarming stain of blood was spreading over the white skin of his abdomen.

Martin put his head down close to Gerrit's. "Are you all right, Gerrit? Can you hear me?"

There was no answer; but he could hear rasping breaths and decided that Gerrit must have fainted from the shock. Starting a quick but systematic examination of the body, he noticed that the sleeve of Gerrit's shirt was in tatters and soaked with blood. He ripped off the remains of the sleeve and saw arterial blood welling from a deep wound.

"Give me a belt—one of you—quickly!" he shouted to the other men.

Ben rushed up, babbling in Afrikaans. He struggled to pull his belt off and handed it to Martin, who strapped it round Gerrit's upper arm and pulled it tight, in the form of a tourniquet.

"Is he all right?" gasped Ben, panting from his exertions with his horse.

"I think he's fainted. His arm's broken—bitten badly—and the lioness clawed his stomach."

Martin used his handkerchief to wipe the blood and ash off Gerrit's torso, and exposed the wounds in his stomach. Some of the deep scratches were open, and blood seeped from the gashes in the white skin. When wiping Gerrit's face he found another scratch on his cheek, which bled heavily, soaking his big beard. As Martin dabbed at the wound with his handkerchief, Gerrit groaned, opened his eyes, and started to mutter in Afrikaans. Then his eyes focused on Martin.

"Two of them—couldn't hit both..."

"You'll be alright," said Martin encouragingly. "We'll get you back to the house." He turned to Ben and Perry. "Go back to the house—

together—fetch the donkey cart—bring a mattress and water." When he saw Ben hesitate, he added, "Both of you go. Guard each other. I'll stay here with Gerrit."

The two hurried off to retrieve their horses; they were grazing nervously on the fringe of unburned grass near the tree line. Martin stood up and shouted after them.

"Ben! Bring your mother with you. Perry, you stay at the house and look after the girls."

He squatted down beside Gerrit, who had lost consciousness again. Taking off his own shirt, he rolled it up and placed it under the wounded man's head. Then he looked apprehensively towards the reeds; there might be other lions unaccounted for, but he suspected they would have been frightened off by the gunshots. He set about cleaning Gerrit's wounds, using his handkerchief first, and when that was saturated with blood, strips cut from his cotton trousers. Remembering that he had a clean spare shirt in his saddlebag he went over to Chandra and fetched it, then he soaked it from his water bottle and washed the gashes in Gerrit's body.

The sun was beating down on them relentlessly, so he walked to the trees and pulled off some branches to make a shade over the supine body. He knew that the Afrikaner could recover from his mauling, but the main risk was infection, so he set about cleaning the wounds again. Fortunately, as far as he could see, the lioness's claws had not penetrated the abdominal cavity. Every few minutes he checked Gerrit's pulse, which seemed strong, though he showed no signs of recovering consciousness. Martin felt helpless, though confident that Jeanne would know what to do.

It seemed longer, but it was only thirty minutes later, when he saw the donkey cart careering along the edge of the *vlei*. In the distance it looked like one of those toy wooden carts made by African children. Ben was whipping the donkeys and as it drew closer he could see Jeanne sitting alongside her son, gazing anxiously ahead. When the cart reached Martin, he helped her to jump down, taking her canvas bag. She was wearing a dark blue skirt and a white blouse, with the sleeves rolled up. She rushed up to her husband, ducking under the crude shelter of branches, then knelt down to take his pulse. Martin was struck by her fragility beside the massive body. Satisfied with the pulse, she felt her husband's limbs for broken bones, probing gently at the fractured arm.

"How long since you put on the tourniquet?" she asked calmly

He replied that it was about half an hour. She tried to loosen the belt, but the leather had soaked up blood and swelled, so he cut it away with his pocket knife. For a moment he thought the blood flow was stemmed, but it soon started to well out from the tattered flesh. She reached into her canvas bag and brought out a bottle of iodine and strips of cloth. After swabbing the wound with the dark brown fluid, she wound a new tourniquet round a different part of the upper arm.

Ben had been poking round the body of the lion that mauled his father. He came to stand behind his mother. "You were very close when you shot this blerry lioness, Martin. The fur on her shoulder is all burnt. We all missed with our first shots—except you. I'm not sure if Perry fired..."

"Keep a look out Ben," Martin interrupted. "There may be others still there in the long grass." He muttered to Jeanne, "It was a shambles. The whole thing was a bloody shambles."

"Never mind." She was working on Gerrit's belly, teasing open the claw scratches with her fingertips, trying to find out whether any of them had penetrated into the abdomen, applying iodine wherever the skin was broken. The blood had clotted, so she asked Martin what he had found, and he told her that the wounds seemed only flesh deep.

She stood up. "Help me get him into the cart."

Ben joined them and they tried to lift Gerrit. He weighed over two hundred pounds, though it was not only his weight but the awkward length of him. Martin took the big man by the shoulders, conscious of his mangled arm, and dragged him to the cart, with Jeanne and Ben helping as best they could. He made Ben hold the donkeys while he unhitched them from the cart, allowing him to tip it up, so that the tail touched the ground. They dragged Gerrit onto the mattress in the cart, before pulling the shaft down to re-harness the donkeys.

They set off with Ben driving the donkeys, shouting encouragement at them. Jeanne sat beside her husband, his head in her lap, trying to prevent him from rolling as the cart lurched along. Martin rode Chandra, and Gerrit's horse emerged from the trees to follow them. Now and then the wounded man let out low groans as the cart jolted. Martin stayed close to the cart, and when Jeanne looked up he could see her face shining with sweat, curls of wet hair plastered on her forehead.

"It's the risk of infection that concerns me," she called to him, her voice calm. "When we get to the house, I need your help to clean the wounds. Ben must look after the farming matters. Louise and Pookie can help, but I need you most." He noticed that she had not mentioned Perry.

It took them fifteen minutes to reach the farmhouse, where a group of about twenty African labourers and servants were gathered in front, standing in silence. Louise and Pookie rushed down the steps, their faces tear-stained, their eyes wide with fright as they saw their father lying in the cart. Perry was standing on the verandah, and watched impassively as Ben, Martin, and two servants carried Gerrit up the steps and into the house. In the living room, Jeanne instructed her daughters to lay sheets on the dining room table, before the men laid Gerrit on it.

"You mustn't stay here," she told the girls, and they went out to the kitchen without reluctance. She sent the servants out, then instructed Ben to take the cattle to water, to ensure that the cows had been milked, and to carry out all the farm chores. He was then to feed and water all four donkeys. "We have to take your father to the mission hospital at Gwelo."

Finally she turned her attention to her husband. "We must clean the wounds very carefully," she said to Martin, "otherwise they'll go septic. A lion's teeth and claws are always very dirty." She shouted, "Perry! Bring boiling water from the kitchen! But I don't want the girls coming in here."

Together, Jeanne and Martin stripped off all Gerrit's clothes, throwing them into a bloodstained heap in the corner. His large naked body lay like a white corpse in a mortuary, all its wounds exposed. Jeanne washed her hands, then placed a clean white cloth over his genitals. While Martin was washing himself from a basin of hot water, he heard Jeanne muttering to her husband. He could not understand the Afrikaans, but it sounded like endearments and encouragement. When he returned to the table he noticed Gerrit's eyelids flutter, and his lips moved.

"It's all right," soothed Jeanne, in English. "You'll be fine." She went to the cabinet and brought back one of the precious bottles of brandy.

Under her instruction Martin started to swab Gerrit, using brandy on a cloth that had been soaked in boiling water. The big man opened his eyes, and Martin felt a moment of elation. "We're just cleaning you up, Gerrit. Then we're going to take you to the mission hospital at Gwelo."

He winced as Martin cleaned a deep scratch. "*Jah, jah.* But it will take two days. Who will look after the farm?"

"One of us will look after it. Don't you worry."

Jeanne called to her daughters. "Louise! Pookie! Go and pack! Take everything we'll need for a few nights."

Pookie called back, sobbing. "Why? Where are we going?"

"To the Gwelo mission. We don't know how long we'll be. Now hurry up girl!"

Gerrit groaned, "You're using my peach brandy. What a waste!"

Jeanne drew Martin aside for a moment. "You must come with us, to Gwelo. We need your help."

"Who will look after the farm?"

"Your friend Perry?"

Martin shook his head. "He knows nothing about farming..."

"Then we'll leave the headman, in charge. But I must have you with us."

They returned to the task of swabbing the patient, starting in the worst affected areas. Martin worked at the belly, Jeanne at the torn arm, where she released the tourniquet again. When he finished the belly, Martin worked down to the legs and feet; Jeanne looked at the groin, which, amazingly, was not wounded, before working on the upper torso, arms and head. Gerrit was semi-conscious all the time, groaning and muttering in Afrikaans. His wife responded with soothing words, now and then pausing to wipe the perspiration from her brow. They evolved a routine of swabbing the wounds with boiled cloths, then wiping with brandy, and finally with iodine. When they finished what they could see, they called Perry to help turn Gerrit, so that he lay on his good side, allowing them to clean his back, where there were a few superficial claw marks.

"I wish I could put his arm in a splint," she muttered, "but it's too badly broken."

Finally, Martin helped her to pull onto Gerrit a clean shirt and trousers. She sent Perry to call for the servants and they carried him gently down to the donkey cart. The movement caused him to recover consciousness and he grumbled and groaned at the pain. While Ben rigged a makeshift shade, Jeanne supervised loading the family luggage. The two girls cast worried glances at their father as he lay on a mattress on the floor of the cart, surrounded by pillows. The young men hastily packed up their saddlebags and prepared to ride along with the Venters. They said nothing to each other, accepting the inevitability that they would stay with the family until they were no longer needed.

Ben returned and wandered around, trying to tell whoever would listen about the instructions he had given: "I've told the headman to light fires around the *kraal* until we come back. I've told him to take the cattle to water every day."

It was nearly noon when they set off for the small settlement at Que Que. Jeanne and Louise sat at the back of the cart, on either side of Gerrit to protect him from the lurches. Ben drove the donkeys, urging them to make speed, with Pookie by his side; the family's horses were tied by long lead reins to the cart, leaving Martin and Perry free to ride on either side. They made slow but steady progress, the tough little donkeys trotting along, hour after hour, pausing only once, to drink from a stream.

It was about ten o'clock at night when they reached Que Que. First they saw lantern lights twinkling through the trees, then the rough track suddenly became more defined, and they could make out a few scattered houses.

"We're nearly there, darling."

Gerrit muttered, "Thank God, I can't bear much more of this."

They went to the small hotel, which catered for travellers on the road from Salisbury to Bulawayo. It was a low grass-thatched building with four rough bedrooms and a large lounge used also as a dining room. Martin dismounted and hurried in, calling for the landlord, Bob Carey, who he knew from earlier visits. A servant ran to fetch Carey, who appeared, smiling and rubbing his hands on a towel. Martin greeted him perfunctorily, and said, "It's Gerrit Venter, Bob, he's been mauled by a lion. We're on our way to Gwelo. We need to stay for the night."

Carey's cheerful demeanour changed to concern. He had lived in Africa all his life, most of it in the Transvaal, and knew how serious a mauling could be. "There's one room vacant—we'll put him in there. Better let me have a look at him; I've worked in army hospitals."

They carried the wounded man to a bedroom, where they laid him down on the large wooden bed. His wife and daughters followed with their cases and saddlebags. The eerie light of the hurricane lanterns threw long shadows on the walls, as the hotel manager bent over Gerrit unfastening the rough dressings.

He drew in his breath. "Ye Gods! You've been knocked about Venter. You certainly need to go to the mission hospital. You need a surgeon for that arm." Looking up at Jeanne, he said, "The girls can go to the kitchen and get something to eat. No, you stay here, Jeanne. Ben, you'd better take the donkeys and horses to the *kraal* at the back. Wake up that idle watchman and make him fetch some scoff for them—there's some mealie meal and hay in the shed. Here—take the key. Take the girls with you."

The three Venter children left quietly and Jeanne urged Perry to go with them. The patient was still semi-conscious, groaning occasionally. Carey ordered his servant to fetch boiling water, then started to remove Gerrit's clothing. Jeanne and Martin, both weary to the bone, helped him as he used medical spirits to clean the wounds again.

"He has a fever," said Carey in a quiet voice.

Jeanne felt her husband's brow and nodded. "I'm afraid an infection may have set in." She looked up at Martin, her eyes full of concern. "I'll stay with him while you find something to eat. Then, please come and relieve me, so I can put the girls to bed on the sofa in the living room."

The other guests had retired long before they arrived. Perry and Ben sat with the two girls in gloomy silence; Pookie was falling asleep, and Louise's eyes were drowsy. When Martin came in from checking the horses and donkeys he drained a glass of water, then told them that he would take over from Jeanne. They looked up without speaking and watched him go. He met Jeanne at the door to her husband's room.

She put a finger to her lips, then whispered. "He's asleep—but he definitely has a fever. I'm very worried about him. I wish we could take him to Gwelo now; but he needs to rest. The donkeys are very tired, but they'll do well tomorrow. You've checked them, haven't you. Ben said they've had a good feed. Now, I'll go and eat." She put her hand on his arm. "I can't thank you enough for helping us, Martin. Goodness knows what we would have done without you. And I haven't thanked you properly for saving Gerrit from the lion. Ben told me what happened."

"I'll stay with you as long as you need me. Now, off you go and eat."

She sighed wearily and went off to the living room, while Martin entered the bedroom and looked down at Gerrit; his face was shining with sweat. As Martin watched him, his body shuddered, and he moaned almost inaudibly.

※～

At dawn next morning they set off for Gwelo, the donkeys plodding along the track through open savannah forest. As before, Gerrit lay on the bed of the cart, but now he was no longer conscious. Jeanne wiped his brow, concern ravaging her face. It was maddening for her that they could go no faster.

It was late afternoon when they approached the little mission station north of Gwelo. Martin rode ahead to warn them, and found the cluster of stone buildings with thatched roofs, set in a large forest clearing. Dr Murray, tall, gaunt and grey-haired, was sipping a cup of tea on the verandah of the hospital. They greeted each other and Martin told him what had happened.

"I know of the Venters," he said gloomily with an Edinburgh accent. "Of course they don't come here. Dutch Reformed, I expect. Sounds bad. Better get prepared in case I have to amputate the arm." He called for his nursing sister, a large Scottish woman in her fifties, and told her to expect a patient suffering from a severe mauling.

"I've seen it in Matabele men, of course. Happens quite often, and by the time I see them, the wounds have turned septic and there's nothing I can do for them. They die quickly."

Half an hour later, the donkey cart clattered up to the mission hospital. Martin and the doctor went to greet them, with two medical orderlies. Murray walked straight to the cart and for a moment looked at the inert figure in the back. After nodding a greeting to Jeanne and her daughters, he signalled to the orderlies to carry Gerrit into the clinic. They took him to a small operating room, with double doors opening onto the verandah. An African nurse, wearing a clean white uniform, prepared the patient for examination, assisted by Jeanne.

Dr Murray washed his hands in an enamel basin, saying to Jeanne. "I've seen several like this—Matabele trying to prove their manhood— with a short spear and a little shield—crazy people. Russell told me what happened."

Gerrit started to shake with his fever, groaning and twisting, and the doctor put his hand on the patient's forehead, then shook his head. "When did you say this happened?"

"Yesterday morning," Jeanne replied. "We had to stop at Que Que for the night—to rest the donkeys".

"Hmm. So, about thirty hours. Well, I'm afraid the blood may ha' been poisoned. Either that, or he has malaria—perhaps both."

"But we cleaned the wounds so carefully..."

"Aye, but you canna' go deep enough—like this one, where a claw has gone into his belly. You did the best you could, lassie, so dinna blame yourself. And he must ha' lost a lot of blood." He tested the broken arm.

"The bones here have been crushed, but they'll mend. It's the fever that worries me. I'll give him some quinine—in case he has malaria."

⤞⤝

Late in the night, Jeanne sat beside Gerrit's bed while an African nurse sat on the floor in the corner, asleep. Mary Murray, the doctor's wife, plump and kindly, came in with a mug of tea for Jeanne.

"You should really try to get some sleep, my dear. I'll stay here."

"Thank you, Mrs Murray, but I want to stay here."

Gerrit started to call out in delirium a ramble of Afrikaans words. Jeanne placed a comforting hand on his shoulder, wincing as she felt the burning heat of his body. She took a wet cloth from an enamel basin, wrung it, and wiped her husband's face. Then she resumed her seat, while Mrs Murray shook her head sorrowfully and left. Her husband had told her the prognosis was not good, but these Akrikaner men were stronger than most.

Jeanne could sense death coming. Her husband had been mumbling about the farm, and about his brother, but his voice seemed to be fading. She kept on wiping the sweat from his face, just to have something to do. Then he stopped speaking, and she woke the nurse and sent her to fetch the doctor. Murray came and took Gerrit's pulse. The burning heat had gone from his body, and Murray could feel only the faintest flutter of the heart pumping. He was struck by the cruel irony that the largest and strongest men, like this one, were no match for malaria. They went as easily as a baby. Of course, this man was weakened by the trauma of the mauling, and the loss of blood; perhaps that had allowed the fever to take hold.

He pulled up a chair and sat beside the insentient man. Looking at the wife on the other side of the bed, he wondered what would come of her. She looked remarkably young for a woman who had grown-up children, and who had endured the privations of living in this remote country. His own Mary also seemed immune to the climate, and, thank the Lord, the fevers.

⤞⤝

Gerrit Venter died shortly before dawn. Dr Murray had dropped off to sleep and woke with a start. He reached out to the patient's wrist but could find no pulse. He checked the carotid artery, then put his ear to the man's chest and detected no sound. When he looked up to tell Jeanne, he saw she knew already, tears streaming down her cheeks.

He spoke softly. "The blood in his urine was not from the wounds, I'm sure. It was the fever. Poor man, strong as he was, he could not fight two enemies at once. They're no respecters of a man's strength."

He went out to fetch his wife, so that she could comfort the widow. On the verandah he stretched his aching limbs and looked out at the dawn light at the horizon. Another day, another death. Catching the scent of pipe smoke, he saw Martin at the far end of the verandah and walked over to the young man, who watched his approach with apprehension.

"He's died?"

"I'm afraid so. I'll go and fetch Mary. Then we must make arrangements to bury him. You'd better go to Mrs Venter."

Martin went into the room, glanced at Gerrit's inert body, then went up to Jeanne. Her eyes were wet with tears when she looked up at him. She gripped his arm fiercely. "Oh, Martin! He fought so hard for his life." Then she broke down, bending her head as she sobbed. "Please call the children."

Ben and Perry were asleep in the donkey cart, and he woke them first. Ben let out a great cry and rushed into the hospital. Martin went next to the Murray's house, where the two Venter girls were sleeping in a *rondavel* reserved for guests. He met Mary Murray, who was about to go to the widow; she went into the *rondavel* to wake the girls. He heard them cry out, then the door burst open as they rushed out, still dressed in the clothes they had worn for the journey, their hair disheveled. Mrs Murray hurried after them, but Martin followed slowly, stopping to re-light his pipe.

During the ride to Gwelo, he and Perry had already discussed what would happen if Gerrit died. The family could not stay on the farm without him; they would have to return to South Africa. Groups of travellers now regularly used the route from Bulawayo to Pietersburg, in the Northern Transvaal. They could make the trek with other people. Martin wanted to go with them, but he had his own farm to look after. Perry had planned to use the same route to Johannesburg; he would escort them.

❧

The burial was at noon, in the little stone-walled cemetery, where Gerrit's grave would be surrounded by those of a few dozen or so men, women, and children, some white, but mostly black, who had died at the mission since it was founded.

That evening, the Venters and the two men ate supper with the Murrays. The small room was lit by a single hurricane lamp, the light playing on their sombre faces as they ate. It was the first occasion when they had talked about the future.

Jeanne sighed. "I wish his eldest son could have been here for the burial—and to help us now. I can't bear the thought of going back to our farm without Gerrit..."

"You need not go back there," said Martin. "You should go straight down to Pietersburg. Perry can go with you—we've already discussed it. I'll take care of your farm."

"But you have your own farm..."

"I've thought it out, Jeanne. I can pack your personal belongings and send them down to you on the coach. Then I'll herd your cattle up to Salisbury and arrange for them to be auctioned. I can send the money to you in South Africa."

"You should do as he suggests, lassie," said Doctor Murray. "A lonely farm in this country is no place for a woman with a young family."

Louise had said hardly anything all day, but now she spoke with a vehemence that surprised them all. "Yes, Mamma. Martin's right. We should go straight to Pietersburg, and then back to the Cape."

"You can take the coach to Bulawayo tomorrow," added Martin, "then wait to join some others for the journey south."

"But we have no clothes..." said Jeanne.

"I have some money," said Martin. "I brought it to pay for the bull, so you would have had it anyway. You take it to buy what you need in Bulawayo."

おんめ

The coach arrived at noon on the following day. An hour later, the horses had been changed and it was ready to leave for Bulawayo. Two men gave up their seats for Jeanne and her daughters; they would ride horses alongside the coach. Ben and Perry took the Venter's horses on leads.

Martin stood to one side, watching the family say their farewells to Doctor and Mrs Murray. Jeanne looked thin and drawn, weary from three exhausting days, desolated by the loss of her husband. Yet somehow she retained her innate poise and dignity. Coming up to Martin, she sighed, with a wan smile.

"How can I ever thank you enough for all you've done to help us." She lowered her voice. "I wish you could come with us now."

"Better I see to your farm and cattle."

"Yes." She nodded, with another sigh. "Yes. I'm sorry for the trouble it will give you." She looked back at the group assembled at the cart, then turned to him again. "Don't lead a sequestered life in Rhodesia. Come down to the Cape and see us soon?" She reached up to kiss his cheek.

Pookie came up to him, and impulsively flung her arms round him. He smoothed her blonde hair and patted her back, before she broke away and ran to her mother. Then Louise took her turn. He held her by the shoulders and kissed her cheek, wet with tears.

"I hope I'll see you again," he said quietly.

She smiled, then turned away. She was afraid of a paroxysm of weeping like the one that engulfed her when she woke that morning. Her emotions were in turmoil.

Ben came up and shook Martin's hand. He said nothing, but his twisted shy smile showed his gratitude.

Finally Perry approached. "Look, I'm sorry about what happened back there. We mustn't allow it to jeopardise our friendship." He looked at Martin questioningly.

"No, you're right. What will you do after you deliver the family to Pietersburg?"

He made his characteristic casual gesture of indifference. "Go back to Jo'burg, I suppose. I've grown quite fond of the place." He gave a hollow laugh. "I'm not cut out for this sort of country."

As he watched the coach move away, Martin wondered if he would see any of them again. It was quite likely he would meet Perry if he stayed in Johannesburg, but the Venters? They would dissolve into the Afrikaner community somewhere, either in the Northern Transvaal, or the Cape; Jeanne's people were there, so the girls would likely stay with her.

He said his farewells to the Murrays and the staff at the mission, then rode off to the east, back to the Venter's farm. He had hired an African to drive the donkey cart, with Scheherazade tied to it, while he rode Chandra. When he spent the night at the Que Que Hotel, he told Carey what had happened, and arranged to leave the Venter's belongings for the next coach to take them to Bulawayo.

He reached the farm by mid-morning of the next day. It already had a desolate air, and he could almost hear the echoes of Gerrit's shouts and the high-pitched laughter of his daughters. Wandering through the house he assessed the amount of furniture and boxes that he would take to Gwelo. It would at least fill an ox wagon, so Carey would have to send the stuff in installments by the coaches. He instructed the headman to bring the wagon to the front of the house, and started the daunting task of loading it with furniture from the house, with the help of a couple of labourers.

Jeanne had given him a list of the pieces that should be sent to her—a large armoire, two chests of drawers, a writing desk, and some small tables—good pieces that the Venters brought into the country from South Africa. All the other furniture had been made on the farm, and Jeanne told him to keep what he wanted, sell what he thought could be sold, and give the remainder to the African staff. He loaded the double bed that Gerrit had shared with Jeanne, and the bed from Louise's room, expecting that Carey would be able to use them or sell them. He packed clothing and linen into stinkwood boxes that the Venters had used on their journey north. Jeanne had stored the boxes in a shed, airing them every year, and re-charging them with camphor to keep boring insects away. Having wiped them clean, and lined them with sheets, he folded and packed the clothes. He left Gerrit's clothes aside to be burnt; it would be a waste, but this was the widow's instruction.

The books and papers filled two boxes. There were novels and technical books in Afrikaans, English and French, books of accounts, and bundles of documents such as bills and receipts. He barely looked at any of them in his hurry to complete the task, but he had nearly finished the task when he saw the small locked tin trunk he had found under Louise's bed. He guessed she would have taken the key with her, but when he cleared out her chest of drawers he found the key among her underclothes. Unlocking the box with some misgivings, he found it contained small bundles of letters fastened with ribbons. On the top of them was a journal written in French, in small round characters that were easy to read. He put it aside and carried on with the clearance.

By sundown, most of the things to be sent to South Africa had been loaded into the ox wagon, and the headman himself undertook to guard it that night. Martin was able to communicate with him quite easily because the Shona and Karanga languages have many similarities. He explained that the remaining household contents, such as the farm-made furniture and some kitchen utensils, were to be distributed to the longer-serving African staff; he would leave the distribution to the discretion of Mapini, after he had gone. He also explained that Gerrit's clothing was to be burned before he left, fabricating an explanation that it was a custom of white people to burn the clothes of those who died before their allotted life span.

Mapini brought him some food, vegetables from the garden, and papayas; also he found a few biscuits in a tin, and some coffee. When it was dark, and Mapini left to sleep in the wagon, he settled on the verandah with a mug of coffee and a hurricane lamp. Lighting his pipe he started to read Louise's journal, intrigued, but uncomfortable to be a sort of voyeur. He was very tired, and it was only his interest in what she wrote that kept his eyes open.

Why did she write it in French? Presumably to keep its contents from her sister. But her mother could have read the journal, so she must have kept it locked at all times. It was a quarto hard-covered notebook, lined, and with a margin ruled by the author. Each entry was dated, and she had not written every day. Some entries were a few lines, others covered several pages. He started at the end and was surprised to find that she had written during the night of the lion shooting. He turned the pages quickly to a place recording his first visit with Perry, when they were returning from the Matabele War.

'Two young men came to the farm today,' she wrote, giving their names and ages, and something of their background. 'They are both tall and nice looking, thin from the privations of the war, but quite cheerful. The American is a bit low-spirited because of some horrible experiences he had in the fighting. He jokes a lot, but one can tell that he is hurt inside. He looks at me in a strange way. The Englishman is quieter, more serious, and pays little attention to us children.' She made no other comments about them, only recording their departure. He moved quickly forward through the pages until his eye caught his name. 'We are to be visited by those two young men that came earlier in the year.' Nothing more until they arrived, then:

'Perry is more full of nonsense than before. He seems to be happier, perhaps because he's returning to South Africa—how I wish I could go too. He still looks at me in that strange way, with his eyes watching my body. Martin is like a deep *well, which is dark inside. But what use is someone when you look into the well but can see nothing. At least his friend opens his character, with all its faults for the world to see. I would like to know Martin better, but he does not make it easy, though at least he treats me as a person now.'* Martin ground his teeth on his pipe. It was the bitter fruit of his prying that he should have to read this young girl's summation of his character.

The final entry: *'The men have gone to sit over the carcasses of oxen that were killed by lions. I trust they will keep safe. This afternoon went with M and P to the spring for a picnic. I went into the water and then P kissed me—and more. M was furious with him and they had a fight. Then M kissed me, which was interrupted by my father coming to tell us about the lions.'* At this point she seemed to have reconsidered her abbreviated style. *'What a strange experience, to be held like that by a man, and to feel his hands on me. I was very frightened, but excited too—aroused. I was even disappointed when we were interrupted. What a strange man M is. I suspect he was jealous of P, but how could that be, when he has not shown that he has any affection for me. Men are strange creatures, so gauche.'*

At that point her journal ended. He imagined her locking it away in the tin box and putting it under the bed, while thinking about the two men who had blundered into her life. He pulled himself up to his feet and went into the house, where he fell on the bed in Louise's room and was asleep within a moment.

At dawn he supervised the final packing and covering of the wagon, and inspanned the oxen. The headman gathered the farm workers so that he could address them. He paid them two months wages, explaining that there was no more work for them, although Mapini and his family would stay as caretakers until the sons of Gerrit returned to the land they had bought and developed.

After they dispersed he told Mapini to collect a monthly stipend from Mr Carey at the hotel. He also told the headman that he would visit whenever he passed on the way between Salisbury and Bulawayo, and might even ask his friends to drop by. In this way, he hoped to ensure that Mapini would keep the place in order. He took six herdsmen to drive the Venter's cattle. The youngest animals were six months old and would be sold in Que Que. The remainder would be trekked up to Salisbury, a slow business. With one of Mapini's sons driving the wagon, and two young drovers whipping on the oxen, they set off.

At the top of the rise, where he had first seen the homestead, he stopped to look back. There was nothing in the scene before him to hint of any change. The farmer had died and his family had gone away, but the house and village, the garden and the cattle *kraals*, were oblivious in the bright sunlight.

☙❧

CHAPTER 12
Elandsfontein – May 1894

One month after Gerrit Venter's death Martin watched the auction of the cattle in Salisbury. In a clearing on the southern outskirts of the township stood two rows of pens, each containing a group of steers, cows or heifers. The auctioneer was a dapper little Irishman wearing a bowler hat, who moved from pen to pen, taking an upturned box, on which he stood, rattling out the numbers like a machine gun. A tall African dressed in ragged khaki shorts held an umbrella to shade the auctioneer. The cattle milled around in their pens lifting clouds of dust, while about thirty white farmers leant over the fence rails to watch the proceedings, some making their bids with raised hands, or by waving the flier that advertised the auction.

It's going better than I expected, thought Martin, satisfied that he was concluding the promise he made to Gerrit's widow. By rough estimates he reckoned that the sale would net nearly a hundred pounds after paying the auctioneer's fees. He would contribute fifty pounds for the cattle he kept for himself, after deducting some costs for veterinary expenses and feed, and the payments he'd made to the herdsmen and workers on the Venter's farm. He had given some money to Bob Carey to pay for the transport of the family's belongings to Pietersburg, but in all there would be well over a hundred pounds to send to Jeanne. He had no idea of her financial status, but imagined that this would be a welcome sum.

Tom Ellsworth came up to join Martin, ambling slowly, never a man to be in a hurry. Like Martin he wore a broad felt hat, which he removed to wipe his brow with a large red handkerchief.

"How's it going, cobber?"

"We'll make nearly a hundred pounds today—a bit more than I expected."

"And you'll send it all to the widow?"

"Yes. I'd like to take it down to her, but I must stay for another season. Missing the last crop hit me hard. Besides, I've heard they haven't reached the Cape yet."

Ellsworth put his hat on and leant back on the fence facing Martin. He pulled an envelope out of his trouser pocket. "Well, I have some good news for you."

"The gold?"

"Yep. The last lot of assays were really good. I reckon we'll clear a hundred each this year."

"That's fantastic; and I've done nothing."

"You staked me when I had nothing, mate," Tom drawled. "If you hadn't done that, I'd have crawled back to Jo'burg, hungry and with my tail between my legs—maybe even to Adelaide!" Ellsworth went on to explain that it might be possible to increase the profit, but it would need more equipment and labour. "It's not a great site, but well worth working for the time being."

When Martin wrote his next letter to his parents, he explained how the mining venture had saved him from financial embarrassment. *The disruption of the War—missing a maize crop—was a serious matter. The vegetables were quite lucrative, but not enough to sustain me for a year. Fortunately, the gold sales have yielded more than enough to buy seed and fertiliser, and to pay my labourers for a year.'*

He wondered how the Venter's were faring in their journey south. He had received a letter from Jeanne, written when they were in Bulawayo. It was polite and rather formal, thanking him for his help during and after the tragic incident with the lions. She ended the letter with an invitation to visit the farm at Franschhoek when he next visited the Cape. She did not mention Perry, and Martin imagined that the American would be chafing with impatience during the long trek, as he had in 1890 when they came up from the Cape. He would hate the privations, the dust and discomfort. On the other hand, he would enjoy looking after an attractive and still quite young woman, and her daughters. Would he try to take advantage of the vulnerable young Louise?

One evening at the farm, as Martin and Tom Ellsworth were drinking beer and smoking their pipes on the verandah, their conversation turned to the future.

"I have this sense that we whites will always be regarded as intruders," argued Martin. "We're like the Romans in Britain, who brought lots of advanced ways of living and fighting, but eventually returned to their homeland. They were bitterly resented, especially at the beginning, and they were always foreigners."

"Do you think the whites can remain here—like the Boers in South Africa?"

"I suppose they may. But it seems wrong that the terms should be so unequal."

"But the blacks have no civilization."

"Because they've been living in a backwater. They had no contact with civilization, except for a handful of Arab traders and white hunters. Surely it's up to us to bring civilization to them, to educate them, and bring them to the same standards as us?"

Ellsworth tapped out his pipe. "Is that possible, mate?" Sometimes he thought Martin was far too serious.

"With time—if we try. But what are we doing now? Aren't we exploiting them?"

"No." Ellsworth was emphatic. "They're no longer preyed on by the Matabele. They've never been better fed. Some of them are being taught to read and write, by the missions, and people like you. Don't take it all so seriously, Martin." He got up to leave. "What you need is a woman, to distract you from all these deep thoughts."

"Well there's another thing. It's a lonely life, with few prospects."

"There's a certain nurse in the town who would argue with you."

"Fiona? She's a great girl, but...well, I have no such feelings for her."

"You're still stuck on Onslow's wife, aren't you? Perry told me about it. There's no sense in that, Martin. You might as well find someone who's unattached."

∾∾

While the cattle were being auctioned in Salisbury, Jeanne Venter, in the company of her children and Perry Davenport, approached the farm of her late husband's family in the Northern Transvaal, near Pietersburg, nearing the end of a long and arduous journey. The first stretch had been by horse-drawn coach to Bulawayo. Her memory of it was vague because her mind was numbed by Gerrit's death. He had been so strong and supportive, and now he was suddenly gone and she was left with four children. She wanted to get back to the Cape as soon as possible, although she knew it was her duty to visit Gerrit's family,.

At Bulawayo they joined forces with another Afrikaner family travelling to Pietersburg, and agreed to share an ox wagon. They had to wait for their personal effects, sent by Martin from Que Que, and it was three weeks before they finally departed on the long and difficult trek. When they finally reached Pietersburg, they hired a two-horse trap to take them to the farm, leaving their heavier belongings to follow on a wagon later.

It was dusk now, and the cicadas were making a tremendous racket as they drove down the dirt track leading to the homestead. Ben announced each familiar landmark in growing excitement, and Louise patiently translated for Perry. The farm was called 'Elandsfontein', because there was a small spring where eland used to come for water. These antelope never came again after the Venters settled there. When the farm buildings came into view Perry was surprised at their size and number, and by the extent of the gardens that surrounded them. Large acacia trees stood near the houses, and beyond them spread an orchard, with oranges, lemons, limes, papayas and mangoes. The imposing big house was stone-built with a thick thatched roof, and was surrounded by deep verandahs.

The Venter family came out to greet them. They already knew of Gerrit's death from Jeanne's letter, sent ahead by the coach. Jacobus Venter—'Cobus'—was an even larger version of Gerrit, his younger brother. He helped the weary travellers up the broad steps onto the front verandah, three servants carrying their bags, dogs circling them, sniffing their clothes and yapping in excitement. Louise and Pookie were crying at the emotion of joining their father's family, and were enfolded in embraces.

On the verandah, Perry was introduced, first to *Ouma* and *Oupa* Venter, Gerrit's parents. *Oupa* was tall and stooped, stroking his white beard with a gnarled hand. His wife, *Ouma*, was short and round, her deeply lined face wet with tears. Cobus's wife, Hannah, was gaunt, her face unmoving as she shook Perry's hand. They had a son, Piet, who was fifteen, and two daughters, Clara and Anna, aged eleven and nine. The family sat in a large circle on the verandah as the sun set, while servants carried drinks to them. Perry could tell that they were deeply distressed. He also sensed that Jeanne was not fully accepted, almost as if she were an outsider; he presumed this was because she was a Cape Huguenot rather than of Dutch stock.

"What took you so long, Jeanne?" asked *Oupa*, speaking in heavily accented English out of politeness to Perry.

"We had to wait for the wagon and oxen to be ready," replied Jeanne. "And Pookie had a fever in Bulawayo. It seemed to take her a long time to recover."

"Poor lamb," said *Ouma*, embracing the compliant Pookie. "She looks very pale."

"Did you leave the cattle behind?" asked Cobus.

"We had to," Jeanne sighed. "But Perry's friend, Martin—a British man—he farms in Mashonaland—will arrange for them to be auctioned." She noticed a shadow of doubt on her brother-in-law's face. "I'm certain we can trust him."

Oupa said to Ben, "Drink your coffee, boy. I wonder when your brother will get here." He turned to Jeanne. "We will have a memorial service for Gerrit. I've spoken to the *dominie* already.... As soon as Hendrik arrives, we'll have it." The old man's voice quavered.

Jeanne nodded, but said nothing. She looked at her daughters, both weary from the journey. Perry was sitting beside Louise, and Jeanne hoped that he would not touch her, because it would offend the grandparents.

Oupa addressed Perry. "And you are American, young man?"

"Yes, sir. And it seems a long time since I was there—four years now."

"I'm sorry my English is so poor. Do you speak Afrikaans?"

"A little. Louise and Ben have been teaching me on the trek."

Oupa cackled. "You call that a trek? I was in the Great Trek, you know. I must tell you about it—me and Paul Kruger were young boys together."

At this point the family interrupted, wishing to spare the visitor from the old man's ramblings, at least for the time being.

᪥᭜

It was a couple of days later when Hannah Venter asked Perry to help her take some food and a mug of coffee to the old man. He had been confined to his bed, and lifted himself up as the young man entered the room. His eyes seemed to brighten, and he reached instinctively for the pipe lying on a bedside table. Hannah started to fill the pipe for him, extracting wisps of tobacco from an ancient stained pouch and pressing them with practised skill into the bowl of the pipe.

"How are you, sir?" asked Perry, deferentially.

"As well as can be expected, young man, considering that I have to stay in this bed. I always hoped it wouldn't happen to me—to die like an old woman in my bed. I wanted to drop dead from my horse, or be shot in a skirmish..."

"But not from a Matabele spear", added his daughter-in-law wryly.

The old man snorted. "No, by God, not that way—though it could have happened to me a hundred times. Did I tell you about Vegkop, young man?"

Perry shook his head politely, and Hannah laughingly said to her father-in-law. "Of course you must tell him, Pa."

Louise came into the room to join them, and the old man grumbled as he lit his pipe with deliberation. Perry glanced at Louise, who smiled and nodded her approval that he should listen to her grandfather's tale. She herself had heard it countless times, but still enjoyed the way it animated the old warrior.

A cloud of fragrant tobacco smoke wafted up as *Oupa* Venter started his story. He spoke in English, occasionally lapsing into Afrikaans, which Louise translated. "It was like this, you see. The Matabele had attacked our people north of the Vaal River. They killed and pillaged, even stole those Liebenberg children—we never found them, you know." He paused, his rheumy old eyes misting with the memories. "Our leader was Potgeiter—I was only twenty then, but married already, and your grandmother, was with child, with Cobus..." He looked towards his granddaughter, then turned back to Perry, encouraged by the young man's attention.

"Potgeiter told all the *volk* to gather together, with their cattle and sheep. He was a wise fellow, that Potgeiter, and as brave as any. He told us that when we were scattered we would be easy prey for the Matabele—like lone *wildebeeste* on the plain when the lion prowls. He said that until the Matabele were defeated we would have to stay together in a big *laager*. So, when we had all gathered, we moved to a low hill where there was a spring of good water—that place is now called Vegkop."

He continued in biblical sentences, as if he were reading the lesson in the *kirk*. "Then Potgeiter called for men to ride out with him, and I volunteered. He said I was too young and inexperienced, but he knew I had a strong horse, so he let me go. We rode out of the *laager* and went north until we found the Matabele *impis*. There were several thousand of them—how many was it?" He looked at Louise.

"Six thousand, *Oupa*."

"Yes, that's right, six thousand. There were so many of them, young man. They were sitting on their haunches sharpening their *assegais*. Then one of their generals shouted and they all stood up, and my heart nearly stopped beating. Even Potgeiter, who was a very religious man, said *'Gott verdomme!'*. All those *kaffirs* were a fearsome sight. They started to shout their war cries and beat their *assegais* against their shields. They could see there were only thirty of us."

"Then Potgeiter lifted his gun and fired at them, and we all fired a shot—we had only muzzle-loading guns then, you know. They bellowed with anger and started running towards us. Potgeiter shouted to us to get back, and we rode away far enough to give us time to reload our guns. Then we waited until they came close enough, and then fired again."

The old man's eyes were bright with the excitement of his memories. "We did this a dozen times, until we were near our *laager*. We were drawing the Matabele in, you see. Then we rode into the *laager*. We had a big outer circle of a hundred wagons, and in the centre there was a small inner *laager* of a dozen wagons, with the old people and the very young children, and the pregnant women—*Ouma* was one of them. First the attackers made a circle round the *laager*. They stayed out of range, but we could hear their *indunas* shouting to them to have courage and kill all the invaders of their land." The old man snorted. "It was not their land—they had been there for only a couple of years, fleeing from their kinsmen, the Zulu. Anyway, when the *indunas* had encouraged them, they started their war songs and they beat their shields. One of our women, who was standing near me as a gun-loader, she fainted with fright." He paused. "Do you know who another gun-loader was?"

Perry dutifully shook his head.

"Why, it was Paul Kruger—the very same man that is now our President. I could see that he was frightened, but he did not flinch. Then the Matabele attacked. It was a terrifying sight when they ran towards us. We waited until they were in range, then shot at them through the loopholes. Then we passed our guns back in exchange for the gun-loaders to reload. After three volleys, some of them reached the *laager*. They tried to climb over the wagons, and they tried to pull away the thorn branches that we had stuffed into the gaps. Some of them threw their *assegais*, but they were not real throwing spears. Even so, several of our people were wounded. I saw one woman pull a spear from her shoulder as if it was a thorn that had stuck in her dress, and she carried on loading..."

"If there were so many of them, why didn't they overwhelm the *laager*?" asked Perry. "When we fought them in Matabeleland, we had machine guns to help us."

Oupa shook his head. "They could have, but it was frightening work for them too. The bodies of their fellows were piling thicker and thicker on the ground, and after the first onslaught they seemed to lose their stomach for the fight. Remember, our men shot well—every shot killed a *kaffir*. The barrels of our guns were too hot to touch—I had to use a piece of leather on my left hand. We had no time to tamp the powder, so we banged the butt of the gun onto the ground. We kept the bullets in our mouths, so our spit would prevent the bullet from sticking in the hot barrel."

"After about half an hour they withdrew. It gave us time to replace the thorns branches where they had been pulled away, and to bring up more slugs from the central *laager*. Then we heard them again; their generals were shouting at the men to have courage to attack. They charged a second time, but it was not so bad this time. We knew that we could keep them out, and they gave up sooner this time. They went off to find our cattle and sheep, which we had left in *kraals*. When we ventured out, we found that they had taken them all—twelve hundred cattle, and about fifty thousand sheep—all gone! Can you imagine—all our wealth? Some of the men wanted to follow the *kaffirs* to get back their cattle and sheep, but Potgeiter ordered them to wait, in case it was a ruse to weaken our *laager*. We had a service then, to give thanks to God for our success in the battle."

He wrinkled his nose. "The stench was terrible. There were several hundred dead *kaffirs* lying outside the *laager*, some of them almost under the wagons, and the vultures started to come down. We had to shoot at them to keep them away. Potgeiter sent out scouts to make sure that the *kaffirs* had truly gone, so that we could unchain the wagons and move to another place. We found over a thousand assegais in the *laager*! Yet only two of our men were killed."

"And what happened after that?" asked Perry, genuinely interested now.

"Well, after that we went back south of the Vaal River, but two months later we came back and found the place where Mzilikazi—the Matabele chief—had his *kraal*. We attacked them, and drove them out—Mzilikazi had heard we were coming and fled. After that, the *kaffirs* went over the Limpopo...to the place you call Matabeleland."

"Before that, they fought with the Zulus, remember, *Oupa?*" said Louise.

"That's right, I'd forgotten. At any rate, we had no trouble from them again—until you tangled with them—with Mzilikazi's son. You must tell me about that".

Perry nodded. "They were never as strong again—after they crossed the Limpopo. I don't think they ever fielded so many men after the Battle of Vegkop. Of course they had guns when we fought them, but they weren't very proficient at using them."

❧❧

On the following day a lone horseman rode up to the farmhouse; he was Hendrik, Jeanne's elder son, a younger version of his father, tall and fair-haired, with the beginnings of a beard. The family rushed out to greet him, and brought him up to the verandah, where he was introduced to Perry. He seemed cold and aloof, and Perry presumed that he was tired after his long journey.

A short while later, when Hendrik was alone with Perry, he said in halting English. "I must thank you for helping my mother on her journey from Rhodesia."

Perry shrugged. "I'm glad I could help." He thought the young Afrikaner was examining him with a rather hostile expression.

"I've heard of your uncle, George Davenport. He's a wealthy man, isn't he? Why have you been wandering in the north?"

Perry smiled. "Wandering with some purpose, I hope. He sent me to report on the prospects for gold mining in Mashonaland."

"We Afrikaners don't like foreigners taking our gold," said Hendrik gruffly.

Perry now laughed. "It's not your gold, Hendrik. Rhodesia is British territory."

"I meant in the Transvaal. The British and Americans should get out of our Republic and go up to Rhodesia."

"But it was the British who developed the gold mines—and the diamond mines. If it weren't for them, there would be little of the wealth you have now."

Hendrik snorted. "We would have developed the mines in time. You people think we're only farmers, but we have many other abilities. And we would not have brought in all the riff-raff—the foreigners, the Indians..." He turned and strode away down the verandah.

❧❧

Perry and Louise were alone on the verandah, waiting for the family to assemble for the memorial service in Pietersburg. Perry had borrowed a dark suit from Cobus, which was much too large for him. Louise was dressed in black, which made her appear even more pale and delicate. She was amused at Perry's appearance and pulled teasingly at the long sleeves.

"I've hardly seen you since we arrived here," said Perry sulkily. "You seem to avoid me. And you're always talking to your relations in Afrikaans."

"Well, you can understand the language well enough now. And I have to talk to my family."

"And when we travel to Jo'burg, you'll turn to me again for company, won't you?"

She put her hand on his arm. "I'm sorry, Perry. What do you want me to do?"

Between Gwelo and Bulawayo, Louise and her siblings had been submerged in grief. However, after a few days in the small town the elder girl seemed to recover her *joie de vivre,* so much so that Pookie chided her for not mourning their father. On the journey south Perry and Louise would sometimes ride their horses at a distance from the wagons, to avoid their noise and dust. He discovered that this young girl was every bit as educated and well-read as the girls he'd known in Boston and London. She could speak three languages fluently, and she patiently coached him to improve his Afrikaans. He was captivated by her spirit and liveliness, and yearned to touch her again; but he could tell that she was nervous about physical contact, afraid of her mother's sharp tongue, and also wary of the lust that she sensed in him. At night, when the camp was lit only by fires, and by a few hurricane lamps, Jeanne kept her children close to her. When they had to relieve themselves, she would always accompany the girls into the bushes. When they went to bed, they were always together. Only twice did Perry have Louise to himself.

On the first occasion, her horse stumbled in an antbear hole. It strained its leg and Louise had to dismount. Perry dismounted too, and examined the horse's leg, pronouncing that she could not ride it. He was helping her to mount his own horse, and stood behind her, putting his arms around her. They were over a hundred yards from the moving wagons and well out of earshot. Louise protested laughingly, but grew subdued when he stroked her breasts. She let him unbutton her cotton shirt and touch the bare skin, turning her head and making small muffled noises into his neck. Only when he started to unbutton the waistband of her skirt did she protest. Her horse grew restless as it saw the wagons moving further ahead, and Perry had to stop.

On the second occasion, a moonless night, he met Louise fetching something from the wagon. The travellers were seated round the camp-fire a mere ten paces away, but he drew her behind the wagon and kissed her. He could tell that she had little experience, but she had a natural exuberance, and copied the deep probings of his tongue. They had to stop when her mother called to ask why she was taking so long.

Now, Perry said, "Spare me a little of your attention, or better still, a lot of your attention, like you did on our way here."

The rest of the family came onto the verandah, halting this conversation, and they all went down the steps. A donkey cart took the sombre party to Pietersburg, eleven miles away. The memorial service was held in the stone church in the small town, the main settlement in the Northern Transvaal. It was conducted in Afrikaans by a minister of the Dutch Reformed Church, and was attended by about a hundred people, mostly members of the farming community. It was a simple service of hymns and prayers. The *dominie* gave an address in which he reminded the congregation that they should pray for Gerrit Venter and his family. Then Cobus spoke briefly about his brother, and expressed his family's condolences to the widow and children.

❦

Jeanne and her children started packing on the day after the memorial service, so that they could set off for the Cape. A couple of days later Louise stopped what she was doing and sought out Perry, finding him on the verandah sitting next to *Oupa*, who had fallen asleep while telling one of his stories. She beckoned to the American, telling him that she wanted to search for old heirlooms before leaving for the Cape. She led him to the back of the house and out to the stables in a rambling stone and thatch building, deserted because the horses were out grazing. She found a stout ladder that led to the loft, and smiled bewitchingly at Perry, before climbing up the ladder. At the trap door above, she took a key from the pocket of her pinafore and unlocked the padlock. She tried to push the flap up, but it was too heavy, so Perry climbed up the ladder to help. When he was beside her, he put his arm round her and they kissed.

She laughed and pushed him away. He lifted up the trap door and they clambered up into the loft.

It was a huge room that spanned the whole area of the stables, and had been used as a storeroom by the Venter family ever since they settled at Elandsfontein nearly fifty years ago. In the dim light from two gable windows, they examined the accumulated flotsam, old saddles, parts of wagons, wooden trunks, some muzzle loading guns, canvas wagon covers that were beyond repair, an old dressing mirror, badly foxed. Louise tried to open the trunks, but some of them were locked, and others contained only dusty papers. In a corner she found one large trunk that she was able to open, revealing some party dresses. She pulled them out with gasps of delight at their quaint shape and fine material.

"*Ouma* should keep these in the house. They're so beautiful."

"They've kept well enough up here. What would she do with them?"

"Oh, I don't know. We could dress up in them for fun. This one is gorgeous; I could take it for myself." She held up a russet velvet dress. The material was filmed with dust, which drifted away in the still air as she smoothed the dress against her, turning to and fro as she watched her reflection in the mirror. "I want to try this. Shut your eyes."

She waited while Perry puts his hands over his eyes. Then she turned away from him and pulled off her pinafore dress; underneath she wore a short white petticoat. Looking towards Perry, she smiled and pulled the old velvet dress over her head. For a moment she was lost in the dress, and muffled coughs came from under the material. Perry laughed at her predicament and went to help her lift the dress off. Her face was flushed, and she squeaked when he hugged her. Then he pulled her down onto a pile of old antelope skins, where she struggled ineffectually as he kissed her.

"Mamma says—I must not lie with you," she gasped as Perry expertly started to remove her petticoat.

He paused for a moment. "Lie with me? Why not?"

"She says I'm too young..." Her eyes were shining.

"*Ouma* told me she was married at sixteen."

"That was in the olden days. Anyway, Mamma made me promise, and I promised."

Undeterred, Perry resumed the removal of the petticoat. "What did you promise? Let's be precise"

Louise was now naked except for her little white briefs. "Perry, you mustn't! I promised her..."

He was kissing her breasts now, taking the nipples in turn and rolling them on his tongue. He stopped to ask, "Promise what? You mean—to make love?"

Her eyes half closed and her toes were curling in response to the exquisite sensations from her naked breasts. She put her hands on his head and pressed it hard against her. "Perry, please don't."

He paused to look down at her. "You like to tease don't you?"

She opened her large eyes in puzzlement. "What do you mean?"

"You know how to excite a man, but you don't understand how it affects him—how difficult it is for him to control."

"Can't you control yourself?"

He smiled craftily. "It's very difficult." Leaning forward he kissed her ear, whispering, "We could make love now and no one would know." He put his hand down to the waistband of her briefs and pulled them down to reveal little wet curls of blonde hair. She wriggled in shyness, but it merely allowed him to pull her pants further down. Then with a few swift movements he pulled off his trousers and underpants, and finally his shirt. He put his hand between her thighs, finding them slick with perspiration. His fingers probed into the soft flesh as she writhed and gasped. Then he lay on her, trying to prise her thighs apart, but she started to resist.

"Please, Perry! I promised Mamma. If we do this I might have a child."

"Not if it's a safe time.".

"There is no safe time—except when I'm bleeding—she told me."

He lifted himself up and looked down at her. Her face was shining with perspiration and he could see the fright in her eyes. Her chest heaved, lifting her breasts so that they gently touched his chest. I'm not being subtle enough, he thought, and moved to lie beside her. She turned her face, her eyes half closed and misted with desire, wondering why he had moved. He put his hand on her and stroked her with a gentle soothing motion as he tried to break down the barrier of her resistance. Sure enough, her thighs relaxed and parted. With great patience, and considerable expertise, he brought her close to an orgasm, watching her breath quickening. Her eyes were almost closed, as if she was being transported to some other plane.

He moved over her again, scarcely able to contain himself, putting his mouth over hers, his tongue probing deeply. Her body tensed under him, and he could feel her thighs tightening as she tried to keep him out. Her hand was on the back of his neck, tangled in his hair, and she was pulling his head back. He moved slowly, hoping that she would relax and yield enough for him push deeper. But she was aware of his subtle invasion and twisted her head away from him her eyes widening in panic.

"We can't stop now," he muttered. "We've never come this far. You have to let me." He tried to push further, but she wriggled away and he lost his position of opportunity.

He sat up. "Very well. It's obvious that you're still a little girl. You're not old enough to be with a grown man."

She stood up, trying to hide her nakedness, stung by Perry's remark. For a moment she debated with her conscience whether to break her promise, wanting to prove Perry wrong, but decided this was not the time. She hurriedly pulled on her petticoat and dress, leaving the loft as quickly as possible, while Perry followed slowly behind.

ॐ◌

All the Venters gathered round the wagon to say their farewells. It was a week after the memorial service and Jeanne's family were leaving Elandsfontein. They would take the donkey cart and ox wagon to Pietersburg, then the train to the Cape. Perry would accompany them as far as Johannesburg.

Oupa was well enough to come out of the house, saying to Jeanne, "I'm sad to see you go, my girl, because I don't know when I'll see you again."

"We'll come to visit you, *Oupa*. And you must come to the Cape. Your cousins always want to see you..."

"*Yah*, but I'm getting too old."

"It's different now," she replied. "You can travel on the train."

He kissed her on the cheek. "You're a good woman. You bore my son four fine children."

The donkey cart set off, with Perry, Hendrik, and Ben riding in escort. The other Venters waved until it was out of sight.

ॐ◌

CHAPTER 13
Reunion At The Cape –
September 1895

Lady Helen Onslow and Perry Davenport walked side by side on the deck of the *Lismore Castle*. It was September 1895, and the liner was a couple of days out of Southampton on the voyage to South Africa. The sunshine was brilliant, but the wind bit harshly, so the two walkers were warmly dressed. The stronger gusts plucked at Helen's hair and pressed the long woollen dress against her tall slim body. Two male passengers passed by with admiring glances.

"I've been meaning to ask you," she said, "whether you've heard anything of Martin Russell."

Perry smiled at Helen's attempt to sound matter of fact; she was so obviously fishing for information. He was surprised that it had taken her two days to find this opportunity to talk to him without Robert listening. "I visited Middleton Hall last week. They'd recently had a letter from him—he plans a visit to England this year." He pushed a strand of hair out of his eyes and glanced at Helen; she was looking steadfastly ahead. He went on, "I calculated that he may even be in Cape Town when we arrive."

She turned her head sharply, then sighed. "Do you remember how we three met at the High Commissioner's Ball in '90, and how we travelled to Palapye together?"

"Only five years ago, yet it seems much longer—so much has happened." Looking at her covertly he observed her reaction. "I seem to remember you were rather fond of Martin."

"He was charming...Yes, I liked him a lot, but I was engaged to Robert then." Her tone was cool. "Also, he sometimes seemed......well, rather angry."

"Angry, or frustrated?"

"Are you still friends?"

Perry shrugged. "We came through a tough time together in Matabeleland—in '93. I admire him, of course. He's a steady character—a good man to have with you when things are looking tough." He told her about the battles at Bembesi and Shangani, and about the loss of Wilson's patrol.

When he finished, Helen said doggedly, "You still haven't answered my question. Are you friends?"

He wondered what she was angling for. "I suppose so. But we've always been wary of each other. He knows all my failings, and that makes me vulnerable. I sometimes find him rather self-righteous...too much the stiff English gentleman."

She faced him, frowning as if she found this criticism of Martin unjustified. "So you're planning to see your Louise?"

"Yes, and I've decided to propose to her before I go up to Jo'burg. She's in Franschhoek staying with her mother. You know, Helen, we could all go there together."

"That would be nice. Tell me about her. Is she like the Afrikaner girls I met last time I was here? They seemed rather...unworldly?"

"Oh no." He laughed. "She's not a little *meisie op die plaas*, if that's what you mean. The de Villiers family are French Huguenots. They have a farm and vineyard at Franschhoek. Louise is very well educated...."

"Why hasn't Martin married?"

"Hasn't had much choice, has he? There aren't many girls in Rhodesia."

"Hasn't he been down to Johannesburg—or the Cape?"

"A couple of times, but he never found anyone—as far as I know. He's not the type to confide, even if we are...sort of friends. I asked his sister Beth—last week. She said he hasn't mentioned a girl in his letters—except Louise." He fell silent, regretting this revelation, which he'd intended as a goad to his companion.

"Why should he mention her?"

"It was only about meeting her at the time of her father's death; that sort of thing. He always said she was a child, but..."

"What?"

"Well, I think he fell for her too. Probably because he hadn't seen an attractive girl for months."

They had completed two circuits of the deck and started on a third, when Helen asked, "Why do you only 'think' he fell for her? Didn't you talk about it, as friends?"

"We were quarrelling. Nothing serious." He frowned as he recalled the incidents.

"Of course." There was an edge of irony in Helen's tone. "How old was she?"

"Sixteen."

She raised her eyebrows. "Yes, that is rather young. So she must be only eighteen now. I suppose that's not too young to marry."

"The Afrikaner girls marry young."

She mused for a while in silence, then said, "I wonder why Martin thought her too young? Perhaps he was using her age as an excuse."

"For what?"

"So as not to stand in your way?"

He laughed out loud at this idea. "Helen, I know you think Martin's awfully noble, and all that. But...no, I expect he has someone else in mind."

"Oh, really?" Trying hard to disguise the depth of her interest.

He was enjoying himself. "There's a girl in England—a friend of his sister. Her name's Amanda; she's a doctor, and an active suffragette. Martin used to write to her when we first went to Rhodesia."

"How interesting." Her face betrayed her jealousy, but before she could pursue her questioning, she saw her husband. "Oh look, there's Robert. He must have finished his game of chess."

Robert Onslow walked up to them, beaming and jovial, and when Helen asked how he had fared, he replied, crestfallen, "Dreadful! I have no talent for that game." His expression brightened as he added, "I say, you two must have worked up appetites. Time to change for dinner, eh? See you later, Perry."

ॐ∽

Martin sat on the verandah of the Mount Nelson Hotel in Cape Town, writing a letter to his parents. He could see Table Mountain to his right, beyond the hotel gardens. To his left was the ink-blue water of Table Bay.

'The journey was easier than I expected,' he wrote. 'I took the new Zeederberg coach to Kimberley. Then I travelled by train, retracing my route in 1890. It's hard to believe that it's five years since I arrived in the Cape. I'm sorry it's taken me so long to fulfill my promise to return to England, but now I'm on my way.'

'The day after tomorrow the 'Lismore Castle' will reach Cape Town, and on board will be Robert and Helen Onslow—and Perry Davenport. It will be marvellous to see them again.'

'I now wait—impatiently—because I was unable to find a berth on the next boat (it will carry this letter). Tomorrow, I plan to visit Jeanne Venter, whose husband died so tragically last year after he was mauled by a lion on their farm in Rhodesia. I have not seen her, or her children, since the day after he died. She lives on her family's farm at Franschhoek.'

Next day, he set out for Franschhoek, stopping at an inn for lunch, and to water his livery horse. The sky was clear, the air brisk, and imposing mountains loomed ahead, their bases fringed with vineyards, green with the soft leaves of spring growth. On the slopes above the vines were pine forests clinging to steep rocky scarps.

He took Jeanne's letter from his pocket to re-read it:

'My dear Martin,'

'I am delighted to hear that you can visit us. Your coming to Cape Town is most opportune, and we would be very pleased if you could find the time to come here. You would be most welcome to stay, for as long as you wish. Louise and Pauline are both here, and looking forward to seeing you again.'

'I enclose a rough map that I trust will guide you to the farm. It will take you about six or seven hours to ride here from Cape Town, so we'll expect you to stay the night at least.'

He set off again, and after another four miles turned off the road into a poplar-lined avenue; it was like the entrance to a chateau in the Loire Valley. Ahead he could see an imposing Cape Dutch farmhouse, with elegant sweeping gables and a wide *stoep* along the front. As he rode up to the house Pookie rushed down the steps; she was fifteen now, taller and slimmer, with curves that she had not had before. She wore her blonde hair in long ringlets that flew behind her as she ran. She slowed her childish charge as she reached him, becoming a demure young woman. He dismounted to greet her.

"We're so glad you came," she said, slightly breathless, then glanced back at the house. "One of us especially."

A Cape Coloured servant came out to take Martin's horse, and now Jeanne approached, holding out both hands; he kissed her. She looked young and happy, and he noticed from her clothes that she was out of mourning.

"It's so good of you to come to see us, Martin."

He smiled, thinking how attractive she looked. "Thank you for inviting me, Mrs Venter."

"Oh, Martin—you used to call me Jeanne, I think. How old are you now?"

"Twenty-nine."

"And I am thirty-eight. So, you see, we're quite close in age. Now, where's Louise?"

Pookie said sharply, "She's *trying* to make herself beautiful."

Jeanne caught Martin's eye, and they smiled. Taking his hand, she led him to the house, up the steps to the *stoep*, and into a large cool drawing room that spanned the whole front of the house. The floor was of polished dark mahogany, scattered with Persian rugs; the furniture was heavy stinkwood.

"My brother and his wife are not here now," she explained. "Our cousins have a holiday house at Sea Point, and my sister-in-law is taking the sea air. So we'll show you the farm."

Louise appeared suddenly through the door at the back of the room. She wore an ivory-coloured dress that showed off her dark hair and olive skin. Her eyes seemed enormous, with long sweeping lashes. The corners of her mouth lifted, and Martin remembered her bewitching smile. He was astonished at her appearance of sophistication.

"Louise. You look so different."

She frowned slightly. "Older perhaps? It's been nearly two years." She came forward and offered him a small hand, cool to touch.

Jeanne gestured for Martin to follow a Coloured maid to his room; his saddlebags had already been taken there. A large window gave a view down the valley. The sun had dipped behind the mountains, and the vines were tinged with reddish gold. He washed, then changed his shirt, thinking about Louise and how she had grown up into a lovely young woman. He remembered, too, the moment at the picnic when he'd held her almost naked body and felt it shudder against him.

In the drawing room Jeanne was pouring tea. She looked up with a smile. "I'm so grateful to you for selling the cattle, Martin, and for sending us the money."

While Louise and her sister sat side by side on the sofa opposite, he told Jeanne how he had visited their farm. "Your old headman has looked after everything quite well." Gently, because he knew it would bring back painful memories, he told them about their house and how Mapini the headman had kept everything tidy, and had looked after the fruit trees.

"We don't know whether to sell it," said Jeanne. "What do you advise?"

He took his cup of tea and walked to the window that opened onto the *stoep*. It was a different world here, not really Africa; more like the Mediterranean. "I presume you don't want to go back there? Then I advise you to sell. Settlers are going up to Rhodesia in great numbers so farm prices are quite good."

Jeanne nodded. "Then I'll sell. How is your own farm?"

He told them he'd had a good maize crop and expanded his vegetable production in the dry season. His herd of cattle had grown, with some offspring expected from the young bull that he purchased from Gerrit.

"And the gold?" asked Louise. "Perry said your mine has started producing."

He explained that the mine on the farm was working now. "My partner, Tom Ellsworth, also pegged a deposit in the Mazoe Valley. I took a fifty percent share, and it's proved, well...a gold mine!" He laughed. "That's how I can afford to return to England—for a visit, of course; I'll be coming back." His eyes were drawn to Louise, who watched him solemnly.

Jeanne said, "Will you meet Perry in Cape Town?"

"Yes, and my friends Helen and Robert Onslow—they're on the same boat." He looked at Louise. "I expect Perry will come straight here?" He saw her blush and turn away.

"I'll bet he's forgotten how to speak Afriks," said Pookie scornfully. "But Louise can teach him again. He's written lots of letters to her..."

"Shut up!" Louise turned on her sister sharply. "We don't want to talk about that. Mama, let's take Martin round the farm. It's quite cool now."

Jeanne and her daughters led him first to see the orderly rows of vines, then to the presses and the cellars, where huge oak barrels stored the wine. There were gabled stables with eight horses, and a rose garden sheltered from the wind that sometimes hurtled along the valley. Many times Martin found himself watching Louise, and admiring her lithe movements.

Supper was brief and quiet. Martin was sleepy after his long ride and three glasses of peach brandy, so he started to excuse himself. Jeanne suggested that next morning Louise should take him for a walk up the mountain before breakfast. She then made the girls go to bed, indicating that she wanted to talk to Martin alone. After they left, she poured him another brandy; as she gave it to him, she led him to the sofa, then sat beside him.

"I'm worried about Perry and Louise," she said. "I feel I hardly know the young man. Oh, I know he travelled with us to Johannesburg two years ago, but I was distraught after Gerrit's death and didn't pay much attention. When he came down to visit us Louise was ill and I scarcely saw him. You know him well, Martin. What do you think of him?"

He tried to hedge. "Has he proposed to Louise?"

"He's written to me, to tell me that he intends to."

"And what does she say?"

Jeanne shrugged. "She won't talk about it sensibly. I think she doesn't know her own mind. I know all mothers feel the same. Perhaps she's too young. I'm inclined to make her wait for a year or two. She's not meeting enough young men." She sighed. "How I wish Gerrit were here to advise me. What do you think?"

His forced laugh betrayed his discomfort. "You shouldn't ask me. I know Perry too well, and...how well does Louise know him?"

"On our way south two years ago he was with us for nearly three months, first in Bulawayo, then on the farm at Pietersburg, and on the treks. He was with us every day. They must know each other very well."

"Then, if they love each other, they should be allowed to marry."

She sighed again. "I suppose so. But I remember so well how I felt about Gerrit. I don't see the same depth of feeling in Louise. She doesn't wait impatiently for his letters. She doesn't talk about him as if he were always in her thoughts. I think her thoughts are elsewhere."

"Perhaps she's hiding her real feelings for him."

Jeanne paused for a moment. "I think she has a strong liking for you, Martin."

Embarrassed, he muttered, "I've noticed nothing."

"I have," she said quickly. "Whenever your name is mentioned she seems to light up. Now that you're here, you can find out what she thinks of you—and of your friend." She poured more brandy into his glass. "What do you feel about her?"

He thought carefully, wanting to evade her direct question. "She's a lovely girl, of course. But when I met her in Rhodesia, I thought she was... well, very young. Seeing her today, I realise she's no longer a child. But I haven't had Perry's advantage of getting to know her."

"You'll have an opportunity tomorrow." Putting her hand on his arm she added, "Most men of your age have married—at least in this country. Why not you?"

"I suppose I've been unlucky. And I've been so busy with the farm. It's habitable now, but it would be a rare woman who would go to live up there."

"I went to live with Gerrit..."

"You had already been married for...?"

"Twelve years. Yes, and a woman will go anywhere with a man she loves."

～∽

Next morning Martin was woken by the Coloured maid, who bore a tray with coffee. When she left, he quickly washed, shaved and dressed, then went out to the *stoep*, where he found Louise waiting. She wore a caramel coloured cotton pinafore, with an emerald-green shawl over her shoulders.

"Pookie is still asleep," she announced, her expression unsmiling. "We're going without her." She led him through the back garden, and along a path lined with vines, where they passed a few Coloured labourers who were walking to the farm buildings to start the day's work. The path became steeper and wound up the mountainside, through pine trees. The girl was silent until at one point she stopped and pointed out the view down the valley, now brightening in the morning sun.

He used the opportunity to start a conversation. "This place is so beautiful. It must have been difficult for your mother to leave and go north."

She looked at him with a hint of a smile. "I doubt if she thought much about it. She was in love."

"Ah yes."

"Have you ever been in love?" She looked at him intently. She had tied her shawl around her waist, and was leaning against a pine tree. Her chest was heaving from the exertion of the climb.

"Once—at least I thought so. It seems a long time ago." He decided he would not talk of Helen.

"In England?" When he nodded, she went on. "And only once in all your twenty-nine years?"

"Isn't quality better than quantity? Besides, for the last five years I haven't had many opportunities, have I?"

She regarded him quizzically. "There are some women in Rhodesia, aren't there? I was there. Do you remember that incident at the pool?"

"I remember it very well."

There followed a long pause before she said, "How is it with your only love—the one in England? Perry told me you wrote long letters to her. You gave him one to carry to England, and that's not long ago. Do you still love her?"

So Perry had given this girl a strong impression he was pining for Amanda. It was far from the truth, although he sometimes wondered if he still loved her. Five years ago he had enjoyed a brief moment of passion, but it lacked preliminaries, and there was no aftermath. Their correspondence was always rather stilted, and he guessed she had lovers. "We didn't have much time together," he told Louise. "I'm not even sure we were in love then. It depends how you define love..."

She laughed, mocking him. "You don't define love. You know it. You feel it. Why are you always so analytical?"

"Have you felt love?"

"Yes," she replied with confidence, moving from her pine tree.

He wanted to ask her for whom, but was reluctant for Perry's name to enter this conversation. "It's a complex emotion. I think men are foolish about it. We're too influenced by physical attractions."

Louise looked at him sharply. "Women feel those too." Now she was blushing.

"Yes, but you have the sense to recognise the difference between the physical and the emotional, and that emotional love is more important."

"Surely you can have both?" She turned and resumed climbing up the path.

He thought he was destined to follow the young girl up paths, unable to see her expression, but inflamed by the sight of her lissom body and supple movements. After another ten minutes the path ended at the base of a sheer granite scarp where there was a narrow shelf that seemed to hang over the valley. The view was stupendous, and they stood together to admire it. Louise pointed with a slender arm to the farm below and the features of the valley.

After a moment of silence, she sighed deeply. "You're right," she said, "I don't think I could leave this place easily."

"Are you saying that you're not in love?"

She shrugged. "I'm not certain." She bent to pick up a stone and flung it over the edge of the precipice. Then she turned to him and asked earnestly, "Do you find me attractive, Martin?"

"You know I do."

"And Pookie?" She was looking at him slyly.

"She's just a child."

"You thought I was a child when we met in Rhodesia, yet you kissed me. I was only a year older than Pookie is now..."

"I'm not proud of what I did. Anyway, you're not a child now."

She shook her head, her dark ringlets flying, her eyes shining. Martin took a pace towards her and pulled her into his arms. She buried her head against his chest, and he held her tightly until she sighed and lifted her face.

"When did you last hold a woman like this?" she asked, her voice straining because he held her so firmly.

"When I held you—in '93."

"No, not counting that. What about that woman—he said you met a friend of his—in Cape Town—and you flirted with her on the train—even though she was engaged.."

"Helen? That's rubbish." He squeezed her, and she gave a little cry of alarm. "God, you feel so...so fragile and light." He lifted her feet off the ground and she laughed.

"I'm actually quite strong." She tried to wrestle with him, and he allowed his grip to loosen before gathering her up again and whirling her round. Then he set her down and kissed her, holding her firmly against him. She returned his kiss, moving her body against him without inhibition. Then she pulled away and stood apart, smoothing her hair and skirt. "I suppose you think I'm wicked and flirtatious?"

"Why should I think that?"

"Because I'm supposed to be Perry's girlfriend."

"Will you marry him?"

"Not yet." She glared at him accusingly. "But that wouldn't matter to you, would it. Like your flirtation with that...Helen." She turned away and looked out over the valley. "I keep forgetting what he's like. It's nearly a year since he left for America. Sometimes I wonder if I was weak because I was distressed—my father had just died. Perry was very kind to me, you know—to all of us. He kept our spirits up." She turned back to face Martin. "What do you think of him? Do you think he would make a good husband?"

He shook his head. "The irony is that you think I'm fickle, whereas I think Perry is the man who seems to avoid commitment. When we first met, he struck me as a swank, and a bit of a gigolo. But I admit he seemed to change in '93, during that awful campaign against the Matabele. He seemed more sober after that—and not over-confident..."

"What about you?"

"Would I make a good husband? I'm not in the husband stakes, am I?"

She smiled, but the tone of her voice was unhappy. "You ought to be. I think you would make a good husband. You have a reputation for being dependable."

"That sounds rather boring."

"No, a woman likes a man to be trustworthy—especially when she has suffered from a man who isn't loyal." She looked at the height of the sun, squinting her dark eyes. "We should be going back for breakfast." She felt her ribs and smiled ruefully. "I think you may have cracked my ribs. You're very strong, and perhaps I'm weaker than I thought."

He touched her side gently. "I'm sorry." His hand moved up to her breasts, and she held it, clutching it to her heart, her head bent. They stood in silence, and then she heaved a sigh, turned away and hurried down the path.

An opportunity had passed. An enchanted moment had dissolved, and they were back in the mundane. He wanted to keep her with him, but she seemed like some ephemeral creature that he could not fathom. Hurrying after her, he called her name, but when she stopped, she looked at him in exasperation, as if he were a child wanting to know the contents of a present.

"What is it, Martin?"

"Why did you allow me...to hold you like that—to kiss you?"

"Allow you? Can't you tell that I wanted you?" She turned and ran down the path.

❧

Martin waited as the *Lismore Castle* docked in Cape Town harbour. He wore a navy blazer and carried a Panama hat that he waved to the passengers lining the boat's rail. He was trying to spot Perry, but could not, so he waited at the place where the gangplank came down to the quay. He had mixed feelings about meeting the American, knowing that he was about to propose to Louise. Yet if he tried to intervene, it would appear that he was a rival for Louise's hand. He suspected his feelings for the girl had more to do with lust than love; she was so mercurial and exquisite.

Perry was one of the first to come down the gangplank. He hailed Martin, "I say, you do look swell. Very different from the ragged settler I remember." After looking over his shoulder he said, "I'm looking out for Robert and Helen." He explained that they were fellow passengers, then drew Martin away and placed a hand on his shoulder. "She asked me all manner of questions about you—all through the voyage. But she's married now—you know that?"

They exchanged news until Martin saw the Onslows on the quay supervising the assembly of their pieces of luggage. They greeted Martin—a hearty handshake from Robert, and a proffered cheek from Helen. Her smile transformed her rather serious demeanour.

"Glad to see you, old boy," said Robert. "Thank heavens you survived those battles with the Matablele...."

"Perry told us you're about to leave for England," said Helen.

"A week from today. I'm staying at the Mount Nelson too, so I hope we can all have supper together this evening."

"Splendid idea!" said Robert. "Want to hear all your news. You know we're heading for Rhodesia? I want to take up where I left off five years ago."

As they walked to the carriages Martin asked after Helen's father.

"He died in July. I couldn't leave him before, even though he urged us to go; he was very dependent on me at the end."

He watched the Onslows depart in one hansom cab, while he and Perry followed in another. It was disturbing for him to see Helen again. In the intervening years he'd thought about her a great deal, despite hearing little about her and Robert. Seeing her now brought back the realisation that he had loved her, though whenever he tried to analyse the reason it seemed almost absurd. She was even more lovely now, with her usual pale complexion lightly tanned during the voyage. But it was more than her physical attributes that attracted him. He knew that she had a warm and sensual side to her.

No sooner had they started up Adderley Street than he told Perry, "The Venters are looking forward to seeing you again."

"Oh? So you've seen them." His friend was dismayed. "How are they?"

He described his visit to Franschhoek, but said nothing of his conversations with Louise. He handed over a letter she had given him for Perry, who tore it open.

"It says only that they are going to stay at Sea Point, with Jeanne's cousins."

"I gather you're expected to visit them there," said Martin, who could see that Louise had written only a few lines. "Doesn't she say she loves you?" he asked provocatively.

Perry replaced the letter in its envelope, glowering at him. "What have you been saying to her?"

He laughed. "She's grown into a lovely young woman. I was trying to protect her from this predatory American."

"You keep away from her." Perry was angry now.

"She doesn't belong to you. Nor to anyone for that matter."

"What's that supposed to mean. Are you telling me that you're free to pursue her?"

Martin shook his head slowly. "No, I'm not saying that. But if you leave an attractive girl while you go off to America before putting a ring on her finger, don't expect to come back months later and find her waiting patiently for you. We both know that she's too lively to sit pining at a garret window."

"Oh? What has she been doing?" Perry was red in the face, but he was prevented from further interrogation by their arrival at the hotel, where the Onslows were waiting for them.

☙❧

At supper Robert tried his best to make the atmosphere convivial. He and Helen had seen Perry's angry demeanour when he stepped out of the hansom cab, and here he was sitting silently, like an ill-omened owl, occasionally glowering at Martin, who had been telling them about life in Rhodesia. Helen wanted to concentrate on what Martin was saying, but she suspected a rivalry over Perry's girl and again felt pangs of jealousy that she knew were unreasonable.

"I'm concerned about taking Helen up to Rhodesia," Robert was saying. "When I was there in '90 it was hardly the place for a woman. What is it like now?"

"You wouldn't recognise it. Salisbury's a real town now, with brick and stone buildings—not many, of course. There are proper houses in the avenues. Bulawayo is even larger."

"And the Matabele? Is there any risk of them causing more trouble?"

Martin stroked his chin while he pondered how to reply. He did not want to alarm the Onslows, yet felt it was important that they should know about the risks. "Yes, I think the Matabele may rise up against the settlers. And not only the Matabele; there are rumblings among the Shona. Mind you, no one seems to pay any attention."

"Is it because the Africans resent the presence of the white people?" asked Helen.

"Yes, there is some resentment. But it's not only that. There are religious undertones that worry me. Perhaps 'religious' is the wrong word—'spiritual' would be better..."

"What do you mean," asked Robert, frowning.

"The *ngangas*—the witchdoctors—are telling the people to drive out the white men..."

Perry snorted derisively. "Witchdoctors? Do you mean those fellows who prance around in animal skins? You can't be serious."

"I am serious." Martin tried to stay calm. "It's difficult for the authorities to understand or control. The *ngangas,* and even more the *mhondoros*—the spirit mediums—are very reclusive. They live in caves and the locations are secret."

"If there was an uprising," asked Helen, "surely there are enough settlers and troops to keep the populace under control—presumably the natives are not allowed to have rifles."

"In essence, I agree," said Martin. "But those most at risk would be farmers and miners living in isolation—they're quite vulnerable."

Robert sighed. "Oh well, it won't stop us going there, will it Helen?" He turned to her and squeezed her hand."

"I wouldn't leave her down here," interjected Perry.

"What do you mean?" asked Helen angrily. "Are you suggesting that Robert can't trust me?"

"No, no." Perry's face reddened, as he became uncharacteristically flustered. "I mean Jo'burg isn't much better for a woman living alone."

Helen turned away and smiled at Robert, but Martin noticed a trace of fear in her eyes. Her husband decided to change the subject and proposed a trip to the seaside. "That would be marvellous," she said, trying to sound enthusiastic. "We could hire a carriage to get there. We could walk on the beach. Perhaps we could swim—the water's quite warm, I'm told."

"Splendid!" added Robert. "We can make a weekend of it—spend a night at the inn at Gordon's Bay. It's a delightful place; I stayed there when I went fishing last time I was in the Cape."

It was agreed that Robert would book the inn, while Martin would hire a carriage; it would have to be large enough for five people, because

Perry wanted to bring Louise, although Helen doubted that her mother would allow her to go.

☙❧

Perry drove out to Sea Point next day in a hired hansom cab. He found the de Villiers's house perched on a bluff overlooking the beach, surrounded by wind-twisted coastal pines. After paying off the driver he walked up the steep path to the entrance, feeling deeply apprehensive because Louise's letter had lacked any affection. Furthermore, he feared that Martin might have spoiled his suit. A Coloured maid showed him in and led him to the living room, where he found Jeanne with her cousins. She greeted him with affection, and introduced him to her brother, Francis de Villiers, and his wife Coralie. Francis was heavy set, with a large dark beard. His wife was pale and seemed frail; they were staying at the coast because of her poor health.

Louise and Pookie were on the verandah. The younger girl offered her cheek shyly and went into the living room, leaving them on their own. Louise looked ravishing in a dark green satin dress. She held out her hand to him, and made it clear that even a kiss was not on offer. Standing beside her, frustrated and awkward, he remarked on the magnificence of the view over the sea.

"You seem to have had a fine time in America," she interjected. "Was it difficult for you to tear yourself away from all those parties in Boston?"

"Not at all." He gave a small laugh. "As a matter of fact, I enjoyed myself more in England."

"Oh, I haven't heard about that. I suppose you saw Martin's family. Is his sister very lovely?"

Annoyed that within a few minutes Martin was featuring in the conversation, he replied, "Not beautiful. I would describe her as good-looking. She plays the piano with great accomplishment. I saw Martin's girl friend too—Amanda Jacobs." He advanced closer to her. "I've missed you, Louise. I've been longing to see you."

She retreated a step. "I still don't know why you left."

"I told you. I had to see my mother, and my family—after four years away. You knew that. Besides, my uncle wanted me to meet his business friends. He's thinking of buying another gold mine on the Reef. He wants to put me in charge."

"Why doesn't he make you manager of his own company?"

"I don't have enough experience for that—yet. But the new company will..."

"What sort of work will you be doing?"

"Managing Director. The investors gave me stiff interviews in New York and London."

"So you'll live in Johannesburg?"

He advanced again, and took her hand. "*We* will. I want you to marry me, Louise, otherwise I would not have come back here. I've already written to your mother. We'll have a big house in Jo'burg, with plenty of servants and a carriage..."

Her cheeks were flushed, and though she smiled, she did not appear as elated as Perry had hoped. "I'm not sure, Perry."

"But we discussed it before I went to America. You seemed sure then."

"That was nearly a year ago." She moved away. "I need to think some more about it."

He frowned in impatience. "Why do you need to think about it? Is there another man? It's Martin, isn't it? I know he went to see you in Franschhoek."

"He came to see my mother, to tell her about our farm in Rhodesia, and to advise us about selling it. Are you jealous, Perry, just because your friend came to visit us—at my mother's invitation? She wanted to thank him for selling the cattle." Louise realised that she had a powerful weapon to exploit, and introduced a little indignation into her tone. "Martin was very charming. My mother thinks he's a real gentleman."

He clenched his jaw to stifle an outburst against Martin. "I'm sorry. Look, Louise, we're all planning to spend a weekend at False Bay—Robert and Helen—you know, my friends the Onslows—and Martin. Will you come too? We'll ride horses on the beach at Muizenberg—we may even swim. We'll spend the Saturday night at the inn at Gordon's Bay. Robert says it's very comfortable."

Her face brightened as he described the proposal, but then clouded again. "My mother would never allow me to go alone with you."

"Not even with a married couple present?"

"She doesn't know them."

"I could introduce them..."

They were interrupted by Pookie, who had come to invite them in to lunch. She was smiling to herself, at first because the courting couple intrigued her, but even more when she realised that they were quarrelling. Perry had surely proposed to her sister, who evidently had not accepted, because he looked so gloomy.

When the family were seated at the dining room table, Perry wasted no time before introducing the proposition that Louise should come with him to False Bay. At first Jeanne was non-committal, asking about the composition of the party. Then she became doubtful, and finally shook her head. Her brother suggested she go herself as chaperone, taking Pookie with her.

Jeanne said, "No, I'm not their generation—but Pookie can go as Louise's chaperone."

Pookie wailed in dismay. "That's a hateful idea. They're all much older than me."

"You'd have a really good time, Pookie," said Perry, whose spirits had risen, only to be dashed by this reluctance from the young girl. "We're going to hire horses—and you like riding, don't you? We need another girl to make the numbers even..."

"Even with who?" asked Pookie with suspicion, frowning.

"With Martin, I suppose. He's the one without a partner."

"He doesn't want me to be his partner. He wants Louise."

"Pookie!" Louise glowered at her sister's indiscretion. "Anyway, Martin is very fond of you. I'm sure he'll look after you."

Pookie nodded ungraciously. "Oh well, I suppose I'll have to go."

చ~కా

Later that afternoon Perry and Louise walked on the esplanade. A strong sea breeze tugged at the girl's skirt, and Perry had to carry his straw boater in his hand. He had mixed feelings about the prospect of the weekend at False Bay. He would have opportunities to talk to Louise, but expected that Martin's presence would complicate matters, and might even dismantle his attempts to secure her agreement to the marriage.

"When we get back to the house," he said, "I'm going to ask your mother formally for your hand in marriage."

Louise edged away and looked out at the heaving sea. "I've already told her I want more time. We need to talk—to get to know each other again."

"What did she say?"

"She wants to talk to Francis and Coralie, and to my brothers..."

"For God's sake! Surely you don't need permission from your brothers?"

"You don't understand," she replied soothingly. "Not permission—approval. When my father died, Hennie became the head of the family." She skipped forward a few steps, then turned back to face Perry. "Don't look so mournful. We have plenty of time. We can enjoy ourselves before we have to consider serious things like marriage." She turned forward again, and skipped among the flagstones like a child. Perry thought she was like a beautiful butterfly, always escaping him.

CHAPTER 14
Excursion To False Bay

It was a fine day, with only a few clouds drifting past Table Mountain, and a brisk breeze whipping small white horses across the bay. The Onslows, Martin Russell, and Perry Davenport, waited on the verandah of the Mount Nelson Hotel. It was warm enough for the men to dispense with jackets, and for Helen to discard her shawl. Conversation was desultory until a small carriage drawn by two matching bay horses came along the drive and drew up at the steps. Francis de Villiers handed out his two nieces and made introductions.

Helen appraised the young girls, judging, somewhat to her discomfort, that they were exceptionally pretty. Their slim figures were evident in light cotton frocks; fashionable, but not too smart for the occasion, with bonnets to protect their faces from the sun. Meanwhile, Louise looked shyly but carefully at Helen, surprised that the Englishwoman was so tall, and her skin so white. Her serious demeanour was rather daunting, and she wondered why Martin was so enamoured of this woman, whose portly aristocratic husband was placing their bags into the larger carriage.

Meanwhile, Perry hovered around Louise, whispering that he wanted to sit with her for the journey to Muizenberg. Although he wanted her to come on this expedition, he was increasingly apprehensive of her reaction to Martin's presence. Would his erstwhile friend pay his attention to Helen, or would he compete for Louise? Both were bespoken, but Perry now knew that Martin would not be deterred.

Pookie stood to one side feeling uncomfortable. She wondered who she could speak to, and wished she had not agreed to join this excursion. She had been embarrassed when introduced as 'Pauline', having to explain that she preferred to be called by her nickname. The English couple looked rather superior, and she could not imagine having a comfortable conversation with them. Meanwhile, Perry was so besotted with Louise that he hardly noticed her. Only Martin had greeted her properly, enquiring after her health and kissing her cheek fondly. She could see him glancing at Louise, but at least he did not position himself next to her sister all the time.

The party said their farewells to Mr de Villiers, who wished them an enjoyable weekend and set off back to Sea Point. They moved over to their waiting carriage. It was large and comfortable, capable of taking six passengers and driven by a Cape Coloured coachman, who had a small black boy beside him as his assistant. There was some hesitation about the positioning of the passengers. Robert insisted that the women should not face forward; he had been taught since his youth that it was impolite for a woman to look into a horse's backside. It was finally agreed that Helen would sit between Robert and Martin. Opposite them, Perry was happy to be between Louise and her sister. Eventually they set off down the hotel drive and onto the road leading to Muizenberg, Robert commenting on the beauty of the passing scenery to his fellow passengers.

Martin caught Louise's eye, and she smiled slightly; then he glanced at Helen who was watching shrewdly. He felt a distinct jolt of jealousy seeing Perry sitting next to the young girl, the side of his body and his thighs touching her. He was also conscious of his own inconsistency; after all he had the woman he loved right beside him. So why should he have any interest in the girl opposite? It must be that Helen was now unattainable, whereas Louise was not yet committed; and the young girl was full of promise. His earlier judgment that she was immature had been overthrown when he realised she was now full-grown, well educated, and delightful to talk to. Besides, her Cape Huguenot culture was not so far removed from his own.

So this is the girl who has captured Perry's heart, thought Helen. She knew that Louise also intrigued Martin, so there must be something exceptional about her. She was undoubtedly pretty, but perhaps in little more than conventional ways. Her skin was lovely, soft and dark gold, complemented by her cream coloured cotton dress. She had an impossibly slim waist and enough bosom to excite men. Perhaps she flirted with them, or teased them; her smile was certainly quick to rise. Her younger sister was lovely too, taller than Louise, with long blonde hair, cupid's bow lips, and flawless complexion. There must be something about the Cape air to keep their skins so free from blemish, or perhaps it was all the fresh fruit. She thought there was something more openly sensuous about Pookie, perhaps because she was just past the stage of puberty; and she seemed less reserved than her elder sister.

"Have you girls been abroad?" she asked conversationally, her tone betraying her unease.

"We've been to Europe," replied Louise. "Five years ago—to France and Holland. We went with our grandparents, to visit the places that our ancestors came from. My father wanted us to hear the native Dutch and French languages, especially Dutch, because Afrikaans is now much different."

"And do you have any family there now?" She directed her question at both girls, attempting to include the younger sister in the conversation.

"Oh no," answered Louise again. "You see, they came to South Africa many years ago—in the last century—even before—so we've lost touch. And what about you, Lady Helen, where have you travelled."

"You must call me Helen, my dear. Well, I've lived in India, and I've been to several countries in Europe. Alas, I haven't been to America..."

"Then you haven't lived yet," interposed Perry quickly.

"And do you speak any other languages?" asked Louise.

"I'm afraid not....a little Hindustani."

Robert interjected with a laugh, "We British are very lazy about learning languages."

"Not all of us," said Helen. "Martin speaks French, and he has learnt the native language in Mashonaland."

"You never told me you spoke French," said Louise looking reproachfully at Martin. She added, in French. *"We could have talked to each other. We can now..."*

"Why would you want to do that?" said Martin.

"Hey, you two," said Perry, laughing uneasily. "We forbid the speaking of foreign languages in this company—don't we everyone?"

Robert and Helen nodded their assent.

࿎

The carriage drew closer to the village of Muizenberg, and the passengers could see a few holiday cottages clustered at the beach and on the overlooking hillside. A long straight beach stretched away to the east, past the small settlement of Somerset West, to Gordon's Bay. The tiny fishing harbour was in the opposite corner of False Bay, so named because it deceived mariners into thinking it was the entrance to Cape Town. The sun was bright, the breeze steady, and regular waves swept in to break frothily on the beach, throwing long strands of kelp onto the sand. A small hotel in the village served occasional visitors from Cape Town and there the party took tea and used the bathrooms. The girls changed into riding clothes and went out to the horses Martin had hired. He allocated them to the six riders amidst much laughter, and some apprehension, though all were experienced. Girths were checked, and the girls helped into their sidesaddles before the men mounted. They set off along the firm sandy beach, the horses exhilarated by the sea air and easily encouraged into a canter. Perry challenged Robert to a race and they galloped ahead, shouting to each other. Helen reined her horse back, and Martin turned to ride beside her.

"Is that saddle all right?" he asked.

"Yes. But it's a long time since I've ridden." She blushed. "Actually, the real reason that I'm going carefully is...I'm expecting a child."

He was taken aback, and for a moment could not find words. Visions of Helen and the corpulent Robert making love raced through his mind. "Then surely you shouldn't be riding at all?" he said with concern. "Robert didn't say anything to suggest..."

"I asked him not to make a fuss. And please don't mention it to the others. I must take it a little easy; but Robert's mother used to hunt into her seventh month."

They walked their horses in silence for a while, falling far behind the others. The lacy foam from the incoming waves spread out before them, in wide curves, and flocks of seagulls rose, complaining noisily as they approached.

"Are you happy?" Martin asked.

She looked at him sharply. "About the child?"

"No—in general."

"I suppose so—moderately." She paused, looking out to sea. "I still miss my father badly."

She reminisced about him, while Martin listened sympathetically. When she stopped talking about her father, Martin asked, "Is it because of your father that you were so equivocal—when I asked if you were happy?"

She looked at him with a steady gaze, and he looked back into her eyes. "You mustn't ask me questions like that—you of all people."

"I can, Helen, and I will. I fell in love with you. Have you forgotten?"

"Of course not! How could I forget? But I'm married now."

They rode on in silence for a while. Helen reluctantly found herself comparing Martin with her husband. Robert's interest in emotional matters was fleeting and awkward. He enjoyed the company of people and animals, and he enjoyed most physical activities, even though he was inept at them. This made her think of her husband's lovemaking, which was brief and energetic, and she was disconcerted when she started to wonder how it would be with this man riding beside her.

Martin had to restrain his horse who was agitated about separation from the others. "When will your child be born?"

"Not for another four months. I expect I'll go down to Johannesburg, or even come here to the Cape."

"That would be wise. Medicine is rather primitive in Rhodesia. Some white children have been born there, but..."

"Are there many women there? What is it like for them?"

"I'm not the best person to ask, Helen. I know a few—cheerful characters—a few nurses, and farmers' wives. They make the best of the life. I think hardship brings people together in strong friendships. We help each other..."

"And have none of them attracted you?"

He laughed. "Only in moments of desperate loneliness."

"And what are the hardships? "

"Oh Helen, so many. But you're used to a hard life. Of course you had good servants in India. We have servants too, but we have to train them ourselves. And language is a problem; very few of the Africans can speak English. I wish I was going to be there to help you."

"So do I! We've timed it very badly. But you'll be back soon, won't you?" She seemed almost to plead.

"In a couple of months. I have to be back to plant my crops in November."

They could see, far ahead, that Robert had turned back and was coming to join them. When he reached them, he was puffing from the exertion of his gallop, his round face beaded with sweat.

Martin said, "I was telling Helen that I have to be back by November to plant my crops. What will you do, Robert?"

"Get a job first—as a farm manager. I don't expect much pay—but I want to learn."

"That's a good idea. You'd have somewhere to live—and time to learn the language. In the meantime you can search for your own farm."

❧

Their carriage had gone ahead and was waiting for them at the small hotel in Somerset West, about half way along the coast of False Bay. They found a sheltered place in the sunny courtyard to eat their hamper lunch, washing it down with local wine, then rested on the verandah talking quietly through the heat of the early afternoon. At four, they set off for a walk on the beach, the six friends coalescing in different groups. Helen chatted with Pookie, and Robert earnestly questioned Perry about the mining industry, while the American glanced back anxiously at Martin and Louise, who had fallen behind.

Louise lifted her skirt above her knees so that she could paddle as they walked. "The sea's quite warm. I wish we could swim now. Why don't we? I suppose everyone would be shocked. I bet Helen would be shocked—she's quite a lady, your Helen, isn't she?"

"She's not 'my' Helen," he remonstrated, with a smile. "Haven't you noticed that she's married to Robert?"

Louise made sure that the others were out of earshot, then said, "I don't know what she sees in him. He's so large and...awkward."

"He's kind-hearted, and he has plenty of money."

"So she married him for his money?"

Martin grasped her hand and turned her, so that she could see his serious expression. "No, I shouldn't have said that."

She smiled archly. "Do you hate to see her married?"

He ignored her question. "I wonder what you'll be like when you're married. When is it to be?"

"I'm not sure about..." She looked up at him sharply. Then she disengaged her hand and skipped ahead of him. At that moment Perry looked back and was reassured to see her leaving Martin's side. He turned his attention back to Robert, and thus did not see Louise pick up a driftwood stick, and circle back to Martin through a shallow spread of wave.

"Does Perry know that you're not sure? He seems to have made up his mind."

"Yes, but I haven't." She laughed gaily, and playfully stabbed at him with the stick, fencing as if with a sword.

"No wonder he looked so glum when he came back from Sea Point. What reason did you give him? That you're too young?"

"Age has nothing to do with it!" she retorted. "I want to be sure I marry the right person. Oh, Martin, why are you so obtuse? Does it have to be spelled out for you?"

She started to write with the stick on the wet sand: 'LOUISE', then a heart; then a wave washed up and wiped away what she has written. She flung the stick into the sea and ran along the beach to join Helen and Pookie. Martin followed at his own pace, pensively.

Perry managed to disengage from his conversation with Robert. He dropped back to join Martin, and said, angrily. "Leave her alone!"

"She doesn't belong to you...yet."

"Why do you have to pursue other men's..." he paused to seek a suitable word.

"What? Other men's what?"

"Sweethearts—worse, their fiancées; even their wives. Why can't you find your own girl, and leave Louise and Helen alone?" He was so angry that his words seemed to tumble out in confusion, and Martin's slight smile was increasing his irritation.

"I'm not pursuing Helen", said Martin calmly. "As for Louise, she seems to be uncertain about marrying you."

"And that's because of you!" Perry shouted. He moved to stand in front of Martin, his fists clenched. "We may as well have it out now. I want you to stop."

"Don't be absurd, Perry!" Martin's voice was raised for the first time. "You can't forbid me like that. I shall talk to her if I wish."

Robert looked back at that moment. He saw Martin and Perry shouting at each other, and caught Helen's arm. "What on earth are those two up to?"

After a pause, while she watched the two men, Helen replied, "I suspect that Louise is the cause of the quarrel."

"Louise? You mean Martin...?"

"Yes, Martin too."

❧⊰

Martin broke away from his wrangling with Perry when Pookie called to him. He walked up to where she was examining a huge jellyfish that had washed up on the sand. It lay in a gelatinous heap, its tentacles spread towards the sea, as if entreating its medium to advance and take it back.

"Ugh," said Pookie, wrinkling her nose in disgust. "Imagine if you were stung by a big one like this—you might even die!" She stood with arms akimbo, her legs splayed. She had pulled up her skirt and tucked it into her belt, exposing long slender legs.

"It would certainly be sore, even if it didn't kill you." He was thinking that she was a lovely girl, and so different to her sister, at least in looks. Where Louise was so like her mother in appearance, Pookie took after her father. Yet she had the same spirited demeanour as Louise. He watched her poking the jellyfish with a piece of driftwood.

Meanwhile, Pookie was very conscious of Martin's attention; with her peripheral vision, she could tell that he was gazing at her. She was confused by her feelings for him, realising that images of him had flashed in and out of her mind for the last two years, ever since he appeared at the farm in Rhodesia. As she grew older these images had sexual connotations, and she had started to fantasise about him, imagining his arms around her, and his hands stroking her. When she lay awake at night she would touch herself and imagine him feeling her. Even now she felt his presence exciting her. Disturbed, she turned without a word to run along the beach.

❧ ❦

After the party had been walking for about an hour, they boarded their carriage. It had followed them on the road running parallel to the beach and took them to the inn at Gordon's Bay. Rust-stained fishing boats clustered in the little harbour. The inn was just south of the harbour wall, overlooking a narrow beach that ran for about fifty yards before petering out in a jutting cliff.

They were the only guests at the inn, taking all four rooms. Robert and Helen had the best room, with a view over the sea. Louise and Pookie shared another, and Martin and Perry each had one of the smaller rooms. With appetites sharpened by their ride and walk, they met for a supper of freshly caught lobster and grilled mullet. Martin and Perry were barely on speaking terms, and Robert tried to raise the spirits of the party by telling jokes. Helen was scrupulously polite, Louise smiled to herself, and Pookie was slightly tipsy on wine, her cheeks flushed.

After the meal they sat out on the verandah where they could see the lights of Simon's Town sparkling on the far side of False Bay. There was virtually no conversation; they were tired, and wary of the tension between the two younger men. Pookie was the first to retire, led off by Louise, and followed soon after by Robert and Helen. When Louise returned she saw only Martin and Perry who were sitting in silence; she backed inside without them noticing.

The two men sat without talking for a long time. Eventually, Martin left the inn by himself to smoke a pipe on the harbour wall. There was no moon, and the sky was brilliant with stars. He thought about his impending visit to England, and how good it would be to see his family and Middleton Hall again. He would see Amanda too, though he doubted they would renew their relationship after five years of only intermittent correspondence. His vision of her had faded and perhaps distorted.

An hour later, he returned to the inn and found the verandah unoccupied. He poured himself a glass of port from the decanter left on the sideboard in the dining room, then sat on a rocking chair and lit his pipe. He heard the door from the drawing room open and turned to see the figure of a woman come through the dining room. It was Louise, wearing a nightgown and a thin satin dressing gown. Her hair was loose and her eyes wide; she regarded Martin with a sardonic smile.

"I couldn't sleep" she said, "And you haven't even tried."

"I went down to the harbour for a smoke. Is Pookie asleep?"

"Like a log. I want to go down to the beach. Come with me?" She did not hesitate to watch him follow, but ran lightly down the stone steps that led to the beach, discarding her slippers at the bottom. The tide had ebbed leaving a broad strip of sand. She strode off towards the cliff at the southern end of the beach. It took Martin a while to untie his shoelaces and pull off his shoes. When he followed the slight pale figure of the girl, she was almost lost in the darkness ahead. He came up to her as she stood facing the sea, her head thrown back, gazing up at the stars.

"It makes me dizzy to see them all, so far away. When I was a little girl my father used to say that God had scattered millions of diamonds in the sky." With a sudden movement she put her arms round Martin. He bent to kiss her upturned face, and she unfastened the sash of her dressing-gown. When he stepped closer to her, pressing her warm body against him, she started to shiver and he held her tighter until she cried out. Then he sank to his knees, pressing his face into her, her warmth and fragrance invading his senses. His lips followed the curve of her body under the flimsy material of her nightgown. He put his hands up her legs, under the nightgown, slipping up the smooth skin of her thighs to her bottom, grasping her tightly and pushing his face into her. She leaned over him, then dropped to her knees in front of him.

"Oh, Martin. You could have me if you wanted."

"I want you. Surely you can tell." He put his hands on her shoulders.

"But not enough to want to marry me." Her tone had a sharp edge, as she fended him away. "You're always looking over your shoulder at other women. You want Helen—oh, you can protest, but I know. And you have some girl in England—that one you left behind. But I'm here! You can touch me, kiss me, make love to me. But I'm not good enough for you, am I? Am I too young? Too immature? Too...foreign? Well, if you don't want me, I'll soon find someone else."

"Even if you don't love him?"

She started to sob. "Perhaps I do love him." She scrambled to her feet. Martin tried to hold her, but she broke away and ran back towards the inn, clutching the gown to her. He walked quickly after her, but by the time he reached the inn, she had disappeared.

⤙⤚

At breakfast next morning the silences were protracted and awkward. It was obvious from the state of Louise's eyes that she had been weeping. Pookie was bored and petulant like a spoiled child. Perry was morose. Helen found the tension between Martin and Louise almost palpable and resented their selfish behaviour. Only Robert remained constantly cheerful, trying to cajole each of his companions in turn.

After the meal they returned to Cape Town in the carriage, sitting in the same formation as for the outward journey; but this time there was hardly any conversation. When they reached the Mount Nelson Hotel the Onslows and Martin got out and unloaded their bags, leaving Perry and the Venter girls to go on to Sea Point.

Martin kissed each girl on the cheek. To Louise, he said, "I'll call to see you when I come back from England."

"Please do," she replied coolly.

He nodded to Perry and watched the carriage until it passed out of the gates. Although he was ready to wave, the occupants did not turn back, and he was disconsolate as he turned to go up the steps.

Helen had been watching him. When she saw his expression, she turned away abruptly. I have no right to feel like this, she thought. Whatever has passed between Martin and that girl is no business of mine—

unless I can help him. But does he need advice? Can't he see that she's not right for him?

❧

Three days later Martin waited outside the hotel for the hansom cab to take him to the docks where he would board the liner to take him to England. Helen came out of the hotel lobby and stood beside him. "Robert had to go off to see someone about our journey north. He'll join us at the dockside. May I come in the cab with you?"

They sat side by side for the short journey to the quay, looking at each other, seeking an easy topic for conversation. Martin was overwhelmed with admiration for Helen's calm demeanour and her cool beauty. Her eyes were soft with sympathy for him, knowing that he was both excited by the prospect of returning home, yet reluctant to leave.

He was the first to speak. "So, Perry and Louise are going to get married. He came to tell me, late last night. It was all agreed yesterday."

She was surprised, not only by the news, but by the way of Martin hearing it. "I thought you two weren't on speaking terms."

"The reason for our dispute no longer exists," he said gloomily.

"And you're disappointed, are you?" Her tone was no longer sympathetic. "Do you wish it was you marrying Louise?"

He looked at her cautiously, warned by the tone of her voice. "I'm glad for Perry. They make a handsome pair."

"He'll make a better adjustment to her culture than you would." She sighed. "You surprise me. You've always been so decisive. You left England to go up to Mashonaland, and you started your farm. But you don't seem to know what you want when it comes to women—and love."

He was taken aback by her outburst of frank speaking. Perhaps she was right. He had not realised that his indecision was so obvious to others. "I know what I want. But unfortunately it's been unattainable. I can't ruthlessly follow my own ambitions. I can't try to sweep aside…"

"Other attachments?"

"Yes—other attachments. I fell in love with you, when we met here five years ago. But you were engaged to Robert; so I tried to behave as a gentleman—and I thought you respected that."

"We never had the chance…to talk about it."

"But you knew how I felt—I told you—that time in the stables at Palapye. You knew, Helen—don't deny it. But you were doing the noble thing, weren't you? Would you have broken your engagement to Robert?"

She shook her head. "It would have devastated my father."

"So now you'll live your life with a man you don't love?."

"Yes, Martin. I don't love him; nor, to be frank, do I admire him greatly." She paused and put her hand to her mouth, as if belatedly trying to stifle her words. Then she turned to him. "It would destroy me if you ever told Robert what I've said."

He laughed bitterly. "You needn't fear that. Men have a certain honour about such things."

"Some men do."

The cab delivered them to their destination. As they stood waiting for Robert at the quay, the great Union Castle liner loomed above them. Passengers and luggage were moving slowly up the gangplank. Voyagers lined the rails, waving and calling farewells.

"Your father must have known that you weren't in love with Robert, didn't he?"

She sighed. "He was one of the school that expects love to grow from co-habitation...and bearing children."

"So, does that mean we shall have to keep our true feelings hidden for the rest of our lives? Would it be better if we lived in different countries? Even on different continents?"

She lowered her eyes in the face of his vehemence. "That's not necessary. I will value greatly your loving friendship. And for that I need you as near as possible. You will fall in love again, I'm sure—as you fell in love with little Louise?"

"Listen Helen, three years after I fell in love with you, I met Louise and was attracted to her. I'd hardly seen a white woman in that time. But you're wrong—I was never really in love with her."

"There's something between you. Anyone could see—even Robert. Is it lust?"

He looked up at the huge liner that would soon take him away. "I'm not sure. She seemed so young and vulnerable, and Perry—so much a man of the world—wanted to take advantage of her. I felt I should protect her."

"Women can use vulnerability to attract men, sometimes subconsciously." Suddenly, tears started to stream down her cheeks. "Martin, I feel so deeply for you—more than you realise..."

She brought her confession to an abrupt halt when Robert joined them, his face red from exertion. "Sorry I'm late, old man." When he saw Helen's tears, he frowned and said, "I say, what's the matter, darling. He's only going for two months."

This brought a weak smile from Helen that reassured her husband. Abruptly, Martin kissed her on the cheek, shook Robert's hand, and strode up the gangplank. Within a few minutes he was waving to them from the rail as the liner moved steadily away from the pier. His last sight was of Helen standing tall and graceful beside her ungainly husband.

CHAPTER 15
Visit To England — September 1895

When Martin's liner docked at Tilbury on a grey day in late September 1895 his father and sister were at the quayside to greet him. Bentham Russell had changed a little in five years; he was slightly stouter, and had more grey in his hair, and he walked cautiously, depending more on his stick. Beth had grown into a handsome young woman of twenty-three, the bone structure in her face more pronounced, her expression more confident. They greeted each other with embraces, then stood talking while Martin's trunk was unloaded.

As they followed the porter to the railway platform, Bentham said, "Your mother has been ill. She's better now, but not well enough to make the journey to meet you."

"I hope it's nothing serious, Father?"

"We think not. Now, my boy, you look in fine health, doesn't he, Beth?" He turned to his daughter for confirmation. "And you're now a squire in your own right, eh?"

Martin laughed at the notion. "I suppose I am—of my three thousand acres anyway. It's not large by Rhodesian standards."

"And owner of two gold mines too," added his sister.

"Part-owner with Tom Ellsworth. Just as well I have the mines. If I'd relied only on the farm, I wouldn't have been able to afford this trip."

"And no more problems with the natives? No more wars to fight?"

Martin's expression turned serious. "Not yet. But there's trouble in the wind..."

"As there is almost everywhere. Come, we must save your news for your mother."

They had a first class compartment to themselves for the journey to Oxford. Bentham slept, his waistcoat unbuttoned. After making certain that her father was really asleep, Beth leaned forward to speak to Martin, in hushed tones, her eyes bright with the conspiracy.

"They're going to try to persuade you not to go back."

He shook his head. "I have to go back. They must accept that..."

"I understand. But you've made it more difficult by taking so long to return. Five years was too long, Martin."

"I know it. But there was a war, Beth. Well, at least *you* know I had good reasons."

"Yes, but they wonder if it will be another five years before they see you again—or perhaps even longer. Can you convince them otherwise?"

"I'll try. Thanks for warning me." He looked at his father who was snoring gently. "I seem to know so little about your life, Beth. I'm sorry you never married Peter Jacobs..."

She smiled ruefully. "In retrospect perhaps it was a good thing. I'm immersed in my music now. I've discovered that I'm a better teacher than player; I wasn't good enough for the top recitals. And now I have enough time to pursue my other interests."

"The suffragettes?"

"Not only that. Arguing for the rights of women in many aspects of life."

Their father stirred and Beth stopped talking immediately.

❧

At the Russell's house in north Oxford, where Martin's parents now lived, the family assembled in the drawing room before supper. Isabel Russell had lost weight through her illness, and her complexion was pallid and unhealthy. Arthur and Sylvia, who now lived at Middleton Hall, were also present, Sylvia expecting a third child and Arthur grown stouter and more florid.

"And when are you planning to contribute some grandchildren, Martin?" asked Arthur jovially. "Your sister shows no inclination to marry—you can't leave it all to Sylvia and me."

"Indeed we should not." Martin laughed. "But I've had scarce opportunities. Any eligible girl in Rhodesia is like a vixen to a pack of hounds. One can be trampled in the rush."

"Then you should use your time in England to advantage," said Sylvia, having heard rumours about Amanda and Martin in 1890.

"That wasn't the prime purpose of my coming back, Sylvia. And it would be a brave woman who would accept an invitation to return to wildest Africa with me."

Sylvia went on, her voice soft and drawling. "You make it sound as if it's a male preserve. When your friend Perry was here, he told us of a Cape Dutch family that he met there. He said he hoped to marry the daughter."

"And he told us about Lord and Lady Onslow's plans to join you," said Bentham, as ever impressed by the aristocracy. "I'm surprised Lady Onslow considers it habitable—from what you say."

"Oh, it's habitable, and Helen is an exceptional woman. But I have only a grass-thatched cottage to live in, and it takes an hour on horseback to reach the nearest town—and that's scarcely the size of Banbury. We have fever, and wild animals, and..."

Isabel cut in, her tone wearily ironic. "Then, for heavens sake, son, why are you so determined to remain there?"

He considered his answer carefully. "I suppose, Mama, it has an attraction that's difficult to explain. Like a woman who lacks conventional beauty, but has character in her face, and an interesting personality."

His mother looked distinctly unconvinced, and Bentham intervened. "When we met at Tilbury, you said that there's trouble in the wind. What did you mean?"

Martin sighed, he was weary from the journey, and felt a trifle resentful of the interrogation. "We've occupied a country which didn't belong to us. It was remote, of course, and sparsely inhabited—by people living in rather primitive circumstances. Even so, it was their country and we took it from them, largely through bravado, and with some force of arms. We had rifles and Maxim guns, while they had spears and *knobkerries*. But we don't belong there—at least not yet...It's rather like the pioneers in America. The Indians resented them and fought them."

"Then why did you buy a farm?" asked Isabel, as Bentham helped her to her feet. "I still cannot understand why you wish to stay there." She led them through to the dining room.

When they were seated, and a maid had served the soup, Isabel Russell reminded her son of her question.

"You see, Mama," he responded urgently, "I think we can share the country with the natives. We have a great deal to offer. In the part of the country where I live, the people used to lead miserable lives—many of them still do. We can educate them, cure their diseases, help them to grow better crops, and to raise better cattle..."

"And the 'trouble in the wind'?" his father persisted. "You haven't answered me."

Martin turned to him. "We've certainly angered some of the natives. I hear stories about the 'spirit mediums' telling them to drive the white men out of the country."

"What's a spirit medium?" asked his sister. "Is it a sort of witch doctor?"

"He—or she—is called a *mhondoro*, a person through whom the ancestral spirits speak—a sort of oracle. Remember these are very primitive people, Beth. Of course, some of us think they are self-serving charlatans, or they may be in a genuine trance..."

"What if the natives decide to follow the mediums' advice?" asked Bentham. "Can you contain them? You white men must be hugely outnumbered."

"We are, but we're still far superior in fire-power. We're well-armed and disciplined, and we can counter great numbers of the natives—as we did in the war against the Matabele in '93."

Isabel shook her head sadly. "It sounds a savage place. I hate the thought that you will return there."

⍤

After breakfast next morning Bentham Russell retired to his study to attend to his papers, and Isabel went to her room to rest, leaving Martin and Beth alone.

"Amanda is staying with her parents this week," said Beth quietly. "Wouldn't you like to see her?"

"My dear sister." Martin laughed. "Are you playing the same game as you did five years ago?"

"That was no game." She was annoyed that he should think her a frivolous matchmaker. She was so genuinely interested in his welfare, and hoped that if he and Amanda could renew their relationship, he might be less determined to return to Africa.

"I'm sorry. Of course I'd like to see her. But I thought she worked in London."

"She does; but there was a conference here, and she stayed on for a few days."

"I'll write a note. One of the maids can take it. Tell me about her. I wrote to her for a while, but then no mail could leave Salisbury for about three months—during the rains—and I suppose she thought I'd lost interest."

"And had you?"

"No. But can one sustain a romantic interest for so long without ever seeing each other?"

He wrote a note to Amanda, and Beth called a maid to whom he gave the note. After she left, Beth asked, "Did you tell her you would return to England? I think she lost hope."

He avoided the question. "Why hasn't she married?"

"Martin, dear!" She smiled, but was quite vehement. "You make marriage sound as if it's every woman's destiny. I assure you it isn't."

"No, I accept that. But surely it's an evolutionary stage in life."

"Yes it is; but for women like Amanda and me, evolution takes us to other interests."

"Presumably you would consent to marry if the right man proposed it?"

She looked at the clock and stood up. "Certainly. We might even propose it ourselves. We might even live with a man without recourse to marriage." Seeing Martin's expression, she added, "I can tell that shocks you. Don't ever tell Mama and Father what I said."

❧

Stepping up to the front door of the Jacobs' house, Martin's mind was awash with memories of his last visit. A maid received him and told him that Mr and Mrs Jacobs were out, but Miss Amanda was in the garden. She led him through the house to the drawing room where French windows opened out to the garden. Amanda, who had been deadheading roses, came across the lawn to greet him. She had changed a little; her figure was more voluptuous, her walk more measured, and Martin thought the blue of her eyes seemed slightly paler. They took each other's hands and Martin kissed her on the cheek.

"It's marvellous to see you again!" said Amanda. "How well you look—so suntanned and healthy."

"I always remembered you—pictured you—in this garden—but at night...so many times I..."

"I expected you would return sooner." Her tone was gently reproaching. "Five years have been too long." She took his arm and started walking him towards the house.

"I wanted to return sooner, of course. But it was impossible to get away..."

She interrupted him, squeezing his arm. "My parents will be here soon. Why don't we walk to The Parks."

They walked slowly, her arm in his. Autumn leaves lay scattered on the pavement, drifting in short movements at the whim of the breeze.

"Tell me about your life," said Martin.

"My life? Oh, it's quite exciting—and rewarding. When I qualified I was offered work at a women's hospital in London. But in the last year I've found myself drawn more into politics...with the Liberals. Most of my friends are Liberals." She looked up at him to judge whether he was interested. "You would be surprised to know how often we talk about South Africa. I have a small house in Kensington. Beth often comes there—she stays with me whenever she visits London. I have a maid to look after me and I'm quite happy. I feel at least that I'm a part of this world—a privileged part, perhaps."

They entered the gates to the park, then strolled along a path leading down to the River Cherwell. Amanda's tone quietened, as if she was uncertain of the new topic she was introducing. "I expected you would have found a wife. I've heard people say that men in the colonies usually take native women. But you wouldn't admit to that, would you?"

"I haven't done that—though others have. There are not many eligible white women there, and I spent only a few days in the cities of South Africa."

"And are you ready for marriage now? It was obvious—before—that you were not yet ready."

He smiled at her. "Yes, I'm ready now. But I have little to offer..."

"Except yourself, and you think that's not enough?" Her tone carried more than a trace of bitterness. "For some it would be enough. You may find a girl who will follow you to your farm in Africa, because she loves you."

"Would I be enough for you?"

"Is that a proposal? Are you asking me if I still love you?" She turned away, and when she continued speaking, Martin could scarcely hear her. "Perhaps you should come to one of our meetings in London. You might be educated by the discussion. And you could contribute from your experience in South Africa."

To Martin's chagrin, she steered him back to the house, walking in silence. They found her parents there and the conversation became general. When he left, he asked Amanda to tell him when her next meeting would be held. She was cool and somewhat distant when she said her farewell.

⊰⊱

Martin entered the meeting hall with his sister; about sixty people were seated in rows. At the far end was a stage, on which stood Amanda and a large woman, talking to three men. She waved to them and came down to take her seat at the front. Beth told her brother that the large woman was Mrs Jasper, who Martin judged to be in her forties. Behind her on the stage, the three men now sat in a row.

"Welcome to you all!" called out Mrs Jasper in a loud contralto. "This evening we will discuss a topic which is increasingly in the news—the situation in the Transvaal. We have three speakers." She turned for a moment to indicate a clean-shaven man on the left. "Mr Douglas Montreath is British, and lives in Johannesburg, where he has mining interests. He will talk about the case of the 'foreigners', or *uitlanders* as they are called by the Boers."

She turned again, this time to indicate the bearded man on the right. "Mr Webster is also British, but he will argue the case of the Boers, who he knows well, having worked as a veterinary surgeon in the Transvaal."

She turned a final time, to indicate the slight, dark man, who sat between the other two. "And finally, as mediator, and to stimulate discussion, we have invited Mr David Lloyd George, Liberal Member of Parliament. David, I leave the conduct of the meeting to you." She led the applause for the speakers, then stepped down from the stage to sit next to Amanda at the front.

Lloyd George stood up and moved forward to the lectern. He took out a single sheet of paper. "Before I offer the floor to Mr Montreath and Mr Webster, let me set the scene—as briefly as I can; and that isn't easy for a Welshman!" He waited for the laughter to subside. "I expect most of you know that the Boers are descended from the early Dutch farmer-settlers, who moved up from the Cape to the Transvaal about sixty years ago—to get away from the British! They settled on the virgin plains and started farming. They fought off the natives, and claimed it as their country—the Transvaal Republic. They set up their Parliament—called the *Raad*—and they have a President—Mr Paul Kruger—and ministers."

"But ten years ago, gold was discovered near Johannesburg, and before that diamonds were found at Kimberley. The great wealth offered by these discoveries have attracted thousands of foreigners—miners, engineers, lawyers, bankers, doctors. They now outnumber the Boer farmers, who call the foreigners *uitlanders*, which, in their language, Afrikaans, which is derived from Dutch, means 'foreigners'. They have accepted the *uitlanders* to do business, but they resent their ungodly ways and they refuse to give them the vote, and therefore representation in the *Raad*."

"But I go too far. Let me ask Mr Montreath to tell you the case of the *uitlanders*. He is, after all, one of them. Mr Montreath."

There followed a scattering of applause to thank Lloyd George and to welcome the new speaker. Montreath stood up and approached the lectern. He was tall, with a serious demeanour, and when he spoke, very slowly, he had a soft Scottish Highland accent.

"Thank you, Mr Lloyd George. As you say, I am one of the *uitlanders*, and have been for the last eight years. I am now a member of the Reform Committee in Johannesburg. Our aim is to reform the constitution of the Transvaal Republic to allow democratic representation. We pay taxes to the Government and we believe we have a right to vote on how much we should be taxed, and on how those taxes are spent. Until now, we have received obdurate resistance from the Transvaal Government. They are unwilling to accept our arguments. We have appealed to the British Government for assistance, but they have no jurisdiction in the Transvaal."

"You may ask, 'What can be done?' We have been asking ourselves that question. None of our arguments have been recognised. Should we leave? That seems unreasonable? We have settled in the country. We have a part to play—a contribution to make. Should we accept the status quo and remain unrepresented? Why should we? Can we bargain? We have already tried and failed. Can we use stronger means of persuasion?"

Montreath continued in this vein for a while, but did not define what he meant by 'stronger means of persuasion'. Eventually, Lloyd George stood up and started to clap, which stimulated the audience to follow suit. "We should hear the other argument—from Mr Webster. Sir!"

Webster came forward to the rostrum. He had a sheaf of papers but appeared to give them no attention. He started speaking quickly with no pause for introduction. "As Mrs Jasper told you, I have worked with the

Boers for many years—nearly twenty years—as a private veterinary surgeon. In order to work with them I learned their language, and I think I know them—the people—quite well. Let me start by telling you something about them."

"The typical Boer man is tall, fair-haired, and strongly built. His wife is also large and fair. Their ancestors are descended from those Dutch pioneers who came to the Cape in the seventeenth and eighteenth centuries. They are hardy people, used to fending for themselves in harsh circumstances. They're deeply religious; they read and follow the Bible closely, often interpreting the scriptures literally. They have fought the natives in South Africa ever since they arrived, and they have become very experienced in such warfare. They regard the native people as inferiors—'hewers of wood and drawers of water'."

"As Mr Lloyd George told you, many Boers left the Cape over sixty years ago and settled in the Transvaal. They regard the Republic as their land, free from tribute to any Imperial country. They see the *uitlanders* as—forgive me, Mr Montreath—a necessary evil, needed to exploit the mineral resources, but unworthy of any permanent place in their nation. Taxes they regard as a fair levy for the privileges of extracting wealth, and enjoyment of the protection of the Republic. Representation they cannot offer without being submerged by the sheer numbers of the *uitlanders*. To lose control of their destiny would be intolerable—unthinkable. That's the main issue: they are determined not to lose control."

When Webster paused, Lloyd George was quick to his feet, again leading the audience into applause for the speaker. When the noise subsided, he took the rostrum. "Ladies and gentlemen, we have heard two excellent expositions of the cases. Now I ask for questions, either to clarify your understanding, or to extract further knowledge. We are also open to further opinion."

He looked questioningly at the audience, but for a moment there was silence. Then Amanda stood up, as if she has been primed to start the questioning. "I would like to ask Mr Webster if the Boer women have any representation in their government."

A ripple of polite laughter followed her question. Mr Webster sprang up. "The Boer women are highly regarded by their men folk, for their endurance. But they do not have the franchise, nor can I honestly say that I ever heard one woman ask for it..."

Polite laughter again pattered around the audience, mingled with muted applause. A tall man stood up, near the rear, clutching a cap in both hands. "One option that has not yet been mentioned is for an imperial power to occupy the Transvaal—by force of arms if necessary—in much the same way as the Boers themselves occupied the country."

For a moment, Lloyd George pondered who was the most appropriate person to answer. He chose Mr Webster.

"You are right, sir. That is indeed an option, and I'm sure the *uitlanders* have considered it. But your comparison to the Boer occupation of the Transvaal does not stand examination. The Transvaal was populated by only a few thousand natives, living in grass huts, warring against each other with spears. In contrast, there are now perhaps one hundred thousand Boers living on productive farms, with large herds of cattle. They are well armed and well organised as a volunteer military force. They have a fighting ability that should not be underestimated. I have only to remind you of the debacle at Majuba Hill twelve years ago. Besides, what excuse could there be for an invasion. Is the lack of a franchise for the *uitlanders* enough reason to use force? Surely not." He returned to his seat, waving impatiently to Montreath to take his turn at the rostrum.

"I do not share Mr Webster's opinion of the invincibility of the Boers," said Montreath. "Nor do I accept that there is insufficient reason to use force, or better still, to threaten it, in order to make the Boers see the reason of our arguments..."

Lloyd George interrupted him. "As mediator perhaps I should not enter into the debate, but I cannot resist a question. Where do we draw the line in our use of force? If twenty thousand *uitlanders* is enough, how about five thousand? Does the fact that we have five thousand Germans in Britain without the vote justify Germany invading Britain?"

❧❧

When the meeting ended, Amanda went forward to congratulate the speakers, obviously warm in her friendship with David Lloyd George. Martin watched as he and Beth waited. Mrs Jasper led the speakers to meet a dignitary from the audience, and Amanda walked back to the main doors of the auditorium. Beth slipped away to leave her alone with her brother.

"I'm sorry to keep you waiting. Beth has tactfully left us alone. It wasn't really necessary, was it? Well, was that interesting?"

"Excellent," he replied, "but the missing voice was the British Government..."

"They would never deign to enlighten us with their policies at a meeting of this kind. Even Parliament scarcely knows how they think." She paused to glance back towards the stage, then back to Martin again. "So, you're leaving on Friday? When will you visit England again?"

"I wish I could say. Perhaps a couple of years from now. So much depends on the farm and the mines. Would you visit me?"

"I'd like to visit South Africa, but I wonder if I could spare the time. If I could, it might be to the Cape—I doubt I could make the journey to Salisbury."

"I could come down to the Cape to meet you."

She tried to sound light-hearted. "We'll see. And now I must go, dear Martin. Look after yourself," her voice thickened with emotion, "and try to come back soon." She reached up to kiss his cheek, and he held her firmly to kiss her lips. She broke away and gave him a look that was both puzzled and disappointed. Then she turned and walked hurriedly back towards the stage.

అ∽ఈ

CHAPTER 16
Return To Mashonaland –
November 1895

Martin's returned to Cape Town in November 1895. It was early summer, dry and sunny, the vines burgeoning. He took a hansom cab to call on the de Villiers house at Sea Point, hoping to get news of the Venter family. Mrs de Villiers received him and served tea in the drawing room.

"Of course you won't have heard, Martin. They have all gone to the Transvaal to plan the wedding. Louise is to be married at the farm—to your American friend Perry. They made the announcement three weeks ago. Her uncle Cobus will give her away, Pauline will be a bridesmaid, with her cousins Clara and Anna."

"When will the wedding be?" He felt a painful welling of disappointment and jealousy that he tried to suppress; he'd had his chance to marry Louise and lost it.

"They said in January. I'm sure you will be invited. Perry has to go to America on business, and wants to take Louise with him—to introduce her to his family."

After exchanging news about England and the Cape, Martin left to return to his hotel. On the following day he took the train to Johannesburg; there he took a hansom cab to the offices of the mining company where Perry was Managing Director. A secretary went off to find Perry, while he pondered the approach he should take. He sensed that he was being left out of the proceedings, but it might be a simple matter of letters missing him.

When Perry came into the lobby he greeted Martin with a handshake that seemed less than enthusiastic, appearing distracted, and avoiding Martin's eye. "We sent a cable to Middleton—announcing the wedding. It must have missed you. Never mind..... Er, you must come—it's in January."

"Of course I'll come to your wedding. I hope we can remain friends. And I regard Louise as my friend too." He added, "I'm sorry I can't stay longer now. I have to get back to the farm."

"How will you travel?" Perry asked hurriedly, his expression betraying concern.

Somewhat surprised at the urgency of the question, Martin replied, "I planned to go by train to Bulawayo. My horses are with a friend there. I have to get back soon—to sow the maize crop."

"So you won't see the Venters." Perry could not disguise his relief.

As soon as he heard that remark Martin realised that Perry feared he might take the coach to Pietersburg, and thence across the Limpopo, on the route through Fort Victoria. If he went that way he could call at the farm Elandsfontein. He decided to say nothing now.

"No," he replied. "How are they?"

"Well enough; you'll see them at the wedding. Now, let me take you to my house. You must be whacked after your journey." He turned to the secretary. "I'm taking Mr Russell home for lunch. I'll be back later." To Martin he added, "I'm my own boss, and I work hard enough to allow a couple of hours for an old friend."

They went in Perry's pony trap to an impressive bungalow in the Bryanston suburb, set in a large garden with luxuriant lawns scattered with beds of roses. A Coloured manservant helped to unload Martin's trunk, and an African maid took his worn leather grip. The two men sat on the verandah with cold beers, Perry smoking a cigar and Martin his pipe.

"It's an idyllic place," said Martin. "So near the city, yet far from the noise and bustle. I expect Louise will enjoy living here."

"Hmm. Pity about the politicking—that's far from idyllic. If only we could just get on with mining and making money—and get on with our own lives."

"What do you think will happen?"

Perry drew on his cigar, and sent out contemplative puffs of smoke. "There's a fight brewing...I trust you not to say a word to anyone."

"Of course. Where do you stand? You're an *uitlander*, but you're marrying into a Boer family."

Perry shook his head. "It sure is a dilemma. I'm staying clear of the Reform Committee and the activists. But now I'm being drawn closer to the Boers. I went up to Elandsfontein last week. The trouble is, they speak Afrikaans—I can understand most of it, but sometimes I miss the nuances."

"Are they politically active?"

"Oh yes! Show me a Boer who isn't. Not so much the older people. But Hendrik is fiercely chauvinist, and anti-*uitlander*...and that includes me."

"Against you? Why?"

"Because I'm a foreigner marrying his sister—defiling the blood. It's not only that; he dislikes me as a person too—because I'm not the brawny farmer type." He gave a hollow laugh. "I think he sees me as an effete intellectual."

"Well, you don't have to live out there with them—in the bushveld. What about the rest of the family?"

Perry shrugged. "They're pleasant enough. They have a sort of old world civility. Louise's uncle—Cobus—and her aunt Hannah, are charming. Jeanne is delightful, as you know, but Pookie is the typical younger sister—moody and jealous."

"And Louise?"

He looked at Martin guardedly. "Sometimes I still feel I scarcely know her. I can't fathom her temperament. She'll dance gaily around, charming everyone, but minutes later she can be sulky and stubborn, or her nose is buried in a French novel."

Martin laughed. "She's a woman, my friend."

The American stood up and threw the stub of his cigar into the garden. "Have you accepted that she's going to marry me?"

"Of course." Martin feigned surprise. "I always knew you two would reach the altar."

"She was keen on you."

"That was just flirting. But you'll have your hands full with a girl like her; she's spirited."

"Don't I know it." He poured Martin another beer. "I always thought I'd settle down with an American, or an English girl. But what about you? Did you see Amanda?"

"I did, but that romance—such as it was—is long dead."

❧

Without telling Perry about his change in plans, Martin took the coach to Pietersburg that afternoon, after despatching a letter to his friend in Bulawayo, asking him to send his horses back to Salisbury. When he reached Pietersburg he took a room at the Grand Hotel, which belied its name, being rather ramshackle. Leaving his trunk there, he hired a horse from livery stables and rode out to the Venter's farm, taking a change of clothes in his saddlebags.

As he rode up to the farmhouse, three dogs came rushing out, barking furiously. He calmed them with a few words of Afrikaans, which he now spoke well. Louise and Pookie were sewing on the *stoep* and looked up, shading their eyes against the bright sunshine. Pookie ran down the steps and reached Martin just as he dismounted. She flung herself into his arms, and he swung her round as she squealed with delight. He set her down gently so that he could greet her sister.

"This is a great surprise," said Louise, trying to be cool and poised, though her cheeks were flushed. "Did you see Perry?"

He kissed her cheek, his lips lingering a moment longer than politeness required. "I come straight from him."

She caught his eyes and gave him a quizzical look. "Come and meet the family."

He was received with more warmth than he expected. Ben had told the family many times how Martin had shot the lions while trying to protect Gerrit, and had been their support during the fateful journey to the Gwelo mission. Furthermore, they knew that Martin had cleared up the farm business, sold the cattle, and given the proceeds to Jeanne. These actions of fundamental honesty were deeply appreciated by the conservative Afrikaner family. When they realised that he spoke Afrikaans well, the warmth of his welcome was sealed. Nevertheless, the conversation soon turned to the conflict between the Boers and the *uitlanders*, and they asked Martin where Rhodesia stood. He explained that the settlers north of Limpopo had so many problems of their own that they would not become involved with affairs in the Transvaal, although they were interested onlookers.

"But what happens here directly affect you," said Hendrik. "Your trade will ultimately pass through the Transvaal. Therefore, who governs here must concern you."

"It does," acknowledged Martin, "but we cannot interfere—at least we should not. It's a domestic matter for your government. We could always use the Bechuanaland route if the Transvaal was closed to us—or even Mozambique for that matter."

"I wonder if Rhodes and Jameson see it like that," mused Cobus.

It was obvious to Martin that these Boers were deeply suspicious of Rhodes and the British. There were so many foreigners in the Transvaal that they were feeling overwhelmed. He was excused from the suspicion, since he'd settled north of the Limpopo, but they regarded Perry as the archetypal *uitlander*.

The Venters insisted that Martin should stay the night; there was a spare bedroom in a guest *rondavel*. He was able to have a hot bath and change into clean clothes. Later, after supper, he stood alone with Louise on the *stoep*. It was quite warm, and she was wearing a simple cotton blouse and skirt. She had tied her dark hair up for supper, and Martin was again captivated by her as she stood at the railing looking out into the darkness. Doubts about his intentions rose up in his mind, mingled with memories of holding her. He wanted nothing more now than to make love to her, but she seemed distant and preoccupied.

"Perry would be very unhappy if he knew you were here," she said at last. "You changed your plans, didn't you?"

"I wanted to see you again." His voice was hoarse.

She glanced over her shoulder at him. "We can't talk here. Come." She led him round the corner of the *stoep* to where it ran along the side of the house. There were no lamps here, and it was much darker. She stopped and put her hand on his arm. "I'm glad you came. I always feel I've missed chances to talk to you."

"The last time—at Gordon's Bay—you ran away from me."

"I don't want to remember that time. What will you do now?"

"Go back to my farm..."

"I know that!" She was impatient. Why did he always exasperate her? Was it deliberate? "I mean, what will you do with your life?"

He smiled. "Do you mean life without you?"

"I mean, you should find a good woman and marry her."

"Spoken like a woman whose head is ringing with wedding bells," he replied, laughing.

"I'm serious, Martin. Don't mock me." She reached forward, putting her arms round his neck. They kissed passionately, but when she pulled away from him, she muttered, "Oh God, what am I doing," then ran along the *stoep* and composed herself before entering the house.

Pookie was in the living room and noticed her sister's distress. She watched with a mischievous smile as her sister went to her room; then she walked out to the *stoep*. At first she could not find Martin, but, walking round the corner, saw him standing in the dark lighting his pipe.

"What happened? I saw Louise come in, looking like a cat that's lost the cream."

"It was nothing." He talked to her for about ten minutes, asking her about her horses. She seemed to change her manner, becoming more mature, though she was only sixteen. She was slightly taller than Louise, and appeared to be a young woman now. Her long blonde hair was plaited and wound round her head in a quite sophisticated style. Her bosom was well-developed, swelling much more obviously than her sister's. Her skin was tanned and unblemished.

When he went inside with her, he excused himself from the company, pleading that he was tired. He was given a hurricane lamp and he strolled in the light of a half moon the thirty yards from the farmhouse to the guest *rondavel*—one of three that stood in a group under a huge thorn tree. He imagined he would sleep here if he came down to the wedding. Thinking about Louise's impending marriage depressed him. Feeling weary, he quickly took off his clothes, washed in the china basin, then blew out the hurricane lamp, and crawled naked under the mosquito net and into the bed.

He was back in Africa again. The Cape was a different country, and Johannesburg was all stone and steel; but here was the real Africa. The walls of the *rondavel* seemed to radiate heat, and the thatched roof was alive with myriads of insects. A cricket somewhere in the room started a harsh persistent chirping. In the big acacia tree an owl hooted, and he remembered the Bantu suspicion that if one settled on the roof it portended death.

He did not fall asleep immediately, his thoughts revolving around Louise and their conversation. She had bewitched him again, as if she were some sort of evocation of his lust that kept returning to haunt him. It was surely too late now; imagine the repercussions if she broke off her engagement, or if they eloped. But it would be heaven to have a girl like that in your bed every night, and to add spice to every moment of your life.

He was almost asleep when the door opened with a slight creak. Looking up he saw a woman's figure silhouetted against the moonlight for a moment. Struck first by his carelessness in not latching the door, he then realised that it must be Louise. The door shut with a click, and the room was enveloped in dense darkness again. Waiting, his pulse racing, he heard his name whispered softly and felt the mosquito net lift. She climbed onto the bed as he made way for her; she wore a thin cotton nightdress, and her warm scent wafted over him.

Without speaking, she touched his naked body at the shoulder, then traced down with her fingertips while his body tensed with excitement. He fumbled for her, finding the hem of her nightgown, and tried to lift it. She pushed his hand away and he waited, sensing that she was sitting beside him, hearing a rustle as she took the garment over her head. He reached out and touched her smooth skin, damp with perspiration. They lay down facing each other, skin to skin. He groaned with the ecstasy of the feel of her, soft breasts pressing his chest, and smooth warm thighs. Her feet pressed against his shins, and her hair fell on his face, drowning him in her scent.

This is madness, his thoughts roared. I am the guest, and I'm lying here making love with a woman engaged to marry my friend. His heart thumped as he thought that at any moment Cobus, Hendrik or Ben could come to look in on him—perhaps they would have seen her come to his *rondavel*. They would find him *in flagrante*. Not likely, he reassured himself, judging by the amounts of peach brandy they'd drunk; they would scarcely make it to their own beds.

He murmured her name, his voice muffled against her; she replied only with his, whispered hotly in his ear, but said no more. When he looked down he could not even see her face in the dark, let alone her eyes or her expression. He bent to kiss her deeply and felt excitement surge through her, making her body arch and her arms tighten round his chest. He stroked her, and her thighs spread for him. He moved over her, keeping his weight from pressing on her.

"I love you," he said, wanting to offer some confirmation that this was not mere coupling in the throes of lust. When she did not reply, he asked, "Please tell me. Do you love me?" He heard a sobbed 'Yes' of acquiescence in the depths of his ear, and the movements of her body were all invitations.

He felt no obstruction, nor did she wince in pain, and he wondered whether Perry had already preceded him. They moved urgently, locked together from mouths to hips. When he could contain himself no longer, he tried to pull away but she bound him fiercely. Moments later, her body lurched and she made a sound close to his ear, a stifled cry as if surprised.

They lay side by side in silence, regaining their breath. He stroked her side, his palm sliding over her wet skin. When he touched her breasts they were larger than he expected.

"Louise?" He was suddenly overcome with doubt. Surely not ...?

"Couldn't you tell? It's me—Pookie." She giggled and put out her hand to touch his chest.

Instinctively, he pushed her away. "You tricked me! I thought it was your sister."

"You wish it was her? Are you disappointed?"

The enormity of what had happened overwhelmed him. Here was a sixteen year old girl he'd just ravished like a man possessed. "I might have made you pregnant, Pookie."

"No. I know about that sort of thing. Don't forget I've lived on farms all my life."

"You're only sixteen."

"Yes, but many girls my age marry and have children. The legal age for marriage in your country is twelve. It wouldn't be made so young if girls were not ready, would it?"

"But we're not married—and you're not even my sweetheart."

"No, but I could be. Please, I'm not too young, Martin—at least not physically. You enjoyed loving me a few minutes ago, didn't you? Are you saying that you wouldn't enjoy it if you knew it was me?" She put her hand down between his legs and held him firmly, and when he tried to disengage her, she prevented him. "You see," she murmured, "I can feel you're becoming excited again."

"Pookie," he remonstrated, "someone could come any minute and find us."

"It's not possible. I put sleeping draughts in their drinks—*Ouma's* special stuff. They're all fast asleep."

"And the servants?"

"They're always asleep at this hour—even the night watchman, who ought to be awake." She laughed.

She sat astride him, bending forward to kiss his mouth. Her breasts brushed against his chest, and he could not resist touching her lithe body, then cupping his hands on her breasts. She wriggled onto him with amateur thoroughness, although he knew he should resist. His eyes were now accustomed to the dark, but he could see hardly anything. His fingers seemed ultra-sensitive, tracing the line of her spine, and moving up to her shoulders and slender neck. Her movements became more and more urgent, until he felt she was urging a bucking pony.

Later, lying beside her he heard the owl hoot again, and far away a jackal howled. Pookie ran her forefinger down the hairs on his torso, which were drenched with sweat, then put her mouth to his ear. "You enjoyed that, didn't you? I shan't tell anyone. My mother would kill me. Louise would hate me. It'll be my secret—and yours. You won't tell anyone, will you?" She kissed him. "I don't want to go. I wish I could stay here forever making love to you."

She left as quickly as she came, reaching down to the foot of the bed to recover her nightgown, and when he tried to restrain her, she slipped out of his grasp. He heard only a soft rustle as she pulled on the garment. Then a rectangle of moonlight appeared as the door opened, and she was gone.

Exhausted, he fell asleep. He woke at dawn, and while dressing noticed a bloodstain on the rumpled sheet. So she was a virgin, he thought, and she wanted me to be the first, not some future husband. He hoped he had done her justice. The sheet could not be left, because the stain would be seen by the housemaids. There was no place to wash it, and he knew that the blood would be almost impossible to wash out, so he folded the sheet and placed it at the bottom of one of his saddlebags.

He had to leave after breakfast, in order to reach Pietersburg for the noon coach. He fed his horse, packed his saddlebags, washed and walked over to the house. The family were already gathering for breakfast, the men complaining sheepishly of sore heads, the women still in the kitchen. Jeanne came into the dining room first, bearing a large bowl of porridge. Louise followed her with a jug of cream, and Pookie with two bowls of sugar. As Louise placed the cream on the table, Martin caught her eyes, and thought he saw signs that she had been crying. He smiled at her, but she did not respond. Pookie brought one of the sugar bowls to him, and as she leaned forward to put it on the table, she brushed against him, and he caught a faint bouquet of her scent. When he looked up at her she smiled demurely before lowering her eyes.

The women sat down and ate with the men, but there was little conversation. Hendrik and Ben discussed with Martin a visit they would make to Gerrit's farm in Rhodesia, to prepare its sale; they asked for his help in choosing an agent in Salisbury. When the meal was over, Martin said his farewells, shaking the men's hands and kissing the women on the cheek. Louise was the only one to come out with him.

"Louise..." he started, when they were out of earshot of anyone on the verandah.

"We can't talk any more," she said hurriedly. "You have made your decision, and I mine. We may regret forever what we're doing." She kissed his cheek, turned and ran back to the house.

"We must talk," he called after her, wanting to follow her, but he knew he could not. He stood watching her dash up the steps. She did not even look back, and disappeared inside. His spirits lifted for a moment when he thought she had come out again, but it was only Pookie, who waved to him. He waved back, then mounted and trotted up the road to Pietersburg.

❧❦

In December 1895, at his farm 'Long Valley', Martin wrote a letter to his parents and Beth. He sat on the verandah, with his ridgeback dog, Lolloper, at his feet.

'My dear Mama, Father, and Beth,

'Well, the maize is sown at last, and now I can sit for a while to write a long overdue letter—too long overdue; my last was from Johannesburg. The farm is in quite good order. My men, with Tom keeping his eye on them, have done well. Petrus, my servant, had the house clean. My ridgeback dog Lolloper is in good health. Chandra is eager for canters into town.'

'The rain came early this year, which helped me to work the fields to prepare for sowing. It came again last night, and I'm confident that the maize seed will germinate well. After that, I depend on heavenly largesse to bring regular showers.'

'The gold mine at Mazoe prospers, but Tom is worried about the labourers. He says they have become surly and unreliable. He has not been able to find out why, but other miners report the same truculence. I know the language much better than Tom, so I should ride around with my ears flapping.'

'My friends Robert and Helen Onslow are here now. He has taken a position as manager for an indulgent landowner—so that he can learn the business of farming in Africa. The house on their farm is not of a high enough standard for Helen, so they live in a small cottage in Salisbury, where I see them at least once a week...'

❧❦

A few days later Martin rode Chandra up to the Onslow's cottage in Salisbury. It was built of red brick, with a thatched roof, and stood in a large garden among *msasa* trees. A young African boy was slashing the grass of the rough lawn with a long iron blade, his bare torso glistening with sweat. Helen came out to greet Martin as he dismounted and hitched the reins so that Chandra could graze.

"How are you—both!" He kissed Helen on the cheek, looking at the bump that seemed larger each time he saw her.

She smiled wryly. "We're both well enough—though I'm just a trifle bored."

Robert emerged from the house to greet Martin. His shirtsleeves were rolled up, his face and arms pink from sunburn. They shook hands, and Martin enquired after his maize crop.

"That rain last night was a Godsend," said Robert.

"Come on, you two farmers!" said his wife. "You need a drink. No beer yet, but I can give you lemon squash."

As the three friends were settling down on the verandah a man on horseback rode up, unhitched the gate, and dismounted in the garden. Robert went out to greet him; it was his employer, Peter Wilkins. He came onto the verandah with Robert, took off his hat and nodded to Helen and Martin. He was in his late forties, thin and stooped, with a drooping moustache and a sallow complexion.

"Helen, Martin, good day to you. Have you heard about the recruiting?" Seeing Martin shake his head, he went on. "The Doctor's recruiting—only experienced men..."

"What for?" asked Martin hurriedly, his heart sinking, as he remembered the Doctor's scheming two years ago for the Matabele campaign.

"It's a bit mysterious," replied Wilkins. "I was hoping you might know. I heard it's to strengthen the armed force on the border in case there's trouble in Johannesburg. We might have to help the British down there, if there's trouble."

"Huh, that sounds just like Jameson," grumbled Martin. "Any excuse to rattle the sabres."

"Yes. A show of strength perhaps," Wilkins seemed to share his scepticism. "Keeping Johnny Boer in his place."

Martin laughed bitterly. "He'd better realise that the Boers are not the same as the Matabele."

"Will you go? I would, if it weren't for my health. I'll never be the same again after that last bout of fever."

They all looked at Martin, knowing he had been an officer in the Matabele War. "I want to hear Jameson's reasons first," he said. "I missed one entire cropping season in '93..."

"And you, Robert?" asked Wilkins. "Don't worry about the farm. I'll keep an eye on it—and your missus."

"Where would we go?" Robert's large round face was full of anxiety. "Where would we live?"

"They might send you anywhere," replied Wilkins, and Martin suspected that he was enjoying his employee's discomfort.

Robert looked unhappy, but tried to hide his feelings in front of the other two men, as they discussed the alternatives that the Administration might chose for people like Martin and Robert, if they were called into service.

ॐ❧

Next day, Martin and Robert rode together up to Dr Jameson's office; he was still the Administrator of Rhodesia. They were shown in, and found the little doctor as dapper as ever, his eyes glinting as he greeted the two visitors. With him was Major Jack Heany, a tough, stocky, moustached officer, wearing a khaki uniform. He was the commander of the British South Africa Police, the para-military force in Rhodesia.

"We want you to volunteer," said Jameson, without preliminaries. "I know you don't want to leave your farms, but the crops are sown, and your labourers can keep the fields weeded while you're away. Russell, I want you to lead a section, and Onslow, you should be his deputy. By the way Onslow, it'll be easier for volunteers to get title to land, I can promise you—in fact it's virtually guaranteed."

"May we know where and why we're going?" asked Martin with deep suspicion.

Jameson sighed. "I'm worried about the Matabele. There are rumours that they're trying to form an alliance with the Sechuana..."

"But the two tribes are sworn enemies!" Martin exclaimed.

"I know, I know. But strange things can happen."

"You haven't said where we'll go," said Robert diffidently.

Heany spoke for the first time since the opening pleasantries. "We can't tell you now, but it will probably be somewhere in the Tuli area. Don't mention that to anyone."

"And who will look after the women here—like my wife—if there's trouble?" asked Robert.

Jameson gave him a little smile. "The men who are left behind—those who are too old, or in positions from which they cannot be spared. Don't worry about Helen."

"Doctor," said Martin, "I expect you've heard the stories going round about the *ngangas*."

"Yes, yes." Jameson nodded impatiently. "But the natives dabble in that sort of thing all the time. Do you have any real concerns about it?"

"Yes," replied Martin emphatically. "I think it would be unwise to dismiss what these mediums are saying. They have a powerful influence over the Shona people..."

Heany interrupted him. "So what would you propose?"

"That you be wary of stripping the country of all its able-bodied men..."

"Hah!" said Jameson, with rising irritation. "Do you really think the Shona would rise up against the whites?" He snorted. "Not the Shona, of all people. I don't believe it! The Matabele perhaps, but never the Shona. You're far too cautious, Martin. This empire was not built on caution..."

Martin stood up angrily. "Was I cautious when I volunteered to cross the Shangani to go to the aid of Wilson's patrol?"

For a moment, Jameson was taken aback, and when he spoke, there was none of the usual bombast in his tone. "Did you? I didn't know that."

"Ask Forbes." Martin turned angrily and left the Administrator's office. Robert was left gaping, and even Major Heany was surprised.

∂∽∾

That evening Martin sat at home with Tom Ellsworth, drinking whisky. It was raining, and rivulets flowed off the thatched roof like a curtain outside the verandah. Mosquitoes whined in the humid air, and both men had rubbed citronella oil on any exposed skin to deter the insects. They were trying to generate a deterrent cloud of smoke from pipe and cigar.

"I have to go," said Martin, "though I have grave doubts about the Doctor's motives. There's some nefarious plan being hatched. Helen begged me to take care of Robert..."

Tom laughed. "So that decided you!"

"He wants to go so that he can get title to a farm. As usual, the Company is bribing the settlers with promises of land."

"Yes, but they keep their promises. Can you afford to be away at this time of year?"

"Hardly. But we may be back in time for the main weeding. And I trust you to keep an eye on my workers."

"That I will, mate. But I fear that I may have the same difficulties with them as we're having at the Mazoe mine. I don't want you to return to a crop full of weeds, but..."

"I must take that risk." Martin paused to re-light his pipe. "You know, Tom, I don't share the settlers' idolisation of the Doctor and Rhodes. Jameson has a wild streak—he's not a statesman. And as for Rhodes—well, frankly I don't trust the man."

"Why not?"

"I met him in Bulawayo when we got back from the Shangani debacle. I thought his concern about the men who died—white and black—was rather superficial. Mostly he seemed obsessed with the enlargement of his empire."

"They say he's a man of vision."

"I concede that," said Martin. "But his vision obscures a sensible view of the native people..."

"So what should he have done about them?"

"Realised that they have rights to the land. For heaven's sake, they may be primitive and uneducated by our standards, but we should be circumspect about trampling all over them. If we abuse our power it's bound to feed their resentment. And it's all very well for people like Jameson to say 'We'll go into *laager*'. It's not simple for isolated farmers to do that."

☞✍

The following Saturday a polo game was played in Salisbury. A crude marquee had been erected to one side of the field, and in its shade sat a group of about twenty men and women, while some other men, and a few African servants and grooms were scattered along the sidelines. Martin and Robert were playing in opposing teams. Among the spectators were Doctor Jameson and Helen. In the second chukka, Martin and his opposite number were riding hard for the ball when Robert clumsily crossed their path. It was an illegal and dangerous move, and they collided. Martin's pony fell heavily, throwing him to the ground, where he lay clutching his arm. Players and spectators quickly gathered round, among them Robert, his large face red as an apple with embarrassment and the exertion of the game. Jameson pushed forward, bent over and examined Martin's arm, while he winced in pain.

"It's fractured. Better get to Dr Fleming; he'll do a good job of setting it. I'm out of practice."

"I'm most frightfully sorry, old man," said Robert, frowning deeply. "Couldn't keep that damned pony under control."

Martin was trying to smile, but grimaced with pain. "Don't worry, Robert—these things happen. How's my pony?"

Someone answered, "Only winded—seems all right. Barlow's pony isn't it. He's leading it off now."

Jameson muttered to the disconsolate Robert, who was hovering nearby. "We must be thankful it wasn't his neck that was broken!"

Seeing his deep distress, Helen took Robert's arm, while a couple of bystanders helped Martin into the Onslow's trap. Helen drove to the little grass-thatched hospital with Robert riding alongside. The young Irish matron helped Martin down, and Helen noticed from the girl's eyes that she was obviously fond of him. She sent an African messenger to fetch Dr Fleming, and they all helped Martin into the doctor's surgery. The matron removed his shirt and started to clean up his arm, gently removing the red mud and dust from shoulder to fingertips. Dr Fleming soon arrived, a stooped Scot, with straggling Dundreary whiskers. He started to examine Martin's arm.

"A self-inflicted wound, eh, young man?"

"Hardly, doctor..." Martin protested, laughing.

"Inflicted by me, I'm afraid," said Robert contritely.

"For goodness sake, Robert, it was an accident."

"Well, it's a nasty fracture," Dr Fleming announced. "I'll give you some morphine while I set it. You'll have to stay here overnight."

Martin asked the doctor whether he could become addicted to morphine, having heard about wounded Civil War soldiers in the United States, but Fleming assured him that it would be a problem only if taken regularly. After thanking the Onslows for bringing him to the hospital, Martin asked them to stable Chandra for the night.

Fleming looked up over his spectacles, and said severely, "No riding tomorrow, young man. Not for a week, at least. And it'll be six weeks before you can use the arm properly."

෧ঌ

CHAPTER 17
The Jameson Raid — December 1895/January 1896

Martin sat astride Chandra, his arm in a plaster cast, supervising a gang of about twenty labourers hoeing the weeds out of his maize crop. He caught sight of the Onslow's pony trap coming along the dirt road from Salisbury; Helen was driving and Tom Ellsworth sat beside her. After giving some instructions to his headman, Martin cantered up to the corner where the rutted road curved round the maize field.

Helen reined in the pony, and called. "Tom kindly offered to escort me out here."

The Australian explained, "I wanted to check the work at the mine, and my best horse has been commandeered for the expedition."

"So they've left already? Robert too?"

"Yes," replied Helen, without enthusiasm. "He's full of excitement, of course. I'm staying with the Carters—they wouldn't allow me to live on my own, though I'd much prefer it."

Tom was watching his partner shrewdly. He had suspected for some weeks that there was something between Martin and Helen. The Englishman wore a slight smile as he watched the girl, and his eyes had taken on a new liveliness.

"He said he'd be back for Christmas," Helen went on, but it was evident from her tone that she doubted it.

"Don't count on it," said Ellsworth. "Now I must get on to the mine."

Martin told him to take Chandra, and dismounted to hand over his horse. He invited Ellsworth to lunch, and the Australian mounted Chandra to ride off to the mine at the far end of the farm.

Martin unhitched the pony and let it graze in the sparse but succulent grass among the *msasa* trees, while Helen sat on a fallen tree in some shade. She took off her large hat and wiped her forehead with a handkerchief, while Martin's dog Lolloper went to sniff her, then settled at her feet.

Martin had been watching her; she looked up to catch his eye and smiled shyly. "This farm seems so peaceful," she said. "I think it has a lot to do with your presence. I feel safe here with you." He sat beside her and she touched the plaster cast on his arm. "How is it?"

"Itchy! Just a nuisance. But Robert did me a favour."

"By saving you from the expedition?"

"No, by giving me the chance to be alone with you."

Her cheeks flushed. "Don't say that, Martin; it may be bad luck. Besides, I won't be able to come again. You know how people talk. I don't want Robert to come back and hear gossip about us."

"You can trust Tom—he's not the gossiping type." After talking about the farm for a while, Martin suggested they walk up to the house. He looked down at her swollen shape. "Would it be too far for you?"

"Not at all. The exercise will be good for me. What about your workers?"

"They've nearly finished. Two hundred yards of hoeing each—I'll inspect it this evening." He hitched the pony to the trap and led it as they started walking slowly to the house. "I'm down to twenty men. The others seem to want to obey the *ngangas*. It seems the village elders go to listen to a particular spirit medium—an old woman—a sort of witch, I suppose. She lives in a cave in the hills, but none of us white people know where. Then the elders come back and pass on her message to the people in the village."

"And she's telling them to rise up against the settlers?"

"That's what I've heard. But my natives don't like to talk to me about it—I have to interrogate them gently. Jameson won't give it any credence, and the Native Commissioner thinks nothing of it. But they can't explain away the deserters from the mines and farms."

"I've noticed that you always use the term 'native', not '*kaffir*'."

He shrugged. "Whatever it's original meaning—infidel—*kaffir* is a pejorative term, and I won't use it."

She touched his arm. "You're a strange man. You don't like to hunt for sport, even though it's almost the only sport here. You treat your servants and workers much as you would in England, even though most of the settlers regard them as inferior beings, and you even start a school for them..."

"...and I'm rewarded with the sobriquet '*kaffir*-lover'!"

When they reached the house a groom took the pony and trap, and Martin led Helen into the cool living room, that seemed almost too dark in contrast with the bright sunlight. He poured her a drink of lemon squash and placed it on an occasional table. In a swift movement, he moved to her, put his arms round her, and kissed her. At first she responded eagerly, holding his face in her hands, but she soon broke away, her face flushed, pushing aside a strand of hair that has fallen over her cheek. She walked over to the sofa, sat down and started to cry, her shoulders shaking. He sat beside her, holding her in an attempt to comfort.

She lifted her tear-wet face to him. "You know how I feel about you. But I won't have an affair, Martin. I suppose I'm old-fashioned; it means I have to live by my principles."

"I'll respect them. I'm sorry; I won't do that again." He pulled a handkerchief from his pocket and handed it to her.

She touched his cheek affectionately. "If you do, I won't be able to see you again—and I'd hate not to be able to see you." She smiled wanly, dabbing away her tears. "I'm very vulnerable too. So I can't allow myself to be in a situation where I may weaken. God knows what you see in me now. I feel—and look—like an elephant."

ȣɈ

A Christmas party was held for the white community that remained in Salisbury after the departure of the volunteers to Tuli. It was held in the Assembly Hall, a long thatched building, and about a hundred white people were present, with a few African servants. The whites were mostly women and older men; the younger men had gone with Jameson. A stocky bearded man in worn khaki clothes played music hall tunes on the piano. Martin sat in a group with Helen Onslow and his friends the de la Panouses; Felix, the French Count, and his young wife Billie, were well-known characters in the town. They married in England, and Billie disguised herself as a young man to follow the Pioneers into Mashonaland.

"When will you go down to Jo'burg to 'ave the baby?" Billie asked Helen. She had a strong Cockney accent.

"As soon as Robert gets back, but if he's not here by the middle of January, I'll have to go on my own…"

"You can't do that, my dear," interjected the Count, who spoke excellent English. "You must be escorted. I'm sure one of us will oblige."

She bowed her head in acknowledgement. "I couldn't ask either of you to take me."

"Speaking for myself," said the Count, "it would be a delightful excuse to visit civilisation."

"And you'd 'ave to take me with you. 'Elen should have another woman wiv 'er for the journey." Billie glanced round the festive room. "Your poor Robert! Fancy being stuck in...wherever. Why is their expedition still so secret?"

"Well you may ask," said Martin.

❧❧

As it happened, a meeting of the section leaders in the Rhodesian expedition was being held in Pitsani, a dusty little town in Bechuanaland. About two dozen men in khaki uniforms sat on bales of hay under a large marquee. Among them was Lord Robert Onslow, and looking round he spotted several men he knew, including Johnny Willoughby and Bobby White. Willoughby, tall and handsome, waved to him and smiled. The men stirred and then stood up as Doctor Jameson entered. Indicating that they should be seated, he took up his position behind a folding table, looking pale and tired, stooping more than usual. With smiles he nodded at familiar faces, then tapped his cane on the table, and started to speak in a strong voice that seemed out of keeping with his small body.

"Gentlemen! I know you're wondering why I asked you to come here. I intend to tell you, but what I say must be for your ears only." He paused for dramatic effect. "I expect you thought we were going to attack Linchwe and the Sechuana? Well, we're not! We're going to Jo'burg!"

Excited murmurs sweep through the audience, but Jameson raised his hand for silence. "We're going to support our countrymen—and the other *uitlanders*."

A voice called out, "When?"

"Tomorrow. Rumours have been getting out. People have been blabbing. We have to move now, before the Boers can prepare themselves." He waved a piece of paper. "I have a letter here. It's from the Chairman of the Committee of the *Uitlanders*. Now listen to this." He read, "'Thousands of unarmed men and women are at the mercy of the Boers.' We can't ignore a plea like that, can we?"

There was a roar of "No!" from the men.

"So, we're off tomorrow, as early as we can. We have to ride hard—straight for Jo'burg. Now I'll hand over to Colonel Willoughby to give you the details."

Willoughby, was thirty-six years old, fair haired and smartly-uniformed. He came forward to take his place behind the table, and started to address the men in a cultured drawl. "We'll have three troops, each with two Maxims and a field gun. They must stay apart, but not so far that they can't communicate, by heliograph or lamp. Our scouts ahead will warn us of any Boers. But we don't expect any resistance, because we have the advantage of surprise—and the Maxims. The Boers won't get together more than a few dozen men before we reach Jo'burg."

"What happens when we're there?" shouted someone.

"Do we each get a gold mine?" shouted another.

Willoughby raised his hand to quieten the laughter. "When we get there we'll join forces with the Reform Committee. They already have stored weapons. Then we take key places—the Post Office, the banks, the mines, the water pumps. The Committee have plans ready."

"The Boers have a commando system—a militia," someone shouted. "They use it to gather their men together in emergency."

Willoughby smiled. "That's why we're taking them by surprise—so they don't have time to mobilise their commandos."

"They're very disorganised," added a staff officer standing beside Willoughby.

Someone from the back shouted. "What makes you think they'll sit back while we occupy Jo'burg. Remember what happened at Bronkhorst Spruit and Majuba?"

Jameson waved for quiet "The point is, we'll take the initiative; then we'll be in a very strong bargaining position if we can capture the key positions in the city. We can then negotiate for better terms. Now, we can't discuss this all night. I suggest you get some sleep. I'll see you all tomorrow."

❧◈

Jameson's troops rode over the rolling *veld*. There were six hundred of them. The countryside was deserted as they rode past fields of young green maize. The only signs of habitation were a few farmhouses on the horizon, well away from the dust of the road. Jameson and Willoughby rode together. Despite his bluff demeanour, Jameson was nervous; he was also very tired after nearly two days in the saddle. It seemed to be going well, but they were venturing into the heart of the Transvaal with virtually no intelligence.

"So far, so good, Willoughby," he said, trying to sound cheerful.

"Yes, but it seems too good to be true. Those Boers who spotted us yesterday are bound to have taken a warning ahead." Willoughby peered ahead to two riders advancing. "Here come the scouts."

The two horsemen reached them, saluted and fell into riding alongside.

"Boers ahead, sir!" said one of the scouts, and when Willoughby asked him how many, he replied. "Difficult to say, sir. 'Bout a hundred."

"Do they have field guns?" asked Jameson.

"No, sir. At least we didn't see any."

"Very well," said Willoughby. "Go and inform the flank troop commanders. And, well done!"

An hour later, Jameson and Willoughby still rode together, watching a line of Boer horsemen on the horizon. "Are they going to stay with us all the way to Jo'burg?" asked Jameson.

Willoughby shrugged. "Perhaps. I suppose they're afraid of the Maxims. I don't blame them."

≈⚬≈

By next morning the Jameson raiders were surrounded by Boers who were sniping into a disorganised *laager*. Bullets fizzed past and sometimes ricocheted with a whine when they hit a metal object. Intermittent shouted orders were mixed with the occasional oath or imprecation.

Jameson was lying under a wagon, watching events with a gloomy expression, when Willoughby crawled up to him, dusty and dishevelled.

"The Maxims are shot out!"

"My God, what do you mean?" gasped Jameson. He'd thought the Maxims were invincible, with their incredible firepower.

"The Boer snipers have destroyed them—persistent accurate rifle shooting. There's nothing we can do; they're beyond repair. We've effectively lost a couple of hundred riflemen. "

Jameson was starting to panic. "What are we to do? Can we escape?"

"I'm afraid not," replied Willoughby calmly. He had already come to terms with impending defeat. "They've got us pinned down. I regret that I must advise surrender, Jameson—before we lose any more men."

"Oh God!" Jameson buried his face in his hands. "It goes against everything I...Can't we make a fight of it?"

"To what purpose? There are hundreds of Boers out there. No doubt hundreds more on their way. They're all crack shots. It's obvious we miscalculated. It would be a waste of good men and horses."

Jameson pondered for a while before saying, "Very well. Send a white flag out—though, by God..."

"I know." Willoughby patted the older man's shoulder. "I know. And have you thought about the consequences?"

"We're soldiers, Willoughby. They'll have to treat us according to convention."

"Remember, I warned you, they may treat us as an unofficial force."

Meanwhile, Robert lay huddled behind a wagon forming the wall of the *laager*. He was dusty and exhausted, terrified of the bullets that hummed around him like vicious wasps. He watched in consternation as the white flag was raised. A trooper lying beside him tugged his sleeve and asked him what was happening.

"I think we've surrendered," he answered, filled with foreboding. At least we're still alive, he thought to himself. I'll be able to go back to Helen. He said to the trooper, "They'll take us prisoner."

"Will they 'ang us, sir?"

"Hang us? Whoever gave you that idea?"

The trooper wiped his nose with the back of his hand. "One of the sergeants, sir—said we aren't under the Queen's orders. 'E said the Boers would treat us like rebels and 'ang us—leastwise the officers—beggin' your pardon, sir."

⊱⊰

Two Boer infantrymen herded Robert into the jailhouse in Johannesburg. His uniform was dirty and tattered, and his head drooped as he shuffled his heavy body wearily forward. He could smell the pervasive stink from his unwashed clothes, soaked with the sweat of fear.

The guards were watching his ponderous progress with some amusement. "This one's a Lord, *boetie*," said one.

"Is it? Maybe they won't hang him if he's a Lord then."

"Why not? More likely him than the others. Make an example of him. I wonder if he knows." He then said in English, "Hey, Lord! You know you'll all be hanged tomorrow?"

Robert turned to him. "We never meant any harm. We only wanted to help our countrymen." His expression was so agonised that the Boers thought of stopping their taunting.

"*Jah, jah*. Save it for the court, Lord." The Boer indicated Robert with a jerk of his thumb, saying to his companion, "This one's shit-scared."

"So would you be, *boetie*, if you knew you'd be strung up."

క్లా

Two weeks after the ill-fated Jameson Raid, on a hot day in mid-January, Martin rode into Salisbury to visit Helen, who greeted him with a kiss on his cheek, and led him to the verandah. She was pale, her eyes tired, growing larger by the day.

"Oh Martin," she broke down sobbing. "Robert's been sentenced—to five years in jail—I can't bear it."

He tried to drive out unworthy thoughts that milled in his mind. Putting his arm round her shoulders he led her gently to a cane chair, and held her arm as she sat down. Then he pulled up another chair to sit near her. "The British Government will get them out. It might take a few months."

She looked at him despairingly. "But they say they won't help—because it was an illegal act."

He responded soothingly, explaining slowly, as one might to a child. "They won't help Jameson, or the senior officers. But those who knew nothing before they left Pitsani will get off—I'm sure. People like Robert were duped. The Boers may be stubborn, but they're not stupid—or cruel."

"Poor Robert," she sighed. "He'll feel so humiliated."

Martin stood up and started pacing the room. "But for grace of God I'd be with him."

She smiled wanly. "You mean, but for Robert's clumsy polo."

"We'll see him soon." He patted her shoulder. "I'll take you there. You're going to Jo'burg to have the baby. While you're there, you'll be able to visit him."

"But I can't take you away from your farm..."

He held up his hand to interrupt her. "I promised Robert I'd look after you. That means taking you to Jo'burg. Besides, I intended to go down for Perry's wedding. Did I tell you? I'm to be his best man." He wondered if she understood the depth of the irony—that he should stand beside his friend as he married Louise.

و&&

The wedding service was held in the Dutch Reformed church at Pietersburg, the same church in which the memorial service for Gerrit had been held in 1893. Martin stood beside a buoyant but nervous groom, wondering why he had been asked to be the best man, and how his friend felt about joining himself to this clan of Boers, some of whom regarded him with suspicion, if not distaste. Still, the important thing was that Louise wanted to marry him, to share her bed with him, and her life. The wheezing organ sounded out an anthem that he did not recognise, and he turned to see Louise and her uncle Cobus advancing down the aisle. A veil hid the young girl's face, and he found himself wishing that some other woman could have been substituted.

But, if Louise were free, would he take her away and marry her? He'd had an opportunity when in the Cape and let it slip. When she drew closer he could see that she was looking at him through the veil. Was she marrying Perry in spite? He wished he had at least made love to her, and that she had given herself to him first. Would it have meant that he was more important to her than Perry? Would it have been a gesture of love, or merely physical attraction? She might not have slept with him unless she knew that he would marry her. How could he have thought it was her who came to the *rondavel* that night? Louise would never have been so impulsive.

Behind the bride were her three maids, Pookie, Clara and Anna. They were dressed in shorter and simpler versions of the bride's dress. In contrast to Louise's pale complexion and serious expression, their faces were sun-bronzed, and their smiles cheerful, as they glanced around. Martin caught Pookie's eye and saw her smile expand. A tremor of excitement passed through him as he remembered their love-making at Elandsfontein three months ago. Would she do it again? he wondered. Probably; she seemed to have a rather amoral attitude to sex.

The service was conducted in Afrikaans, but though he understood the words, he paid them scant attention. His thoughts wandered to the other girls he'd loved, Amanda and Helen. Those splendid women were lost to him, and here he was at twenty-nine, with no prospect but to live on his farm as a lonely bachelor.

When Louise lifted her veil to kiss the groom Martin could see there were tears in her eyes. The bridal couple went ahead into the vestry to sign documents, while he looked back down the aisle. Perry's uncle, old George Davenport, had been unable to come to the wedding, and there were only a handful of friends and colleagues from the mining company in Johannesburg to support him. All the other guests were Boers, most from the Pietersburg district, and a few from the Cape, from the bride's family. Jeanne Venter came into the vestry to join them, kissing her newly-married daughter, her new son-in-law, and the best man. Pookie followed close behind, and when it was her turn to kiss Martin she whispered hotly in his ear, but he could not catch what she said.

The reception was held in the garden at Elandsfontein where over a hundred guests gathered to celebrate, all in their best suits and dresses. The men looked uncomfortable, their high white collars contrasting with red sunburned faces. The women wore large bonnets with trailing ribbons, and busied themselves laying out the food on long trestle tables covered with white cloths.

Martin handed Perry a glass of punch. "You look so satisfied—like a cat with a bird."

The American looked handsome in his wedding suit; his slender frame had filled out after months of easy living in the city. With a sardonic smile, he said, "And you think it might fly?"

"What do you think?" Martin looked across the crowd at Louise, who was talking to some cousins. She caught his eye, or was it Perry's, and smiled.

"She loves me now. I don't have to shackle her."

"No." Martin thumped him on the back. "I envy you."

Perry looked at him shrewdly. "What will you do now?"

"Go back to Jo'burg tonight, look after Helen until she's well enough to return to Salisbury."

"Is there anything between you two?"

"No". Martin thought he must sound unconvincing. "I like her enormously, but she's committed herself to Robert, and that's that."

Pookie came up and took his arm. "Come along, you have to join in the dancing." She pulled him into a throng of whirling couples, and was surprised to find that he could dance better than the Boer men. He explained that there were several Afrikaner couples in Salisbury who were very hospitable to single men and taught them folk dancing.

"And no single girls?" She pulled close to him to make herself heard, talking in Afrikaans.

"A few."

They were in the dark margin of the dancing area, where the lights from the verandah could not reach. She moved closer until her body was pressed against him. "Why don't you stay tonight?" she asked. "Is it because of Louise? Are you too jealous to stay?"

"I have to get back to Jo'burg. I promised to look after Helen Onslow."

"Are you in love with that Englishwoman? Louise says you are?"

He did not answer, but asked instead. "Don't you have a young man, Pookie?"

"I've already given myself to you. No one will have me now."

"Why did you do it?"

She laughed and started talking in English. "Because I'm a woman, and I wanted to find out what it was like. I've always wanted you, Martin, but you've never noticed me because you've never been able to see past my sister. But now I've slept with you and she hasn't. Just think, I might have had your child; what would she have thought then?"

"So you did it to spite her?"

"No, that wasn't the reason. I was excited by the thought of you lying alone in your *rondavel*. Everyone was sleepy, because they drank too much brandy—even Louise. I drank none, only lime juice, and you drank only two glasses—I noticed. So, I put *Ouma's* powder in their drinks. Then I lay awake until they were all asleep, trying to work up courage to visit you. I thought I would talk to you—perhaps flirt a little. But when I felt that you were naked, and...excited, I had no hesitation."

"Even when I thought you were Louise?"

"Even then. I thought you would guess, despite the dark. I'm taller, and my breasts are larger. Anyway, I have no regrets. I would even do it again." She reached up to whisper in his ear, "Stay tonight and I'll come to you. While Louise is with Perry, you can have me."

Despite the enticing invitation, Martin decided to leave immediately after his conversation with Pookie. He made his farewells to his hosts, and Jeanne, and finally the bride and groom, and when they asked him to stay longer he explained that Helen was expecting her child soon, and was relying on his support. He spent the night in Pietersburg, took the train to Johannesburg next day, and went straight to the hotel where Helen was staying, finding her well, but frustrated because she had not managed to obtain permission to see Robert. The Transvaal government was taking its time.

❧❦

Two weeks later, after Perry and Louise returned from their honeymoon, Martin paid them a call. He found Louise in the garden and walked with her as she cut some roses for the house. It was late afternoon and long shadows stretched across the lawn.

"It's good of him to take Helen to the prison," he said.

"Why didn't you take her?" asked Louise.

"She asked me not to. I think she was afraid that Robert would feel jealous. He knows I've spent a lot of time looking after his wife."

She looked at him, searching his face. "And are there grounds for jealousy?"

"None at all." He laughed, wondering if his denial rang true.

"One can be jealous of thoughts as well as actions, you know."

"Then it's Perry who should feel jealous." He tried to give the words emphasis.

She stopped and turned to face him. Although still only eighteen, her face has matured to that of a lovely young woman, with clear olive skin and defined cheekbones. Her large dark eyes regarded Martin for a while. "I know you're in love with Helen."

"I might have been if she was not so firmly married. But it's you who excite me."

She blushed. "But if you had the chance to make love to me you wouldn't take it. I know you, Martin. You'd decline because it would dishonour your friend—and you would think less of me."

"If I had such high principles I wouldn't be talking like this. I don't know the limits of my self control, and it's let me down with you before. You'd be surprised how often I've thought of you and regretted the chances I had—at Franschhoek, and at Gordon's Bay."

When she spoke, her voice was tinged with bitterness. "A chance for what? To have my body? How important is that? I wanted more than that, Martin—some commitment. I knew that you weren't prepared to give me more. Nor are you now."

"How can I? You've married my friend."

"Your friend? You've always despised him?"

He was genuinely shocked. "What on earth gave you that idea?"

"Women are intuitive. I know you both quite well. You told me once that you thought Perry was like a gigolo..."

"That was years ago—when I first met him. I don't think that now—he's changed, you know."

"When he was with you in the Matabele campaign, you despised him—because he wept."

"Did he tell you that?"

"Not in so many words. But he's told me a lot since we married. The sad thing is that he admires you. He aspires to be like you—brave and dependable."

"You called me that before, and I told you it sounded boring."

She shook her head. "Perhaps it isn't the right word. 'Trustworthy'? Could I trust you?"

"For what? With what?"

"My love?"

"I don't know what you mean."

"I love you, Martin," she said, slowly and deliberately. "I know now that I've really loved you, ever since that time you came to Franschhoek..."

He swallowed, a little awed by what she was saying, conscious that her marriage was scarcely two weeks old. "And Perry?"

"I love him too...but in a different way. And I'm growing to like him—as a friend. I think you would like him better now."

"I do like him now, Louise—I wish you could believe me."

"But could he trust you?" She was teasing now. He could see the familiar sparkle in her eyes.

He shook his head slowly.

ॐॐ

They sat in wicker armchairs in the lounge of the Victoria Hotel in Johannesburg, Perry, Louise, Martin and Helen, drinking tea. A palm court trio played quietly in the background, while African servants in white uniforms padded silently around the guests.

"I've decided to stay here after the baby is born," Helen was making the announcement to her friends for the first time. She spoke calmly. "At least until Robert's released."

"That could be months," said Perry. "Sorry, Helen, but we must be realistic—the Government is in no hurry. You can't stay in this hotel.

Why don't you come and stay with us?" He looked at Louise for confirmation. "What do you say, darling?"

"Of course, you'd be welcome, Helen," she replied, but Martin could tell that she was less than enthusiastic.

"Thank you both," said Helen, smiling graciously, "but I wouldn't dream of imposing myself on you, especially a newly married couple. No, I've already found a small house to rent. Martin took me to see it today."

"Well, I hope we'll see you often," said Perry. Then he turned to Martin and said. "Can't you stay any longer?"

"No. Must get back to the farm. I've been away far too long."

"When will we see you again?" asked Louise. "It would be easier for you to come down here, than for us to travel to Salisbury."

"I wanted to fetch Helen, with her baby, but if she insists on waiting for Robert...I don't know. Next year, perhaps, when I plan to go to England again." He looked from Louise to Helen, thinking that he now had two very good reasons to visit Johannesburg.

❧

CHAPTER 18
Trouble Brews In Mashonaland —
June 1896

On a cold misty morning, Martin sat on the verandah of his farm-house, sipping from a mug of coffee as he wrote a letter to his parents. Part of his letter contained the following:

'I saw Helen last week. You asked why she changed her mind and decided to come back to Mashonaland after the baby was born. She told me that she felt her closest friends were here, and she needed them, whereas she was allowed to see Robert only once a fortnight. Now she has had a cheerful letter from him. He thinks he may be released from prison next month—although there is no certainty. She decided to come back here, not having any liking for the regime in the Transvaal, though I must say, I think they have treated Jameson's raiders quite fairly. I would be interested to hear your opinion.'

'The news from Bulawayo is all bad. The Matabele have been raiding isolated farms. I don't want to alarm you, and you must remember that it's a long way from here. They have killed several settler families. The Administrator has ordered all settlers to come into a huge laager in Bulawayo, where they can be protected.'

'I must reassure you that we are well prepared for trouble here. Some say that the Shona people will always be too cowed to attempt an uprising. Others, like me, feel they may be encouraged by what they hear about events in the Matabele country. So we need to be wary.'

He noticed a huddled figure under a tree at the edge of the lawn. When he called out the figure emerged, now recognisable as Mpata, the son of the honey gatherer Nyendi. The young African approached cautiously, then stood at the foot of the steps, looking around furtively.

"Are you well?" Martin asked, in the Chishona greeting ritual.

"I am well. Are you well?"

"I am well. How is your father?"

"He is well. He wishes to speak with you."

"Where is he?"

"He is waiting for you at the place where you shot the sable bull."

"Why does he not come here?"

Mpata looked away, embarrassed. "I do not know. He asked me to say it is very important. He will wait until noon; then he will leave."

Martin nodded. "I will go now."

He rode Chandra to a small clearing in the woodland that covered the ridge, where he found Nyendi squatting at the base of a huge spreading *mpondo* tree, his spear protruding from his ragged cloak. As Martin dismounted, the Shona man stood up and walked forward to greet him. Martin took out his tobacco pouch and offered it to the little black man, who helped himself and lit his pipe. He lit up too, and their smoke curled up together in the still air.

"So what do you wish to speak about, Nyendi?"

The honey gatherer looked down, and poked at a leaf with his spear. "There is trouble around, Rusli. I came to tell you that some of the Zezuru want to make trouble for the white men."

"Why?"

"Who can tell." he shrugged his bony shoulders. "There are some who say that the white men have taken their land, and have caused their crops to fail, and their cattle to die."

"Do you believe that?"

"No, Rusli. But when powerful people say these things, they are heard. There is a sorceress—Nyanda is her name—who is telling the Zezuru that they must rise up against the white men, as the Matabele have done."

"Have you heard this sorceress yourself?"

"No. I have heard about her from other people."

"What do these people intend to do?"

Nyendi looked away. "Who can tell? I am saying this to you, in case you should move to the town where the soldiers will protect you."

Martin smiled. "So you think they will come here to attack me? Well, thank you for warning me, but I will stay here, because this is my home."

"As you wish. I must go now. Do not tell anyone that I spoke to you. The Zezuru would be angry if they knew, and they would kill me."

"I will not tell about you. Thank you. Go safely."

The honey gatherer pulled his cloak around him and limped away through the trees, followed by his son. After watching them out of sight, Martin knocked out the ash from his pipe, and ground it into the earth with the heel of his boot so that there was no possibility it could start a fire. Then he mounted Chandra and rode back to the homestead.

That afternoon he rode up to the Carter's house where Helen was staying until Robert returned. Betty Carter was also without her husband, imprisoned with Robert in Pretoria.

Helen came out to greet him, and held Chandra while he dismounted. "What makes you look so serious?" she asked.

"I've been talking to a Shona man I know. He warned me about the possibility of attacks against settlers."

"Not just rumours? Come inside. I have news for you. Would you like some lemonade?"

As they went into the house together, Martin said. "I'll come in for a short while. Then I have to tell Judge Vintcent. Where's Betty?"

"She's gone to the store. She heard today that our husbands have already been released. They're on their way here—they arrive next week."

Martin looked into her eyes. She ought to have been excited, but there was no spark there. She announced the news with no more enthusiasm than if some friends were coming. He went over to the crib, where Helen's baby daughter Clare lay sleeping, and said, over his shoulder, with luke-warm enthusiasm, "That's good news for you." Then he added. "As for me, it means that I'll see less of you."

"Martin...you promised." She smiled ruefully.

"That was before Robert was taken prisoner, and you came back with this little girl. Has nothing changed?"

"I'm still worried about Robert—and I'm so grateful to you for your comfort, and for talking to me all those long hours."

"And for holding you while you cried your heart out."

She bowed her head. "Yes, for that too. But do you want some reward?" She looked up at him, her eyes moist. "What do you want of me, Martin? You know that I'm not free to...be your lover. As it is, people have talked about us. And you may be sure that Robert will hear of it. But at least I know my conscience is clear."

He went up to her and put his hand on her shoulder. "I'm sorry. Helen, I'm really concerned about you and Betty living here alone. I would come to look after you, but I don't want to add fuel to the rumours about us. Could you not stay in a house where there's a man to protect both of you—and the baby, of course."

"Betty says she's as good as any man. And I'm going to Marandellas tomorrow on the coach..."

"That's not wise. What about Clare?"

"Betty promised to look after her. I'm going to see my friends there—only for a day. I refuse to stay cooped up in this town, just because there are rumours. Why should they have any more truth than the rumours about you and me?"

He made her sit down and spoke to her earnestly. "What I heard today gives me much stronger suspicion than I had before; that's why I want to see the Judge. I must go now. I want to warn Billie too—the Count's away, so she's on her own too. Be careful, Helen."

He rode up to Count de la Panouse's house on the ridge known as Avondale, to the north-west of Salisbury. Countess Billie came out to greet him, shielding her eyes from the bright sun as she looked up at him.

"Martin! Wha' a pleasant surprise. Come in." Her hands were covered in flour.

"I won't come in, thanks. Where did the Count go?"

"To Chimoio—in Mozambique, to buy maize." She lowered her eyelids, and spoke to him with mock seduction. "Does that change yer mind about coming in?"

He laughed as he dismounted. "Yes, but only to talk to you seriously."

She feigned disappointment. "I can't compete with the fair 'Elen, can I?" She led Martin into the little house and seated him in the cool, dark drawing room. It was furnished in a strange mixture of locally made furniture and ornaments from Europe.

"Please don't add to the rumours about me and Helen."

"M'dear man, anyone can see that yer in luv with 'er. An' she may do 'er best to conceal 'er feelings for you when in public, but I've seen yer both in this 'ouse, and I know she luvs yer."

"Then you know more than I do..." he said, without conviction.

"A woman doesn't 'ave to use words, Martin. She says it wiv 'er eyes, wiv 'er expressions." She started to giggle. "Like yer can tell from me eyes that I'd luv for you t'fling me onto this sofa for a passionate embrace."

He laughed with her. "Before you get carried away, let me deliver a solemn warning. I've heard this morning from a reliable Shona man that some natives may try to attack settlers."

Her expression immediately turned serious. "Young Talbot, you know 'im—the Norton's farm assistant—'e came here this morning, on 'is way into town. 'E told me that none of their labourers came to work this morning. Mr Norton sent 'im to tell the Native Commissioner."

"You see." Martin pounded his fist into the palm of his other hand. "The evidence is piling up." He stood up. "I must go to see Judge Vintcent. Now, be careful, Billie."

She followed him out, saying with a giggle, "I think yer should come and look after me tonight."

"I'd love to," he called, as he mounted.

"But yer farm's more important," she shouted after him, with another peal of laughter.

≈◈≈

Judge Vintcent stood looking out of the window in his spacious office, his grey hair stirred by a chill breeze. He was acting as Administrator of Rhodesia, because Dr Jameson was still in prison in England, convicted by a British court after the ill-fated raid. Vintcent knew Martin quite well; he was highly regarded in the white community, having escaped the opprobrium of involvement in Jameson's ill-judged venture into the Transvaal, though he was considered to be a trifle eccentric in his liberal attitude to Africans.

After listening carefully to Martin's story, Vintcent asked, "Is he a reliable source?"

"Very." Martin was sitting opposite the judge's desk, watching his reactions carefully. "But he made it clear that he was only passing on what he'd heard."

The Administrator nodded gloomily, then lifted his head as he heard a commotion outside followed by urgent knocking on the door. He called out a command to enter, and a BSAP trooper plunged into the room, saluted Vintcent, then turned to Martin and nodded.

"There's been—trouble—at Mazoe—sir..."

The judge held up a calming hand. "All right. Take it easy, man. What happened?"

"Mr Ball—sir—the Native Commissioner; they've taken 'im prisoner. Come quickly.

They hurried to the police compound where they found Rogers assembling a posse to ride out to Mazoe. The policeman drew the Administrator and Martin aside and told them, "This woman, the witch Nyanda, told the villagers to kill Ball. She said that his blood had to be

shed, like the blood of the Shona people had been shed by the white men."
He paused, looking into Vintcent's eyes. "They cut off his hands and feet,
and he bled to death."

"God!" Vintcent's exclamation was like a gasp. "Are you certain?"

"I believe our informer was telling the truth."

"What else?"

"Nyanda has gone up to the hills north of the Alice Mine, where
there are many caves..."

Martin interjected, "I know the area quite well; I've prospected in
the hills with my partner, Tom Ellsworth."

"And Ball's body?"

"We don't know."

"All this is third-hand information," said Vintcent impatiently.
"What do you think, Martin?"

"What concerns me is that the Shona villagers were prepared to do
something like that, at the bidding of the witch. They would know what
a serious act they were committing, with great potential for official retri-
bution, but they still went ahead with it. Now this sorceress will probably
sit like an evil oracle in the Mazoe hills, urging them to commit more
atrocities."

Vintcent started to pace around, stroking his chin as he thought.
Then he announced. "If I have any evidence that this is a wider rebellion
I shall call all the settlers in central Mashonaland into *laager* in Salisbury."
To Captain Rogers, he added, "We'd better go over our plans." Then he
turned to Martin, and said, "You'd better not say anything about this
Ball incident—not while it's unconfirmed."

∾∾

CHAPTER 19
Mashonaland Rebellion — 1896

In her house on the Avondale ridge Countess Billie de la Panouse cooked herself some supper—a vegetable stew—by the light of a paraffin lamp. She was never happy on her own, being a gregarious young woman, and she missed her husband badly. She was humming a song to herself in an attempt to kindle her spirits when she heard the sound of a horse outside, and in some alarm opened the curtains. A young policeman had ridden up to the front of the house. She went to the door, finding that the trooper remained mounted; although she knew many of them, she did not recognise this one.

"Evening, ma'am." He made a half salute. "Captain Rogers asked me to tell you that I'm on my way to the Nortons—to bring them into town. After what Talbot told us about their men not showing up for work, he doesn't want to take any chances. The captain said the Nortons might want to come into town and stay with you."

"Oh yes, of course. Please tell 'em they'd be most welcome—even if they 'ave to sleep on the floor! And you be careful, too. Bye." She waved as the trooper wheeled and cantered off.

She ate her supper and tried to read for a while, but her thoughts kept straying to her friends the Nortons. There was something ominous in what Talbot had said about the labour on the farm. There had been so many rumours of unrest, and the possibility that the natives would turn against their white employers. Now there was this message from Rogers, and he was not a man to react to rumours. Surely he must have good reason to send a trooper all the way out to the Norton's farm. It would be sensible for the family to come and stay with her, especially as they had a young baby. Eventually she fell asleep in her armchair in the living room.

She awoke on hearing a commotion outside, and then heard a white man's voice asking her night watchman to wake her. Trying to clear her thoughts, and with rising agitation, she picked up the lamp, adjusted the flame, and went to the front door. Opening it, she saw Talbot and the young trooper; disheveled and exhausted, they bent forward over their horses' withers.

"Whatever's the matter, boys!" she called out. "Where are the Nortons?"

"They're dead, Billie," gasped Talbot. "Murdered."

"Oh m' God!" She put her hand to her mouth and leant back against the door post. "What 'appened?" Her voice was almost inaudible, and she could feel her heart thumping.

"We don't know," said Talbot, sighing heavily. "It happened while I was in town. When I got back to the farm, I found them all dead— Mrs Norton, Molly, Gravenor, the baby. It was awful. Mr Norton wasn't there—at least we couldn't find him. Perhaps he escaped. We hope so."

"Oh, poor boys. Yer must be done in. Can I get yer somethin'? No, yer'd better go on and tell Captain Rogers." She waved them on. "Thanks fer stoppin' to tell me."

They rode off and she went back inside the house, bolting the door behind her carefully. She sat in her large armchair and started sobbing. The settlers had been expecting an uprising, and it must have started. Now, here she was, all on her own, with her husband miles away. At least Rogers knew she was here on her own. So did her friends, including Martin Russell, but she felt so alone now. She contemplated leaving the house to go to Betty Carter, or one of the other houses that was not so isolated, but decided that she must be brave and stick it out, at least for the rest of this night.

After a few moments, she got up and poured herself a glass of whisky. Then she unlocked a cupboard and took out a hunting rifle. Her husband had taught her how to use it, and she ensured that there was a cartridge in the breech. She went to the bedroom, unlocked a trunk, and found a revolver wrapped in a length of oily cloth. After loading the revolver with great care she put spare ammunition in her pockets and paced tearfully in the living room, wondering whether she would be competent to defend herself. Her greatest fear was that she would be raped, and she debated whether to shoot herself with the revolver if that became a prospect.

Her watchman and her servant were outside, as were four young men from the Zambezi Valley, who her husband employed for loading and unloading wagons. These men slept in a small outhouse, and she was confident they would warn her if any strangers came onto the property.

Suddenly, to her great alarm, she heard noises outside. Her heart pounding, she tiptoed to the window and peered out through a gap in the curtains. Seeing shadowy figures moving outside she grasped the rifle and ran towards the front door, but, as she did so, someone tried to open it. For a second she considered firing at the door, but that would have meant re-loading. Instead, she turned and fled into her bedroom. The only way out was through the window. She closed the door between the living room and the bedroom, plunging the room into darkness. Then she opened the window, and climbed out.

It was pitch dark. She tried to adjust her vision, searching for figures in the gloom. Seeing no one, she stumbled away from the house towards a tree at the edge of the garden. Suddenly a dark figure loomed out at her, and she stifled a scream as she brought the rifle up. Just before she pulled the trigger she recognised her kitchen servant, Amos, shivering in a thin blanket. He seemed in a trance, unable to move, like a mouse mesmerised by a snake. Pushing him in front of her away from the house, she groped in the dark, dredging her memory of the garden. She guided her servant to a small stone-walled enclosure at the end of the garden; it had been built a couple of years ago around the grave of a settler. They scrambled over the wall and huddled inside.

જન્જ

Martin lay asleep, fully clothed, in the spare room of Tom Ellsworth's house in Salisbury. He slept fitfully, as he always did when in strange surroundings, and conscious of a dangerous situation. Urgent rapping on the front door woke him. Tom's sleepy voice called, "Who is it?"

Martin buckled on his belt and revolver and went to join the Australian at the front door.

Outside, a mounted BSAP trooper told them. "The Norton family have all been murdered. I'm warning everyone—Captain Rogers' instructions." Seeing Martin, the trooper added, "Mr Russell, he wants you to report to him—on horseback." He saluted quickly, turned his horse, and cantered away into the darkness.

"It's started," said Tom gloomily as he came back through the front door. "What you feared. What I thought were rumours have started coming true. You were right."

"Sounds like it. I'm worried about the women on their own. Can you go and warn Betty. She's looking after Helen's baby? I'll go up to the ridge to warn Billie; she's much more isolated."

"You have to go to the police compound," Tom reminded him.

Martin's mind was full of thoughts about what might have happened to the Nortons. He had met them several times, and knew that they had a young child and a governess. All the outlying farms would be vulnerable to the same sort of atrocity, and not only the farms, even the houses outside the town centre like the de la Panouse's. He finished dressing before grabbing his shotgun. He ran out to the back of the house, where he saddled a disgruntled Chandra. After galloping along deserted roads to the police compound, he came to a group of men standing outside Rogers' office. Most of them had bicycles because many of the men who owned horses had gone on the Jameson Raid. Through the window he could see Rogers pointing at a map on the wall; he looked up and saw Martin, and came outside.

"Russell! Can you ride up to the Count's house? We've heard there's been some trouble there. I've sent four men with cycles, but they may get lost in the dark. You know the way. Maybe you can get there faster."

Martin nodded and wheeled Chandra round. The horse had woken up now, and was game for a gallop to the Avondale Ridge. Dawn was lightening the sky behind him an ominous red, as he peered into the gardens and behind trees on his route, half expecting to see armed men. He knew that if rebels had gone to Billie's house she would be an easy target. She was such a cheerful, courageous soul, and he couldn't bear the thought of her being harmed.

Reaching the base of the ridge he made out four white men standing with their bicycles. To his great relief, Billie was with them, barefoot and clutching a large bush jacket round her small body; it must have belonged to one of the men. She was arguing fiercely with them, and turned to Martin as he approached. "Oh, Martin! Thank 'eavens y've come. I want to go back to the 'ouse, but these men won't let me."

One of the men was a tall black-haired Irish miner, who Martin recognised as a frequenter of Meikles bar. He said in a disgruntled tone, "Our orders are to take everyone back to the police compound."

"I left my wewolwer in the bedroom," pleaded Billie. "And m' sewin' machine's there. They may be stolen if I leave them there. Please, Martin, it won't take long."

"Come on." He lifted her up to sit behind him on Chandra and they started trotting up the steep slope towards the Count's house. Billie felt very cold against his back, but was clearly enjoying the adventure. She gripped him tightly.

"It's all right for you, mate," shouted one of the men after them, "on yer bloody great horse. You 'aven't tried to ride a bike up that 'ill."

While they rode up to the ridge Billie told Martin what had happened; she spoke in short bursts right into his ear. Chandra was a strong horse and hardly noticed the extra weight. By the time they reached the house it was light enough to see clearly. She slipped off the horse and hurried towards the door, but Martin signalled for her to wait. When he dismounted, he moved cautiously round the house, holding his shotgun at the ready in one hand and the reins in the other. The door was open and there might be rebels inside; if so, they might be armed, although the police had taken pains to prevent rifles getting to the Africans. Noticing that the servants' quarters were at the rear of the house, he circled round, with Billie close behind him. Letting loose Chandra's reins he pushed the door open with his foot. Lying on the floor were the bodies of several Africans, and he backed out to prevent Billie from seeing.

At that moment, the volunteers arrived on their bicycles. He helped the men to pull the bodies out of the room. They were four Africans, stiff and cold.

"Oh, m' God!" Billie had her hand to her mouth, as she looked on, aghast. "They're our Zambezi boys. Poor fellows." She started sobbing.

The tall Irishman was bending over one of the bodies. "Stuck with *assegais*—looks like," he called without much emotion.

Billie led Martin to the house but he insisted on entering ahead of her, probing each of the three rooms with great caution before allowing her in. She told him that nothing had been disturbed, and when she started sobbing again, he put his arm round her and spoke soothingly until she recovered. Then he carried out the precious sewing machine, which he gave to one of the cyclists to carry. He again lifted Billie up to sit behind him, and they set off down the hill towards the town.

She was uncharacteristically quiet. Eventually, she said, "Wha' a night! I wonder wha' the Count's doin'. 'Ope he 'asn't 'ad any trouble."

"They'll send a warning telegraph message to Umtali."

She started to cry, putting her face against his back. "If it weren't for those poor Nortons and my Zambezi boys, I'd...I'd almost be enjoyin' this."

⚭

On 18th June 1896, two days after his wife Billie's lucky escape, of which he was unaware, Felix, the Vicomte de la Panouse was on his way back to Salisbury from buying maize at Chimoio, in Mozambique. Reaching the small settlement of Marandellas, about forty miles from Salisbury, he stopped to feed the teams of donkeys pulling his two wagons. He was a tall, slender man, with a quiet patrician manner that disguised an adventurous spirit that had brought him to the heart of Africa through considerable privations. He was about to set off again when the coach drew up. It was travelling west, which puzzled him, and he watched the driver rein in his horses. A man climbed out, short and neat; the Count knew him slightly, and remembered that his name was Lamb.

"*Bon jour*, Mr Lamb." He walked over to shake the man's hand. "Why are you going in that direction?"

"We've decided to go back to Salisbury. The telegraph office had a message saying the Shona around here are in revolt."

The Count drew slowly on his cigarette. "Is that so?" Like most of the settlers he had been expecting some sort of trouble. He was cogitating the news when, to his surprise, Helen Onslow climbed out of the coach. He doffed his hat to her. "My dear Helen. What a pleasant surprise. What brings you here?"

"I came out to visit friends," she replied, with a wry smile, "but now I want to get back as quickly as possible. Can we join forces with you?"

"Of course, my dear, but the coach would be much faster without me. My wagons move very slowly; heavily laden, you see."

"Yes, but..." Lamb intervened. He paused, glancing at Helen, not wishing to alarm her. ".... safety in numbers, sir."

After pondering for a moment, the Count said. "There are plenty of weapons and ammunition here in Marandellas. Perhaps we should stay here until we get more news. We don't want to expose the young lady to danger."

"I must get back," protested Helen. "My baby daughter is in Salisbury."

"Well that settles it, my dear." He could see that she was agitated. A great weight of fear descended on him as he imagined surging hordes of natives, shouting and waving spears. What could he and Lamb do to fight them off. It would be hopeless.

They were about to leave when a heavily loaded wagon lumbered up, drawn by oxen. The owner, Fred Carstairs, called to the Count, asking if he might join them and the Frenchman waved him forward with a magnanimous gesture. Thus, the ill-matched convoy set off, with its variety of vehicles, drawn by horses, donkeys, and oxen. The road to Salisbury wound through huge castle *kopjes*, gigantic tumbled heaps of grey granite boulders. As Helen looked at them with apprehension she imagined that behind them lurked their enemy, and her thoughts veered towards her baby daughter. It was agonising to think that she might never see her again, and she berated herself for leaving the town.

After about five miles, that took them two hours, they reached a roadside store where they found the owner, a tall Scot named Graham, barricading the building, working alone.

"Why don't you join us, Mr Graham?" called the Count.

"Thank you, sir," Graham replied, "but I'd rather look after my stock. My men have disappeared, but I'll manage somehow."

As he set off again the Count was full of misgivings. He was a realist, and pragmatic. He knew, though he did not reveal his thoughts to his companions, that this motley slow-moving convoy presented an attractive target and would be extremely vulnerable to attack, simply because they had no means of escape. The horses that pulled the coach had no saddles. The three white men were not well armed, having only four rifles between them. He would ensure that they sold their lives dearly, and even considered that he might have to shoot Helen to prevent her falling into the hands of the rebels.

A few miles further on they saw groups of Africans lurking among the trees, and the Count commented to Helen, who sat beside him on the bench seat of his wagon, "They're out of range. Too frightened to come nearer, I suppose. But they look a bit sinister, don't they?" He tried to sound calm, though he was extremely concerned.

"Can't we go any faster?" she asked, her voice shaking.

"I'm afraid not, my dear—unless we leave our wagons and ride ahead in the coach. But I'm damned if I will abandon my purchases to those devils."

After another four miles, they stopped near a stream and outspanned the draft animals. It was a risky procedure, and the Count arranged guards from among the African drovers, instructing them to stand on the wagons and warn him about approaching rebels. He was reluctant to put such trust in natives, but they must know they risked sharing the same fate. Soon after, one of the drovers shouted that a white man was approaching on horseback. To the Count's great relief he recognised Martin on Chandra. Now their capacity to resist onslaughts had risen by much more than the addition of a single rifle.

Martin dismounted and greeted them. "I came to warn you, Helen. Judge Vintcent has ordered that all settlers should come into town. They're setting up a *laager*." He turned to the Count. "Billie's safe—she's staying with Betty Carter."

Felix de la Panouse expelled air in a huge sigh. "Thank you for that news, *mon ami*. I'm so relieved that you have joined us, Martin. You will take command, eh. How is the road ahead?"

"I don't know. I came by short cuts, through the bush." He saw that Helen was trembling as if she had fever, and he could imagine that she was terrified.

They inspanned the wagons and coach and the convoy set off again, Martin riding alongside the wagon, on which Helen sat. He wanted to talk to her, but was constrained by the Count's presence, and he had to resort to casual conversation. Eventually, an opportunity came when the Count jumped down to walk forward and give instructions to his other drover.

"You shouldn't have come all the way out here", said Helen in a low voice. "You were taking a great risk. I'm sorry I ignored your advice." She bombarded him with questions. "Will we be all right? I'm afraid for my baby. If anything happens to me, will you take care of her—and Robert?" He tried to reassure her, but her eyes were wide and casting around as she looked for rebels among the trees and rocks. "Please! Promise me."

"Of course. I promise."

About an hour later, they came to an isolated store by the road-side. Seeing no sign of life, they assumed that the owners must have gone into town, but decided to check the compound. The Count, Martin, and Carstairs went to the front door of the store and saw immediately that it had been broken. Carstairs kicked the door open and when they went inside the store it was obvious that it had been looted. Sacks of maize meal had been dragged out leaving trails of white flour; tins and bottles, pulled off the shelves, lay scattered on the counter and the floor.

Martin went through the back door. It led into a yard, with the small house of the owner situated on the far side. Lying on the ground in front of the house were four bodies, a man, a woman, and two children. He hurried across the yard, followed by his two companions. They checked the bodies for signs of life. The family were dressed in their nightclothes, and they had been speared in the chest and throat. Flies moved busily over their faces, and Martin bent down to close the wide dead eyes of the little girls.

"*Mon Dieu*, those little children!" exclaimed the Count.

"Bastards!" muttered Carstairs.

"We have no time to bury them," said Martin, straightening up, "but we should at least bring them inside the house."

"You're right. You check outside, and make sure the young lady doesn't see this."

He returned to the wagons where he found Helen keeping watch, a rifle across her lap. He told her, without detail, what they had found.

She put her hands to her face in horror. "Did you know them?"

"No. Carstairs knows who they are." He looked around warily. "Any sign of rebels?"

"No, thank God. Martin, how awful. How many more families...?"

"You may as well know. The Nortons, their governess and the manager."

"Oh! The poor things." She bent her head, her face in her hands, and started sobbing. All her pent-up reservations about coming to this country were justified now. How irresponsible of her to bring a tiny baby to live in this wild place, where savage Africans rose up to kill and rape. While she was agonising, she remembered that she had to keep a lookout, and wiped away her tears. She realised that Martin's presence changed everything; he would protect her, and even if they were overwhelmed by rebels, she would die with the man she loved.

The Count and Carstairs returned from their grim task, and the little convoy started forward again. Their progress was painfully slow, as the heavily-laden wagons lurched along the rutted road, the donkeys straining, the drovers whistling and cajoling. Martin could see scattered groups of rebels in the bush, keeping their distance from the lumbering vehicles. Then, suddenly, a shot was fired, followed by several more. The bullets fizzed harmlessly by, but the occupants of the wagons bent lower, and the drovers moved closer to the shelter of the wagons.

Martin wondered how the rebels had acquired their rifles. It was some consolation that the incoming fire would not be very effective at long range, but there was always the risk of a bullet finding a target by accident. He pulled four bags of maize meal onto the bench of the wagon, building them into a barricade; then he made Helen sit between them. Carstairs called to Martin and complained about their slow progress. After explaining that it was the Count's heavy load of maize, and the relative lack of strength of the donkeys, that caused the wagons to move so slowly, he decided to suggest that the Count should jettison some of his load. Getting down from the wagon he ran past Chandra, back to the Count.

"I think you should lighten your load," he said. "You'll have to drop off some of those sacks."

"*Mon Dieu*, Martin! Do you not realise I have brought those sacks all the way from Mozambique! Do you think I'll just drop them on the ground for those murdering savages to eat?"

"If you don't, Felix, all our lives will be jeopardised."

The Frenchman looked around for sympathy, but all he saw were anxious faces, watching him expectantly. Eventually he heaved a Gallic shrug of resignation, and ordered his Africans to remove most of the sacks, dropping them on the road. The wagons moved forward again, and the Count looked back with chagrin to see a dozen or more rebels emerge from the bush to slit open the fallen sacks and carry off the maize and meal.

Even with the reduced load the Count's wagons could not keep up with the coach and Carstairs' ox-wagon, so they stopped to double-harness the donkeys, leaving one of the de la Panouse wagons behind, then started again. As they moved forward, the Frenchman turned and fired his rifle at the rebels who emerged from the bush to loot the abandoned wagon. While the Count and Carstairs walked, to reduce the load, Martin remained on Chandra, because his height gave him an advantage spotting rebels. Furthermore, he could take messages along the convoy.

To their great relief they reached Law's store at dusk, but found it had been looted; there was no sign of the storekeeper. The men set about barricading the store building, and built a thorn zariba round the wagons, which they positioned in front of the store. The animals were brought into the small yard behind the store, where the men lit a circle of fires.

Inside the storeroom, the Count, Carstairs, Lamb, Martin and Helen, ate scraps of food in the light of a hurricane lamp. Martin spoke quietly to the Count, hatching an emergency plan, which would entail riding the horses back to Salisbury. Helen could ride Chandra, and the four white men could ride the coach horses. They were broken, but had no saddles, so the men would have to ride bareback. It would mean abandoning their African drovers.

"Why don't the rebels attack us?" asked Helen.

"They know we have rifles," muttered Carstairs. "They're afraid."

Martin explained to her. "They don't have much experience of weapons, unlike the Matabele, who fought against Boer rifles—and against us in '93. They think our rifles have magical powers—which I suppose they do, in a way."

"Then that means they won't attack Salisbury?" she asked.

"I'm willing to bet on that!" said Carstairs, and Martin nodded his agreement.

The men arranged two-hour watches, while Helen slept on a pile of empty maize sacks, exhausted both physically and emotionally. Martin could not get to sleep, and when it was his turn on watch, he moved around, checking the integrity of the zariba, and stoking the fires. He spoke with the drovers, who were all Shona men; they professed not to know why the rebellion had risen. Martin suspected that they knew, and he was suspicious. He made them sleep together in the courtyard, where they could not communicate with rebels, and could be seen in the fire-light.

৵৽

Next morning, at first light, they set off again. The shots from the rebels in the bush intensified and two of the oxen were wounded. One of Carstairs' dogs ran squealing into the trees after being hit by a ricochet bullet. About an hour later they came to a group of about two dozen rebels blocking the road ahead. Martin stopped the convoy and ordered the occupants to take shelter behind the wagons, where they kept a lookout. He climbed on top of the coach with his hunting rifle and shouted at the rebels ahead in Chishona, warning them, that if they did not clear off, he would shoot at them. He could see them chattering among themselves. They were about a hundred and fifty yards away, and he could not hear what they were saying.

Suddenly one of the rebels fired a shot, which fizzed past the wagon. Martin lay down on the roof of the coach, wriggled into a comfortable position, and started firing methodically at the rebels. They were easy targets, and two men fell in seconds. A third appeared to be exhorting his companions to attack, but Martin felled him, and they dragged the wounded man away, eventually leaving the road clear. He expected that their suspicions about the magical powers of the white man's rifle would be heightened now.

The convoy lumbered forward once more. They were now only five miles from Salisbury, but the firing from the rebels was growing more intense. This was quite the opposite of what Martin expected, and he was concerned that large numbers of rebels might have gathered on the outskirts of the town in preparation for some attack, or to loot houses in the suburbs. If so, they would be approaching from the rebel rear.

Lamb, who usually said little, suddenly shouted in a high-pitched voice. "In God's name, why don't our people send a rescue party?"

"They don't know we're here, do they?" Carstairs growled. He turned to the Count. "I think we should release some of the oxen. The *kaffirs* will chase them. It'll distract them."

"You do that," replied the Count hastily. "They're your beasts."

Carstairs quickly unhitched four oxen and they lumbered off, bewildered by the rifle fire. Whooping rebels ran out from the trees to try to capture them. Using this opportunity, the convoy hurried forward again. Helen insisted on walking, and Martin stayed beside her, keeping the wagon on one side of her, and Chandra on the other, to protect her from the flying bullets.

At last they reached the outskirts of the town. All the houses seemed deserted; the occupants had gathered in the town centre where they could make a better defence.

"Perhaps they've all been murdered!" whined Lamb.

"Shut up, man!" shouted Carstairs. "Of course they haven't. There! Look!"

Sure enough, a party of a dozen mounted police troopers trotted down the road towards them shouting greetings. Helen flung her arms round Martin.

෨෴

Two months later, when Martin sent his regular letter home, he wrote: *'The rebellion is officially over. Judge Vintcent gave a speech at the club last evening. Nyanda, the spirit-medium is to be tried, and they'll certainly hang her and the other ringleaders. It's been a dreadful time—here, and in Matabele-land. I can't help wondering how long it will be before the natives rise up again. We must think of ways to make them see that we are their partners, not their enemies.'*

He had told his family little about the harrowing journey from Marandellas to Salisbury, not wishing to alarm them, and mentioned

Helen only in terms of her courageous demeanour throughout the troubles. He thought frequently about her, remembering with admiration how she had sat upright on the wagon, a rifle on her lap; she indulged in tears only twice, and then only under extreme duress.

He remembered her smile that spoke of close companionship at least, but wondered whether there was still love there. His frustration was a constant irritant. She was well and truly married, now with a young child, and he knew she would not have an affair. Even if she weakened, it would be a hollow relationship. As long as Robert lived, Helen was denied to him except as a friend. He found himself fantasising about ways that Robert might conveniently shuffle off his mortal coil. He might die of fever—the most likely threat—or he might suffer a heart attack, something that often seemed possible when Robert exerted himself. He might have an accident, fall down a mineshaft, or off his horse. He might even be murdered, but Martin tried to shake that unworthy thought out of his mind.

CHAPTER 20
Prelude To The Boer War — 1898

Two years had passed; Martin was thirty-two years old. He was on his way south to the Cape, from whence he would take the boat to England for his second visit in the eight years since he came to Africa. Arriving in Johannesburg by the Zeederberg coach, he checked in at the Grand Hotel in the centre of the city, unpacked, bathed and shaved, then dressed in clean clothes. Finally, he opened a letter from Perry, which he read, not for the first time; written a month ago, it reached him on the farm just before he left.

'If you visit Jo'burg on your way home,' Perry wrote, *'come and stay with us—we have plenty of room. I can't think you have a good reason for wishing to stay in a hotel. Just turn up—if you don't mind putting up with the children. We are all well. Little Gerald gives us great pleasure. I expect he will be delighted to see his godfather. I wish I could spend more time with him. Baby Rosemary is Louise's delight, and very placid—for which I'm grateful! My work has been very demanding—Uncle George would have been proud of me, God rest his soul! But the political situation, with all its meetings, seems to take most of my spare time. I'll tell you all about it when we meet, and look forward to hearing about your farming endeavours.'*

Martin closed the letter and left the room. It was five o'clock in the afternoon, and he surmised that Perry would have left his office. He hailed a rickshaw, which took him along leafy avenues to Bryanston, where the Davenports lived. When he reached the house, he paid off the rickshaw man and opened the gate into the large garden, where long shadows spread over the lawn. He heard a small child's voice call demandingly, and a woman replied, laughing. A huge tawny ridgeback rushed out towards him, barking ferociously. When it saw that the visitor was a white man it slowed and started to wave its tail in greeting.

Louise emerged from behind a rose bed to see why the dog was barking. Her toddler son Gerald followed, holding her skirt as he watched the stranger with large solemn eyes. She unconsciously put her hand to her hair and smoothed her skirt. It was nearly two years since Martin had seen her. He held her by the shoulders, and she smiled at him in a questioning way, her head tilting as he kissed her on each cheek in turn. Her hand lingered on his arm as he bent to take the tiny hand of the child.

She was intrigued to see how Martin had changed. He was leaner and his skin was the colour of teak. He had grown a moustache that made him seem older and disguised his smiles, so that she had to look more to his eyes. When he spoke, in his measured way, he seemed to making sure that his words were well chosen. All her longings for him flared up as she watched with both affection and desire as he paid attention to her son.

"You don't know your godfather, do you, little man?" He turned to her. "Where's Perry?"

"On his way to America."

"Good Lord!" he exclaimed in surprise. "Why? He said he'd be here."

"It happened suddenly. Come and see the baby."

The baby girl was in a portable cradle covered with netting, in the shade of a nearby tree. Louise lifted her out for Martin to inspect, then led the way into the house through a large hallway into the spacious drawing room, while her son trotted unsteadily by her side, looking back with apprehension at the man who followed. She stopped to pick up some toys, and Martin admired her lithe movements. Her figure had not been affected by bearing two children, and her hips and thighs were as slim as he remembered.

When they were seated in the drawing room, Martin answered her questions, while an African maid brought lemonade on a tray.

"You always look so well. Are you still pining for Helen?" She smiled at him, her dark eyes sparkling with mischief.

"No, I'm not pining." He laughed, not aware that Louise's simple questions were part of a deep strategy.

"So she's still devotedly married?" Her tone was full of irony. "And Robert?"

"They're both well—and send you their love. They have their own farm now." He laughed wryly. "Robert seems to have an inexhaustible supply of money. Just as well...he's not a very good farmer. Now tell me about Perry."

She held up a small slender hand, on which a diamond ring flashed. "First, you stay for supper?" When he agreed, she called the maid, and gave her instructions in Afrikaans. When she had finished, and after the girl left the room, she turned to him, and said, her voice slightly hushed,

"He's gone to find out what support we can get from the Americans. I can't tell you more than that—and you must never repeat what I said. You know how things are."

She came over to sit beside him on the sofa, and put her hand on his arm. "I don't know where your allegiance lies. But in any case, I gave him my word. Surely there are other things we can talk about?"

He asked her about her family and she told him that her mother was trying to decide whether to marry a rich wine producer. "I think she should marry him; he's a decent man. It's almost five years since my father died. Why should she live a widow for the rest of her life? Pookie is unhappy about it; I'm not clear why. You should see her; she's eighteen— tall and striking; quite beautiful. She's training as a nurse in Cape Town. You could see her when you go there."

"And your brothers?"

"Ben's an advocate now, practising in Cape Town. And Hendrik? Well, he's supposed to be farming—up at Elandsfontein, with my uncle. I'm told he spends all his time training his commando. He thinks war is inevitable."

"Do you?"

She heaved a big sigh, as if the question was far too large for her. "If Perry were here I'd let him answer. Yes, I think it is inevitable, and the British imperialists will be to blame. They can't leave us alone. They have their huge empire—on which the sun never sets—but because we've had the good fortune to find gold and diamonds they want this country as well."

"I'm afraid so." The current sabre rattling by the British was a matter of great concern to him.

She nodded as if to acknowledge his honesty in admitting the avaricious intents of his countrymen. "I must put this little chap to bed. Who do you think he looks like?"

Martin looked down at the little boy. He had fair hair and strong features. "He has a look of your father."

"I think so too." She was pleased. "Say goodnight, Gerald." She helped the little boy to wave his hand as she carried him to the nursery.

Left alone in the drawing room Martin wandered round looking at silver-framed photographs and Perry's few modest hunting trophies. There was a wedding photo on a sideboard that brought back memories of the occasion. I look so young, he thought. Louise looks just the same; the photo might have been taken that day. Perry was looking at Louise with longing, as if he knew that at last she would belong to him. Pookie was grinning mischievously.

When Louise returned she poured him a glass of cool white wine, and he told her about his farm and about the rebellion in Mashonaland. Her eyes widened when she heard about the murders on isolated farms, about the attack on the Alice Mine, and Martin's experience on the road from Marandellas. When the African maid, Cecelia, came to say that supper was ready they moved into the dining room, which was lit by candles, and they were served a simple meal.

"You must be very well off now," said Martin, "—with Uncle George's millions. Does Perry think it was worth it? I remember so well his doubts about coming to Africa. He said the old man was bribing him."

She laughed. "He hated that trek up to Rhodesia—and putting up with you. You could be quite difficult, Martin. He says your standards were sometimes rather demanding."

"I did him a great favour! If he hadn't come north he'd never have met you. In fact I might have gone on my own to buy your father's bull."

She stood up and led him to the drawing room. "And what might have happened then?"

The maid served them coffee, and Louise thanked her, saying she could go. She waited for the maid to leave. "Do you ever remember how we met?"

"Yes, of course."

"Because I've never had the chance to ask you before—when we met in the Cape it was too recent—did you guess how I felt about you then?"

"I know how you felt about me. You thought I was 'deep and silent, like a well, with nothing to say'."

She put her hands to her face, her cheeks red. "You read my journal! Martin, how could you?"

"I read only the parts about me and Perry. I'm sorry, it wasn't noble of me." While she was still trying to recall what she'd written, he went on, "I thought you were rather unsure yourself...you seemed very young and vulnerable. And you turned to Perry."

"Only when you showed me you weren't interested in me." She poured him a liqueur. "And there was always Helen. Where do you and I stand now?"

"Now? You're married to my friend, and..."

She sighed deeply. "Oh Martin. You're impossible." She walked abruptly across the room to the large mirror over the mantelpiece; then she turned to face him, her eyes shining. "Is there anything of what you felt before? Why is it so difficult for you show your feelings? Is it perhaps that you don't have very strong emotions? Do you wish to keep all your thoughts to yourself, like some miser, to gloat over in your privacy?"

He was taken aback by her outburst. Until now he had enjoyed the banter, but here she was, becoming serious. "You know that none of that is true," he countered. Then he decided he had nothing to lose by telling her. "Very well, you shall hear it all—since you seem so determined to know."

"Every woman wants to know."

"When I first met you, and again at the Cape, and at Elandsfontein, I wanted to make love to you. At first I thought it was just lust... heightened because I'd had—well, no opportunities in Rhodesia. And also I thought it had much to with your youth, and your apparent innocence and vulnerability. I thought it was because you were physically very attractive..."

Her lips twitched as she enjoyed the praise. "And why didn't you—make love to me?"

"I told you. Because you seemed so vulnerable, so much younger than me."

"And so inexperienced? You can't think those things about me now."

"No, but in a way I still think of you in those terms. But it hasn't diminished the strength of my feelings for you."

"Is it still lust?"

He shook his head, stood up and walked over to her, putting his hands on her shoulders. He looked into her eyes trying to assess how she was thinking. Then she kissed him with surprising strength. He lifted her off the ground and carried her to a room that she indicated with touches of her hand.

The guest room had two single beds that had been moved together but not made up, draped with a bright patchwork cover. There they lay together embracing and kissing, but saying nothing, thinking their own thoughts. After a while, Louise went to look after her children. When she returned she was wearing a cotton dressing gown, but underneath it she was naked.

⟋⟍

Later, after they made love, they lay in each other's arms.

"We can never be to each other what we could have been. I could have matched you in all your endeavours. I have the strength of generations of pioneers. I was yours forever, Martin, just for the asking. Now I have been yours, but only for a tiny sliver of time."

"And I've never really known you. You always seemed to be darting away, like a little bird—elusive and rare, seen only in indistinct glimpses. Even now, when I'm as close to you as two people can be, I feel I don't really know you."

"You'll never have the time to know me now. We could have grown to know each other, but it's too late now." Her tone was not accusing, only stating facts as she saw them. "You wanted me, and now you've had me, but I fear you will not want me again. Are you a man who tastes and then seeks a new flavour?" When he denied it, she said, "At least we ought to see each other again. And when we do, we can remember that we've loved and felt each other's hearts."

They made love again, she sitting on him, moving slowly, savouring the sensations, the touch of his hands on her breasts. He spoke to her as he caressed her. When they had finished she fell asleep for a while, then woke, fearful that morning had come. She went to find out the time on the clock in the drawing room.

When she returned she said, "You must leave before Cecelia comes to work—another two hours. Perry must not hear that you stayed the night."

It was the first time his name had been mentioned. Martin pondered the implications of her adultery but said nothing about it. His hands were feeling her warm body again. She lay down beside him and he kissed her body, starting at her neck and working down to her toes, then he turned her over and stroked her with his lips and tongue. He realised that he was trying to store sensations of her, and images of her body that he might never feel and see again.

⟋⟍

CHAPTER 21
The Boer War Starts — 1899

Perry Davenport sat in the Pretoria office of Jan Smuts, the Attorney General of the Transvaal, his brother-in-law Hendrik Venter sitting next to him. It was a large airy room lined with long shelves of legal books bound in leather. Through the window, Perry could see imposing stone buildings on the far side of the street that seemed to have the same solidity as the Afrikaner people. Yet Smuts was not a typical Boer—a neat, dapper figure behind his huge desk; he watched Perry keenly, with clear blue eyes that held much humour.

"Mr Davenport, answer me truthfully," Smuts asked, "if there is another war with the British, on whose side would you fight?"

"I wouldn't fight against my wife's people, of that you can be certain...", answered Perry indignantly.

"Why not?"

"Because they're my family now." Perry glanced at Hendrik, who sat impassively, and evidently awed by his surroundings; this young man was now his 'family'.

Smuts nodded with understanding. "And could you fight against the British?"

"I don't know, Mr Smuts. I can't answer categorically. It would depend on the circumstances."

"Which side do you think is in the right?"

Perry looked directly into the lawyer's eyes and saw a man who was deeply intelligent. "Yours, of course. I'm certain the British are spoiling for a fight. They're looking for some excuse to annex the Transvaal—and probably the Free State as well. The problem is, your people are doing their best to give them an excuse..."

Hendrik seemed to come to life, turning to him angrily. "What do you mean?"

"By treating them as aliens." Perry ignored his brother-in-law, looking only at Smuts. "By not sharing some of the wealth of the Rand."

"Why should we share it?" Hendrik almost shouted.

Smuts raised a restraining hand to Hendrik while still speaking to Perry. "We do share it, Mr Davenport. The foreigners who work here earn good money—far more than they could get elsewhere. Investors make good profits and dividends, and we allow them to take their money back to their own countries."

"*Verdomme!*" Hendrik's face was suffused with anger. "We fought for this country. Our forefathers were killed in battles for it. Are we to hand it over to a rabble of grasping Jews and drunken Irish labourers?"

"Then keep them out," replied Perry calmly, without looking at his brother-in-law. "Dig out the wealth yourselves. But, if you allow them to help you, give them some rights. I don't say you should hand over the country—that would be absurd..."

"They have the right to live here," said Smuts quietly, "but we will not allow them to vote. Their numbers are growing so fast that their votes would outnumber our own. We could never allow that."

"You could give them some seats in the Raad. They could appoint their own representatives. At least it would give them some say."

Smuts shook his head. "It would not be acceptable."

"You can see he's not entirely committed to our cause," said Hendrik bitterly.

"Are you committed?" asked Smuts, looking at Perry searchingly.

"I believe the Afrikaners have the sovereign rights to the Transvaal," replied Perry. "I deplore the British designs to take control of the country..."

"What evidence do you have—of their designs?"

The American shook his head, wishing he could offer more. "Only hearsay. But there's plenty of smoke...And remember that I've moved freely among people who are influential."

"You mean Fitzpatrick and his cronies?"

"Yes, and Frank Rhodes, and Beit."

"And they talk freely with you, even knowing that you're married to a Boer?"

"They don't allude to my wife—and I don't remind them. They know I'm interested and want to hear more."

Smuts stood up and walked to the window behind his desk. He looked out, deep in thought, before turning back to face Perry. "Do they know you've raised support for us in America?"

"Of course not..."

Smuts stood up. "By the way, your help is deeply appreciated. Will you help again, Mr Davenport?"

"The question my backers ask," answered Perry, wryly, "and I can never give them an adequate answer, is what chance have you of winning?"

"Let me tell you about the stakes. You know, from your wife's family, how the *volk* have struggled for their homeland. Now we have peace and have found great wealth in the earth under us; maybe it's a reward. We can use that wealth to develop the country—to build roads and railways, schools and hospitals, to become a nation that can hold its head up with any others. But no sooner does this happen than Britain comes sniffing at our door—like a great dog that has smelled the savoury meat inside. Not content with their own empire—the wealth of India—Canada—Australia—they want more!" For the first time, Smuts' eyes showed a flash of anger. "We defeated them at Majuba, and Gladstone let us keep our independence. Now they're back again. They never stop! Look at the Jameson Raid. Yes, and you know the thinking of the British establishment. Do you think it's fair? Do you think the Chamberlains and the Milners of this world have the right to take our independence away? To deny the heritage of the Venter family— your wife—of Hendrik here, and of all the thousands of Afrikaners like them?"

"You haven't answered my question," said Perry stubbornly.

"Mr Davenport, I'm not a gambler, but I know the odds are on our side, for the simple reason that this is our country, these are our farms, our mines. We'll fight to the last man to keep them. And we know how to fight!" He thumped his fist in the palm of his left hand.

When Perry stood up to leave, Smuts came round the desk to usher them out. At the door, he shook Perry's hand. "I hope that you stay with us. We need help."

తొలోగ

Martin walked with Amanda in Green Park. He had been in England for two weeks, staying with his family in Oxford, and had come to London on the previous day to see Amanda. He took her to lunch at a fine restaurant and she invited him to her flat for coffee. She was now thirty, unmarried, a beautiful woman, and here she was, her arm in his, warm and close, but unattainable.

As if sensing his thoughts, she asked, "Why are you surprised that I don't have you as a lover?"

"Do I seem surprised?"

"Piqued? What happened between us nine years ago doesn't really have any significance now, does it? We're worlds apart—in several senses."

He saw little humour in her expression. "Don't you feel anything?"

"Of course I do." She squeezed his arm that was held firmly against her side, strong and reassuring. "I still find you very attractive."

"Whatever you feel for me, I'm full of admiration for you. You may remember, I was never against you suffragettes."

"I know, and I'm grateful for that. So you must understand that a woman like me doesn't have to have a husband—or a lover. She can have friends, as you and I are friends—or even an occasional liaison, as you and I have had—without tying the package in pretty ribbons." She paused. "By the way, I'm sorry for Beth. I think she fell rather heavily for your friend Perry. It was a blow when he turned up a married man."

"But she knew—from my letters."

"Yes, but to see him again was a shock. I was in Oxford at the time, when he and Louise called on their way to Boston. He has changed, don't you think? Grown up? More of a man—and he's much more attractive, which made it all the more upsetting for Beth." She looked at him carefully, almost an examination. "You've changed too. You're harder. Not as light-hearted as you were."

He felt uncomfortable hearing her analyse him. "Amanda, I've decided to try and join up."

"Oh!" It came to her as a real surprise. "I thought you were so opposed to what's happening out there."

"I am, but I feel it's my duty. Colonel Adams, who was my Adjutant in India, wants me to apply for a staff position with General Buller. He says they need people with experience of Africa."

"And you have plenty of that," she added, with a trace of bitterness.

☙❧

Perry sat on the verandah of his house in Johannesburg, reading a letter from Louise.

'Dearest Perry,

'Oupa is still alive, though very frail, and seems to be indestructible. The children are both well. I miss you so much, and wish that you could be with us instead of living so far away.'

'The news is alarming. We hear that British troops are being sent in great numbers to Natal, and also that the Raad is talking more than ever about the prospect of war. This is news from Jan Smuts himself, who came to the farm yesterday to pay respects to Oupa. He spoke well of you and sends his regards to you.'

'Hendrik tells us that a war is inevitable and every able-bodied man must take up arms. He asked what you would do, and I said that I did not know. What will you do? Write soon and tell me.'

જ્જી

At General Buller's headquarters in Aldershot Martin was introduced to staff officers by Colonel Adams, under whom he served in India. These formidable men sat at a long table opposite; Adams had joined them. Martin, who was alone on the other side, felt at a disadvantage, wearing a tweed suit while they were all in uniform. They were talking to each other and ignoring him. On the surrounding walls were portraits of those who had served their country before. Nevertheless, seeing all the trappings of the military he almost regretted his decision to enlist

"Gentlemen," said Adams, calling for attention. "Russell is known to me personally, from his service in India. He is already a seasoned campaigner in Southern Africa, having fought in the Matabele War of '93 and the rebellion in Mashonaland in '96. I strongly support his application to join our group."

A brigadier spoke from the centre of the formidable row of staff officers; they seemed stern behind their bristling moustaches and mutton-chop whiskers. "Yes, thank you Colonel. We've read your outline, Russell. You have certainly seen plenty of action in Rhodesia, but not, I think in South Africa?"

"That's correct, sir, but I've travelled extensively in South Africa, and I've fought alongside Boers, so I know something about their tactics and attitudes—and I can speak Afrikaans quite well."

"And why do you wish to join us here," asked a florid-faced colonel, "rather than go back to the outfit being assembled in Rhodesia."

"I don't want to be baulked in an attempt to travel north."

"What d'you mean?" asked the brigadier sharply.

"The Boers will almost certainly cut the railway line through to Bulawayo. I could travel by road, but it would take ages to get back to Rhodesia."

The brigadier glanced uneasily at the other members of the board, then turned back to Martin. "And where d'you think they'll cut the railway?"

He asked if he could indicate on the map, and when the brigadier nodded his assent he walked over to a map of Southern Africa that hung on the wall. "Somewhere around Mafeking probably. Here, I think. They'll cut the other railway lines of course."

The staff officers raised their eyebrows in unison. Such sweepingly pre-emptive action had not occurred to them. "Of course," said the brigadier. "Very well, Russell." He bent and whispered to his colleagues, who nodded. Then he said to Martin, "We've decided that you should join our staff group, as an intelligence officer...er, with the rank of Captain. We'll prepare to travel to South Africa at short notice."

❧⊱

In late September 1889, Perry and his younger brother-in-law, Ben Venter, rode along the dusty road from Johannesburg to Pretoria, the American on his bay gelding Rollo, wearing smart riding clothes that contrasted with the casual khaki trousers and shirt worn by Ben. The young lawyer was shorter than his companion, thin and wiry, riding a Basuto pony of less than fifteen hands.

"You know, I'm glad we're going to have a real war," said Ben. "This trouble's been brewing for almost as long as I can remember. It has to be concluded. Blood has to be shed to find the solution."

"I'm surprised to hear you—a lawyer—advocate bloodshed." Perry was in poor humour, because he was even further from seeing his wife and children.

"We've tried everything else. This is the only alternative left to us. If we can show the British they can't dictate to us, they won't bother us again." He looked at the American carefully. "Why didn't you go up to the farm to see Louise? Is there something the matter between you two?"

Perry shook his head slowly, his mood worsened by Ben's sudden change of subject. "It would have taken too long," he lied. "I'll see her again when she goes down to Franschhoek—if I can get leave." He really wanted desperately to see his wife, to hear her say the words she wrote, to start again, to make love to her. Yet here he was, riding off to a war with no certain outcome, but bound to cost many lives.

That evening they fell in with a group of a dozen Boers from the Louis Trichardt commando, who were hurrying to join their comrades. They shared a makeshift camp, with a big fire in a clearing, a thorn *kraal* for the horses, mutton and *boerwors* cooked on the coals, and two bottles of fiery *dop* passed round to wash down the meal.

One of the Boers said to Perry, "Who are you *rooinek?*"

"Hey, hey, man," intervened Ben. "He's my brother-in-law."

"Shut-up!" said the Boer. "Let him answer for himself. Come on then, man. Who are you?"

"I'm American," Perry answered calmly. "I'm on your side."

"How do we know you're not a spy?" asked another Boer.

"You don't," answered Perry, and there was a roar of laughter from the others. "But I'm not. You'll just have to trust me."

"Where do the Yankees stand?" someone shouted. "Are they on our side?"

"They haven't taken sides. I doubt they will. They have their own problems."

৵৵৵

About two weeks later, on 8th October 1899, Perry and Ben rode into the centre of Pretoria and found the town in turmoil. Men were gathered in small groups, laughing and calling to each other with the shivering excitement of impending action. They repeatedly cleaned their rifles, counted their ammunition, packed and re-packed saddle bags, filled and re-filled water bottles, and endlessly rubbed down their horses. Perry and Ben found the Pietersburg commando to the east of the town, near the road leading to Volksrust. They reported to the commander, Viljoen, a short burly farmer with a reputation for hard drinking.

"What can you do, lads?" asked Viljoen, in Afrikaans. "Fought before?"

Ben laughed nervously, and pointed to Perry. "He was in a war already."

Viljoen spat into the dust a stream of saliva yellowed with nicotine. "Where was that, *kerel*? In the kitchen?"

Perry smiled. "In Rhodesia in '93—the Matabele War."

"Hah! That was a skirmish, lad. Against a rabble of *kaffirs* too. *Agh!*" He spat again. "This will be a real war, against real soldiers—with rifles. Can you shoot, lad?"

"Of course!" Ben replied.

"He's alright, Viljoen," said a stocky young man from the back of the group. "I know the family."

Viljoen ignored the intervener. "Can you ride?" he asked the two companions.

Ben laughed. "I've just ridden all the way from Pietersburg! What do you mean?"

"I mean hard riding, *jong*—over rocky, hilly country—scouting, and carrying messages."

"We can do that," said Perry.

"Why are you with us, Yankee?" Viljoen eyed Perry sourly.

"He's married to my sister. Be careful, Viljoen; don't doubt him."

"Shut up! Let him answer for himself."

"I believe in your cause," said Perry quietly. "Otherwise I wouldn't think of fighting."

Viljoen nodded. "All right—we'll see." He turned to the men around him. "Get some rest, *kerels*. We have a long ride ahead."

❧❦

The grand parade was held next day, a march to honour the Boer commander, General Joubert. The word was passed around that President Kruger had finally given an ultimatum to the British Agent in Pretoria, telling him that unless Britain withdrew the new troops from Natal within forty-eight hours their actions would be regarded as a declaration of war. A great murmuring swept through the thronging men. There were ten thousand of them, the largest body of armed soldiers ever gathered in Southern Africa.

"Will the British back down?" asked a young Boer near Perry.

"Not likely!" said another.

"Then it's war tomorrow."

Someone laughed. "We'll sweep them into the sea—like rubbish!"

"May not be so easy," said Ben. "They're not a bunch of *kaffirs*."

"Not much better!" This remark was followed by a deluge of raucous laughter.

"They have ten thousand men too," said Perry.

"We'll have twice that number!" said a bearded Boer. "And better men than the English. You beat them, didn't you, Yankee?"

"The British can't shoot much better than *kaffirs*..."

"Remember Majuba!"

❧❧

Martin stood on the deck of the ocean liner *Dunottar Castle*, on its voyage from Southampton to the Cape. They were getting underway after a re-fuelling stop at Madeira, and he stood with a group of young staff officers. With them was a civilian, Winston Churchill, correspondent of the Morning Post. They were discussing the news they had picked up from the telegraph office in Madeira. With the sole exception of Martin, they were eager for action and resentful of their slow progress to the theatre of war.

"I expect by the time we get there it'll all be over," said one of Martin's fellow officers. "We'll head straight home again."

"How did the old man react to the news?" asked one of his friends, referring to General Buller.

"No reaction at all, as far as I could see," said Churchill. "Keeping his own counsel as usual. By the way, I wouldn't be too sure that the Boers can be beaten so quickly. Remember they're fighting in their own country."

"We know that, Winston," said a tall captain, "but they're not a real army, are they? They're just farmers who've volunteered."

"Perhaps, but they're very good shots and they fight in small tightly knit groups. What do you think, Martin?"

"My sense is that they'll be very difficult to defeat—if they fight a guerrilla war, which seems probable."

❧❧

Two days before the liner was due in Cape Town, the same group of young men were on deck, eagerly watching a freighter approaching, heading north.

"We should stop her to get the newspapers, or at least talk to the captain," said one officer.

"I've just heard," said Martin. "Buller won't allow it."

"I think it's ridiculous," said Churchill, "that we can't stop her and get some real news."

As the freighter drew closer, they saw a large blackboard hanging over the side of the freighter's superstructure, bearing the message: 'BOERS

DEFEATED—THREE BATTLES—PENN SYMONS KILLED'. The young men watched the passing ship in silence, then turned to look at each other.

"Well that's it, my friends," said a lieutenant, breaking the silence. "When we reach Cape Town it'll be 'about turn'."

"Three battles, by God! They must have really got stuck into each other!"

"Poor old Symons. I never met him. Heard he was a good man."

"Not so old either. How did the Boers get to him? A sniper perhaps?"

જ્જ્જ્જ્

When the liner reached Cape Town, Martin rode in a carriage with fellow officers in procession up Adderley Street to the cheers of a small crowd, some of them waving Union flags. He recalled the first time he drove up this street, with Perry in '90. He could never have anticipated all the conflict in the intervening years, and least of all this monstrous confrontation that threatened the whole region. Later, they attended a staff meeting in Cape Town Castle, when a brigadier explained the war status. It was their first opportunity to hear a definitive account of the action.

When the murmur of voices subsided the brigadier moved to a large war map. "The Boers are trying to get to the coast at Durban. They know we're sending reinforcements there so they want to stop us landing. Sir George White is in Ladysmith—that's a small town here..." He pointed to the map.

"Sir, is it true that they're under siege?" came a voice from the back.

"Yes," was the brisk answer, "and an immediate objective is to relieve them." The brigadier pointed again at the map. "The Boers have also invaded the Cape Colony, and have laid siege to Kimberley. So that's our second objective."

Several arms were raised by questioners, and the brigadier pointed to one.

"Is it true that the High Commissioner wants us to stay here to defend the city?"

After waiting for laughter to subside, the brigadier replied with a sardonic smile. "An idle rumour—you'll hear a lot of those. General Buller has split the army, to follow those two immediate objectives of relieving Ladysmith and Kimberley. He's chosen to go with the force to Durban. The dispositions are..."

એ∞ન્ફ

Sir Alfred Milner gave a splendid reception for the staff officers of Buller's army. As Martin entered the huge ballroom at Government House, his thoughts were invaded by waves of memories—his first sight of Helen with the young ladies, his meeting with her father, and the waltz round this room with her. He had not seen her for five months, and there had been no letter to meet him when he docked. Mingling with the guests, nursing a glass of red wine, he noticed Lady Violet Cecil, who he knew slightly from a dinner party given by his parents in Oxford in '95. He greeted her and asked her how she came to be in the Cape.

"Hello, Martin. I thought you were farming in Rhodesia."

He explained how he came to be on General Buller's staff, and repeated his question.

She was tall and blonde, with a patrician nose, and spoke with an aristocratic drawl. "I'm actually trying to help H.E. The poor man's having a difficult time."

"I suppose he's worried that the Boers will sweep south?"

"Worse than that." She looked over her shoulder. "Don't repeat this, Martin. You army people seem to forget that there are lots of Boers in the Cape. The whole countryside is populated with them. They could rise up at any moment. But, if we send troops to garrison the *veld*, it will only antagonise them. They may have to garrison this town."

"But the Prime Minister's a Boer," Martin protested. "Won't he be able to control them?"

"Schreiner? Oh, he says he won't side with the Transvaal Boers. But he's sitting on the fence. If he saw a main chance, he'd go with it. Poor Alfred has to go and talk to him nearly every day to find out what he's thinking."

Martin was not a chauvinist, in the sense that he valued the opinion of women like Violet who were close to the centre of policy. "So what's your best guess about what will happen?"

She, in turn, appreciated that one of the General Staff should ask her opinion. "I'm sure it will all be over by the end of the year, Martin. The Boers must come to their senses when they see the might of the British Empire lined up against them. Don't you think so?"

He shook his head. "No, but I'm a lone voice in the staff room. In my opinion the Afrikaners are too stubborn to give in so easily." Fearing that he might sound subversive, he changed the subject. "I heard that you're staying here in Government House?"

She drew him aside, to avoid a young officer who was approaching. "Actually, I've moved out to Groote Schuur."

"Isn't that Rhodes' house?"

"Yes, but of course he's not there now, poor dear. He's besieged in Kimberley. It must be driving him mad."

"Why did you leave here—if you're being such a tower of strength to H.E.?"

She smiled wryly. "Because Mrs Chamberlain has come out from England?"

"You mean the P.M.'s wife?"

"No darling, his sister-in-law. You know her husband, Richard, died? Well, she's come out here to throw her cap at poor Alfred." She leaned closer to him, to whisper. "She's a dreadful woman. I decided to get out from underfoot. Of course Alfred and I still play tennis together...". Another officer approached them, and she altered her tone from conspiratorial to jocular. "I say, Martin, whenever are you chaps going to have a go at the Boers. Surely Buller can't be happy hanging around here?"

It was over a week before Martin found a sound horse, and an opportunity to visit Franschhoek. He sent a telegram to Jeanne, who replied that she would be delighted to see him. She was still staying at the de Villiers estate, and he rode out as before. While they walked slowly through the beautiful garden in front of the Cape Dutch mansion she told him she had decided not to marry the wealthy farmer who had been courting her. Martin told her how he had joined the British army; he expected Jeanne to be critical, but she merely nodded, as if she understood that it was a natural course for him.

After a while, she said. "Perry decided to join the Boer army. Are you surprised?"

Martin whistled. "I am. I expected he'd stay in Jo'burg and organise weapons from America—or some civilian role like that."

"I thought so too. He's had a quarrel with Louise. I don't know the reason. In her last letter she said that Perry had refused to go up to the farm. I expect she'll see him when she comes here." Looking at him shrewdly, she added, "Do you know why they've quarrelled?"

"How would I know?" he blustered, immediately suspecting that Perry had discovered Louise's infidelity. "I haven't heard from Perry since I left for England."

"But he was in America, when you left—when you saw Louise in Johannesburg. Could that be the reason for the quarrel? I know Perry's jealous of you."

"I hope not, Jeanne. If there was something between me and Louise, it's over now." He knew he was failing to disguise his guilt.

She shrugged. "Well, whatever the reason, I hope they patch it up soon."

❧

CHAPTER 22
Elandslaagte – October 1899

Perry Davenport dozed fitfully in the shade of a tall eucalyptus. There were a few flowers left on the tree and when he was awake he could hear the drone of bees as they moved busily above him. The air was still, and some of the fragrance of broken leaves and scented wood smoke tingled his senses. Someone was cutting wood and the regular whacking sound echoed up to his position. A horseman clattered up; Perry sat up and reached for his rifle. The young messenger's thin chestnut horse was lathered with sweat near the girth, and stood with nostrils flaring and flanks heaving.

"Yankee! General Meyer wants to speak to you," he announced in Afrikaans, adding, "You'd better hurry!" He took off his slouch hat and wiped his brow with the sleeve of his khaki shirt.

Perry stood up, and stretched his back. "Where is he?"

"You have to follow me."

They set off at the steady canter the Boers typically used. Riding his big gelding Rollo, Perry followed the young messenger up the hill and along the edge of the eucalyptus plantation to a group of small stone cottages where Meyer's command group was bivouacked. Dismounting, he held Rollo's head, stroking the sheen of the horse's neck.

The broad-chested bearded General Meyer was inside one of the cottages talking to his commando leaders. Looking harassed, he turned to look for someone, then called for a staff officer who informed him that the messenger had returned. When he came out, Meyer wiped his mouth with the back of his hand, then noticed Perry and nodded, exchanging a few words with the staff officer that Perry could not hear.

After a few moments Meyer looked up at him and beckoned him forward. "Davenport?" He shook Perry's hand. "I want you to ride down to Dundee. Find out what you can about the numbers of men and guns, and where they are—their state of readiness—prospects of reinforcement. Anything you can find out. Do you think you can do that? You must return by tomorrow evening, before midnight—without fail. Go to Smith's farm, which is on the hill overlooking Dundee. Give us a duck whistle..." The general imitated the call of a flying duck, a sound that would not normally be heard at night. "The password is *klipspringer*. You will take this man de Wet with you." He pointed to the young messenger. "His English is not good; so be careful if you have to do any talking. Do you have any questions?"

"Are we spies?"

"Yes—and you risk being shot if the British catch you." He looked keenly at Perry. "I can't force you to go. I recommend you wear a uniform shirt with badges under your jacket, and throw the jacket away if you're caught."

Perry shrugged. "I could be shot anywhere." He mounted and wheeled to ride away.

"Good luck!" Meyer called after him.

At the outset of the war Perry decided that he would not spy, feeling that it would somehow be reprehensible to seek information from men who had been friends and colleagues. However, in this context of military operations, he accepted a role of providing information about the enemy. Uniforms were generally worn only by officers. If he was caught he could always argue that he had never been issued with a uniform. Besides, he felt fatalistic. Death in front of a firing squad held no great fears. It would be a death with honour, and Louise would grieve for him.

They found a clump of trees at the outskirts of Dundee, with a large ditch running through it towards the road. Here they rested and buried their rifles in shallow depressions covered with dead leaves. They walked with their horses down to the town, where they booked into a small hotel of a sort frequented by commercial travellers. There Perry had a long hot bath, his first for a week, and later joined de Wet at the bar.

An elderly man nursed a pint mug of beer in the corner of the bar. After looking over the visitors with careful appraisal, he asked, in English, "Going to Durban, lads? Saw you ride in."

"Yeah," replied Perry, not trying to disguise his American accent, "there's no sense in staying in Jo'burg. It's a ghost town now. Maybe I'll go back to America and come back when it's all over."

The old man cackled, sputtering phlegm. "It'll be over before you get there—if the English troops I've seen here are to be believed. Name's Jenkins." He pointed to himself. "Welsh, from way back."

Perry did not introduce himself. He wondered if this man held some grudge against the English, and could be pumped for information. "I haven't seen any troops yet."

"Oh, they're full of confidence. To hear them brag, they'll be in Jo'burg next week. Mind you, there's a lot of them here—about five thousand, they say—and another ten thousand coming up the road from Durban."

"Ten thousand? That'll take them a long time," said Perry. He glanced at de Wet, who was listening, but by their prior agreement remained silent.

"At least," agreed Jenkins. "They're having all sorts of trouble with their baggage—so they say—and they won't go without it."

The barman came to join them. "Soft, they are." He spat, with a curled lip of disdain. "Put them in the sun for a couple of hours and they'll melt into a puddle. Rotten shots too. Mate of mine saw them on the range—they could hardly hit the targets, let alone the bull's eye!"

This conversation continued for about ten minutes, until Perry and his companion finished their drinks and left.

&∘&

Next morning Perry and de Wet explored the town on the pretext of looking for provisions, which were extremely scarce. They watched some of the artillery teams practising limbering and un-limbering their guns, while the day passed slowly. As soon as it was dark, they unearthed their rifles and returned to the hills. When they reached the rendezvous near the eucalyptus plantation, de Wet sounded the duck whistle. A sentry called to them and de Wet gave the password. The sentry led them to a small stone cottage, which was Meyer's HQ, where they were ushered in, finding the general smoking a pipe, in discussion with one of his commanders. He immediately sat them down, sent an orderly for mugs of coffee, and while they drank he listened to their accounts, first Perry, then de Wet.

When they were finished, Meyer said, "Well done lads! Now, ride back to the railway and give the information to General Kock."

So it was that on the 21st of October 1899, Perry and his companion found General Kock near the Elandslaagte Halt on the line of rail. It was not a station, merely a place where goods could be transferred, on the main line between Durban and Johannesburg. The general, with a staff of about a dozen Boers, had his headquarters on a *kopje* overlooking the Halt. The two messengers gave the password, and after a screening by a staff officer, were ushered into the general's tent. Exhausted after their

ride through the night they gave him their account of the British dispositions in Dundee, as well as sealed messages from General Meyer; then
they collapsed into sleep among the rocks.

❧ ☙

Next morning, news of a British attack filtered through the Boer
encampment; opinions varied about enemy numbers and whether cavalry would be involved. There was plenty of bravado and allusions to
Majuba, but Perry detected some nervousness about the sheer numbers
of the opposition. By afternoon, he was lying behind a rock, watching
the British forces advancing. It was obvious that his Johannesburg commando was heavily outnumbered. When the firing started, despite the
wide front of the attack, the Boers were unable to hold the advancing
British troops at bay. Perry sniped from behind his rock, with young de
Wet a few yards away. The American was not a good shot, and his aim
was affected by an intense fear, mitigated by simmering disdain for the
men advancing towards him. They were kilted Gordon Highlanders who
bounded forward from rock to rock, often exposed to the accurate Boer
fire. They were getting closer all the time, but at the expense of heavy
casualties.

A message to withdraw was shouted through the Boer ranks. Perry
wriggled back from his position trying to shelter from the British fire.
He saw General Kock, a commanding figure in his frock coat, marshal-
ling his men back. There was something deeply impressive about this
patriarchal figure that gave Perry heart. A huge storm approached as
the afternoon light faded; deep grey clouds loomed above, and lightning
flickering above the hills. At half past four the rain started, and he was
quickly drenched, while young de Wet was cursing as he huddled to a
boulder. Perry ran back to Rollo, who was grazing loose, and soothed the
big horse as thunder reverberated over them.

A dishevelled Boer ran past shouting "We've had it! Let's get out of
here!" Another man followed soon after. "There are too many of them!"

The Boers started to mount their horses for escape, but Perry
returned to his former position beside de Wet where he could hear General Kock shouting to rally his men. An aching fear wrenched Perry at
his guts. The situation was hopeless. The Highlanders were everywhere,
scurrying and squirming forward, seemingly oblivious of the Boer commando's fire, although it was now weakening. About ten minutes later

Perry heard the General's order for a withdrawal. Yelling to de Wet, he ran back to his horse. Suddenly, as he mounted, there was a shout from another group of fleeing Boers.

"Cavalry! Look out!"

Looking to his right he saw a wave of Lancers thundering towards him. For an awful instant he weighed his chances of out-galloping them, but the way to the rear was strewn with rocks, and the Lancers had effectively cut off the Boer retreat. He dismounted and slapped Rollo across the haunch with his hat, shouting "Go Rollo!" The big horse lunged away into the driving rain, stirrups flapping.

He took a firing position behind a boulder and watched the Lancers grouping about a hundred yards away, their horses plunging and tossing their heads as they were reined in. Blinking through the unremitting rain, he could just make out an officer shouting orders. Then they charged, the troopers' lances lowered, the sabre blades of the officers glistening in the damp evening light. His stomach knotted tighter, but his sphincter loosened and he felt a warm flow down his thighs. He imagined the lance thrust through him, and the sabre slash against his neck. When he ran out of ammunition for his rifle he pulled out his Colt revolver and waited for the thundering line of charging Lancers. The ground vibrated with their hoof beats, and the air reverberated with their shouts as they urged each other on.

When the Lancers were twenty yards away, Perry fired his first revolver shot. He just had time for a second shot before they were all around him. A sweeping sabre slash from a young moustached lieutenant just missed him as he ducked away. Only moments left before I die, he thought, and time seemed suspended while a feeling of serenity came over him. In his peripheral vision he could tell that all the Boers and their servants were dismounted, some of them lying stricken on the ground, others groaning from wounds. A few waved white handkerchiefs as they tried to surrender.

He heard a hoarse cry and saw de Wet crawling towards him, his arm dangling loosely in a blood-soaked sleeve. He had lost his hat, and rain streamed down his agonised face. "Yankee! Help me, for God's sake! *Agh*! They're coming again!"

Perry dragged the Boer to the shelter of his boulder only moments before the second charge descended on them. Distinctly, he heard the shouts from the Lancers: "Good pig sticking, lads!"; "Tally-ho, and at them!"; "Remember Majuba!"

He fired at point blank range into a tall captain of the Lancers, who was leaning from his horse as he swung his sabre. The shot hit the officer in the chest, but he still delivered the sabre blow; the blade turned so it was flat when it struck Perry in the face. He fell to the ground, stunned, and for an instant, as his thoughts faded, he saw de Wet reaching towards him while a lance was driven through the young man's body. A Lancer trooper pulled out the point with a sickly sucking sound, then turned to answer a shout from his officer. Perry lost consciousness.

∂∿∾∾

Darkness was relieved by a quarter moon, and a chill mist drifted over the battlefield. Coagulating moisture dripped slowly from the brim of Perry's hat onto his face, reviving him. He lay on his side near the boulder, and as he opened his eyes he saw lights moving around him. He tried to move, thinking of escape. The body of the Lancer captain lay some ten paces away, and memories of the sabre slash returned, as he crawled to the corpse to pull off the officer's jacket, fumbling with the large brass buttons. After putting it loosely over his shoulders, he removed his bush hat and stuffed it in one of the large pockets.

One of the bobbing lights approached and a face peered at Perry. With one hand the medical orderly held up his hurricane lamp, with the other he pointed a revolver, and with strong Scottish accent, he said, "You've been 'it on the cheek, sir."

"I'm all right," whispered Perry hoarsely, concealing his American accent. "Just a graze. See to the others."

"You're sure, sir? All right, I'll come back later." The orderly moved off into the gloom.

Perry raised himself shakily to his feet and stumbled back to de Wet's body, finding it cold and stiff. Then he started to trudge painfully in the direction of the Biggarsberg. His cold wet clothes clung painfully to his aching body, and when blood started to seep from the wound on his cheek, he tried to mop it with his handkerchief. Some time later, the mist thickened and he had to stand and wait while he tried to regain his bearings, shivering uncontrollably. He could no longer see the lamps of the medical orderlies on the battlefield, nor was there any vestige of sound. Moving on, every now and then he stopped to give Rollo's whistle, but felt certain a fleeing Boer had taken his horse.

A clatter of stones startled him. The huge figure of a horse loomed out of the mist; it was Rollo. The big gelding snorted in greeting and started to nudge Perry in the chest so hard that he fell over. He scrambled up and caught the reins, then led the horse to a rock where he clambered up to mount. Once in the saddle, he slumped forward over Rollo's withers, feeling the warmth seep up through his wet clothing, breathing in the horse's familiar odour. Then he lapsed into unconsciousness again.

He woke to a shout in Afrikaans. "A khaki! A wounded bastard." The Boers used the name 'khaki' as a term of derision to describe the British soldiers.

"I'm not a khaki," he called back in Afrikaans. "I put on this jacket to escape."

"Hell, man, I could've shot you," said the guard, coming closer, rifle at the ready.

Perry had reached a Boer encampment. One of General Joubert's scouts had seen him come through the mist. They took him to the *laager* where men gathered round; some of them knew him as the American messenger. They plied him with questions about the battle, and before long, Ben Venter appeared and took care of him. The wound on his face was a mat of blood congealed in his beard. Ben's African servant cleaned it with surgical spirits and then applied a bandage, wound round his head. During the day the servant fed Perry and changed his dressings, muttering soothing words.

With little enthusiasm, he tried to write a letter to Louise:

I feel so frustrated, sitting here, while the war is being fought a few miles away. I can hear Big Tom, our huge howitzer, shelling Ladysmith. General Botha has taken command, but I've heard that Kruger's insisting on a defensive role. Goodness knows why! They say Joubert was too slow and cautious...

It then occurred to him that censors would not allow such statements in a letter.

I'm sorry I said those things about you and Martin. I was jealous. I want to see you, so we can talk about it without anger.

Ben took him to meet General Botha. A group of men surrounded the young general; Louis Botha was thirty-seven, a farmer, and a member of the Raad. He shook Perry's hand, and with a broad smile said, "So Davenport. I see a British sabre has wounded you. I hope you live to tell your grandchildren about it."

"So do I, sir."

"I'm afraid you'll carry the scar for the rest of your life. Now I want you to tell me what happened at Elandslaagte. My intelligence staff have already reported to me—what was it the Lancers shouted—when they charged?"

Choosing his words carefully, Perry replied, "I definitely heard them say 'No prisoners'."

"And you say they attacked the servants too?"

"Yes, sir. They showed no mercy to them, although they were unarmed."

Botha shook his head in disbelief. "I heard these accounts from other survivors. I'm truly surprised—and shocked. What do you think of their behaviour? Do you think it was justified by the heat of the battle?"

"Definitely not, sir!" Perry shook his head, but soon regretted the gesture as pain pounded through it.

"In God's name, I hope we never behave like that! Now, young man, I want you to ride with my command group. You could be very useful—when you're fully recovered."

☙❧

The Boer column set off before dawn on the 15th of November 1899, and near the Blaau Kranz River they heard the puffing of the armoured train that was sent north from Estcourt by the British. Waiting by a low *kopje* they watched the train shuffle past—an armoured locomotive with three trucks in front and three behind; one of them carried a field gun. When the train was out of sight, General Louis Botha ordered the men to pile rocks on the line just beyond a bend where the returning train could not see the blockade until the last moment. Then he and his troops waited further up the line, in swirling mist. About two hours later they heard the train returning, the panting of its engine muffled by the heavy air.

"Wait for our guns to fire!" shouted Botha.

As the train came past the Boer field guns each fired a shot. They missed, but the locomotive driver accelerated, and the train clattered round the bend and into the rock blockade. The front truck toppled off the rails and the two behind it were partially dislodged, but the locomotive, tender, and the rear trucks stayed on the rails. Perry could hear faint shouts from the British while he fired occasionally to give cover for a Boer raiding party, but the range was too great for their rifles. They advanced slowly, picking their cover as the troops in the train fired back at them. Perry could see figures around the engine, which was shunting backwards and forwards in an attempt to push the forward trucks off the line. After more than an hour the British were able to get the engine and tender free, but the rear trucks were now abandoned. The locomotive set off for Chieveley, festooned with wounded soldiers.

"Let it go!" shouted Botha. "It's taking wounded away."

White flags were being waved from the abandoned trucks as the Boer raiding party approached. Perry rode alongside Botha to see the prisoners and to help with interpreting. As they approached, they noticed that one of the British men was not wearing a uniform.

"Are you a spy?" asked Botha in English.

The man was indignant. "Certainly not. I'm a newspaper correspondent."

"What newspaper?" Botha seemed amused.

"The Morning Post. My name is Winston Churchill."

Botha turned away to supervise his men, but Perry stayed and stared at Churchill. "When you write about the war," said Perry, "ask about what happened at Elandslaagte."

"What about it? It was a good win for us." Churchill cocked his head to one side. "Are you an American?"

"Yes. It's not a game, man. There's no winning; only losing." Perry turned his horse and rode after Botha.

&∘&

CHAPTER 23
The Battle Of Colenso –
December 1899

Perry sat in the Boer camp near the Tugela River, writing a letter to Louise: *'I've been with Botha for four weeks. galloping with messages. Usually I wait for hours while lengthy meetings are held. Then suddenly I'm ordered to ride off with a message. We're digging in behind the Tugela and we'll wait here for the British to attack...'*

The great British army was assembling on the other side of the Tugela River in Natal, near the village called Colenso, and the sight unnerved some Boers, who started to return to their farms. A commando that had been sent across the river to hold Bosch Kop returned to join their friends, arguing that their only hope was to stay together.

At the same time, Martin arrived by train at the small township of Frere, bored with the long journey from Durban. A hot wind rolled off the bushveld as he climbed down at the little station and stretched his stiff limbs before walking to the horse truck to find his old chestnut gelding Chandra. The old horse had been with him since he bought him near Palapye in 1890. On his way to England, Martin had ridden Chandra to Johannesburg, and when he knew that war was imminent, had telegraphed the livery to send the horse to the Cape. Now, he was glad to have his trusty companion for the campaign ahead.

Chandra whickered as Martin approached to speak to him, stroking his head and neck. Then he rode up to General Buller's headquarters on a small hill south of Colenso. Leaving Chandra with an orderly he entered the tents, which swarmed with staff officers. He had to work his way through the security net of warrant officers until he reached a friendly ADC who showed him to a sleeping tent with a spare corner, where he dropped his saddlebags.

After watering his horse he rode back to Buller's headquarters, where he stood with his fellow officers looking out with his field glasses towards the Tugela River. They could see the dull reddish *kopjes* on the far side. There the Boers had placed their defensive line, and the British force had to cross the river and fight its way through to reach beleaguered Ladysmith. Knowing the shooting capability of the Boers, Martin realised that it was a daunting task.

A young fellow officer, Lieutenant Freddy Roberts, son of General Roberts, came up to Martin and clapped him on the shoulder. "Can you see them?"

Lowering his field glasses he replied. "Hello, Freddy. No I can't. You have a look."

"They have a camp over by that far *kopje*," said Roberts, peering through the haze. "To the right of the road to Ladysmith. But they're dug into the base—and the hill tops for all we know."

"Where's Ladysmith?"

Roberts pointed. "Over there. It's about twelve miles from here. We can see their heliograph easily."

"Do we have any intelligence about the Boer positions?"

"Too much." Roberts laughed quietly. "I don't know how much is believable. Care to go over and have a look?"

"Seriously, what about using native spies? They must be moving across the river..."

"Pretty scarce now. Besides, our chaps seem to have decided that they're not reliable enough." Roberts handed the binoculars back to Martin. "Come on, let's go and have a bite to eat."

The two officers went into the mess tent and helped themselves to some slices of beef and bread on covered plates on a trestle table; there was a jug of fresh orange juice and another of water, from which they poured drinks. Later, they went to a table and sat down with a staff officer colleague.

"Have you chaps heard the news from the Cape?" he asked. "There's been a battle at Stormberg. Five hundred of ours killed or wounded. There's a rumour they got lost in the night and were surrounded."

Martin was struck more and more by the inevitability of being drawn into the conflict, and wondered why he'd volunteered to serve. He could now be on his farm in Rhodesia, smoking his pipe and drinking a beer with Tom Ellsworth. Better still, he could be visiting Helen, who was now on her own—Robert had volunteered and was now besieged in Mafeking.

He stayed up late at night talking to the officers with whom he shared his tent, Freddy Roberts and Wally Congreve. Their hurricane lamp guttered and their shadows shivered on the inside of the canvas.

"Can't extend the line too far," Congreve was saying. "The Boers could nip round and cut off the supplies."

"Surely we have enough men to ensure a defended line," protested Roberts. "The longer we wait, the more opportunity we're giving to the Boers to prepare."

Martin left the tent and walked to the horse lines to check on Chandra, stopping to talk to one of the grooms who was rubbing down a horse.

"Which one's yours, sir?" asked the groom, then hearing Chandra whicker, he added, "Well, at least 'e knows you."

Martin laughed. "So he should. He's been mine for nine years." He gave his horse a piece of sugar, and stroked him.

"Salted, is 'e?"

"Yes, before I bought him. I'm lucky to have him here. I rode down from Rhodesia a few months ago, and had him railed to the Cape."

"Aye, well 'e looks none the worse for it."

≈∞∞

At dawn on the morning of 15th December, Martin sat mounted on Chandra on the HQ hill, a few yards from General Buller and his staff officers. He was waiting to take a message to General Hildyard, and Freddy Roberts beside him also waited for a message. Martin had confided to his fellow officer his apprehension about the attack, and the tendency for the staff officers to underestimate the Boers' capabilities.

"We've been shelling them for an hour and not a sound from them," countered Roberts. "Do you think they've gone?"

"I doubt it," answered Martin gloomily. "But they must have suffered terribly."

The British regiments advanced through the long brown grass towards the river. A cloud of dust rose above the infantry and hung like a mist over them, while across the river loomed the steep rocky *kopjes* where the Boers were entrenched. As the Irish Brigade approach the river, a dense crackle of rifle fire broke out.

Roberts shouted excitedly, "I say, look at that! There goes Long!" He pointed to the plain ahead where Colonel Long led the artillery forward, twelve field guns at the front, followed by six naval guns. To Martin the cavalcade seemed completely out of control.

A major rode up to join them. "Where the hell is he going?" Together they watched the progress of Colonel Long's battery.

"He's going too far," muttered Roberts.

The major shouted ineffectually at the far distant Colonel Long. "Stay behind the infantry, man!"

Long's force was two miles away. The staff officers watched through binoculars as the guns were unlimbered, as if on a parade ground. The limbers were taken to the rear in regulation style, and the guns started to fire. When the assembled staff officers saw the little puffs of distant smoke they started cheering, and seconds later they heard the reports echoing over the dusty plain. Suddenly another ominous sound came to them; the boom of a Boer howitzer echoed across the valley, and a dense fusillade of rifle fire broke out from across the river, where the Boers had lain hidden.

General Buller shouted to one of his staff captains, "Go and see what the guns are doing. They seem much too close to the river. If they're in trouble, tell them to withdraw at once."

Twenty minutes later, the captain returned, his horse half blown, his face flushed with excitement. "They're all right," he gasped.

"Surely they must be under heavy fire?" protested Buller.

"They are, sir. But they seem quite comfortable."

The general shook his head in exasperation. "Comfortable?" He gazed gloomily down at the battle scene. He could see clearly that this valuable battery of artillery was within range of the Boer rifles from across the river. "The guns are too far forward," he grumbled. "He's completely in the wrong position."

"They've stopped firing," announced Roberts. "Something's the matter."

Buller turned his ruddy face to the young officers. "Come on, we'd better help them."

The general and his staff officers mounted their horses. Martin rode with them down the hillside in choking dust. After about a mile, they met two captains, dishevelled and almost falling off their horses, galloping towards them. They stopped when they saw Buller and almost incoherent words poured out.

"The guns are out of action, sir!"

"They need more ammunition, sir!"

"The men are done, and all the guns!"

Buller grunted in annoyance and brusquely signalled to his party to ride on with him. Reaching the point where General Hildyard was preparing to make his advance, the two generals conferred for a few minutes, out of the hearing of the staff officers. When Buller returned to his staff officers, he announced, "I've called off today's attack. Now let's see what we can do about those guns."

They rode on urgently to a deep *donga*—a steep-sided ravine—behind the naval guns, which were about four hundred yards behind Long's battery. They put the horses into order and then led them up from the *donga* towards the guns. They were a thousand yards from the river, but the Boer bullets fizzed around them. When they reached the guns, they limbered them and dragged them back towards the *donga*, hunching against the crackling rifle fire. A trooper fell with a groan. Spurts of dust flew from the ground where bullets struck. Shells landed amongst them too, and General Buller was hit by a piece of shrapnel. Martin saw him rub his ribs briskly, as if a wasp had stung him.

Eventually, the naval guns were dragged down into shelter. The rescue party now moved further along the *donga* towards Long's twelve field guns. A shell explosion nearby startled Chandra; he jinked and tripped, then started limping. Martin dismounted and followed the others on foot. By climbing the wall of the *donga* he could see the guns. Strung in a lonely line on the plain, about four hundred yards away, were the prizes waiting to be won. The rifle fire from the river was vicious—to leave the *donga* would be suicidal.

About a hundred yards ahead of Martin, General Buller urged some men to volunteer. For a moment there was no response. They all knew they would be subjected to a hail of Boer bullets. Then a group stood up. With Roberts and Congreve leading, they rode out of the *donga*, galloping forward to the guns. Almost immediately, some of the horses and men fell in a welter of dust.

Martin soon reached their point of departure from the *donga* and decided to follow them. He left Chandra, thinking him too lame to be of much service. As he emerged onto the plain he could hear the bullets crack as they passed him, and for a moment he lost sight of the guns in the dust. Then one of them loomed ahead.

Others had already reached the limbers and were starting to harness their frightened horses. Martin joined them, and at that point noticed that Chandra had followed him. He hitched the horse's reins to his belt, and started to help one of Buller's ADCs, Captain Lee, to attach horses to the guns, struggling with the leather harnesses. Boer bullets cracked as they passed. A trooper beside him was hit in the head and fell to the ground with blood gushing from his nose and mouth. Lee was shouting instructions, encouraging the men to hold on.

Suddenly, Chandra screamed as a bullet raked through his chest. He reared up and crashed to the ground. Martin scrambled round his horse's body, trying to find the wound, and in a moment discovered the point of entry and realised the wound would be fatal. He held Chandra's great head on his lap, and felt in vain for a pulse in the horse's neck. The eyes were shut, and after a moment the body shuddered. He knew that Chandra had died.

A sergeant crawled up to him, his face caked with sweat and dust. "Bad is it, sir?" He looked down at the stricken horse. "Oh dear, 'e'll never make it. Better put 'im out of 'is misery." He glanced towards the river. "God knows why we 'aven't all been 'it."

Martin left Chandra to go forward to help limber one of the guns. Within seconds, his helmet was knocked from his head as if swatted off by some giant's hand, and he ducked involuntarily. The lead horses of the gun train strained into their harnesses, but the gun refused to budge. Martin shouted encouragement to the horses while he bent and grasped the lead traces, helping Captain Lee to heave them forward. The horses strained again and the gun moved.

"Come on Russell!" shouted Lee. "Let's get out of here while we can."

Martin called back, "My horse is wounded. I'll follow you."

"You're crazy! Come on!" Lee joined the gun train, gathering speed as they fled from the deadly swarm of bullets.

Martin crawled on his hands and knees back to Chandra. He wanted to be certain that his horse had died. He felt again for a pulse but could find none. Sitting disconsolate with head bowed, tears starting in his eyes, he stroked Chandra's broad neck, and muttered, "Goodbye, old fellow."

At that moment he heard a groan from one of the fallen men, and scrambled over to find it was Freddy Roberts, who has been wounded in the chest. Pink blood oozed out of the stricken man's mouth; his skin was deathly pale under its coating of dust.

"Hold on, Freddy!" urged Martin. "We'll get you back."

Roberts tried to shake his head. "I've had it—can hardly breathe..."

"Take it easy." Martin looked around and saw another limbered gun and crew turning to flee. He hailed them, shouting, "It's Roberts—wounded."

The gun team drew up, and Captain Schofield ran up to Martin, hunched in fear of the flying bullets. "How bad is it?" he shouted above the din.

"Chest wound," Martin replied. "In the lung, I think. He's conscious, but he'll have to be carried."

"Right. Can't put him on a horse. Can't wait for a stretcher. We'll take it in turns—fireman's chair. You and me start."

The men took it in turns to lift their wounded colleague onto linked hands, and half ran, trying to keep up with the gun train. As they approached the *donga*, other men hurried out to help them.

❧

It was late afternoon, but still hot. They were out of range of the firing now, and officers gathered round to congratulate the men who had rescued the guns. Another group sorted out the wounded.

"We've got to get the rest of Long's men out before it gets dark," said a Colonel.

Martin volunteered wearily, knowing they needed a man who had been forward and knew the way. The Colonel told him he could have a dozen men, and within half an hour they reached the place where he had crouched in the *donga*. The firing from across the river had virtually stopped. Ambulance men, white and black, moved up the *donga*, occasionally making sorties onto the plain to carry off bodies on stretchers. Martin worked his way further along the *donga*, and rounding a bend, came on a huddled group of wounded men. One of them was Wally Congreve, with a bloody bandage tied around his leg.

Congreve smiled weakly. "Good to see you, Russell. My damned leg's caught it. You look done in."

"I'm alright, but Freddy's wounded in the chest—it looks very bad."

"Oh, hell!" Congreve seemed to collapse. "Poor fellow. He was so...." His voice faded.

Martin helped a thin Indian ambulance man to lift Congreve onto a stretcher. There was no one else to help, so he took the other end and they started a slow journey along the *donga*. Martin's thoughts swam, and he felt exhausted. The two men trudged for nearly two miles with their heavy burden, stopping occasionally to rest. On the first of these occasions, Martin offered his fellow stretcher-bearer a drink from his water bottle, and tried to speak to him in Hindustani, and was surprised when the Indian replied in perfect English. He was thin, with a drooping moustache, and wore a khaki uniform with a Red Cross armband.

"Dreadful carnage, Captain," said the Indian. "A pity that your differences can't be decided in a more humane manner."

Martin nodded, regarding the other man with interest. He noted that the Indian had a cheerful expression, although obviously exhausted from carrying the stretcher. During the next hour, as they toiled along the *donga* towards Buller's HQ, and while they rested, Martin discovered that he was a lawyer from Durban.

When he finally reached the headquarters hill Martin slumped onto the ground, his back against a saddle. His thoughts were of Chandra: so many years they'd been together, so many miles they'd travelled. The horse had taken him into Mashonaland, through the Matabele War, the Forbes Column, and their adventure with the lions, when Gerrit Venter died. They had escorted the coach and wagons into Salisbury in the '96 Rebellion. There had been countless rides around the farm, and to and from Salisbury. If only the big horse had stayed in the *donga*; he was too loyal to let his master venture out alone.

☙❧

At Buller's headquarters Martin stood outside the hospital tent with other officers waiting for news of Freddy Roberts. A Colonel came out and told them that their fellow officer had died.

A young lieutenant said to Martin, "I don't envy Buller having to tell Lord Roberts that his only son's been killed. You were there? How did it happen?"

"We were trying to get one of the guns back."

"I say, what's that blood on your arm?"

Martin craned round, but could not see where the lieutenant was pointing—to the back of his upper arm, near the shoulder. The young man prodded gingerly and Martin winced.

"Better go and see a doc," said the lieutenant.

Martin walked to the hospital tents, but saw many wounded men crowding round the area waiting their turn. Some wore rough bandages on serious wounds, while others lay on stretchers. An orderly told him there were hundreds of wounded and they were dealing with the serious cases first, so Martin walked away. At his tent, he found the batman he shared with Congreve chatting to a friend, the smoke from their pipes drifting into the evening air. Martin took off his sweat-stained jacket.

"Harris, have a look at this, will you?" he asked the batman, offering his blood soaked sleeve for inspection.

Harris sucked in breath through his teeth. "You've bin 'it, sir. Bit 'o shrapnel most likely. Blimey.... 'ang on, sir; Mister Congreve keeps some medical stuff 'ere. 'E won't mind if we take some'at."

He waited until Harris emerged with a small wooden box, which he put onto the canvas chair that stood outside the entrance to the tent. The orderly opened the box and took out some spirits and cotton lint. Then, with the assistance of the other batman, he wet a clean handkerchief from a water bottle and proceeded to clean the wound, finally putting a cotton swab onto it, and tying a rough bandage round the arm and shoulder.

"That'll 'elp for a while, sir, but you'd better get it cleaned proper."

A warrant officer approached and told Martin that all staff officers were required to attend a meeting with General Buller—at once. He draped his filthy jacket over his shoulders and hurried along the lines of tents towards Buller's headquarters. The younger staff officers stood in a throng outside, while Hildyard, and the brigadiers, waited under the verandah flap of the marquee. All of them were talking about Freddy Roberts' death, and how Buller would have to break the news to his father.

Buller stood alone, gazing out into valley, the light fast fading. He looked up and noticed Martin, beckoning him to approach. "Russell, what's happened to you? You were with us down there. Schofield says you were with young Roberts."

"Yes, sir. I didn't see it happen. But I heard him call...."

Buller nodded as he interrupted. "You've been wounded yourself."

"It's nothing serious, sir. Probably a bit of shrapnel..."

"Better get it cleaned thoroughly. Were you a friend of Freddy?"

"We met on the boat coming out."

Buller looked Martin in the eyes. "Be good enough to write to his family, would you." He turned to General Hildyard. "When we have time I want to record the efforts of officers like Russell—rescuing the guns."

Martin saluted and went to join his fellow young officers. He noticed that Captain Lee was watching him, and waiting for a lull in the conversation so that he could make an announcement. When that moment came, Lee spoke in a loud voice. "Buller may think you're great, Russell, but I don't like the way you behaved out there."

There was a moment of awkward silence as the officers stopped talking.

Martin was genuinely puzzled. "What do you mean?"

"You were more interested in your nag than helping us get the guns out." Lee stared at Martin, waiting to see what reaction his words would elicit.

Schofield retorted, "What the hell are you talking about?"

Martin went red in the face and stated slowly, "My horse was wounded, Lee. I wanted to see if he had any chance. As it happens, he was fatally wounded."

Lee gave out a hollow laugh. "You're talking about a horse, man, for God's sake!" He looked around the group for support. There were a few sniggers.

"Yes, a horse. But he wouldn't have abandoned me in the heat of battle."

Lee laughed again, full of scorn. "You should hear yourself. The sun must have got to you."

In a quick movement Martin advanced a couple of steps and grabbed Lee's jacket. He lifted the other man up so that his feet barely touched the ground, while feeling a searing pain in his arm. He was about to strike him, but the other officers rushed in to separate them. The two antagonists faced each other, red faced and panting.

Schofield explained to the group, "If Russell hadn't stayed he wouldn't have found Freddy Roberts."

The quarrel was interrupted by Buller's command for attention.

⤳⤙

Next day Martin had a fever and by midnight he was delirious. Harris and another batman carried him over to the hospital tent, where an exhausted doctor examined him. The shrapnel wound in his shoulder had become septic. Without ceremony he was heaved onto a table, a wad soaked in chloroform was pressed onto his face, and the surgeon set about cleaning the wound. Working quickly and crudely, he cut away the septic flesh and reamed down to clean muscle. Then he swabbed the wound and sewed it up. Wiping his brow with one hand he waved the limp body away.

When Martin woke he was vomiting. Although his fever had declined slightly he could not move, and Harris had to give him food and water. Congreve limped into the tent to see how he was faring, accompanied by Schofield. They congratulated him for his part in the attempt to rescue the guns.

"Well done, too, for finding poor young Roberts."

Martin smiled weakly. "Actually, I was staying with my horse, Schofield, as you very well know."

"That's not how I saw it—and there were other witnesses."

"Sorry about your horse," said Congreve sympathetically. "Had him a long time, right?"

"Nine years. He carried me through the Matabele War in '93. I can't bear to think of his body lying out there for the jackals."

"They've all been buried," said Schofield. "Men and horses. Too many by far. By the way, Buller wonders if you can dictate a few words for me to send to Freddy's family. He knows you're not in a fit state to write a letter. But you were one of the last to see him conscious."

⤞⤝

Martin was sent to Durban a week later, still with a temperature and his shoulder aching. A hospital train took him south from Durban, and on arrival in Cape Town he was admitted to Groote Schuur Hospital, where he spent ten days. Towards the end of this period of recuperation, he heard of his promotion to Major, and his award of the Distinguished Service Order in recognition of his efforts to rescue the guns at the Battle of Colenso. Poor Freddy Roberts had received a posthumous VC.

He was invited to a reception at Government House, and attended in uniform, his jacket over his shoulders because he had a bandage on his upper arm and shoulder. The reception was held in the ballroom where he first met Helen; it was filled with officers in dress uniform, and their ladies. He secured a glass of wine and wandered towards the verandah. He had not gone far when he was greeted by Lady Violet Cecil.

"Martin, dear," she gushed. "I heard you'd been wounded. I've been desperately worried." She pulled him by his good arm to a group of officers. "Gentlemen, this is my friend Major Russell. He was wounded at the Battle of Colenso."

Feeling uncomfortable, Martin muttered that it was only a small shrapnel wound that went septic. He knew well that Colenso was now regarded as a debacle for the British.

"At Colenso was it, Russell?" asked a major of the Royal Horse Artillery. "Were you one of those with Freddy Roberts when he was wounded?"

When he nodded, he was bombarded with questions about the battle and the incident of the field guns. These men were itching to get to the front, and hungry for news from someone who had already seen action.

Seeing that Martin was wearying of the questions, Violet Cecil drew him aside. "I heard that your sister's coming out to the Cape."

"Yes. She's to give some recitals for the troops."

"We know that's not the real reason." Violet smiled archly. "She'd like to see how her brother's recovering from his wound. Now, I want her to stay with me at Groote Schuur—and you too. I would have invited you before, but now Beth can be chaperone. We can ride together—Rhodes' horses need exercise."

"What news of him?" Martin knew that Rhodes was besieged in Kimberley.

"Very frustrated, as you can imagine—and not behaving very well. But perhaps it'll do him good to be confined for a while. Certainly Alfred isn't disappointed to have him out of the way; he was rather a thorn in his flesh. You know what Rhodes is like, always interfering." She paused before adding, "By the way, did you hear that Robert Onslow was killed at Mafeking? You knew him—Beth told me—and you knew he was in the besieged town?"

Martin was momentarily dazed to hear this news. He had not heard from Robert and Helen since leaving Mashonaland. Tom Ellsworth had written to him saying that Helen was pregnant with her second child, and that Robert had joined up.

"His wife—I met her only briefly—what was her name? Anyway, she has a daughter of three, and a baby girl. Poor woman."

An ADC came up to whisper in Lady Cecil's ear, and when he left she patted Martin on the arm and moved away. He wandered over to the bar, but stopped in his tracks suddenly as he saw the dapper figure of Frank Burnham in sharply creased army uniform. Astonished to see the American scout, he went forward to greet him, noticing that he wore major's crowns on his epaulettes. They shook hands and grasped each other around the shoulder, Martin wincing at the pain.

"Burnham! A major in the British Army—an American? I can hardly believe it."

Burnham laughed, his blue eyes shining. "You a major too, I see. I'm Chief Scout to Lord Bob. Why are you so surprised?"

"Well, I know you're well qualified, but...our army usually lacks the imagination to take on foreigners. It's good to see you again, Frank. I want to hear what you've been doing."

"Talking of foreigners—your friend, and my countryman, Perry Davenport, is on the Boer side." He could tell that Martin was interested, and went on. "Yes—amazing, isn't it. But, he's playing a dangerous game. We've heard that he's a galloper—carrying messages for the Boer leaders. Evidently they trust him, and supposedly he can pass through the country with less suspicion. If he's captured, he'll be treated as a spy."

"Surely not if he's only been a messenger?"

"Depends if he's in civilian clothes?"

"But most of the Boers don't have proper uniforms."

"I know...well, I'm telling you what the Intelligence guys are saying. They're on the lookout for the American."

They walked to the verandah and had been talking for nearly an hour when an ADC approached and told Martin that a Colonel Haig wished to speak to him. After smiling wryly at Burnham he left to follow the ADC, who led him to the stocky figure of Roberts' staff officer. The colonel shook Martin's hand and without a word led him to a private room, where Martin saw Field Marshal Lord Roberts, recently arrived in the Cape. The Commander in Chief of the British Army, stood at a window looking out over the moonlit grounds. He turned, coming forward to greet Martin, who noticed from the corner of his eye that Haig had left them alone. Roberts was short and stocky, his face weathered to the colour and texture of a ripe old apple. Martin noticed the magenta Victoria Cross ribbon at the end of an impressive row on his chest. He seemed older than Martin had imagined, his white hair and whiskers shaggy, and his eyes tired.

"Major Russell. I thank you for the letter you sent me about my son," Roberts said. "You weren't close friends?"

"No, sir, just fellow officers. I'm very sorry about what happened."

The Field Marshal nodded. "Hmm. Tell me about it, Russell. Were you volunteers—to rescue the guns—or under orders?"

"Volunteers, sir."

"And how great were the risks?"

"Looking back now, I realise they were very great. But at the time, I...well, we didn't appreciate how great the volume of Boer fire would be from across the river—nor how accurate."

"Was there any alternative?"

"I wondered about waiting until dark. But there was a risk that the Boers could come across the river to spike the guns..."

Roberts interrupted, "I mean, could a larger force have helped?"

"I doubt it, sir. You can only use so many men to limber field guns."

"And covering fire?"

"It would have taken a long time. There was virtually no ground cover—except in the *donga*. There might have been much greater loss of life."

"Why was Freddy left behind?"

"It was all very confused, sir. Men and horses were falling—dust and smoke everywhere—shells bursting."

The Field Marshal turned away. "And if you hadn't found him?"

"Others would have."

"Did Freddy say anything to you?"

"No, sir. He was scarcely conscious. And the noise was overwhelming." He paused. "I wish I had more to tell you."

Roberts turned back to face him again, and Martin noticed that his eyes were wet, as he tried to smile. "I heard how you were in that campaign against the Matabele. We're grateful that you volunteered for service for this war—we need experienced officers." He held out his hand. "I expect we'll meet again. If I can be of help, you must ask."

ॐ◌ॐ

CHAPTER 24
Prisoner At Paardeberg — 1900

Martin Russell stood with officers of General Kitchener's staff on a *kopje* overlooking the Modder River; Lieutenant-General Kelly-Kenny and Kitchener were at the front of the group, while Martin and the other staff officers waited behind at a respectful distance. The river below them meandered through a dusty plain like an olive-green snake, its skin the stunted willows that sucked thirstily from its ephemeral waters. The storm floods of centuries had gouged a bed for the river deep enough for the Boer General Cronje to shelter his men, his wagons and all the women, children, cattle, and sheep that travelled with them. They could not be seen from the *kopje* because they were in the lee of the river bank.

Kitchener turned to address the staff officers, his tone formal. "Gentlemen, as you know, our plan has succeeded. We have surrounded Cronje's force and we prevented them from getting help. But we must be on our guard. Large commandos under de Wet and Ferreira are approaching. Some of you have advised me that Cronje is in a good defensive position that is difficult to attack. You have suggested that we should starve the Boers into surrender while shelling their position relentlessly. However, there's always the possibility that Cronje will bolt from his rabbit hole. I will not allow him to escape. General Kelly-Kenny will put the Sixth Division into attack. With good fortune we should be back in *laager* by ten-thirty."

The staff officers applauded politely, and one of them turned to Martin, whispering wryly, "I think I've heard that sort of promise before."

"I heard it at Colenso," agreed Martin.

So the attack went forward across the dusty plain. As soon as the British troops came within range of the Boer rifles a dreadful attrition started. The advance slowed and then stopped. The soldiers lay baking in the sun, unable to move, their water bottles insufficient for their terrible thirst.

Martin was told to report to the Oxfordshire Light Infantry to interrogate prisoners; this had become his intermittent task since his knowledge of Afrikaans became known. He went to the 13th Brigade's tented headquarters, where Major-General Charles Fox was in command, and was given a makeshift trestle table. A sergeant waved forward a dirty, uncouth Boer.

In slow, precise Afrikaans, Martin asked, "Who is your commander, *minheer*?" When he heard the sullen response, 'Cronje', he said, "I mean, who is in charge of your commando?"

"Van Tonder. He's only a farmer, man. What is it to you?"

"How many women and children are there in the *laager*?" continued Martin.

"Plenty. I don't know how many. You people are killing them with your shells. Innocent women and children."

Later, Martin interrogated another prisoner, an educated man, a lawyer who spoke English well. He was dressed in a frock coat of good quality that was heavily smeared with mud and dust. After some introductions and preliminaries, he said, politely, "Major, there are wounded men left behind in the trenches you captured."

"It was impossible to take them out under fire, Mr Coetzee."

"You could use a flag of truce now."

Martin considered his reply, then said, "There have been too many instances of such flags being dishonoured."

"Then I will go with you," Coetzee pleaded. "One of the wounded men is the leader of a commando."

Martin gave the lawyer a searching look, and concluded that he was genuine. Knowing the risks, he questioned him further and then agreed. Feeling fatalistic about the concept of going forward towards the Boers, he led the small medical party to bring the wounded prisoners from the trenches. He was accompanied by Coetzee, and another Boer prisoner, a field cornet, while a British corporal walked ahead carrying a pole with a white towel tied to it. This was a dangerous task, as the Boers had been known to shoot such heralds. Martin made Coetzee walk beside the corporal with his hands tied behind his back. The remainder of the party was made up of a young lieutenant, a sergeant, and some stretcher-bearers. It was three o'clock and the blistering sun roasted the little group as they shambled over the dusty plain toward the river.

The sergeant turned to Martin, "'eard we'd be back in our bivvy for lunch. Is that right sir?"

"They certainly expected the battle to be over before now."

The party moved through scattered British troopers, who lay on the ground, some trying to find shade and shelter behind anthills and rocks. The desultory firing had almost stopped. A voice came from one of the prone figures, having spotted Martin. "Not surrendering, are we, sir?" Martin shook his head and smiled in the direction of the voice. The stretcher party was now in front of the British lines, at the trenches that had been captured in the rush forward and then abandoned.

A white flag appeared over the river bank three hundred yards away and a Boer rescue party emerged. The two groups, each numbering about twenty, converged on the forward trenches, meeting over one containing three bodies, all dead. The Boers jumped in and started to lift out the corpses. The leader of the Boer group, black-bearded, and wearing a drooping slouch hat, started talking to Coetzee in rapid Afrikaans. Martin went forward to remonstrate.

Speaking to the leader of the Boer party, the lawyer, Coetzee, said, "This is the British intelligence officer. He speaks the *Taal*."

The Boer leader eyed Martin cautiously, then said, in matter of fact tones, "You will come with us, Major."

At first Martin was puzzled, but then he realised that he was being captured. He was furious. "What do you mean? We're here under a flag of truce!"

The Boer shrugged. "All is fair in love and war—as you English say. Your people can keep Coetzee. He's one of our intelligence officers. A fair exchange, *jah*?"

Martin glanced at Coetzee, who did not look at all pleased about what was happening. The lawyer's hands were still tied behind his back. At that moment the Boer leader moved swiftly behind Martin and poked him in the back with his rifle. The British lieutenant cried out in alarm and raised his pistol, but his sergeant placed a restraining hand on him. They were only a few paces from Martin.

"Is there anything we can do, sir?" muttered the sergeant.

"Nothing," Martin laughed with bitterness. "Unless you shoot them all. They deserve it for breaking a truce."

"Then 'e'll kill you, sir."

Martin shrugged and watched the sergeant and lieutenant confer, then shake their heads. To his relief they had come to the same conclusion, that a shoot-out would be a pointless waste of lives; enough had been wasted already in this war. He was led away, blindfolded, with hands tied behind his back. At the bank of the Modder he was bundled over, stumbling down a steep slope and into air that reeked with cordite. An artillery barrage from the British started almost immediately and he experienced his first British shell explosions. He was led, and roughly pulled, for about ten minutes, sometimes dragged sideways into vertical cuts in the riverbank. After progressing like this for about a mile, he heard voices in conversation, but could not make out what they were saying.

Suddenly, his guard removed the blindfold, and he found himself near a wagon, tucked under the riverbank. There were dozens of other wagons on the sandy shelf that stretched down to the water. Scattered around were the bodies of dead animals killed by the British shelling. Scores of carcasses of draught oxen, horses and sheep lay bloated and stiff-legged in the afternoon sun. The Boers had dug into the riverbanks like a colony of rats. The women and children were deepest, and were mostly unscathed, but the men were outermost and many of them were standing up near the rim of the bank, where they could fire on the British lines stretched out across the plain. The ground at the base of the sand cliff was littered with spent cartridge cases. Boer women wearing big white *kappies*, their traditional bonnets, were tending wounded men.

Pretorius, the Boer leader who captured Martin, delved into the prisoner's pockets, removing his penknife, pipe and tobacco, as well as two letters from home, which Martin knew contained nothing of interest to the Boers.

"Come along, Major," said Pretorius. "You are to meet our General."

He led Martin for a few yards further along the bank. Here there was a deep, long gully running up into the sand cliff. Only a direct hit from a shell could harm the occupants. General Cronje sat in a chair made from animal hides, his wife statuesque behind him with two of his staff. Pretorius pushed Martin forward in front of the old general, who watched him intently, signalling for a chair to be brought. He was a bulky man, with a full beard shot with white hairs; he wore a heavy frock coat and a black felt slouch hat.

After a while, Cronje asked, in Afrikaans, "Major, how is it that you speak the *Taal*?"

"I have a farm in Rhodesia," Martin replied. "I learned there—from Afrikaner friends."

"If you have Afrikaner friends, why do you fight with the British?"

"Because I'm British." Martin looked directly into the tired eyes of the Boer General. "I don't like fighting against your people. This war should never have been fought."

Cronje nodded slowly. "*Jah*, you are right. How many British are there with Kitchener?"

"You know I cannot tell you, General, but there are many. I beg you to give up the fight, to prevent loss of life."

"We cannot surrender—and I think that more of you British are losing your lives."

"Your man Pretorius behaved with dishonour by capturing me from a white flag party."

Cronje smiled. "He did. But he meant well. He said you might have news of importance, since you are an intelligence officer. He does not appreciate that we will not torture you for information. So your capture served no purpose." The old man paused to light his pipe, then asked, "Are you a man of honour, Major?"

"I would like to think so, sir. Why?"

"Because I will remove your bonds, but you must promise not to escape. I could put you with some other prisoners that were taken today, but as you were captured unfairly I will let you walk about freely. However, I tell you that if you do escape I will shoot one of the penned prisoners—a fair exchange?"

"I don't believe that you would do that."

Cronje laughed, a deep rumble that ended with a wheezing cough. Then he shouted, "Pretorius! Undo his bonds."

Pretorius, who had moved a few yards away and turned, incredulous, did nothing.

Impatiently, Cronje told him, "Do as I say, man. I have decreed that he should be untied – and return his belongings. You captured him unfairly, so he is not to be treated like the other prisoners. If he runs away, you may shoot one of them in reprisal."

Muttering protests, Pretorius untied the wrist thongs and gave him his knife, pipe and letters. Martin rubbed his arms, then thanked the general and walked away.

❧

At about this time, Frank Burnham was sitting in a makeshift office in General Kitchener's staff headquarters. The general fiddled with a penknife as he listened to Burnham, while the other officers wore expressions that varied from amazement to disbelief.

"I've thought it out carefully," said Burnham. "The river flows at about one mile an hour. If I set off shortly before dusk, I should reach the Boer *laager* by dark, when they're cooking their evening meal."

Kitchener watched the American with a half smile, wondering why one of his own officers had not come up with this idea. "Surely you can't swim all that time—can you?"

"No, indeed, General." Burnham leaned forward eagerly, his eyes shining. "So I will use an inflated sheepskin. It's a trick I learned from the Apache Indians."

A colonel on Kitchener's staff intervened. "It's a brave plan, sir. But will Burnham be able to gather any useful information?"

The general looked at Burnham with an interrogative lift of his eyebrows, and Burnham replied, "I could assess the extent of damage caused by the bombardment. I could make a rough estimate of the numbers of surviving men. I might be able to gauge something of their food resources. And if they're planning a breakout—well, it should be obvious."

Kitchener suddenly snapped the penknife shut and stood up. "Yes, you can go, Burnham—and good luck!" He stepped forward and shook the American's hand.

Burnham had been exasperated with his duties, and had surplus energy in plenty. As soon as he devised his scheme of floating down the river past the Boers, he knew he would have difficulty persuading the British command to agree. Now, as he prepared to enter the river, he was elated at the prospect of the adventure. Others from the Corps of Scouts assisted him as he hung his binoculars and revolver round his neck, wrapped in oilskin. Then he entered the sluggish water, and buoyed by the inflated sheepskin, floated off down the river.

᷂᷃

In the Boer *laager*, beside the banks of the Modder River, Martin watched as two young women collected driftwood and lit a fire nearby. They started to cook pieces of meat and sausage on spits. It was dusk now and the firing from both sides had petered out. The moans of the wounded became more audible, mixed with shouted orders and the strains of a hymn. Martin felt a deep sympathy for these people, who were being hounded by a massive British army. He still believed the Boers had earned the right to their republic, by occupation of virtually unpopulated land, and also by their war against the British twenty years earlier.

A stout woman came to him with a tin of water and offered it to him to drink. "Where does the water come from?" he asked her in Afrikaans.

"From the river, of course. Where else? It has been boiled. There's nothing else to drink."

Putting the dish to his lips he found the water tasted of mud, and thought about the risk of dysentery, which the British called 'the Modders' after this very river. Nevertheless, he drank.

☙❦

While Martin brooded by the guttering fire his thoughts were dominated my memories of Louise and Perry. He had achieved an uneasy friendship with Perry and now it was strange that they should be on opposing sides. And what of Helen, now that she was a widow? Would she stay in Mashonaland? He thought it more likely she would go to England, where Robert's family would take care of them.

He stood up, feeling that he should at least reconnoitre the camp. He walked past groups of Boer men and women sitting round small fires cooking whatever food they had. The scent of grilled meat and sausages mixed with wood smoke made his stomach grumble. He'd had nothing to eat since breakfast, but he could not stop and join these groups, nor did they invite him; indeed they seemed oblivious of him. He wore his army uniform, but it was not unusual for Boers to wear their captors' jackets. He approached a field hospital, a huddle of open tents against the high bank, lit by hurricane lamps. Shadowy figures of doctors and nurses bent over bodies on the ground. He was reluctant to move into the area, suspecting his presence as an enemy prisoner would be much more resented; they would see him as an agent of their death and suffering.

He sat near the river shore. The stars were brilliant, and he could see their reflections in the slowly moving river as he cogitated about his lot. He could not escape, because, though unlikely, the Boers might shoot a prisoner in retaliation. If he waited, he might be killed in tomorrow's bombardment. But if he survived, and the Boers surrendered, he would be able to return to his own side.

For about an hour he sat like this, and then watched some nurses walk towards the medical area. A short while later, another group of women left the hospital tents, and he presumed they had been relieved from their shift. As they came closer, he thought there was something familiar about one of them. She was wearing a white uniform, stained with blood and soil—it was Pauline Venter.

She was now eighteen, and her figure had filled out. Though she must have been tired, her step was jaunty, reminding him of the spirited girl he once knew. Her blonde hair escaped from under her white cap, falling below her shoulders.

"Pookie!" he called softly, and watched her look around. "Here!" he called, standing up.

She stared at the dark figure standing against the bank, narrowing her eyes to peer into the dark. "Who is it?" she said in Afrikaans.

"Martin Russell."

"Martin?" She stepped towards him, then, recognising him, she ran up to him. "What are you doing here? Are you spying?" She spoke in an urgent whisper, her eyes wide.

"I'm a prisoner."

"Why aren't you tied up?"

He explained what had happened, and as she listened she nodded, and put her hand on his arm. When he finished, she said she had six hours to rest before going back to duty. They walked together along the sand strip.

"Why are you fighting with the British?" she asked, with curiosity rather than animosity. "Surely you know that they started this dreadful war?"

"I know it, Pookie. I have no conviction. I want it to end."

"If you have no conviction, why are you in their army?" She asked the question quietly, and he sensed that she was genuinely interested, and not accusing him of perfidy.

"Because it's my duty..."

She snorted. "Your duty to fight for people who are in the wrong? I cannot understand you, Martin. I always admired you, because you were so upright and brave."

He said nothing, and they walked in silence for a while, before she said. "What happened between you and Louise? Did you have an affair with her? I think you did." She paused. "They haven't seen each other for ages. Louise and I had to go to Elandsfontein because *Oupa* was dying—he died, you know. Then she stayed there to help *Ouma*, while I went to Pretoria to continue my nursing training. I don't think she's seen Perry since he joined the commandos."

They were now near Cronje's headquarters and stopped to stand near a dying fire that had no people around it. When Pookie threw some pieces of driftwood on the embers the flames revived, and Martin's captor, Pretorius, who had been watching them with interest, walked over to where they stood. He peered at the young nurse, who frowned at him, her face flushed from the heat of the fire.

Pretorius beckoned to her. "Miss, can I talk to you for a moment?"

She looked at him with suspicion as she moved round the fire to his side. "What is it?"

Pretorius drew her further away from the fire, and whispered, "Do you know this man?"

"We knew him in Rhodesia."

"It was I who captured the Englishman." Pretorius glanced at Martin to make sure he could not hear. "He's an intelligence officer on General Kitchener's staff. Cronje will not allow us to try extracting information from him; he says we captured him unfairly. But he must know a great deal about the numbers and dispositions of their troops. Do you think you can get him to talk?"

She turned to look at Martin, who was poking at the embers with a stick, watching the small cloud of sparks drifting up. So she was being asked to wheedle secrets from him. How could she possibly persuade him to reveal anything? He was the personification of honour. Or was he? He'd thought Louise had come to his bed. Perhaps Martin's morals failed him when women were involved. She started to wonder if she could seduce him.

Turning back to Pretorius, she said, "I can try, but I doubt he would tell me anything. Why should he?"

The Boer smiled lasciviously. "Because you're a woman...."

She interrupted him with her laughter. "He has no interest in me. Look at me."

"You undervalue yourself, Miss. Don't underestimate the lust of men. He has not seen a woman for weeks."

"Oh yes, he has! He's been with the smart women of Cape Town—the British bitches that sleep with any man while their husbands are fighting—all scented and with beautiful clothes. No, he won't talk to the likes of me—a sweating, stinking Boer girl. Besides, how could I pretend to want him?"

"Will you not even try? For our country? For all these people?" Pretorius swept his arm round in a gesture that encompassed the whole camp. "Don't you have loved ones who are suffering? It might help us to get out of here."

For a while she stared into the fire, then shrugged. After nodding to Pretorius she went over to Martin and stood beside him while the Boer walked off into the darkness. When she knew they were out of hearing she suggested that Martin come with her to the wagon where she slept. He asked her about her conversation with Pretorius, but instead of answering, she asked him if he had been fighting with the British since the war started. He told her about the Tugela campaign, and how he was wounded and then posted to Kitchener's staff.

"Where were you wounded?"

"At Colenso..."

"No, silly man, I mean where on your body?"

He laughed. "Oh, here—in the arm—shrapnel. It went septic."

They came to a broken-down ox wagon with two wheels missing; it leaned at a drunken angle. Pookie explained that she and other nurses used it for sleeping at night; it was too dangerous during the day, when all the Boers huddled into the riverbank to shelter from the British shelling.

They lit a fire near the wagon, and Pookie brought out some *boere-wors*—Boer sausages—and they cooked them on sticks. The fat from the sausages dripped onto the fire, causing the flames to flare fitfully. She had a small bottle of home-brewed brandy, and mixed the harsh liquor with boiled river water. After they had eaten, she went to the wagon, and Martin lay down beside the fire on a rain cape. He listened to the sounds of the wounded moaning and the oxen wheezing. Voices of men and women at their fires drifted on the night breeze. Some were doing chores that were denied them during the days of shelling. Not far away a group of Boers smoked their pipes, talking in low voices about the day's battle.

When Pookie returned she had changed out of her uniform into a dark skirt and blouse. She had washed herself, and her hair was wet, hanging in tight ringlets. She said softly, "I'm sorry I sounded as if I was against you. I was upset after nursing wounded men. I know you're a good man, and I certainly don't hold this war against you." She sat on the rain cape beside him, smoothing her skirt under her. "Can I get you some more brandy—or something more to eat? There's not much, I'm afraid—just rotten meat and filthy water. Your British out there on the plain are crazy with thirst; we've even allowed them to come to the river to drink."

"War is strange, when men try to kill each other with bullets, then offer to keep each other alive."

"*Jah*, it is strange." She put her arms around her knees.

"So your sister's at Elandsfontein?"

"Mm. I expect she'd rather be in the Cape. She doesn't like the Transvaal." She paused to look at him closely; he was gazing into the fire, as if his thoughts were far away. "I think she loves you."

He shook his head vehemently. "She may have thought so. She was confused, I think."

"No, stupid." She leaned over and punched his arm playfully—luckily for him the good one. "She still loves you. She told me. But she said your heart is in England, or perhaps with that woman Helen. Where is she?"

He told her that Helen was in Mashonaland, and that her husband Robert had been killed in the siege of Mafeking. She poked at the embers, wondering how she could have a more intimate conversation with him; she now regretted reminding him of her sister.

"Would you like to rest? You can come into the wagon."

"Why are you helping me?"

"I said I was sorry."

She explained that at the beginning of the Battle of Paardeberg there had been three nurses sharing the wagon. One ran away to her home, and another became ill with dysentery, and was taken away. "That leaves me on my own," she added wryly, "but the wagon won't go anywhere now." A bucksail was rigged beside it, giving a degree of privacy. "This bucket has soapy water for washing." She explained with a giggle, "You must use this flannel to wipe over your body. We have no more water after that bucket is finished, and who knows how long we will be here."

He waited for her to leave, but she stood watching him, and laughingly said, "I don't trust you to use only a little water. You may bathe now. Don't be shy; I've seen many naked men in my work as a nurse. I've even seen you naked before—remember?"

"It was pitch dark then." He laughed and turned away from her, unbuttoned his tunic and then hung it on the side of the wagon. "Do you sleep in the wagon," he asked, taking off his trousers.

"Huh! What sleep? I'm usually working with the wounded men. Only tonight they sent me away to sleep." She noticed his scar. "Is that your wound?" She stepped forward to touch the wound, then said with a laugh, "It's only a scratch."

"I know, but it became septic." He started to wipe himself with the flannel, feeling shy to be naked with her, even though his back was to her.

"I want to talk to you. We've never been alone before." She handed him a small towel.

"Except at Elandsfontein?"

"...when you thought I was Louise."

He dried himself, then reached for his soiled tunic, but she put her hand on his arm. "Take this sheet. You can sleep here. Dress in the morning." Handing him a folded sheet, she added, "It's the last clean one."

He unfolded it and wrapped it around himself like a toga, watching her arrange a sleeping place for him in the wagon. When he suggested that Pretorius would wonder where he was, she told him the Boer had gone on watch with his men. He sat down on the bare mattress, which was shaped in a 'V' inside the listing wagon. The roof cover was still in place, though with many gaping holes. It kept out some of the night noises giving the impression of a quiet haven. The girl sat beside him, and the sloping floor forced her to be near him.

"You wanted to talk to me."

She sighed. "Yes. Tell me how long this war will last."

"Your people are heavily outnumbered now. If you continue fighting there will be more loss of life. But I think the war could end in a few months. What do you think?"

"Some of the men say they'll go on fighting until you British are tired, and then there'll be an agreement to stop. I don't know. I wish it would end so we can all go back to what we were doing before the war." She shivered suddenly. "I'm afraid, Martin."

He put his arm round her, and she rested her head on his shoulder. "You must shelter in the sandbanks when the shelling starts again." The thought that she might die suddenly became unbearable—she was so young and lively.

"I have to do my work," she said scornfully. "I can't spend all day cowering against the banks. Besides, a shell can land anywhere. It's fate I think." She turned her face into his cheek. "I don't want to die, Martin. I'm just a young girl. I haven't lived yet."

He hugged her in an attempt to reassure. "You won't die. This will soon be over. What will you do when the war's over?"

"Go back to nursing in Pretoria I suppose. What will you do?"

"Go back to my farm. I often wonder what's happening there. I left nearly a year ago. My partner Tom Ellsworth is keeping an eye on it."

Pookie started to take off her dress, but weariness overcame her, and she sagged down, her shoulders bent. "I wanted you to tell me things that would be useful to our side."

He laughed quietly. "Oh, so that's why you asked me to come here—to seduce information from me. I might have guessed that it wasn't concern for my well-being." He sat up, but she pulled him back beside her.

"Don't go. I haven't asked you for anything specific, have I?"

"I couldn't tell you anything that would be useful. In battles like this a day is a long time. My information is already stale and useless."

At that moment, several rifle shots crackled from the sandbanks nearby, and she said that men were shooting at shadows. "I'm sorry for the reason I brought you here, but I'm glad you're here."

"You haven't been a very good spy, have you?"

She put her mouth to his ear, and whispered, "Could I seduce information from you?" When he did not reply, she asked, "Are you asleep?"

"I was. I'm sorry."

"Martin, we have to get out of this place—or surrender. Can you help us get out?"

"How could I help?"

"You know where your regiments are."

"I don't know..."

She moved up to him and put her arms around him. "If you tell me, I will allow you to make love to me." Although she tried to sound serious, she spoiled the effect by giggling.

"You're not very good at this," he said, laughing.

"You mean I'm not seductive?"

"No, just an inexperienced spy."

"I hate you, Martin." She kissed him. "You're a horrible *rooinek*." She was quiet, and he realised she'd fallen asleep.

❧

Waking in the cool dawn he found that Pookie had gone. People were moving from their sleeping places to the shelter of the sandbanks as rifle fire started. A shell exploded on a wagon about a hundred paces up the river, sending fragments of wood flying into the air. After hurriedly putting on his clothes he walked to the tall sandy bank. A Boer slid down beside him, his face coated with dust, making his eyes shine white like a coal miner's.

"They've had enough," said the Boer. "They're not going to attack on foot. Just shelling. We can hold out, eh?"

He nodded, and the man stumbled away. What the Boer troops and Martin did not know was that Lord Roberts had come up to Paardeberg from Jacobsdal. At first he wanted to attack the Boer *laager* on the Modder River, but he received a message from General Cronje asking for a truce so that the dead could be buried. Messages passed between the two commanders for most of the day; Cronje wanted assistance from British doctors, but Roberts refused, and eventually decided not to hold a truce. The Boer general wrote his last message:

'If you are so uncharitable as to refuse me a truce as requested, then you may do as you please. I shall not surrender alive. Therefore bombard as you please.'

෴

It so happened that at this time Perry Davenport was lying among the rocks in a *kopje* south of the *laager*, listening to General Christiaan de Wet, who was saying, "I don't understand why Cronje doesn't get out. The corridor's open now."

"Maybe they're just too weary?" suggested a Field Cornet standing beside the general.

De Wet shrugged. "I give them a chance—they ignore it."

Perry turned over, pulling his slouch hat over his face to block off the sun. He fell asleep and was woken after a few minutes by a commotion. Sitting up he saw two Boer commandants, strangers to him, talking to de Wet. About a dozen men had come with them and threw themselves on the ground near Perry; they exchanged greetings in Afrikaans.

One of the men said, "We were in the *laager*, but we decided to get out while there was a chance. Cronje will not budge, but the food is running out. They will have to surrender, or starve."

෴

Martin worked his way slowly along the river until he came to the field hospital where he had found Pookie the night before. Now, he watched her bathing wounded men, gently removing their bandages and replacing them with clean ones. She looked up when he called her name, then frowned as she went to him.

"What do you want? I'm very busy."

"Is there something I can do to help? I can't sit around all day doing nothing."

She pointed to some buckets. "You could help fetch water from the river, for boiling on the fire—and gather firewood. There are pieces of driftwood near the river, and pieces blown off wagons."

He started to carry buckets of water from the river, and when the big cast-iron pots were full, he collected firewood, building a pile near the fires. At midday some soup was cooked, using meat from animals killed in the previous day's bombardment. More meat came from wounded animals that had died during the night; they had been left half alive so that their meat would be fresh. This day there was no bombardment, while the generals negotiated.

When dusk fell, Pookie came up to Martin as he deposited another armful of wood. "You can rest now," she said. "You've done good work today, Martin. Go to my wagon; you can sleep there again tonight. I don't know when I'll get away from here."

He went to the wagon, stripped and washed his body clean, then wrapped himself in the sheet. He fell asleep almost at once, but being a light sleeper, woke when the girl came. He listened while she undressed and washed herself, but could not see her in the dark. She crawled into the place beside him and breathed a heavy sigh. He pretended to be asleep, and soon could tell that she was.

They were woken by an artillery barrage that started at first light, and struggled into their clothes, bumping into each other with their elbows. She asked if he would help with the water again, and he went with her. Columns of dirt spewed into the air from the shell bursts. They could sometimes hear the whine as a shell came over and threw themselves to the ground, then scrambled up to hurry forward. The wounded were being moved back into the shelter of the sand cliffs. As they arrived at the field hospital, two wounded men were carried into the enclosure, the first casualties of the day.

The previous day's pile of firewood had gone, and Martin went out from the lee of the cliff to start collecting more pieces. The stench of death hung sickly and heavy in the air, oozing from the scattered carcasses of dead oxen and horses. Pookie called to him when he came back with his first armful of wood, asking him to stop, because it was too dangerous. He shrugged and picked up two buckets, walking down to the river as if there was no point in running. A piece of shrapnel whined past him.

Shells landed with terrifying frequency. The river was sluggish brown with an oily sheen. There were carcasses rotting in it—animals that had been killed while drinking. Now their putrefying corpses made the water unusable unless it was boiled, but the only place where this could be done was at the little hospital.

On his second journey to the river Martin was knocked over by the blast from a lyddite shell. He picked himself up and saw Pookie running towards him. He staggered up waving her back to the bank.

"You've got to stop!" she shouted above the noise.

"You have to have water!"

"Not if it means you're killed!"

He went again and again, slowly filling the cast-iron pots. He saw nearly a hundred wounded men in the vicinity tended by ten women. More wounded lay further up the river. He made three more trips to the river in the afternoon and survived. A Boer commandant clapped him on the shoulder, thanking him, not realising that he was British and a prisoner—his uniform tunic had disintegrated, leaving him in vest and khaki trousers.

At the field hospital he found that Pookie has fainted from exhaustion. One of her fellow nurses, a large fair-haired girl, was wiping her face with a wet cloth. Her eyelids fluttered and then her head fell back again.

"Poor girl," said the nurse. "She has worked far too long, and nothing to eat. We'll let her sleep here."

When it was dark the barrage stopped, and he lifted Pookie to her feet. He led her to her wagon, she stumbling by his side, her arm round his neck. Miraculously her wagon is still in the same state, broken but habitable. He helped her into the little enclosure, where she found the washing bucket, a cloth, and a folded sheet.

"I must clean myself," she said. "I can manage."

"No you can't." He made her stand in the bucket, then gently removed her garments, while she leaned on him. No one could see, because it was dark, and there was a bucksail between their wagon and the sand cliffs. Using her cloth, he wiped her naked body, starting at her face and working down. He could scarcely see her, but he could feel the curves and sometimes her smooth skin where the tips of his fingers slipped from the cloth. Aroused, he touched her breasts, and she laughed into his neck where her face was nestled.

He wrapped her in the sheet, and led her to the wagon and settled her in the mattress valley. After wiping himself clean with the remains of the water in the bucket, he took his sheet from where it had been folded, and shook the dust off it. He crawled to his place beside Pookie, expecting to find her asleep.

She sighed and said, "I don't think of you as enemy any more. You seem to be one of us. It was brave—what you did today. Rather foolish, but very brave."

He put his arm round her. "I thought you were asleep."

"I'm stronger than you think. I'm a Boer girl, not one of your weak little English roses." She pulled him closer. "You see, there is life in me yet, and in you too."

Very slowly and patiently, conscious of each other's aches and pains, but growing more passionate, they made love. As before, when she had come to his bed that night at Elandsfontein, he was struck by the urgency of her love-making, as if she thought that their time was finite. In this way she was so different to her elder sister, who had been more passive and leisurely, and happy for him to take command.

Later, as they lay in each other's arms, they heard voices near the wagon.

"Did you hear?" a man's voice said, "Cronje says we have to surrender!"

"We have no alternative," another man grumbled.

"Then for God's sake let's get home."

His companion laughed. "You won't find it, *kerrel*. The khakis will have burned it down."

"Maybe. We can build again. But we'll have something to eat first? I've heard the *rooineks* feed their prisoners."

In the wagon, Pookie kissed Martin. "Now you'll be free, and I'll be the prisoner."

"Perhaps you'll be able to get away. The British don't want women prisoners. Will you go back to the farm?"

"Yes, I must help Louise. It's not good that she should be there alone with *Ouma*."

They got up and dressed, exchanging wry smiles in the first light. Then they joined the throng gathering near General Cronje's headquarters. Men were climbing up the bank with white flags. Martin went with Pookie to the place where the wounded lay, and stayed with her until some Boer men, prisoners now, brought stretchers and carried the wounded away. The other Boer men sat in rows on the sand.

He put his arms round Pookie. "Take care of yourself."

There were tears in her eyes. "I hope I'll meet you again when this is all over. Even as friends?"

He walked over to one of the British guards. The corporal pointed his rifle at the tall unshaven man, and shouted to him to get back.

Martin smiled and said firmly. "I'm a British officer."

The Corporal snorted. "Oh, yes? And I'm the Queen of Sheba. Now get back there."

"Really, Corporal. I'm Major Russell, Intelligence Officer with General Kitchener's staff. I was captured three days ago. Please call one of your men to take me to the officer in charge."

❦

CHAPTER 25
Elandsfontein - 1901

Louise was now living at Elandsfontein, the Venter family farm in the Northern Transvaal. Her grandfather had died, leaving her uncle Jacobus heir to the farm. He had gone to fight in the war, and Hannah, his wife, who had cancer, had moved off the farm with her two daughters to stay with another relative near Pietersburg. Thus Louise cared for her grandmother on her own. Her two children, Gerald and Rosemary, were too young to be of any help, but one of the family's African servants remained; Ephraim was a house servant, and his wife Miriam did the washing; they had a young daughter, Rachel.

Louise was content on the farm, enjoying her children and their open-air lifestyle, but she yearned to see Perry again. Most of her letters reached him, because the Boers had an efficient system of communicating between the commandos and their home districts. She had received several letters from her husband, and was relieved to read that he was hoping to visit, whenever his commanders gave him the time.

One day, while walking in the garden cutting flowers, she looked up and saw her sister ride up to the house. Greatly surprised, since she had heard that Pookie was a prisoner of the British, she dropped her basket and ran to greet her. Pookie slipped off her horse, and hugged Louise, thinking that she looked tanned and healthy from the good life on the farm. They walked side by side into the house, exchanging news, Pookie telling how she had escaped from the British a few days after the surrender at Paardeberg; she did not mention meeting Martin Russell.

Louise showed her sister into *Ouma's* room. The old lady was asleep, and they soon left, Louise explaining that the old lady had lost her will to live. "Poor dear, she hardly knows where she is. I hope you can see if there's anything we can do—I'm sure you know about these things, now you're a nurse."

"She's very old. People often fade away when their spouse dies."

The two sisters sat on the verandah, sipping lime juices, watching the two young children playing. Louise was avid for news. "Tell me, have you heard anything about Perry?"

"Better than that—I met him!"

"No! Where?"

"In Pretoria." Pookie explained that after she escaped from Paardeberg with some other women, she travelled to Pretoria where they put her to work in the main city hospital. When off duty, she made a point of finding news of her brothers, Hendrik and Ben, and also Perry. One of the officials told her she should enquire at General Botha's headquarters, and there she was told that Perry was asleep in a house nearby, where she finally found him.

"Did he say anything about me?"

Pookie was glad to be the bearer of so much news. "He said that if I saw you, I should tell you that he loves you."

"Didn't he give you a letter for me?"

"There was no time for writing letters." She paused for a moment. "Martin was in the *laager* at Paardeberg."

"Martin?" Louise was incredulous.

"He was a prisoner—but Cronje let him stay loose, because he was taken under a white flag."

"You spoke to him?"

"More than that." Pookie smiled to herself.

"What do you mean?"

"I was asked to get information from him..."

"You mean....you seduced him?"

Pookie giggled, deciding to keep something to herself. "I fell asleep. He said I was no good as a spy. You know, Louise, I started by... well, thinking of him as a typical *rooinek*. Then I realised he's...."

"Yes?"

"Well, he's a good man."

"Oh, Pookie! You made love. I can see it. That man!" She was somewhat dismayed that the man she once regarded as her lover should be so free with his favours—and with her young sister too. She had never thought of him as a womaniser, quite the contrary. He always seemed so reticent.

"Well I was very tired." Nevertheless, Pookie's smile indicated much satisfaction.

Louise's mouth opened. "You might have a baby...."

"Not possible. I know, I'm a nurse."

"I'm really surprised at you. You're always so anti-British...."

"But Martin isn't really the enemy. I mean, he's always been our friend. He helped us so much—you remember."

"Yes, and you always fancied him—even when you were a little girl." Louise sighed. "Well you've had him now."

"It was just a strange situation," Pookie mused. "Of course he'll marry Helen now. You know her husband was killed in the siege at Mafeking?"

Louise had not heard. Now she knew Martin would pursue his English rose. He would seek her after the war, and they would surely marry. Of that she was certain—and disappointed, having expected Helen and Robert to live a sort of indefinite Darby and Joan existence. It would have been rather pleasant to keep Martin as a distant but still potential lover.

☞◦☜

Ouma died only two weeks after Pookie came to the farm. The old lady had no will to live after her husband died. She lapsed further into incoherence and incontinence, and though Pookie used all her nursing skills, it was to no avail. They buried her under the big acacia tree, next to *Oupa*, feeling that an era had ended, now that both grandparents were dead.

Louise was in the habit of going for long walks round the farm. Dressed in old worn-out clothes she would skirt around the now abandoned maize fields, her *veldschoen* scuffing the dusty farm tracks. Pookie preferred to ride—there was only one horse left on the farm, old Roode, who was too old to go with the fighting men—and she always took a loaded revolver with her. Sometimes she went beyond the boundaries, occasionally visiting the neighbouring farms where now only women and children lived. There she sought the latest news of the war and drank coarse coffee with them before Roode carried her slowly home.

On her return one day, Pookie told her sister she had heard from the De Bruyns that British soldiers were burning farms on the other side of the river.

"Bastards!" growled Louise. "What shall we do if they come here?"

Her sister shrugged. "What can we do? Fight them? Perhaps they won't come as far as this."

"I won't stand by and let them burn this farm."

"What would be the sense of fighting? They would simply kill you, and for what purpose? You want to see Perry again, don't you?"

Louise sighed. "I'm beginning to think I'll never see him again."

❧

One morning Pookie came across a band of marauding Africans crossing the farm. She saw them first and stopped behind a large thorn tree to watch. There were six men, all young and dressed in trousers and jackets that she presumed were stolen from farms. They moved in a swift furtive way, and there was something menacing about their loping walk, like a pack of hunting dogs. Two of the men carried spears and one a bow.

She wheeled Roode round and cantered back to the farmhouse, where she found Ephraim's little daughter Rachel playing with Louise's children on the *stoep*. When she shouted for Ephraim he came out, drying his hands on a dishcloth. He told her that Louise had gone for her usual walk, he thought to the *vlei*.

"There's a gang of *kaffirs* near the *vlei*," she told him. "I can tell they're up to no good. Get Miriam to the house and put the children inside. Keep a watch! Get *Oupa's* gun ready. Hurry, Ephraim!"

She rode off to look for her sister, alternately trotting and cantering so she did not tire Roode. As she approached the *vlei* she saw the gang of Africans standing in a circle watching something in the centre. Then, to her horror, she saw they were looking down at Louise, who was fighting with one of the Africans. He was lying on top of her, positioning himself to rape her. The other members of the gang watched, grinning and shouting encouragement. The slightly-built white woman was obviously exhausted, her struggles feeble. Her khaki trousers and belt were gathered in a dusty heap round one ankle, and her white shirt was torn open at the front, exposing her breasts.

Pookie pulled Roode to a stop about a hundred yards from the group. Taking her revolver out of its holster she calmly checked that there were cartridges in all cylinders, then trotted her horse closer to the group, stopping about thirty yards away.

The marauders were so engrossed in the impending rape that they did not notice the horse approach. When she judged herself close enough, Pookie took aim at the group of Africans and fired the revolver.

The sound echoed across the *vlei*. One of the gang screamed, clutching his shoulder. They all looked up and towards the sound of the report. The man who was trying to rape Louise scrambled to his feet, struggling to pull up his trousers.

The horse Roode may have been old but he was very experienced. He stood rock steady as Pookie aimed and fired her second shot. It missed, but the gang broke up. At first they tried to surround Pookie, holding their spears menacingly, but she quickly fired two more shots, one of which dropped the tallest member of the gang. The others ran off into the trees, with the man who had tried to rape Louise running after them, trying to hold up his trousers. Pookie approached her sister who had turned on her side into a foetal position. She dismounted, and keeping a careful watch on the Africans, who she could see lurking in the trees not far away, she re-charged the cylinders of the revolver from her bandolier, before firing another shot in their direction.

"Louise!" She stood over her sister's body. "You have to get up."

Louise sat up slowly, recognised Pookie, and then looked fearfully around her. After struggling to her feet, she picked up her trousers and walked slowly over to her sister, sobbing, her shoulders convulsing.

"Stinking *kaffirs*! Shoot them. For God's sake!"

Pookie shook her head impatiently as she mounted her horse. "If you don't hurry, they'll attack us. Here, put your foot in the stirrup. Get up behind me!"

Wearily, Louise heaved herself up behind her sister as the gang of Africans, realising that the horse would be slowed by its double burden, rushed out from the trees. Pookie turned quickly and fired deliberately at them twice, hitting another man. They retreated reluctantly and watched as the two women rode away as fast as the old horse could take them. The gang had lost one man, fatally wounded, but of the other five, two had only flesh wounds. They followed the white women at a respectful distance.

On reaching the farm Pookie reined in behind the big acacia tree where Louise slipped off the horse and pulled on her torn trousers, not wishing the servants to see her half-dressed.

"Don't tell anyone. He didn't rape me, but I don't want anyone to know that anyone tried—especially the children. Please, Pookie. We can tell them I fell off the horse."

"So they didn't...?"

"No, thank God you came! He was the first. If they had raped me, I'd have asked you to shoot me. But I feel...agh!—so dirty."

They gathered Ephraim and his wife into the house with all the children, and bolted all the doors and windows, leaving only the upper loopholes open. Only then did Louise go off to bathe herself, while her sister stood with a rifle trying to spot the group of Africans. Louise joined her, and they waited with pockets full of cartridges and full bandoliers hanging beside them.

"There they are!" Louise shouted angrily. She took aim and fired at the Africans sheltering in the trees about a hundred paces away. The marauders scrambled for cover and a momentary silence followed. Pookie spotted a wisp of smoke; one of the gang was lighting a brand on the end of an arrow, to try to set fire to the thatched roof of the farmhouse. She held her rifle ready. Both sisters were good shots, having been trained well by their father.

One of the men emerged from behind the trunk of the big acacia tree that dominated the farm compound. Pookie promptly shot him in the leg and he dropped the smoking brand, limping away. The gang seemed to decide that the risks were too great. After a short while, they moved off through the trees in a westerly direction.

"They're heading for the Bredenkamps," muttered Pookie. "We must warn them."

"You can't go out now. Please don't leave us."

"I must, sis. Otherwise they'll catch the Bredenkamps unawares."

"And what about us? What if they double back?"

"I won't let them see me leave. Besides, I'm sure they've had enough here."

The young woman went out to the back of the house where Roode was still saddled, munching on some hay. Looking up at the sun as she rode out, she estimated it was near noon. She had her rifle now, slung over her shoulder, and the revolver on her hip.

It took her an hour to reach the Bredenkamp farm using a circuitous route along bush tracks that she knew well from childhood rides on the farm. When she reached the farmhouse, she found, as expected, that they had no inkling of the approaching gang of Africans. Maria Bredenkamp was hanging clothes out to dry, while her two teenage daughters, Cecelia and Rowena, were making the butter that they sold in the district. They listened in dismay as Pookie told them about the approaching gang. The household had only one gun, an ancient muzzle loader. There were four servants, who were brought immediately into the house to help with barricading.

"Come with me to Elandsfontein," suggested Pookie.

"We have no horses," said Maria Bredenkamp. "We cannot walk so far, my dear. We're grateful to you for warning us. God will be with us. You go now."

Shaking her head, Pookie said, "I hate to leave you with only one gun. Keep water ready in case they try to set fire to the thatch."

She had deep misgivings about leaving them, requesting again that they go with her. It seemed to her that Maria had learnt nothing about defending a farm house, and her daughters, who were much the same age as her, were naïve and would be almost helpless if an attack came.

捘捘

CHAPTER 26
Scorched Earth — 1901

Lieutenant Hensman rode through the bush with his Afrikaner guide Willie Kok and several British troopers. When they reached a low rise he saw that the guide had spotted something. He ordered the troop to rein in and they dismounted. It was only then that Hensman saw the ragged little group of Africans approaching, and realised to his horror that they had two young white girls with them, who stumbled along, clothing ragged, their hands tied behind their backs.

"*Verdomme!*" growled Kok. "They've got white girls!"

Hensman's sergeant, who was standing beside him, added quietly, "And one of the men has a gun, sir—must be stolen."

"Gather here!" commanded Hensman quietly, and the sergeant and troopers clustered round him. "Kok, call to the natives to lay down their weapons. I expect they'll make a run for it. You men then ride them down. Kill them if they show any resistance. Be careful, and take care not to harm the girls. Right, Kok. Go ahead!"

The Afrikaner guide called out in a mixture of local languages, but, as the lieutenant expected, the gang immediately scattered into the trees leaving the two bound girls standing on the path. Hensman imagined the Africans would hope that retrieval of the girls would satisfy their pursuers. However, the troopers charged down the slope, whooping as they chased the members of the African gang, who were dodging through the trees like startled rabbits.

One by one the troopers shot them down, as Hensman watched with an expression of distaste at the excesses of his men. He then rode down to the two girls and was able to guess what had happened. Their clothes were torn and barely covered their young bodies. The buttons and other fastenings had been ripped off and they had not been able to hold the clothing together because their wrists were bound together, so they were half naked. He dismounted and as he walked towards them they huddled together, the younger one leaning on her sister, her tearful eyes face watching the approaching officer with apprehension.

"Do you speak English?" he asked gently, and when the elder girl nodded, he turned to his sergeant. "Ross, keep the men well away while I talk to the girls."

He was distressed to see the condition of the two young girls, seeing many abrasions and knife wounds where their white skin showed through the lacerated clothing. They were clutching their torn blouses in an attempt at modesty as he cut their bonds with his sheath knife. The young officer tried to suppress an unwelcome feeling of arousal from the knowledge that the innocent girls had probably been raped.

"My mother is injured—back at the house," said Cecelia Bredenkamp in slow, awkward English. She pointed back along the path.

"How far?"

"About...about twenty minutes walking."

Hensman shouted commands: "Sergeant Ross—go to their house—about a mile down the path. Kok and I will bring the girls. Their mother's at the house, injured." He turned back to the girls. "You must tell me what happened. You see, I have to make a report. Please sit down."

The girls were glad to sit on the ground and haltingly Cecelia told her story, prompted frequently by Hensman, who was disgusted at himself for his prurient interest. He heard that the Bredenkamp's had tried to prepare for the marauding gang, after a warning from their neighbour Pauline Venter. When the gang arrived, the family had fired shots, but very slowly, because their gun was loaded at the muzzle. Then the gang rushed the house and broke in. They sent the servants out under threat of death, and ransacked the house for food and liquor. After eating what food they could find, they drank some brandy, then stripped the two girls of all their clothes and raped them. When their mother tried to intervene, they knocked her unconscious, then raped her. The five men took it in turns raping the young girls, over a period of about two hours, then made them dress and finally tied their wrists. They were taken away from the house as chattels.

The two girls were obviously traumatised by their experience, holding each other tightly and weeping. Although they had strong physiques, they were exhausted, their faces swollen and stained with tears. Hensman knew they needed medical attention, yet there was no one in his troop who could provide it. When he had heard their story, he said, "Kok, let's put the girls on our horses, but keep a good hold on the reins."

Cecelia shrank from the lieutenant as he tried to help her onto the horse. He had to explain that they would reach her mother sooner, before she would allow herself to be lifted up. He noticed how she grimaced with pain because she had to sit astride the saddle. He led the horse along the path, followed by Kok with her sister Rowena.

It took them nearly half an hour to reach the Bredenkamp homestead to find that the troopers were already there. Maria Bredenkamp was alive but unconscious. Her long skirt had been torn off, and her petticoat pulled up above her waist. Her legs were splayed apart, but the British troopers had covered her. There were bruises on her head, and blood had seeped into a cloth tied round it. Gently feeling her skull, he thought he detected a place where it had been cracked. He gave instructions for one of the trooper's horses to be harnessed into the Bredenkamp's spring cart, and Maria was laid on a mattress in the cart, while the girls sat beside her. Rowena sobbed uncontrollably; Cecilia, more stoical, held her mother's head in her lap. Two of the family servants walked beside the wagon as they set off towards the neighbouring farm, Elandsfontein.

Sergeant Ross rode up to Hensman. "What about the farmhouse, sir?"

The lieutenant shook his head. "Those girls have had enough horror without seeing their home burning down. Wait until we're out of sight."

$\approx$ $\prec$

Pookie sat on the *stoep* at Elandsfontein, her rifle on her lap, keeping a close lookout in case the marauding gang returned. She was the first to see the little column of British troops approaching, with a spring cart behind. For a moment she watched the horsemen as they rode up the road from the barren maize fields, then she jumped up and shouted for Louise and the children. She watched as the officer gestured to his men to fan out. They circled the farmhouse cautiously, searching the outbuildings for people and arms.

The young lieutenant rode up towards the verandah, with the Afrikaner guide a couple of paces behind. Pookie went out onto the verandah, holding her rifle, looking down at them.

"Is this Elandsfontein Farm?" Hensman called out. "That belongs to Jacobus Venter?"

Pookie nodded, holding the children close to her side; little Rosemary burrowed her head into her aunt's skirt.

"Don't you speak English?" Hensman stood up in his stirrups and stretched his back. He hated this business of questioning Boer women.

Their English was often non-existent or atrocious, and they could be obdurate and even rude—not surprising, really, when they realised what they were in for.

"I do," she answered curtly. "Do you want food and drink?"

"Thank you—in a minute. Are there any men here—I mean your white men, not servants or farm workers?"

"Of course not. Do you think they would have let you ride up here?"

Hensman sighed patiently. "Where are they?"

"I don't know—and that's the truth."

"We know that Jacobus Venter is with a commando. Is he your husband?"

Pookie flushed. "No! My uncle."

"Are those your children?"

"No—my sister's. She's inside, but she's not well. She fell from her horse."

"Where is your husband? What's his name?"

"I'm not married, mister. And I'm getting bored with your questions."

Hensman sighed again. "Very well." He turned. "In the cart..." he waved it forward. "...is a Mrs Bredenkamp and her two daughters—I expect you know them."

"Well, let them come into the house, man!"

"I'm afraid they've been..." He stopped, seeing Louise come onto the verandah.

"What do they want?" whispered Louise.

Pookie ignored her sister and turned back to Hensman. "This is my sister. She has two children. We have one servant, and he has a wife and child. No farm workers—they've all gone."

Meanwhile, the spring cart drew up at the foot of the steps. When Pookie saw the Bredenkamps, she shouted at Hensman, "I suppose you've burned their farm!"

He nodded wearily. "Yes Miss, we had to...orders." He pointed to the women in the wagon. "They were attacked by a gang of natives." He walked towards Pookie and lowered his voice. "The girls have been...er... violated. I would be grateful if you would..."

"Oh, my God!" Pookie rushed down the steps of the verandah and ran towards the wagon, holding up her skirts.

Hensman took off his hat and wiped his forehead with a white handkerchief. He was deeply thankful that were woman here who could deal with the Bredenkamps. Looking up, he saw that Louise was standing at the top of the steps wearing a dazed expression as she watched her sister lead the two girls from the wagon. Pookie was calling orders to the two Bredenkamp servants and Ephraim, instructing them to carry Maria up onto the *stoep*.

The lieutenant dismounted and handed his horse to a trooper, then turned to his sergeant and ordered, "Put out guards, Ross, and let the men have some rest and food, while we attend to these women. We may have to stay the night here." To Kok, he said, "Interrogate the servants. I want to know if there are other gangs of natives around here."

He followed the women onto the *stoep* and then into the house, watching closely as Maria Bredenkamp was placed on a bed. Pookie started cleaning the contusions on her head, while Louise led the two Bredenkamp girls to the bathroom.

"How serious is her injury?" he asked.

"Very serious," snapped Pookie impatiently. "She needs a doctor, but she shouldn't be moved. I could get Dr Pieters from the town."

"I'm sorry, Miss, but I have orders to burn the house and the farm buildings. We will then take you to an assembly point in one of your wagons. From there, you will be taken to a camp, where you will be looked after until the war is over." He hated delivering the ominous words.

She looked at him with distaste. "I expected this! We've heard about your destruction of our properties. But if you move this woman now she will die. Don't you realise, her head is seriously injured."

"I'm sorry. I do realise, but I'm only carrying out my orders. I expect there will be doctors at the camp. It might be better to take her there quickly. And those two girls should be seen by a doctor."

"Where is the gang of *kaffirs*?" asked Pookie.

"We killed them."

"Good!" She looked down at Maria, then turned to Hensman. "Can you at least give us until morning? It would give us a chance to pack our belongings."

"Yes. But we must leave at first light."

❧

Pookie joined her sister in the bathroom, where Louise had undressed the two young girls and thrown their filthy bloodstained clothes in a pile on the floor. She started bathing the girls in the tin tub, while her sister fetched clean clothes. She extracted the story of what had happened on their farm, while she and Louise listened in horror. Then, after they dressed the girls, Pookie drew her sister aside and said, "The British are going to burn the house. They are going to take us with them—at first light."

Louise slumped against the wall, wiping the back of her hand on her forehead. "We can't leave here—not now."

"Don't you understand? They'll set fire to this house. They're going to take us to a prison camp. You must help me, Louise. We have to pack whatever we can take on the wagon."

Her thoughts were now consumed with an idea of slipping away under cover of darkness. She was determined not to be taken into captivity again, and decided she would have to leave on foot, because Roode would make too much noise. The British would not expect a woman to walk off into the night. Yet she was deeply concerned about leaving Louise, who seemed sapped of energy. She also felt it would be abandoning the Bredenkamp's, especially Maria, though there was little she could do for the older woman.

When the Bredenkamp girls had gone to be with their mother, Pookie drew her sister aside again and told her the plan. "You must not breathe a word about it, sis. I won't tell you when I'm going. You do understand, don't you?"

"Yes—but if they catch you, they may shoot you." Louise's eyes were wide and fearful.

"I doubt it. Anyway, I'll take the chance. They'll be asleep except for the guards, and they can't watch every corner."

"Where will you go?"

"Better you don't know. I'll find my way back to a hospital and I'll go back to nursing. I'll try to find out where you're taken—there must be people who will know. Perhaps I could ask Martin to help." She laughed.

"You can't ask him—he's the enemy! Anyway, he wouldn't help you would he?"

"He wouldn't see me as the enemy. He thinks I'm just a poor nurse. Anyway, if he still loves you, he'll want to find out where you are, and how you are." She kissed her sister lovingly. "Take care of yourself, and those kids."

∽∾

An hour after midnight Pookie made a last reconnaissance. The troopers were asleep on the verandah except for two guards, one at the front of the house, and one at the back. The guard at the rear of the house was sitting on a chair, his back to the wall. He had his rifle on his lap and looked very sleepy. Pookie filled her pockets with biltong and dried fruit, intended to be her emergency rations. Tucking her revolver into the waistband of her skirt she slipped quietly out of the back door, as if to go to the 'little house' where the toilet was situated. She hoped that the guard would be asleep, but he greeted her.

"Where are you going, Miss?"

"To the toilet. I have stomach cramps."

"Watch out for snakes. Hah, hah."

She went into the brick shit house, where there was a wooden toilet seat like a throne with a hole, built over a pit as deep as a well. Behind the throne was a large shutter in the wall, put there when Louise wanted to use a bucket instead of the long drop; she was afraid that Rosemary might fall down the hole. The opening was just large enough for Pookie to squeeze through. Keeping the little house between her and the guard, she backed slowly and silently away until she was in complete darkness. With only starlight to see by, she took a wide circuit round the buildings and set off down the farm road towards Pietersburg.

Meanwhile the guard fell asleep. When he awoke he knocked on the door of the little house. Receiving no answer, he assumed that the girl had returned to the main house while he was asleep.

☞⚮

Next morning, the Venter's smallest trek wagon with only four of the usual eight oxen, led by Ephraim, waited in front of the house. Maria Bredenkamp, still unconscious, was carried down from the verandah and laid on a mattress in the wagon; her two daughters sat with her. Louise's two children sat at the front of the wagon with Miriam and her daughter. Louise elected to travel in the Bredenkamp's spring wagon.

It was at this moment that Hensman asked Louise where her sister was. "She's not here," replied Louise.

With a sinking sensation, Hensman said, "She ran away? Where to?"

Louise shook her head. "She never told me."

The lieutenant called Kok and Sergeant Ross and held a conference with them. "I have to report this incident. There will be an enquiry and I'll be held responsible. Ross, you must speak to the guards." He mounted his horse near the spring wagon and shouted to his men. "Come on then. Get the wagon moving."

Kok shouted at Ephraim, who climbed up on the driver's seat and cracked his whip. The oxen lumbered forward with the wagon in tow.

Hensman called to Louise, "You'd better follow them. We have to set fire to the house." He was despondent at having lost one of his prisoners and in no mood to debate.

She shook her head. "I want to watch."

"Very well." He turned to his Sergeant and said, "Ross! You can start now."

"Pity to leave those cows, sir."

"It would slow us down too much to take them. They can't trek like these oxen. I expect they'll be killed and eaten by the local natives."

Ross went up to the house and supervised his troopers as they threw burning brands onto the thatched roof of the homestead. Within a few minutes the house was swathed in a cloud of cherry red flames, and oily black smoke curled around the walls. The British troopers stood watching silently, glancing now and then at the Boers to watch their reaction. Louise wept quietly as she watched. Then Hensman shouted the orders to leave and she clucked at the horses until the spring cart lurched forward. She glanced back occasionally; the last time she saw the roof timbers collapse sending up a shower of sparks.

෴

They reached the railway station at dusk and found the platform littered with little groups of dishevelled Boer women and children, and a few African servants. Cooking fires guttered and sparkled in the surrounding *veld*, and beyond were the stronger picket blazes of the British troops who had brought them there, and who now guarded them. Hensman rode up to the station office, where a Quartermaster Sergeant sat behind a desk.

"Four more Boer women for you, Sergeant, and two children. My Sergeant Ross will give you the details. One of the women has a serious head injury. Do you know where they can find a doctor?"

The QMS shook his head. "Not 'ere, sir. There're plenty of sick women and children, but we're not allowed to let 'em leave the station."

"When will the train come?"

"Tomorrow afternoon, sir—so I'm told."

Hensman nodded and left. He found Louise unloading the wagon, and told her that she could send it back to the farm with Ephraim and his family. She looked at him for a moment trying to fathom his generosity and motives, then thanked him.

"I'm sorry," he said. "Good luck."

She found Ephraim and told him to go to the farm and stay there. "We'll come back," she added. "The *baas* will come back from the fighting. Tell him what happened." She knew that Ephraim and Miriam would stay at the farm since they had nowhere else to go. They had been born there and knew they were assured of jobs and food for the rest of their lives. Indeed their daughter would probably work for the Venter family when she grew up.

Louise now found a small clearing behind the station platform, not too far from one of the larger cooking fires. There she discovered a family she knew—the De Bruyns—who invited her group to sit near their fire. There were scarcely enough twigs to keep the fire alight, and the families huddled together in a circle around it, too shocked and cold to talk.

At dawn, a huge sun, reddened by dust, loomed up to warm them. A party of troopers from the British camp brought some provisions—a sack of maize flour, and two milk churns filled with water. These meagre rations had to be shared between about thirty families, and old Mrs De Bruyn was asked to divide it fairly. As the sun rose higher in a cloudless sky, the heat became oppressive. There were only patches of shade near the station office, and the Boer families had to rig makeshift shelters by hanging clothing on sticks. Early in the afternoon, a young Boer lad shouted that he could feel the rails vibrating, and soon after that a train approached across the plain and stopped at the little station with squealing brakes and hissing steam.

A platoon of soldiers climbed off, humping their kitbags while a sergeant shouted orders. When the train was empty the Boer families were ordered on board. They piled in all their possessions—makeshift bundles, battered suitcases, old trunks, sacks with biltong and beans, and baskets of chickens. Maria Bredenkamp was carried unceremoniously into the guard's van, where her two daughters were allowed to look after her. The guard party of British soldiers shouted at them to hurry. The engine driver tooted his whistle, and amid a flurry of jumping on board the train jerked forward.

In their carriage Louise shared out precious food between the two children and the De Bruyns, telling them that they would soon be at the camp where there would be some shelter and rations.

It was dark when the train reached Grootfontein, where the Boer women and children stumbled out, stiff and weary. Standing on the platform was a British civilian, a round little man with mutton chop whiskers, holding a speaking trumpet.

"Put together what you can carry," he called, in English. "You have to walk to the camp. You'll be allocated tents. It's a mile away. Leave the things you can't carry on the platform—we'll arrange for them to be brought to the camp."

Louise shouted to him, "What about the sick woman in the guard's van?"

"Don't you worry about anyone else, Miss," was the immediate reply. "Look after yourself. We'll see to her."

She hastily separated essential belongings from the bundles, but the trunk posed a problem. If they carried it between them, they could take little else, yet it contained personal items that she did not wish to leave behind—things like her photographs, and letters from Perry.

"Come along now!" shouted the little man. "We haven't got all night."

She had to leave the trunk behind, wishing that Pookie had been there to help her. She slung a bundle of clothing over her shoulder and the children each carried a small load. They set off down the dark dusty street that led from the station through the town. The bedraggled group moved slowly through the town, as men and women standing on their verandahs watched idly. A few Africans jeered at them, calling "Where's your pass?". Several times, Louise had to stop to ease off the weight of her bundle. A housewife brought out a jug of water and some mugs to drink from, muttering words of encouragement.

After nearly an hour of walking, over a brow of a low hill, they caught their first sight of the ghostly rows of tents stretching in lines down the far slope into the darkness. A few points of light flickered among the tents, but there were no lamps to light the paths between the rows. Two shabbily dressed Afrikaner men approached the procession when they reached the perimeter fence and pointed out where they should go, telling them that there was only one tent for each family. Louise and the De Bruyn family found adjacent tents; each was large enough to take eight people, so there was plenty of room for them.

Louise went in search of food and found near the closed gate one of the men who had guided them to the tents. He regarded her with a bored expression when she asked where she could buy food.

"You're not allowed into the town."

"Then how are we to eat? My children have not had a proper meal since breakfast yesterday."

"You will all be given food tomorrow. Until then, I suggest you chew some biltong. I expect you have some of that. If not, someone will give you some."

"What about water?"

"There's a tap at the bottom of each line of tents. Be careful not to waste it. There's little enough to go round." As Louise turned away, he added, "It's only for drinking—not for bathing, or for washing clothes."

෨‿ᕥ

Next day they lined up for food—it was only maize meal porridge—and each prisoner was given a ladle full from large steaming cast-iron pots. When Louise asked if there was milk for the children, she was told that they hadn't seen milk for over a month.

The round little man who had met them at the station approached with his speaking trumpet. "We had a case of typhoid fever identified in the camp yesterday. You must only drink water from the tap, and if you can, you should boil it first."

Louise reacted angrily. "How can we boil water! There's no wood."

"We will try to bring in some loads of wood. You must remember that there's a war going on."

When they returned to their tents to eat the porridge they found Cecelia and Rowena Bredenkamp, their faces tear-stained. Louise embraced them, guessing their news.

"Mama died on the train," sobbed Cecelia. "They've taken her away to be buried—we don't know where. They said she may have had typhoid, but we know..."

"Stupid bastards!" muttered Louise. She tried comfort the girls while she shared their meagre food. Later, she went to carry a bucket of water from the tap at the bottom of the slope, little Gerald trotting beside her.

"Mama, why can we wash only once a day?"

"Because we're only allowed one bucket of water a day."

"Auntie says we'll start to smell like *kaffirs*."

"She doesn't really mean that—and you shouldn't say such things." She felt her forehead—it was on fire, and her brow was wet. She remembered a time when she'd had fever in the Cape. The thought of typhoid crossed her mind, and when she looked down at Gerald she thought the children were so vulnerable. Their little bodies had such weak defences. Then she remembered something her mother had said—that children had a tremendous ability to survive, otherwise the human race would have disappeared a long time ago.

CHAPTER 27
The Last Throes Of War – 1901

Louis Botha's army retreated towards Pretoria after the defeat at Doornkop. The situation was confused, and the British seemed mesmerised by their success in occupying Johannesburg and the gold mines. The Union flag was hoisted in the city and a ceremonial march past held, with Lord Roberts taking the salute. Meanwhile, President Paul Kruger was spirited away towards the Mozambique frontier. The Boer forces were on the verge of collapse and men were starting to return to their homes and farms.

One evening, as Perry walked outside the Pretoria municipal hall, where a *kriegsraad,* a war council, was being held, he saw Ben Venter approaching. They greeted each other warmly. Perry had always liked Ben, for his good humour and lack of prejudice, which contrasted so much with his elder brother's dour attitudes.

"Have you heard the news?" said Ben. "Smuts and Botha have advised *Oom* Paul to surrender!"

"What do you think we should do?"

"If we can get honourable terms we should make peace. But I doubt the British will agree to our terms. They think they've won. They'll want their revenge."

Smuts and Botha emerged from the hall and the two generals shook hands before walking off in different directions. Then Botha noticed Perry and came up to him. "Well, Yankee, I have another task for you. Come and join me for some food while I write the message."

Botha shook Ben's hand. "This Yankee is a brave man, Venter. I dread the day he may be caught by the British. Well now, come and join us."

They walked in silence towards the old house where the general was billeted, and Botha invited Perry and Ben inside. Two *fraus* were cooking his supper and they brought some coffee to the three men, who sat in the living room in wooden chairs with leather thongs. Perry regarded the weary face of the general who was still only thirty-eight but now seemed ten years older. He remembered how Botha hated the war and its terrible cost in lives.

The General sighed heavily. "We've decided to fight on. What do you think of that?"

"We can fight a guerrilla war now...," said Perry. When he paused Botha indicated that he should continue, and he added, "It's our great strength—mobility. We may not defeat them, but we can prolong the war. That will bring better terms than surrender now."

"You're right, Yankee. But I'm not sure that we can retain our mobility. Our commandos have to eat and feed their horses."

"From the farms, sir?" said Ben. "There should be food enough."

Botha smiled wryly. "And do you think Roberts will allow a commando to come and feed at a farm at will? No, my friends; he's putting a stop to that." He sighed again, and drank some of his coffee. "We shall see."

One of the women came to say that the meal was ready and the men went to wash their hands. When they returned, Botha stood at the table to say grace, and then the women brought plates of grilled meat and *boerewors*. As the three men started to eat, they heard a knock on the door; Botha signalled to Perry to open it. He admitted a messenger, a thin young man in dusty khaki uniform. Botha gave him a sausage to eat while he read the message in silence, then continued his own meal.

"Yankee," said Botha, after a while, "I want you to take a message to General De Wet. But this time I want you to stay with him. He's a good man, a good leader, and I think you will be a great help to him. I doubt he has anyone that can get through the lines as well as you. Stay with him for a while until he trusts you. Get to know his staff. Then you can move between us. You see, the telegraph lines are lost to us. We have to rely on men like you. You can bluff your way past any British patrol." He pushed his plate aside, heaved his saddlebag onto the table, and took out his leather writing case and started to write a message. Finding the light too dim, he called to the women and one of them brought a paraffin lamp to set on the table beside him.

When he had finished writing, General Botha sealed the letter, and gave it to Perry. As he watched him leave, he thought about the dangers his messenger faced. It was one thing to risk death in warfare, but the American risked a firing squad if he was captured.

अ⬧

At about this time, Martin met Frank Burnham in a mess tent near Kitchener's headquarters. They had not seen each other since a few days before the Battle of Paardeberg. The American was as slim and dapper as ever, his blue eyes shining, his teeth gleaming in a broad smile.

"I heard about your float down the Modder River," said Martin, after they exchanged greetings. "You know I was a prisoner there?"

"Yes, I heard. In fact I saw you..."

"You saw me?"

"Sure did. At first I couldn't believe it was you—because you were walking free."

"I was allowed to—by General Cronje."

"And who was the girl?" Burnham smiled slyly.

"That must have been Pauline Venter..."

"A friend? You were talking very intently."

He laughed. "You don't suspect anything, do you?"

Burnham shook his head. "I did for a while. I made no mention of it in my report." He paused. "You remember when I came back with the message from Allan Wilson? Did you suspect me then—of running away?"

"No. Did you run away?"

"No. But I'm afraid the suspicion will dog me all my life." Burnham laughed openly. "At least we can believe each other. So who was the girl?"

"She was the younger sister of Perry Davenport's wife—you remember Perry?"

"Sure." Burnham frowned as he calculated the relationship. Then he said, "You know Davenport's a messenger for the Boers? We've known about him for months. If he's caught, I'm afraid he will probably be shot. Some of the Boer messengers wear British uniforms taken from prisoners because it's all they can find to wear. They cut off the buttons, but many of our officers treat them as spies."

"God, I hope he's careful—he has children now."

☙ ❧

Perry found General Christiaan Rudolf De Wet near Heilbron, where the *vechts-general* had about eight hundred men. They were tough, hardened fighters, but Perry was struck by their poor morale and their shortage of materials, particularly ammunition. The cornet who led him into the *laager* was morose as he showed Perry the way to De Wet's tent. The general was of medium height, with a jutting chest and thrusting beard, his eyes fierce, and bloodshot with fatigue. He nodded a greeting as he cast a searing look at Perry, took the letter, then tore it open and started reading. The cornet tried to lead Perry away, but De Wet waved his hand to indicate that he should stay where he was. After a while, the general tossed the letter onto the camp table and shouted for one of his staff officers. Two came, both tall bearded men.

"The American here has come again," De Wet told them, "with a letter from Botha asking that he stay with us." The Boer officers looked at Perry with curiosity and suspicion, and De Wet went on. "The first time I had some doubts. If you're to stay with me, I must be sure. Which family have you married into?"

"The Venters, sir; from Elandsfontein Farm, near Pietersburg. That's Gerrit Venter, who went to Rhodesia, and Cobus..."

De Wet held up his hand to interrupt, then turned to the staff officers. "Get someone from Pietersburg." He continued glaring at Perry, then pointed at his cheek. "That wound—I remember—you got it at Elandslaagte?"

The two staff officers returned with a burly heavy-bearded man who Perry did not recognise. When De Wet asked the man if he came from Pietersburg he replied that he did, and his name was Wessels.

The general turned to Perry. "Go on. You said you married into the family of...?"

"Gerrit Venter, sir. He went to Rhodesia where I first met his daughter, Louise. We married in '95."

"Gerrit Venter died," said Wessels to Perry. "What was his family farm in the Transvaal?"

"Elandsfontein—near the Bredenkamp's farm."

"*Jah*, I know it. The old man fought at Vegkop."

De Wet nodded with a slight smile. "With our President, eh?"

"I believe President Kruger was a child in the *laager*, sir. Old Venter died not long ago."

"Yes, very well, Yankee. You had better get something to eat. General Botha has urged us to continue the fight. Tomorrow you'll see how we fight here. It may be different from what you're used to."

꙳

Next day the Heilbron commando ambushed a supply convoy of fifty-six wagons on its way to the British General Colville. They took over a hundred prisoners without a shot fired. Three days later, Perry rode again with De Wet, this time to Roodewal. At first the Boer general was furious because his scouts had informed him that the guard on the railway bridge was only of company strength, whereas he soon realised that the British force consisted of a battalion of the Derbyshire Regiment. But the British troops were inexperienced and had not set up an adequate defensive perimeter. The Boers surrounded them with a ring of deadly fire, and after about three hours they surrendered. The Boers rode on to Roodewal Station where the opposition was negligible, and by midday had surrendered. They took away huge quantities of ammunition for their captured rifles, and as much food as they could carry. They then set fire to the rest of the supplies, which set off a series of huge explosions.

After some weeks, General De Wet sent Perry with a message to Cyphersfontein, where there would be a meeting of the Boer leaders. His message was to say that he was coming, but might not be able to reach them for another four days. As he handed Perry the message, De Wet said, "You know why I selected you, Yankee?"

"Because you think I'll have a better chance of bluffing my way through British patrols?"

De Wet nodded with a rare smile. "Not just that. I thought you should visit your wife. You haven't seen her for many months—I know, because you've been around here most of that time." He sucked noisily at his coffee mug. "And Yankee—if you want to stay there—I mean with Botha—you can. You've done well here, but it's only fair that you should take the chance to be near your people. They will have difficult times ahead."

❧❦

When Perry rode into the farm Cyphersfontein, the Boer aides wanted to take De Wet's message and dismiss him. An argument ensued, and voices were raised, when at that moment, a slender man with piercing blue eyes came to the edge of the verandah. Looking up, Perry recognised Jan Smuts.

"What is the explanation of this argument?" asked Smuts sharply.

"This messenger is from General De Wet," said one of the aides. "He insists on seeing General Botha."

"Then why are you arguing?" asked Smuts of Perry.

"My orders are to deliver it personally into General Botha's hand. Here, read this pass."

Smuts eyed him keenly. "You're not an Afrikaner—don't I know you?"

"Perry Davenport, sir. We met in Pretoria—just before the war."

"Ah yes, I remember. You're the American. You'd better come in, Davenport." Smuts waved the aides aside to allow Perry to come up the steps.

Taking off his hat and brushing his hair back from his forehead, Perry went up onto the verandah, where Smuts shook his hand and led him through the hall, which ran the full depth of the house. They emerged at the rear onto another verandah that looked out over a garden with a huge lawn. Under a spreading flamboyant tree, in deep shade, stood a large table surrounded by cane chairs, on which sat President Steyn, and two generals, Botha and De La Rey.

As Perry walked across the lawn with Smuts, Botha looked up, then smiled and rose to his feet. "Well, well—it's the Yankee. You must have come from De Wet." He clapped Perry on the shoulder, and beamed. "How are you, then?" He turned to the other Generals. "This man was my galloper through the first half of this year."

Perry thought that Louis Botha had grown younger again. His face was less drawn, and his eyes brighter. Still standing, he opened De Wet's letter and scanned through it, then turned to Perry and said, "Well, you'll have to tell us about what's been happening there—but later. Go and have some rest—and something to eat. And find your brother-in-law—he's on Smuts' staff now."

"General," said Perry, "may I stay in the Transvaal? General De Wet said that if there was an opportunity I should take it..."

"*Yah*, he mentioned it in his note. Very well—I'll speak to Smuts. Now off you go." As Perry walked away, Botha called after him, "Yankee! Do you still have that big horse?"

Perry turned. "I do, but I had to leave him on a farm last night—he was worn out."

When he found Ben Venter, he was eating in the big dining room of the homestead, with other staff officers. The young Afrikaner jumped up and hurried forward to embrace Perry. He then told how Louise and the children had been taken to a concentration camp, while Pookie escaped and was now in Pretoria. "The farmhouse has been burned down." Ben grimaced. "I got all this information from Pookie a few days ago. She ran away during the night, to escape the British. She managed to walk for two nights, lying in the bush during daylight, until she reached the De Bruyn's farm. It was burned down, but she found a donkey and rode it to Pietersburg. Then she travelled down to Pretoria—she's an amazing girl."

Louise and the children were incarcerated—that was all Perry could think about. He'd already heard that these camps were getting a reputation for diseases and malnutrition. He entered a lengthy discussion with Ben, during which they agreed that one of them must seek leave and find the prisoners.

They rode together towards Elandsfontein. Perry had slept through most of the last few days. Ben told him, "They're right to continue the war. I think it was Steyn who was instrumental in the decision. From what I heard Botha was worried about making the *volk* suffer more."

"He was one of those most opposed to the war. He knows it's the women and children who'll bear the main brunt of a guerrilla war."

"We're going to invade Natal and the Cape. The British won't burn the farms in the Cape. They don't want to risk a rebellion of the Boer population there."

When the two men reached the farm, they dismounted and walked separately among the ruins. Ephraim came out to meet them and told how the British had come to burn the farm house, and how they had taken the women and children away to the railway station. He had heard that they would be sent to a place called Grootfontein.

"Was Miss Louise well when she was taken away?" asked Perry.

"Yes, *baas*."

"And the children?"

"Yes, *baas*, they were all well."

Perry turned to Ben. "Where is Grootfontein?"

"North of Paarl. They'll be all right. Don't worry, they'll be with other families. They'll help each other."

❧❧

A couple of weeks later, Perry rode down the spectacular Drakensberg range, searching for General Botha. Veils of mist drifted down from the crags, and he hunched lower under his cape as droplets of condensed mist dripped off the rim of his slouch hat. He knew that Botha's commando moved quickly and quietly, striking wherever they could find a lightly defended target. There were British everywhere and he had to stay alert.

He searched for two days before he found the Boer camp, where they gave him a warm welcome and were glad to hear about the plundering of a British convoy in the Magaliesberg. He stayed with the commando as they followed the Drakensberg to Piet Retief, then east to Utrecht. Using mules and horses to carry their supplies, they travelled fast and light, with not a single field gun. The spring rain was relentless, but they had to keep moving. Perry scoured the open *veld* with his field glasses, keeping carefully in touch with the scouts.

On 17th September 1901, Botha's force reached the farm Blood River Poort, near the confluence of the Blood River and the Buffalo River, where his scouts found a British force under the command of Major Hubert Gough. Unusually for this war, the Boers outnumbered the British. Perry rode with Botha as they encircled one of Gough's companies, astride a ridge, and in a sharp fight the Boers took the ridge. Below them on the plain were Gough's main force and two field guns. The mounted Boers poured down from the ridge and overwhelmed the British force, capturing a large quantity of rifles, ammunition, and two hundred horses. The British prisoners were stripped of their weapons, ammunition, and field glasses, then sent back to their base.

Soaked and chilled, cheered only by their victory, Botha and his men rode south along the Transvaal-Natal border. Everywhere there were British troops. One evening, Perry was sought by General Botha and found him in despondent mood.

"Yankee, where will all this lead to? I'm afraid our attempt to invade Natal has failed. The British are closing all our options."

"We're always too heavily outnumbered."

"I hate to see my men and horses suffering like this. This war has turned sour—burning farms, shooting prisoners—*agh*, man, is it worth it? Sometimes I feel we're like animals being hunted. I tell you, Yankee, if we were offered an honourable peace, I would accept it." Botha sighed. "I want you to find De Wet. I want to know how it fares with him. My last message was that the British had him surrounded near Basutoland. But he's a wily fox."

⊱⊰

Perry rode alone on the open plain of the Orange Free State. To his left rose the mountains of Basutoland, their tops lost in the clouds. He had few clues about the whereabouts of De Wet's force, and for all he knew they had surrendered, and that might bring the war to an end. Many Boers were saying that as long as De Wet fought there was a chance of better terms.

Suddenly he caught sight of horsemen on the horizon, about two miles away. Pulling out his field glasses he saw that it was a British patrol of six men. Evidently they had seen him and were giving chase. He galloped up to a brow to get a better view of escape routes, but when he reached the crest he found a long fence of barbed wire. These fences had been strung out by the British to prevent Boer commandos from free movement across the *veld*. The wire was too high for his horse to jump, so he turned left towards the mountains. The British patrol anticipated his move and turned too. Perry realised he had no escape.

As they approached, the British patrol commander, a young lieutenant, shouted at Perry to drop his weapons. The American took his revolver out of its holster and dropped it on the ground.

"That was sensible." The lieutenant pointed his own revolver at Perry. "Who are you?"

"I'm an American. I'm trying to find an old friend."

The lieutenant laughed. "A likely story. But you do sound like an American. Your name? And where were you coming from?"

"Davenport, and I've come from Natal."

"Davenport?" The lieutenant turned in his saddle. "Hey, Potgeiter!"

A tall bearded man rode up from the back of the British patrol. His long legs hung down below his horse's belly. He regarded Perry cautiously with rheumy eyes.

"Do you know this man?" asked the lieutenant.

The Boer screwed up his eyes as he examined Perry. Then he shook his head.

"Wasn't Davenport one of the names we were given at the briefing?" The lieutenant fumbled inside his jacket and brought out a wallet. He extracted a paper, which he unfolded and examined. "Yes, here we are. An American named Davenport—a messenger." His demeanour changed suddenly. "Right, Davenport! Get off your horse—and no trouble, or I'll shoot you."

Perry, filled with foreboding, slid off Rollo and stood still while a sergeant searched him. He had no papers on him except a letter from his wife, because he had been expecting this situation for months and committed all his messages to memory. He knew that he might be shot as a spy and felt fatalistic, drawing some comfort from the thought that Louise might think more of him if he died for the Boer cause.

When the sergeant reported that Perry had no papers on him, the lieutenant asked Perry what message he had been given to remember. When Perry refused to answer the lieutenant ordered, "Tie him by a lead rein to his horse. We'll walk him back to camp." He thought that exhausting the prisoner might make him more amenable for further interrogation.

The sergeant tied Perry's wrists together, and then attached a lead rein. He grabbed Rollo's reins and the party set off, with Perry running to keep up. After about four miles, he fell down in exhaustion and Rollo stopped, refusing to drag his owner. The sergeant detached the lead rein from the big horse and attached it to his own pummel. They set off again, with Perry stumbling and falling. Eventually he fell again, and they could drag him no further.

The lieutenant dismounted and walked up to Perry's prostrate body. "I ask you again, Davenport. What message do you carry?"

"I have nothing to tell you," muttered Perry, his lips swollen.

"You really are one of them, aren't you." The officer turned to his sergeant. "We shouldn't damage his clothes any more, Sergeant. I think this one is heading for the firing squad. You see he's not wearing a uniform. A spy to all intents. Right, tie him onto his horse—I want to get back for some supper."

∽∾

CHAPTER 28
Finding The Prisoners

Martin had been given two weeks leave and would then start a new staff job in the army HQ in Cape Town. He found two letters from Helen waiting for him. In her first letter, not realising that he already knew, Helen told him that Robert had been killed in the siege of Mafeking:

'Poor Robert, he was walking back to his billet after breakfast when a Boer shell exploded nearby and a fragment of shrapnel hit his head. He was killed instantly. I'm glad he didn't suffer, or have a disabling wound. I think I had a premonition that something would happen to him, so it wasn't such a shock when the news came. Dear Robert, he was always so prone to accidents—you remember. Very few men were killed in the siege, but he was one of them. I had such a nice letter from his Colonel. He said how much everyone liked Robert, and I believe it. I mourn him as my husband of nearly ten years, and the father of my daughters. He was a kind and generous man.'

She went on to tell Martin about conditions in Rhodesia, and about the state of his farm, which she had visited with Tom Ellsworth. *'I found everything in order. It's as if frozen in time, and waiting for the owner to return and bring it to life.'*

Her second letter was about her plan to visit England. *'I have no family of my own, as you know. But I owe it to Robert's parents to take their granddaughters to see them—they're not well enough to travel out to South Africa. We will take the coach to Bulawayo, and thence by train to Mafeking, where I will visit Robert's grave and arrange for a photograph to be taken.'*

'I hope, dear Martin, that I'll be able to see you in Cape Town, if your duties permit you to be there, and give you sufficient time. I need to discuss my future— whether to stay in Rhodesia, or move to live in England, or even in South Africa.' She gave him the expected date of her arrival in Cape Town, and said that she would be staying at the Mount Nelson Hotel.

It was there that Martin met her, with her daughters, Clare, aged five, and Flora, aged two. She seemed to him lovelier than ever, still with the same upright bearing and slim figure. The same slow smile lit up her face, and her complexion showed no sign of the ravages of the sun; indeed she and her daughters might have walked out of an English garden.

"So you're going back to England?" he said as he embraced her.

"Only to show the girls to their grandparents. I think we may come back to Rhodesia. We have a farm too!"

He smiled at her, wanting to know more. "Do you have someone to help you?"

"I have a manager, if that's what you mean."

He laughed nervously. "Helen, that's not what I mean."

She smiled fondly and touched his cheek. "No, Martin. There's no one else."

He asked her when her ship would leave and she answered, "On Friday. We had great difficulty finding berths. So many people are leaving now the war's coming to an end. We have three days to do some shopping, and to rest after our long train journey."

"I hope you'll spare me some of your time. Where is your farm, Helen? Do I know it?"

"Yes you do! It's next door to yours. We bought Henry Borrow's farm. So you'll have to put up with me as your neighbour."

He had tea with them, and between entertaining the little girls, they told each other about their lives in the last three years, and exchanged news about their friends. While Helen gave her daughters an early supper, Martin went back to Rosebank, where he now shared a rented house with his sister Beth. He changed, and returned with her to the hotel to dine with Helen.

They discussed the plight of Louise and her children. "Pookie has spoken to me," said Martin. "She wants to persuade the authorities to release Louise on the grounds that she's married to an American. But Perry cannot be found—to confirm his nationality. The issue is complicated by his involvement with the Boers. We know he's a messenger and I've asked Major Burnham to trace him. The problem is that if he shows his face he'll be arrested immediately."

Helen was shocked to hear that Martin was so involved with Louise and her sister, remembering all too easily how enticing he had found the Afrikaner girls. For all she knew, he had taken Louise as a lover. Meanwhile, she heard that Pookie had become engaged to a young doctor at the Groote Schuur hospital, where she was a nurse.

Though somewhat mollified that her potential rivals seemed bespoken, Helen was next dismayed to learn that Amanda Jacobs, Martin's old flame in England, would soon visit South Africa, ostensibly to investigate conditions in the concentration camps. Listening carefully she detected in Martin's demeanour that he might be excited about Amanda's visit. She felt particularly vulnerable, knowing that she would be in England at the time.

Next day, Helen arranged for a governess to look after the little girls so that she would be free to be with Martin. They walked up to the Kirstenbosch botanical gardens, where they could speak freely in idyllic surroundings, with a stupendous view of Table Bay and the mountain behind them, walking arm in arm along the gravel pathways.

"I'm still in love with you, Helen. I loved you all the years you were married to Robert." He held her, as they stood in the shade of a huge magnolia.

"You must have had relationships with other women in that time, but I don't care, as long as you have no commitment to anyone now." He assured her that he was not committed and she went on. "Amanda Jacobs? She'll be here while I'm in England. How can I be sure that you won't renew your affair with her?"

"Because it's over—it happened years ago. I know she's not interested in..."

"How do you know?"

"She made it plain to me when I saw her in England."

"So you tried to renew your affair?"

"Not with any conviction."

She tried to accept his statement and that evening, after supper, she invited him to have a nightcap in her room. She had a suite, with the little girls in another bedroom, and ensured that they were fast asleep before giving her attention to Martin. She felt that she was worked up into a state of tension about making love with Martin, having experienced only one man in her life, the last time over two years ago. Imagining that he would have had many and varied women, she felt she was somehow on trial.

As it happened, Martin was very capable at soothing her. It was easy for him, because he recognised that Helen loved him deeply, and was not the least selfish. Thus they made love in mutual desire to please each other. She realised that her latent sexuality and excitement was at last released with this man, and her responses surprised her with their intensity. They stayed together until it was almost dawn, and she could scarcely bear him to leave.

Before she left for England, Martin proposed, in the garden at the Rosebank house. She embraced him, and answered. "I want to marry you, my darling Martin."

❧❦

Beth and her brother met Amanda Jacobs at the pier in Cape Town as she disembarked from the liner. While Beth was hugging her friend, Martin observed that Amanda was as attractive as ever. The bones in her cheeks were more prominent, but this only enhanced her looks. Her blonde hair was as full and fine as ever, and her eyes intensely blue in the bright sunlight. He felt a momentary pang of longing for her, but knew that there could no longer be any romantic contact between them.

Amanda glanced at him over Beth's shoulder and smiled. She was delighted to be in his company again, but only because she liked him, and not with any sexual attraction—that was long gone. When it was his turn, she kissed him on both cheeks, and said, "I have letters from your parents." When Beth asked after them, she added, "They're well enough. Your mother asked me to persuade you to come home—and to bring Martin with you." She turned to him. "How are you? None the worse for your capture by the Boers?"

"No—but guess what—Perry is now a prisoner of the British."

"He was fighting on the Boer side?"

"Not fighting—that's the trouble. He's suspected of spying. I'm trying to help him—I'm hoping to have a meeting in a couple of days time. I don't want there to be some hurried judgment..."

"They wouldn't execute him, surely?"

Beth started sobbing. "It's quite possible."

❧❦

That evening, in Beth's house in Rosebank, the three of them had supper, served by a Coloured maid. A toast was drunk to honour their visitor from England, and another to Martin, and in absentia to Helen, congratulating them on their engagement.

Martin asked Amanda about her plan to visit the concentration camps that held the Boer women and children. "I have letters of introduction—from high places," she replied. "I hope to see Sir Alfred Milner, and General Kitchener. Being a doctor will help—I mean, it will seem less politically motivated."

"Do you expect obstruction?" asked Beth.

"Oh yes. I've had difficulties already, but I'm not surprised. They don't want a woman snooping around the camps."

"We hear conditions are dreadful."

Amanda patted Beth's hand. "That's why I'm here, dear. I must discover whether the conditions should or could be better. We must strike a level of humanitarian adequacy. If we haven't, I shall say so."

"Oh, good for you, Amanda. What do you think, Martin? You've hardly said a word."

He smiled. "It will be helpful to have an objective report from someone well qualified like you, Amanda."

"Can you help her?" asked his sister.

"I'll help so far as I can. But remember that I'm a mere Major in the outer circle of staff officers. We can try to help Louise and her children. They were taken into a concentration camp months ago. I was told this by her sister Pauline."

"Which camp are they in?" asked Amanda. "Perhaps I could find them."

"They're in Grootfontein...it's somewhere north of Paarl."

"Then I will see them—it's in my plan to visit the camp at Grootfontein. What did Pauline say?"

"Louise and the children were taken from their farm—the house was burned down."

"Hmm. Kitchener's scorched earth policy. Do you approve?"

"No. But if you tell anyone I said that, I'll deny it. I still think we can negotiate a surrender."

Beth interjected, "But the scorched earth policy will bring them to the table sooner—that's what the officers say."

"Perhaps," replied Martin, "but with deepened hatred. And what will that serve in the aftermath—which there must be? It will simply increase the amount of reparations."

"Did Pauline say anything about conditions in the camp?" asked Amanda.

"Yes. They don't have enough food. And there's typhoid."

Sipping her wine, Amanda asked about Perry Davenport, and Martin replied, "I was told he's...well, downcast. Apparently he was carrying messages between the Boer generals. They wouldn't have allowed him to do that unless he'd proved himself loyal and capable. He wasn't wearing a uniform when he was captured, but many Boers are dressed in old civilian clothes, or even British uniforms with the insignia and buttons cut off. Our authorities have a strong case against him and I'm not sure that I can do much to help. I have a meeting tomorrow with the United States Consul, and I'm hoping he'll ask Sir Alfred Milner for clemency. You see, the war will end soon and I'm pretty confident there'll be a general amnesty. It would be tragic if Perry were executed now."

≈≪

Louise huddled in her tent, sheltering from the cold wind that swept through the camp, and looking at the thin bodies of her children. They had lost their energy and liveliness and sat listlessly watching the adults. Louise put her hand to her face. She had no mirror, but she knew her skin was sallow now, and her hair straggling. Looking across the tent she watched Mrs De Bruyn, who also seemed tired and lifeless. Finally, she pulled herself to her feet and beckoned Cecelia Bredenkamp to come with her out of the tent.

"I think I have a fever," she announced quietly.

Cecelia put her hand to her friend's brow. "Yes, you have. We'd better keep the children away from you, for the time being. You haven't had the runs, have you? Then it can't be dysentery."

"Do you think Perry's had my letter?"

"Maybe. But he wouldn't be allowed to visit you here."

"He could say he's an American."

"You have to have papers to move anywhere. Maybe he couldn't prove he's American"

"Perhaps he has some—forged papers—so that he can carry the messages around."

"I'm sure he'll come if he can."

≈≪

Amanda Jacobs sat in the small wooden office at the entrance to the camp, talking with the camp supervisor, a stocky grizzled Yorkshireman. Beside him was Mr Potter, the little man with mutton-chop whiskers who had greeted the Boers on their arrival at the station. Assigned to accompany Amanda was an eager and admiring staff officer, Captain Michael Nabarro.

She had been given minimal information by the camp supervisor, laboriously extracted. He was on the defensive, because the statistics of deaths in the camp were difficult for him to defend, and he did not disguise his resentment of this visitor who probed so persistently into his affairs.

"Thank you for all the information, Mr Trevor," said Amanda, with a hint of sarcasm. "Before I leave, I would like to speak with a family called Venter..."

The Yorkshireman replied with undisguised bitterness. "Friends of yours, are they, Miss Jacobs?"

"It's 'Doctor' Jacobs, Mr Trevor. And, no, they're not friends, but they are known to me, and they're in this camp—I've already made certain of that."

"We don't allow visiting friends."

Amanda stood up. "Mr Trevor, I have a busy itinerary. I have the authority, too, you know. Are you suggesting I may not see them?"

"No." Trevor shook his head wearily. "If I did, no doubt it would appear in your report."

"I've already explained—I'll report objectively about conditions in the camps - and the way they're being managed."

Trevor heaved himself from his chair with an exaggerated sigh. "Yes, I'm sure. Well, come along then."

He and Potter led the visitors along the long lines of windswept tents until they reached the Venter's. On entering, Amanda saw a young dark-haired woman lying on a low camp bed, with another younger woman squatting beside her. Both were emaciated, and the prone one was perspiring heavily despite the chill conditions, as if she had a fever.

"Do they speak English?" asked the supervisor of Potter.

"Yes, they do," interrupted Amanda. "Hello, you must be Louise Davenport. I'm Dr Jacobs. I'm making a survey of the concentration camps. Martin Russell told me you were here, so I decided to find you..."

Cecelia Bredenkamp regarded Amanda with sullen suspicion. "She can't hear you—she has typhoid. If you're a doctor, can you help us?"

Bending down to examine the patient, Amanda found her brow was burning, and her lips moving as she verged on delirium. Turning, she said to Trevor, "She should be in the hospital."

"The hospital's full—as you've just seen. Potter tells me this woman"—he pointed to Cecelia—"is a friend. She's not one of the Venter family. There are two young children."

"Yes, I am Cecelia Bredenkamp. I know a little about nursing. My mother died in the train that brought us here, because she received no medical attention..."

"Yes, yes," interrupted Trevor impatiently. "Where are this woman's children?"

Cecelia pointed with a movement of her head. "Outside." She added, "We have no medicine."

"Nor in the hospital," muttered Trevor.

Cecelia said to Amanda, "The medicine all goes to the khakis, doesn't it?"

"They have priority. There are typhoid epidemics in two of their camps." Amanda got to her feet and addressed Trevor with authority. "I want to take this woman back to Cape Town with me."

Trevor was incredulous. "You can't do that! It's not permitted for Boers to leave the camp precincts, except to go to the hospital."

"And that's where I'm taking her—to hospital in Cape Town."

Trevor shook his head emphatically. "Not unless you have written authority, you ain't."

"Very well—I'll get the authority." She turned to Nabarro. "Michael, can we contact General Kitchener by telegraph?"

The young captain smiled, captivated by this authoritative young woman. "Er, I don't know, Dr Jacobs. We could try. But I don't think he'd deal with you, would he?"

"We'll see about that. Come on." She nodded in farewell to Cecelia and strode out of the tent, the three men following. She insisted on going to the British Army camp on the outskirts of Grootfontein, where Captain Nabarro was able to get her into the Adjutant's office. She dictated a telegraph to the operator:

"Message to General Kitchener, through Major Martin Russell. From Dr Jacobs at Adjutant's Office, Grootfontein. Dr Jacobs requests permission for patient Louise Davenport to be moved to hospital in Cape Town, together with her two young children. Patient is..."

Trevor interrupted. "I thought you said her name was Venter."

"That's her maiden name," Amanda replied calmly. She turned back to the telegraph operator. *"Patient is an American citizen by marriage, and is suspected of having typhoid. She should be admitted to the infectious diseases hospital in Cape Town. Your urgent attention would be appreciated."*

Nabarro's frown submerged his habitual smile. "We may have to wait ages for a reply."

It was over an hour before the telegraph started clattering. The operator wrote the message on a pad and handed it to Captain Nabarro, who read it, and handed it to Amanda.

"Unable to grant Dr Jacobs request until we know details of patient's citizenship, and reason for special treatment. Dr Jacobs will know that there are hundreds of British soldiers suffering from typhoid, with unfavourable conditions. General Kitchener, through Major Russell."

"Well, at least he replied," said Captain Nabarro gloomily.

Amanda started scribbling on a notepad. "I want to send my answer immediately," she said, and then started to announce her message to the telegrapher: *"Patient was visiting farm when taken in by troopers. No reason for special treatment except to save the life of someone who perhaps should not be there. Your urgent consideration requested."*

The telegrapher sent the second message, and Amanda and her escort maintained their vigil in the telegraph office. It was three hours before the reply came, again read to them by the Adjutant.

"Message from Major Russell: 'General Kitchener not available. General Hildyard has taken decision that, in view of doubt about the patient's citizenship, she, and only she, and her two children, should be released to Dr Jacobs."

To Amanda, he said, "Well, there you are Dr Jacobs, you've got what you wanted."

"I hope we're not too late." Amanda turned and strode out.

࿐

Amanda and her escort returned to the camp, where they found Louise no longer delirious. She regarded Amanda with large dark eyes.

"I don't think she should be moved now," said Amanda, "—perhaps in the morning if her fever has reduced." She stopped, hearing that Louise was speaking.

The voice was scarcely audible. "Martin used to love you. Maybe he still does. I never knew."

"I never knew too," said Amanda kindly.

Louise slowly shook her head, then turned to Cecelia. "I'm frightened. I don't want to leave the children. Will you look after them if I die?"

"Don't be silly, Louise. You're not going to die. Dr Amanda is going to take you to the hospital in Cape Town—and the children. You'll soon be better."

"I want to see Gerald and Rosie."

"I'll bring them to the door, but better you don't touch them now, dear."

"We'll give her some more powder in about an hour," said Amanda. "I'm going to stay."

Cecelia grudgingly thanked Amanda for her help. They stayed with the patient through a long night, taking it in turns to sleep, sitting in a camp chair that was brought to them by Captain Nabarro. Next morning, Martin arrived at the camp and Amanda pointed out Louise's children, who were playing outside on the muddy path between the lines of tents. Louise was asleep, thin and wan, her brow damp. Amanda felt her pulse and checked her heart with a stethoscope.

Cecelia completed packing the patient's belongings. To Martin, she said: "She's sick because of you British. You realise that don't you. If it weren't for your people she'd be living happily in Jo'burg with her husband. And where's he? He's fighting your bloody soldiers. Helping us to keep our land." She strode out of the tent.

෨ॐ

CHAPTER 29
The Fighting Ends — 1902

The war was nearly over, and Martin returned to Cape Town with good news about the peace talks. He was anxious to see Amanda before she left for England. He spent his first night at Beth's house, before helping her to chaperone the High Commissioner, Sir Alfred Milner, and Lady Violet Cecil, on a ride in the parkland at Groote Schuur. When they reined in from a canter, Milner manoeuvred his horse beside Martin's.

"I heard something interesting, Russell. An American has been fighting with the Boers—name of Perry Davenport. Know him?"

Suspecting that Milner knew the answer, Martin could see no sense in concealing his friendship. "Yes. He's an old friend. I heard he was a courier for General de Wet."

"For Botha too—when we captured him."

"Then what will happen to him?" asked Beth, who, with Lady Cecil, had ridden up beside the men. "Where is he?"

Milner smiled sardonically. "A friend of yours too, Beth. Is this wise, I ask myself, for the High Commissioner to socialise with friends of a Boer spy?"

"Don't be ridiculous, Alfred," said Violet Cecil. "There are hundreds of foreigners fighting with the Boers. Furthermore, one of your Generals told me that a third of the Boers are fighting with us!"

Milner ignored her, and asked Martin, "Why is he with the Boers?" When Martin told him about Perry's marriage into the Venter family, Milner asked, "Do you think you'd have a better chance of getting information from him—than the other Intelligence officers?"

"I might." Martin shrugged. "I was going to ask you, sir...I'd like to see him, if only to tell him about his wife. Amanda Jacobs was able to extract her from the camp at Grootfontein."

"God, that woman! She's coming to see me tomorrow. Very well, Russell, go to see your friend and tell me what you hear. Come on then, we'd better get back. Lunch awaits us." He led them in a canter back to the house.

❧❧

Next day, Milner sat in his office, with his Private Secretary hovering at his shoulder. Facing him on the other side of the desk were General Kitchener and his ADC.

"I'm going back to England next month...." Milner told them.

Kitchener tried to stifle a smile. "For good?"

"No, no," replied Milner, missing the innuendo. "My job here isn't finished. However, one subject on which I must agree with the CIC is that we can't afford to keep an army of a quarter of a million men here in order to subdue twenty thousand Boers."

"Until the Boers are defeated," said Kitchener, "we have to maintain the army here. What alternative is there?"

"There will have to be an alternative. One is that we keep a reduced force to protect strategic locations."

Kitchener snorted. "That would simply allow the Boers to build up their strength. You would be faced with an indefinite stalemate. I've heard that Botha has been consulting with President Kruger about entering into peace negotiations."

"Hmm. Yes, I saw that report. How reliable is it?"

"As you know, we've decoded their messages. I regard it as reliable. But there have been messages from Steyn suggesting that the war be continued."

"It must not be continued indefinitely. You've had the warning, General."

❧❧

Perry Davenport sat at a deal table facing three British officers. Gaunt and weary, he still retained a trace of his former swagger. He was dressed in a loose fitting prison uniform of coarse cotton that might once have been white, but was now a dirty yellow.

The captain in the centre of the group was interrogating Perry. "You don't seem to understand, Davenport. Prisoners taken in your circumstances have been shot as spies."

Perry glowered at him. "You don't frighten me. My wife is dying in one of your disgusting camps. It would not matter much to me if..."

"You have two children; don't you want to see them?"

"Are you bribing me?" Perry's eyes were hooded in fatigue.

"No—but you do have them to live for. If you cooperate with us, it may help you to avoid the firing squad. I'm serious, Davenport. It's not an idle threat."

An orderly came into the room and handed a note to the captain, who read it, and said, "Ask Major Russell to come in." The officer was irritated at this interruption from a senior man, although he admitted to himself that he was making little progress with the American prisoner.

When Martin was shown into the room, he was given a chair to the side of the main table used by the tribunal. Glancing at Perry he smiled, trying to hide his dismay at the American's appearance. Perry's face was expressionless, pale and gaunt, his eyes sunk deep and dull. Martin was shocked to see the scar on the side of his face, wondering how and when the wound was inflicted.

"Thank you for coming, sir," said the captain. "I understand you know the prisoner." A smile lurked at the corners of his mouth.

"I do."

"Do you know the nature of his activities?"

"Not in detail. I heard he was a messenger."

"He was. Wouldn't you agree that he could get through our lines more easily that a Boer?"

"Yes, I suppose so."

The captain turned to Perry and the smile twitched again. "Why weren't you carrying papers?"

"What papers? We didn't have papers..."

"And you didn't have a uniform?"

For a brief moment Perry smiled. "I had one, but it disintegrated."

"So there's nothing to distinguish you from a common spy? In terms of the conventions of war, personnel who do not wear uniforms are either civilians or spies. You were not a civilian..."

"I was not a spy. I told you, my duty was to take messages."

"But you posed as a civilian in order to pass through our lines. That constitutes spying." The captain swivelled to face Martin.

"Look, Captain Slater," said Martin. "I have no doubt he was a messenger. There's no evidence that he spied."

The captain closed his file with a flourish. "Very well. We'll have another hearing a week from now. In the meantime, I want to have further evidence. A decision may be made then to hold an execution tribunal." He turned to a sergeant. "Take the prisoner away."

෬෧

Amanda was shown into Milner's office. She wore a long pale blue dress and her blonde hair was tied in a thick plait that swung across her back. The High Commissioner's Private Secretary admired her appearance as he showed her to the seat recently vacated by Kitchener, then left the room reluctantly. Milner, dressed immaculately in a dark suit, stood near the window.

Amanda started diffidently. "I'm grateful to you for sparing the time to see me."

"I'm very busy, Dr Jacobs." Milner smiled ungraciously.

She nodded. "I wanted to do you the courtesy—and you did request it—of talking to you, before I return to England and make my report."

"Very well. Thank you. Do continue."

"The camps where Boer women and children are held are a disgrace."

"We are at war, Dr Jacobs." He sighed heavily. "Our resources are not unlimited."

"Yes, but if we bring these people into camps, we accept the responsibility of looking after them, just as if they're prisoners of war. Yet the standard of care is appalling."

"Care? May I remind you that they are the enemy. I have to care for a quarter of a million British soldiers. They are my first priority."

"We all know that, Sir Alfred, but the balance of resources has been tipped unfairly. I can only report that conditions in the camps are awful. Thousands of women and children are dying. I do not exaggerate. The British people will not tolerate it."

Her comment about the British people caught him unawares. There had already been some unfavourable articles in the home newspapers, most of them generated by an earlier visit by a woman named Emily Hobhouse. "Is that what you will report? How will you offer your information?"

"To the Prime Minister, and to politicians..."

He walked forward to his desk and sat down. "They have already heard the same comments from Miss Hobhouse."

"Then they shall hear it again, from me," said Amanda with great determination. "And I have the advantage over Emily that I'm qualified medically. The death rates are appalling. The whole mess is an indictment of British policy. As the representative of the British Government here, you should be ashamed."

Milner's eyebrows rose and his fists clenched. He was furious at this woman, but he knew she was right—about conditions in the camps. When he spoke, it was as if he were reciting from a document. "Dr Jacobs, when a country is at war, the main priority is defeat of the enemy. Inevitably the civilian population suffers. That has happened in wars throughout time. What you have observed, and describe in such intemperate terms, is such suffering. We are all distressed that women and children should have to be put in camps. But you must remember that they were providing succour to the enemy."

"That's not sufficient reason for us to fail in our treatment—in my view."

"In your view—and I suppose you'll be reporting to Mr Lloyd George?"

"Yes. He's one of the politicians who will listen to me and read my report."

"That sounds like a threat."

She stood up to leave. "No, just a statement of fact."

❧

A week later, Martin again visited the prisoner-of-war camp where Perry was detained. He was in sombre mood because he'd been informed that a summary tribunal would be held the next day. He had also been advised that the prisoner was likely to be convicted and would then be executed the following morning. While waiting in a sparsely furnished anteroom, he wondered how he could reach a final rapprochement with his friend. Whatever suspicions Perry might have about his behaviour in Johannesburg, he was determined not to reveal what had happened, judging that Louise had said nothing, and had reconciled with him.

When a sergeant brought in the prisoner, Martin stood up and indicated that Perry should be seated. "I'm very sorry. It looks as if they are going to press the spying charge."

Perry shrugged and looked at Martin for a moment without speaking.

"Amanda managed to get Louise and your children out of the concentration camp at Grootfontein."

"She wrote to me," Perry interrupted in a flat voice. He slumped forward, and there followed a long silence. Eventually, he said, "Can you help me to see them?"

"I'll try. She's is in the hospital at Groote Schuur, but the children are with Jeanne at Franschhoek. Perry, I must ask you some questions. It's just for our records. First, how were you captured?"

"I see. This is really an interrogation, is it? Very well—I ran into one of your patrols. There was too much barbed-wire for my horse to jump through."

"Do you think De Wet will join peace negotiations?"

Perry glanced at the sergeant. "If I'm to answer questions like that, we must be alone."

"All right. Sergeant, you can leave us." Martin turned back to Perry. "Well?"

"You must remember that I never attended any councils-of-war. But to answer your question—to give you my personal opinion—yes, I think De Wet will negotiate. All will depend on the terms. If they're humiliating, he'll carry on fighting."

"Have you any ideas of the sort of terms he wants?"

"Only the things one talks about round the campfire. They want their farms of course. And the money to re-build the destroyed houses..."

"And what form of government?"

"As you'd expect, they want to go back to where they were when the war started."

"Hmm. I doubt Milner would offer that. He seems obsessed with the 'rebels'—as he calls them—in the Cape."

"Surely he can pardon them?"

"There's no realistic alternative."

Perry sighed, and asked grudgingly, "How are Beth and Amanda?"

"Amanda went back to England after she finished her review of the civilian prison camps. She's breathing fire about the conditions in them. You know she has influential friends, including Lloyd George. Beth's still in Cape Town, pursued by officers, but not really interested in any of them. She always asks fondly after you. She's trying hard to ensure that Louise isn't sent back to the camp when she recovers. We're using the argument that she's an American citizen. But the High Commission argues that because you fought on the Boer side, it invalidates the citizenship argument."

"Surely only for me?"

"Precisely. We'll keep trying." Martin stood up to leave.

Perry looked up at him, and for the first time smiled. "Thank you, Martin—I mean for not trying to bribe information from me."

They look at each other in mutual understanding, and Martin realised that the years they had known each other had evolved the sort of friendship that could endure. For a while they recalled their meeting in England, the long trek to Salisbury in 1890 and the Matabele War. They'd been through hard times together.

As Perry was led back to his cell, he pondered his attitude to Martin. He tried hard to suppress his jealousy, realising that his friend was now sure to marry the widowed Helen. The two of them had been near death, yet they managed to survive. Perhaps if he was acquitted they could live in peace. There was no sense in recrimination and resentment.

☙❧

Martin went to see Louise in the Groote Schuur hospital, to give her news of her husband, fearing that it might not assist her recovery. He found her in a room of her own, sitting up in bed reading a newspaper. She smiled, her large dark eyes shining, and indicated that he should sit in the wicker chair near the window.

He told her about his discussion with Perry, then added. "The news is not good. He'll be tried soon. They may postpone it if peace negotiations start."

Louise started to weep and shortly after Pookie came into the room, wearing a nurse's uniform. Her hair was short and she looked younger. Martin greeted her with a kiss on the cheek and explained the reason for his visit.

Pookie then told them she had heard that Louise would not be returned to the prison camp. "Because you're now an American citizen—or at least there's sufficient doubt about your status."

They talked for an hour, reminiscing about their times together, and about their friends. He learned that Pookie planned to marry her young doctor soon. Then Pookie decided that her sister was getting tired, and she ushered Martin out.

As they walked down the corridor, she took his arm. "We had our times, Martin, didn't we?" Then she took her arm away hurriedly. "I must be careful now. I'm an engaged woman." She reached up to kiss his cheek and ran down the corridor, leaving him to find his way out alone.

☙❧

Martin decided to visit Jeanne Venter, for no reason other than he felt he should make his peace with her, the mother of two women who had been entwined in his life, however briefly. He rode out to the farm at Franschhoek and found her looking much the same as when he last saw her. Perhaps she was a little stouter, but she had the same fine complexion and pretty eyes.

She thanked him for his efforts to save Louise and her children from the concentration camp. Gerald and Rosemary were staying with her while Louise was still in hospital. He watched them playing among the flowers in the garden, they reminded him of his visit to Johannesburg; Rosemary was a baby then, and here she was, three years old.

They walked slowly towards the house. "I've been so far from all that's happened," said Jeanne. "I've felt so helpless. We tried to visit the camp, of course, but it was hopeless—they wouldn't allow it. I feel cold all over when I think that Louise nearly died." She paused, then added, "She loved you, Martin."

He laughed nervously. "Not really..."

"Oh, don't deny it. And you never returned her love." She puts her hand on his arm. "I'm not blaming you for rejecting her."

"I didn't reject her," he protested. "It wasn't like that, Jeanne. I was uncertain what to do. I thought her interest in me was...well, immature—a sort of young girl's infatuation. I admit I was attracted to her, but..."

"I don't blame you for being attracted to her—and...giving in. Yes, dear Martin, she wrote and told me what happened in Johannesburg. No one else will know."

Martin reddened. "It's all over now, Jeanne. We made a mistake. She really loves Perry now. Now I'm someone from the past. It won't happen again."

"Yes, I think they've made up their differences. If he's released and they can be together again, it will be much better. They can work at healing their marriage."

࿓

The tribunal at the prison in Paarl was a brief affair. A Colonel and two Captains heard the evidence and concluded that Perry Davenport had acted as a spy. He offered nothing in his defence and he was sentenced to be shot by a firing squad the following morning. Before the court adjourned, Martin requested a postponement of the execution on the grounds that peace negotiations were in progress, and that the prisoner was an American citizen. The Colonel listened impatiently and replied immediately that no postponement would be granted.

Martin glanced at his friend, who looked pale and defeated as he was led away to the cells. Shocked by the sudden turn of events, Martin went to a nearby regimental office and sent a telegram to Beth urging her to go to Milner and Kitchener to request a postponement of the firing squad on both grounds. He then decided to seek help from Field Marshal Roberts, who had returned to England after handing over command to Kitchener. After making enquiries about Roberts' probable whereabouts he sent an urgent telegram:

"Major Martin Russell requests Field Marshal Roberts' urgent help as offered in Cape Town in 1900. American citizen Perry Davenport sentenced to death by court martial for spying was used as messenger by Boer generals, not a spy. Please postpone execution pending peace negotiations."

He had little hope that his plea would reach Roberts, nor that the Field Marshal would interfere. He decided to wait in Paarl, finding a spot near the regimental telegraph office. He slumped in an uncomfortable chair, alternating between dozing and jumping to his feet when the machine chattered. Afternoon turned into chilly evening. He had not eaten for hours yet did not want to now.

At nine o'clock the telegraph broke silence and the corporal who manned it beckoned to him. The message was from Beth:

"Milner and Kitchener obdurate. They saw me, but will not budge. Sorry. Beth"

He could imagine her distress, knowing her strong affection for the doomed man. He fruitlessly searched his mind for ways to stop the firing squad. He then instructed the telegrapher to send any messages for him to the prison. It took him two hours to ride there; then he started pacing up and down the corridor outside the telegraph office. The telegraph machine was silent, and this was the only way that a message could come to save Perry.

⊱⊰

Perry sat in his cell, his head bowed. He was not afraid of the execution. He had none of the fear that virtually paralysed him in the *laagers* at Bembesi and Shangani, and when the Forbes Column was fleeing the Matabele after the Wilson patrol was slaughtered. It was nothing like the enveloping terror of the cavalry charge at Elandslaagte. Something must have changed in him Now he faced certain death, whereas in the other events he was merely at risk.

He pondered whether to dispense with the blindfold. Around the Boer campfires they'd discussed the British predeliction for execution and the details of the methods – how one man in the firing squad was given a blank round, so that you could never be sure you had killed the prisoner. How bizarre and typically British.

He thought about Louise and his children, regretting that he would not see them again. It was ironic that, when he finally achieved her love and affection they were dashed from him. He felt confident that they would remember him. Louise would always see him in her children.

̅̅

Martin must have fallen asleep some time after midnight. He was awoken by a commotion somewhere in the prison and went to investigate. A group of army officers were in heated discussion which appeared to centre on a piece of paper. The Colonel holding it saw Martin walking towards him and left the group.

"Russell!" The Colonel shook his hand. "I remember you from Colenso." He flourished a telegram. "I'm Lord Roberts' Liaison Officer in Cape Town. He has ordered me to take Davenport to Cape Town Castle, where he'll be held pending further enquiries." He laughed. "These fellows are not pleased. Nor is Kitchener—he's hopping mad. I don't know if you plan a future in the army, but you'll have a tough time if Kitchener has anything to do with you." He paused. "You look done in. Better get some sleep."

̅̅

At her Rosebank house, three weeks later, Beth greeted her brother, who had returned from the peace negotiations at Vereeniging. "Well, what can you tell me? Is it good news?"

He hugged his sister. "Marvellous. The draft terms have been drawn up. Milner won't like them. He'll say that the Boers have won all the concessions they wanted."

"And Kitchener?"

"It's what he wants. He's a soldier after all. He doesn't want to rub the enemy's nose in the dirt. He just wants to get out with his reputation intact and go to India."

They moved out to the verandah and she handed him a glass of wine. "When we will peace be declared?"

"Before the end of the month, I guess. That's about when Helen will return."

☙❧

It was in June 1902 that a horse-drawn trap brought Helen Onslow and her daughters to the Rosebank house, where Martin and Beth came out to greet them. It was a sunny but chilly Cape winter day. They went into the sheltered garden, where the maid served coffee.

"It's so good to see you again." Martin was hardly able to contain himself as he kissed Helen.

She told them about her visit to Robert's family, and then to the Russells in Oxford. There she found that they had already received Martin's letter telling them that she had accepted his proposal of marriage. She felt gratified that they welcomed her as a prospective daughter-in-law. Turning to Beth, she said, "I have to fulfill my promise to your parents—to persuade you to return to England. Martin, you must go too, at least for a visit. I'll go with you."

Beth said, "Well, as you know, Helen, I'll go as soon as I can buy a berth—now that I can leave Martin in your capable hands. "

☙❧

Before Beth sailed back to England, it was arranged that Louise and Perry would come to lunch. When they arrived, Beth, who had not seen Perry since his visits to Middleton, was surprised at how he had aged. She was also shocked to see him so thin, his hair prematurely greying. The scar on his face was livid and caused her to shudder. His jacket hung loosely on his shoulders and his eyes, usually so animated, were sombre, and deep in dark sockets. Louise was weak and pale, walking slowly and leaning on her husband's arm. They kissed Helen and Beth and introduced their two children, Gerald and Rosemary, who then ran off to play with Helen's girls.

Martin kissed Louise's cheek, and when he shook Perry's hand he could detect no evidence of animosity as they looked into each other's eyes. How he has changed, he thought. The frivolous foppish young man he'd met in London in 1890 had been transformed into a mature man in his mid-thirties, with deep lines in his face. His eyes were glistening with the emotion of meeting old friends, but seemed to have lost their youthful sparkle. He has endured much hardship and sorrow, Martin thought, but it has made him a better man.

When he watched Louise, he estimated that she was now twenty-five. Her expression, especially in her eyes, was more serious and her voice was deeper and softer. She stayed close to her husband's side, and often gazed into his eyes, smiling when he looked at her.

Helen had last seen the couple at the time of Robert's trial in Pretoria, and she told them the story of how he had been killed at Mafeking. Martin then reminded them that Helen had agreed to marry him, and a bottle of champagne was opened.

"To my old friends, Martin and Helen," said Perry, his glass aloft. "We wish you good fortune in your married life in Rhodesia!"

She will keep him from straying, he was thinking. She's a strong woman, and he will probably be satisfied with her. I've come through hard times with him during the last twelve years, but we survived, and now we have women to be grateful for, and to be proud of. "And thanks to my old friend," said Perry hoarsely, "for saving me from a firing squad."

"To my old friends, and former prisoners, Perry and Louise," said Martin. "Celebrate your freedom!"

He wished at once he'd not mentioned they were prisoners, but no one seemed to mind. He thought, Perry is mature and sober now, quiet and thoughtful. She is subdued and maternal. They seemed the most damaged of all, Perry with his scar and his emaciated body; Louise still convalescent after suffering illness near to death. They were the ones who had changed most, not only in appearance—which might be their present condition—but also in character. He was reminded of Rudyard Kipling's verse from Gentleman Rankers: *'And the measure of our torment is the measure of our youth, God help us, for we knew the worst too young.'*

"To Beth," said Louise quietly, holding up her glass. "Our deep thanks for all your efforts to get me and the children, out of that camp—and to dear Amanda—God Bless her." She wondered whether Beth would marry in England; she was thirty now, not quite too old, and in any case she looked younger. She looked at Martin; he would always be her regret, but she would not allow it to sour her life, because she loved her husband.

"What will you two do?" asked Helen.

Perry laughed, a little like his old self. "The company beckons. They say mining will boom again, and I don't doubt it. But first we'll take the children to England and America, to see my family." He paused, regarding Martin with a smile. "Will you live the rest of your life in Rhodesia?"

Martin looked across at Helen. He wanted nothing more than to return to his farm and live with her. She was the only woman he wanted.

෨෧

Epilogue

Martin Russell and Helen Onslow married in Salisbury later that year. They amalgamated their farms, and had three sons. Martin fought with distinction in East Africa in the First World War, ending the campaign as a Colonel. He was prominent in resisting the amalgamation of Rhodesia with South Africa in 1923. He died on his farm in 1938; Helen lived another ten years. Several of their grandchildren still live in Zimbabwe, but most are scattered in England, Australia and America.

Perry Davenport became Managing Director of Consolidated Mining. He and Louise kept houses in Johannesburg and London. They had two more children, and their grand-children still live in South Africa.

Beth returned to live in Oxford, where she married a don at the University. Hendrik Venter became a prominent and successful farmer in the Northern Transvaal. His brother Ben was elected to the South African parliament, and became a Deputy Minister of Justice under Smuts. Their sister Pauline (Pookie) married a doctor and lived in Cape Town, becoming the matriarch of a large family.

☙❧

Glossary

(Afr. = Afrikaans [the language spoken by Afrikaners in South Africa] which evolved from Dutch; 'Bantu = the group of languages spoken by Bantu people in Southern Africa)

Afrikaner	people of Dutch descent living in Southern Africa
assegai	Bantu: 'stabbing spear'
boerwors	Afr. 'farm sausage'.
boetie	Afr. 'little brother'
dagga	Afr. 'mud', as in wattle and daub house
disselboom	Afr. 'towing pole' for wagon
dominie	Dutch Reformed Church minister
dop	Afr. alcoholic spirit made from distilled fruit juice, e.g. peach brandy
highveld	pron. 'highfelt' – the high country – the plateau area of Southern Africa, as distinct from the 'lowveld'
induna	Bantu: 'chief' or regimental commander
kaffir	Arabic: kafir: 'infidel' or 'non-believer', became a derogative term often used by Afrikaners for Bantu people
kappie	Afr. large hooded bonnet worn by Afrikaner women
Karoo	Khoisan: semi-desert natural region in South Africa
kerel	Afr. 'guy'
kopje	Afr. 'small hill'
kraal	Afr. 'corral', enclosure for animals
laager	Afr. circular defensive enclosure, often made with wagons
melktert	Afr. 'milk tart'
mhondoro	ChiShona: 'spirit medium'
minheer	Afr. 'mister, sir'

mopane	*Colophospermum mopane,* forest tree species indigenous to Matabeleland
mpondo	*Julbernadia globiflora,* large spreading tree, indigenous to the highveld in Rhodesia
msasa	*Brachystegia spiciformis,* large spreading tree, indigenous to the highveld in Rhodesia
nagapie	Afr. 'little night ape' nocturnal primate from the family Galagidae
nganga	ChiShona: 'witch doctor'
Oom	Afr. 'Uncle'
Ouma	Afr. 'Grandma'
Oupa	Afr. 'Grandpa'
rondavel	Afr. round house or room, usually with a conical thatched roof
rooinek	Afr. 'red neck', used, often derisively, for a white person other than an Afrikaner
stoep	Afr. 'porch', 'verandah'
taal	Afr. 'language', 'the Taal' being the Afrikaans language
trek	Afr. 'long journey'
uitlander	Afr. 'foreigner', term used by the Boers for expatriates working in the Transvaal
veld	Afr. lit. 'field'; pron. 'felt' – commonly used for the African bushveld (countryside)
veldschoen	Afr. 'bush shoes', made with soft leather
vlei	Afr. pron. 'flay' - a low lying marsh or poorly drained grassland area, generally with no trees
voortrekker	Afr. those who trek ahead, i.e. pioneers

ঽ৽৽ঀ

Short Biographical Notes

Botha, Louis (1862-1919) Boer General, became a member of the parliament of the Transvaal Republic in 1897. He fought in the Second Boer War at Colenso and Spion Kop, and when General Joubert died was made commander-in-chief of the Transvaal Boers. After the fall of Pretoria in March 1900 he led a concentrated guerilla campaign against the British. He was involved in the peace negotiations of 1902, and was a signatory to the Treaty of Vereeniging. When he travelled to London seeking loans to assist his country's reconstruction he met Winston Churchill, whom he had captured during the war. Botha became Prime Minister of the Transvaal and in 1910 the first Prime Minister of the Union of South Africa. At the outbreak of the First World War in 1914 he sent troops to take German South West Africa (now Namibia), a move unpopular among Boers that provoked the Boer Revolt, which he defeated.

Buller, Sir Redvers Henry (1839-1908) British General, educated at Eton and commissioned in 1858. He took part in the Second Opium War and the Ashanti campaign, and served in South Africa during the 9th Cape Frontier War (1878) and the Zulu War (1879, when he was decorated with the Victoria Cross for bravery under fire). He was Sir Evelyn Wood's chief of staff in the First Boer War (1881) and took part in the expedition to relieve General Gordon at Khartoum (1885). He was sent to South Africa as commander of the Natal field force on the outbreak of the Second Boer War, and was defeated at the Battle of Colenso. Further defeats at the Battles of Magersfontein and Stormberg also involved forces under his command, and because of concerns about his performance and negative reports from the field he was replaced in January 1900 as overall commander in South Africa by Lord Roberts.

Burnham, Frederick Russell (1861-1947) was an American adventurer who served as a scout and tracker for the US Army in the Apache and Cheyenne Wars. In 1893 he sailed to South Africa with his wife and young son, then joined the British South Africa Company as a scout and headed north to Rhodesia, where he took part in the Matabele

War (1893). In March 1896 the Matabele rebelled against the authority of the British South Africa Company fomented by a spirit medium named Mlimo. A turning point in the rebellion came when Burnham found the cave where Mlimo had been hiding and killed him. Later, he was appointed Chief of Scouts by Lord Roberts in the Boer War and spent much time behind the Boer lines gathering information and blowing up railway bridges and tracks. He was twice captured and twice escaped, and was awarded a DSO for heroism during the March to Pretoria. Burnham had made friends with Baden-Powell during the Matabele Rebellion and was influential in the formation of the Boy Scout movement.

Cronjé, Pieter Arnoldus (1836-1911) commonly known as Piet was a general of the Boer military forces during the First Boer War (1881). He was in command of the force that rounded up the British force at Doornkop at the conclusion of the Jameson Raid (1896). During the Second Boer War he was the general commanding in the western theatre of war and began the sieges of Kimberley and Mafeking. He was defeated at the Battle of Paardeberg (1900) where he surrendered with 4,150 of his troops after being enveloped by Lord Roberts' forces. After his surrender, he was imprisoned on St Helena until the conclusion of peace negotiations in 1902.

Churchill, Winston Leonard Spencer- (1874-1965) is so well known that this section deals mostly with his visit to South Africa in 1899 as a war correspondent for the Morning Post, a British newspaper. He was captured by Boer forces commanded by General Louis Botha and imprisoned in Pretoria. He escaped and travelled to Lourenco Marques, then returned to join General Buller's army. He was commissioned in the South African Light Horse and was present at the relief of the siege of Ladysmith. He then returned to England on the *Dunottar Castle* (a fellow passenger was Frederick Burnham) in July 1900. Soon after, he was elected to Parliament for the first time. He was the first person to be made an honorary citizen of the United States, and was awarded the Nobel Prize for Literature (1953).

De Wet, Christiaan Rudolf (1854-1922) Boer General, rebel leader and politician. He was born in the Orange Free State. and served in the First Boer War (1881) when he fought in the Battle of Majuba, in which the Boers achieved a victory over the British forces. He took part in the early battles of the Second Boer War and became an expert in guerilla warfare. He was active in the peace negotiations of 1902, in the role of Acting President of the Orange Free State. He was one of the leaders of the Maritz Rebellion (1914) and was defeated by General Louis Botha.

Jameson, Leander Starr (1853-1917) also known as 'Doctor Jim' and 'The Doctor'. British colonial statesman; went to South Africa in 1878 and practised medicine in Kimberley. In 1888 he successfully exerted his influence with his patient Lobengula to persuade the Matabele chief to grant concessions to the agents of Rhodes, leading to the formation of the British South Africa Company. In 1891 Jameson succeeded Colquhoun as Administrator of Mashonaland. He was sentenced to fifteen months in jail for involvement in the ill-fated Jameson Raid, but soon pardoned. Later, he had a successful political life and became Prime Minister of the Cape Colony (1904-1908). He was buried near Rhodes' grave at Malindidzimu Hill.

Kitchener, Herbert, 1st Earl Kitchener (1850-1916) first won fame for his leading role in the Battle of Omdurman (1898) and securing control of the Sudan, after which he was given the title 'Lord Kitchener of Khartoum'. As Chief of Staff (1900–02) in the Second Boer War he played a key role in Lord Roberts' conquest of the Boer Republics, though he was much criticized for the failed frontal assault at the Battle of Paardeberg. He succeeded Roberts as Commander-in-Chief in South Africa and expanded the successful strategies devised by Roberts to force the Boer commandos to submit, including concentration camps and the scorched earth policy. He was later made Commander-in-Chief in India (1902-1909). At the start of the First World War he became Secretary of State for War and organised the largest volunteer army that Britain had seen. He was killed in 1916 when the warship taking him to negotiations in Russia was sunk by a German mine.

Kruger, Stephanus Johannes Paulus (1825-1904), better known as Paul Kruger and affectionately known as *Oom Paul*, was President of the South African Republic (Transvaal). He was born in the Eastern Cape and his family joined the Potgeiter *voortrekkers* that crossed the Vaal River in 1838. He was present at the Battle of Vegkop. He was a deeply religious man and claimed to have only read one book, the Bible. He rose to become Commandant-General of the Transvaal's army. He was the leader of the resistance movement when the British annexed the Transvaal, and played a critical role in the negotiations with the British, which led to the restoration of the Transvaal's independence. He was elected President of the Transvaal in 1880. He fled the Transvaal in May 1900, travelling to Mozambique, France and Germany, finally dying in

Switzerland in 1904.

Lloyd George, David (1863-1945) British politician and statesman, Prime Minister of the United Kingdom (1916–22) during the First World War. Widely regarded as the founder of the welfare state., and the only British Prime Minister to have spoken English as a second language (Welsh being his first). He was elected to Parliament in 1890. He opposed the British government's actions in the Boer War, mainly because he thought the franchise issue was a false excuse, and also on the grounds of cost. He was also highly critical of the conduct of the war and the imprisonment of Boer women and children.

Lobengula (Khumalo) (1845–1894) the second and last king of the Ndebele (Matabele) people, who were an offshoot of the Zulu nation; they fled north under their leader Mzilikazi, during the reign of Shaka. In the late 1830s they settled in what is now called Matabeleland in western Zimbabwe. After the death of Mzilikazi in 1868 the chiefs offered the crown to Lobengula, one of Mzilikazi's sons from an inferior wife. He mistrusted visitors and discouraged them by maintaining border patrols to monitor travellers' movements. Early in his reign he had few encounters with white men but was tolerant of white hunters and prospectors. The Matabele War (1893) led to devastating losses for the Matabele warriors. Lobengula fled and is thought to have died in early 1894, although the cause and the place are unknown.

Potgeiter, Hendrik, born in the Cape Colony and grew up to be a wealthy sheep farmer; left the colony in 1834/5 and moved inland to the present Free State. In October 1836 the Matabele attacked Potgieter's laager at Vegkop, near the present-day town of Heilbron, and were defeated. In 1838, after other Voortrekker parties were attacked, Potgieter and another leader, Pieter Uys, assembled a military force; they were lured into an ambush by the Zulus at Italeni, and both Uys and his son were killed. The Boer force fled, and Potgieter was criticized for his actions; the force was called *Die Vlugkommado* or The Flight Commando. Potgieter subsequently founded Potchefstroom and Zoutpansbergdorp (later renamed Schoemansdal).

Milner, Alfred, 1st Viscount Milner (1854-1925) British statesman and colonial administrator. Educated at Oxford and qualified as a lawyer. Served as under-secretary of finance in Egypt for four years. Selected in 1897 by Joseph Chamberlain, the Foreign Secretary, to be High Commissioner in South Africa He had an unfavorable view of Afrikaners and saw the British as a superior race. He was influential in Britain's belligerence towards the Transvaal Republic that led to the outbreak of the Boer War in 1899. During his civil administration a number of concentration camps were created where 27,000 Boer women and children and more than 14,000 black South Africans died. At the start of the First World War he was made a member of the five person War Cabinet under Lloyd George. In 1921 he married a widow, Lady Violet Gascoyne-Cecil.

Rhodes, Cecil John (1853-1902) English-born businessman, mining magnate, and politician; founded the diamond company De Beers. He supported the failed Jameson Raid and was forced to resign as Prime Minister of the Cape Colony. Rhodesia was named after him. Northern Rhodesia became independent as Zambia in 1964, and Southern Rhodesia was thereafter known simply as Rhodesia, which became Zimbabwe in 1980. He was buried at Malindidzimu Hill, or World's View, a granite hill in the Matobo National Park, 40 km south of Bulawayo.

Roberts, Frederick Sleigh, 1st Earl Roberts (1832-1914) British Field Marshal, born in India, educated at Eton and Sandhurst. He fought in the Indian Mutiny (1857/58) including the siege of Delhi and the relief of Lucknow; he was awarded a Victoria Cross in 1858. In 1879-1880 he served in Afghanistan, and in 1881 as Governor of Natal and Governor and Commander-in-Chief of the Transvaal. He became Commander in Chief, India in 1885. In December 1899 he returned to South Africa in command of British troops fighting in the Second Boer War; he was succeeded in the command in December 1900 by Lord Kitchener. Roberts died of pneumonia in France while visiting Indian troops fighting in the First World War. Both his sons predeceased him, including Frederick Hugh Sherston Roberts who was killed in action at the Battle of Colenso (Roberts and his son were one of only three pairs of fathers and sons to be awarded the VC).

Smuts, Jan Christiaan (1870-1950) South African statesman, military leader and philosopher. Prime Minister of the Union of South Africa (1919-1924) and (1939-1948). He led commandos in the Second Boer War. He served in the British Army in the First World War, and in the Second World War as a Field Marshal; he was in the Imperial War Cabinet under Winston Chuchill. He was the only person to sign the peace treaties ending both the First and Second World Wars, and was the only person to sign the charters of both the League of Nations and the UN.

രു‰

Made in the USA
Coppell, TX
03 October 2023